"On meeting a person for the first time, I often wonder
what they see, how they feel, what they think, and
what makes life worth living for them.
These books are an exercise in answering
those questions for all of us.
We have choices."

GONE TO GLORY

ALLEN STEPHENS

The New Western Series

FLOWERS OF THE SPIRIT LLC
Sherwood, Oregon, USA

1st Printing, 2006
© 2006, Estate of Allen L. Stephens
© 2003, Allen L. Stephens

Published in the United States of America
by Flowers of the Spirit LLC
P. O. Box 1028, Sherwood, Oregon

This book is a work of fiction. Characters, names, locations and inci-dences are the product of the author's imagination or are used ficti-tiously. Although the author enjoyed history, including The West and Native American History, and his wife is part Cherokee, the story is a work of fiction. The author of this book also does not provide medical advice.

Cover Photograph & Design, and Book Editing by Sheila Stephens
Final poem used with permission from Sheila Stephens.

ISBN 0-9761022-2-6
LCCN 2005934319
Flowers of the Spirit™

For more information,
VISIT the Website: FlowersOfTheSpirit.com

It was Allen's greatest wish
to dedicate this artistic work

To his wife, Sheila, his true love
To his son, Julian, his sunshine vision
To his son, Jim, his gentle blessing

Thank you, Allen
for letting each of us know
we are thoroughly, joyfully,
unconditionally loved

Contents

Road to Nazareth

May 1868 — Sunset

Sometimes good men do bad things. War is the usual excuse. For Johnny Lobo the moment blurred with conflicting emotions. He had a hard time remembering who he was before he'd killed his first man. Now Johnny was just one of the many young men from whom the South's attempt at secession had stolen youth. Although the hostilities had ended, Lobo felt trapped, reluctantly using the skills of war to earn a living. Squeezing his eyes tightly shut, Johnny cursed bitterly beneath his breath and mumbled with resignation, "All this thinkin' gets a man nowhere."

Glancing over his shoulder Johnny saw the sun hanging stubbornly along the rim of distant blue mountains, unwilling to abandon its dominion over the world of men. The waning light cast by that golden orb found Lobo slightly below the crest of a small hill, crouched low among the green-tipped branches of late spring sage. Turning again to the task at hand, he sought a target among the distant horsemen only now appearing on the long stretch of road down from the old mines.

Last summer's brittle grass rustled beneath his worn boots as he fidgeted. After all these years Johnny Lobo remained nervous before an action, shifting his weight from one bent knee to another. The sun behind him cast its fading strength into the eyes of the approaching party. Don't think of them as people, only names, he told himself. Some more famous than others.

Johnny was here for just one reason, to make sure that Jake Tallon was the first to die. Ambush was a stinking way to do a good man. But for this man, Johnny preferred the better odds over principle. Few men dared face Jake Tallon head-on and today Johnny just didn't feel that lucky.

Tense with waiting, he cradled the forty-caliber Blue Mountain Squirrel Rifle in the crook of his arm. The solid weight of the piece lay across the sleeve of his threadbare blue wool jacket, comforting somehow.

Johnny had refitted the old flintlock with a modern percussion lock when his daddy died and left him with this family treasure. After that one

1

change, his long rifle remained the most accurate, and now the most reliable weapon he'd ever owned.

Time slowed to a crawl. Johnny caressed the burled maple stock affectionately. Ordinary skin oils had darkened the wood from blond to ebony over the last thirty years.

He remembered the day his daddy, Bryce Lobo, promised him the weapon. He'd called it a sweet rifle, crafted to a one-of-a-kind perfection seldom matched by a gunsmith more than once in a lifetime. His father explained how the lans and grooves were cut slowly, with deliberate perfection, and the steel stained brown to uniform consistency along the entire length of the barrel. Daddy was a little bit of a gunsmith himself, Johnny remembered. The tone of affection he'd used in describing the process had not been lost upon the son.

This day especially, he was glad this gun shot true every time. It had cost a year's wages new, a huge purchase for Papa Bryce, only a part-time farmer.

Johnny shifted his weight again, hating this assignment. During the war, his long rifle made Lobo a reputation for always dropping his man. He moved the piece from the crook of his arm to a more upright position, with the butt plate dimpling the dust before his boot toes.

Looking up, he saw individual horsemen distinguish themselves among the approaching group as bobbing black specks against the cloud of gray-brown dust rising around the cantering hooves of their mounts.

The percussion lock solved whatever problem he had with his squirrel gun, Johnny thought. If the fight got ugly, beside him on the ground lay his big-bore Spencer Repeater with its seven-shot capacity. That would never happen. Once Tallon fell, Johnny's five friends, positioned to either side, were more than equal to the four insignificant horsemen who rode with Tallon. Each rifleman had an assignment, with one shooter left over for backup, Elmer Gammel.

Johnny wondered why he bothered with Gammel, even as he remembered that Gammel had brought the money and this assignment, and had insisted on being in on the ambush as part of the deal. Johnny knew that Elmer's real job was to make sure Johnny did his.

Lobo's eyes flicked quickly to either side as the other men moved into place, making small noises in the dry grass and brush around him. Though he liked none of them personally, Johnny trusted each one to do his job. All had seen action in one war or another. All had long since forfeited the innocence of their youth and their principles, as had he.

The air seemed thick in Johnny's lungs. Idly he scratched at the trickles of perspiration in the dark hair growing across his chest under his shirt. There was money enough in this one job to let him live differently for a time. Johnny alone knew about the gold that Tallon carried in his leather saddlebags. This job could be richer than anyone else suspected. Maybe he could buy his own spread. Maybe he could afford a real life.

Squinting, he distinguished individual faces among the approaching party, now only two hundred yards out and approaching at a canter. Not yet, he cautioned himself. Still too early.

He ran his tongue across dry lips and consciously blinked his eyes to keep them moist. If he could bark a squirrel at fifty paces, he could sure 'nough unhorse a full-growed man close up. Looking to his rifle, Johnny deliberately thumbed back the hammer with a distinctive double click, checked the cap and settled into a final firing crouch with his elbow on his left knee. As if on signal, he heard other clicks and more subtle movements from the brush nearby.

"Get ready," he mumbled into the warm wood of the rifle stock as the target distance melted quickly away. "Let me shoot first."

Lining up his sights on a spot just below the shining hatband of his target, Johnny Lobo focused down the thirty-nine inch octagonal barrel. His guts cranked themselves into painful knots as they did just before he killed a man. With conscious effort he released the knots and centered his entire energy on the target. Dust tickled at his nose as he drew in a breath and released part of it.

What will this cost me, Johnny wondered briefly, as he let the hammer fall.

The Claim

Earlier that morning, at the Harmon diggings
deep within the foothills of the Basin Range
...

The sound of the exploding charges echoed back from the surrounding cliffs a hundred times, almost all at once. Much of the dust and concussion went straight up the chimney under which the mine had its first shaft, but Jake Tallon was still close enough to feel the slap of hot air across his exposed skin.

As the wind scoured away the smoke from the blast, Harry and Manuel dropped a homemade ladder down the hole, and with wet kerchiefs tied around their lower faces, hurried to clean debris from the exploratory tunnel at the bottom of the shaft.

"You should see this, Jake!" Harry yelled upward, over a shoulder sprinkled with new rock dust. "Yellow runs through the rock like a ribbon, just like I figured. Those last charges really opened it up good."

"Never doubted you for a moment," Jake smiled down at his friends as they energetically shoveled broken rock into sturdy wooden buckets.

One at a time, Jake cranked each ninety-pound container upward with the noisy ratcheting of the crude windlass. "Why do you have me doing all the hard work?" he challenged them.

"Because you're the one with all the brawn!" Harry barely stopped to look up, jamming the sharp point of his shovel yet again into the pile of shattered rock.

"Yeah, and you're the one with all the mouth!" Jake returned the compliment, swinging the load toward himself and lowering it carefully to the solid ground beside the edge. Bending to the bucket, he unhooked the cable, released the ratchet on the windlass and fed the line into the hole below.

Sweating over the windlass, pulling up another load, Jake found himself hard-pressed to keep pace with the three men in the pit.

"Take a breather," he yelled, dumping the last bucket into his wheelbarrow with a surge of his muscular shoulders. Drowning out all thought, the falling debris rattled loudly against the heavy metal of the barrow. The vertical rock walls rising closely around the hole on three sides only amplified the racket.

4

As Jake set the bucket down with the others, he stretched his painful back and looked upward to the small patch of sky floating like a blue island between tops of the tall cliffs more than eight hundred feet overhead. "Maybe we've done enough for one day," Jake considered, "What do you fellas think?"

"I thin' that m'be you are a chil' playin' at hard work." As Manuel's brother, the wiry Esteban, spoke, he didn't bother to pause in his work.

"I think the breather is more for you than for us." Hands on hips, Harry looked upwards from the bottom of the dusty pit. "Maybe, like Esteban says, you ain't the man we thought you was."

"Don't worry," Jake returned the good-natured ribbing, "I don't give you that much credit for thinking, one way or the other."

Filling his lungs with high mountain air, Jake turned away from the hole, lifted the handles of his barrow and stepped, almost ran, behind the downhill plunging load, his third.

As Jake ran, the scent of honey reached him from the timber above. The wind carried that sweet smell with it as it swept down the slopes to follow the course of the stream next to the diggings. Mornings and evening he smelled that honey. Jake knew he could look for the source of the honey smell and not find it. Somehow that smell just snaked down from the trees, tormenting his curiosity. His brow furrowed in frustration at the small mystery.

That he didn't need the money from this mine was beside the point. Jake loved gold for its unusual weight and the bright yellow luster the metal possessed in even the smallest pieces. He loved breaking, hauling and washing the rock for the final reward of precious metal. He liked the accumulation in long, heavy sacks.

To him, the very process of mining was an act of creation on the level of painting the image of a beautiful woman or a great landscape on canvas.

As though it possessed a life of its own, the wheelbarrow in Jake's hands thumped and bumped on the dried mud ridges in the deeply worn ruts as it pulled him down the narrow path toward the waiting hardwood sluice box. The noise of his passage echoed back at him from the hills on either side. No secret to anyone that I'm coming, he thought.

Jake felt the healthy pull and strain of the weight of the load against the muscles of his legs and shoulders. Yellow metal liberally speckled the dirt and rock in the barrow. Without half trying, he saw it gleaming back at him.

It hadn't started out that way.

In the beginning Harry Harmon had only a red-haired, Welsh miner's hunch where that gold lay buried. Prospectors who had come before had found everything laying about on the surface and dug for the easy-to-find pockets and veins, yet much gold went undiscovered still. Harry studied the stress lines in the rock, the very way in which the hills walked down from the high mountains, and figured where the gold flowed, a hot and heavy liquid when the Earth spewed it forth. Harry guessed how the yellow metal might stop to rest and cool.

There he would dig!

Didn't much matter to Harry who had come before. Harry always said there was enough gold for everybody who cared to look. There would always be more if you made it your friend. "Lookit all those men swarming over the river and hills," he observed on occasion with disgust. "They'll dig up only a fraction of the treasure, no matter how hard they look. The rest may lie buried forever, just out of reach, waitin' for 'em." Yarning away an afternoon, Harry went on at length to Jake about the crafty ways of precious mineral as though it were a living, breathing being.

Harry so loved the rock, he worked it until the hills he'd befriended gave up their most treasured secrets. The placer miners came and went in their greedy, drunken rush, never stopping to talk to the mountains themselves with such courtesy as did Harry. By itself, that explained Harry's success.

Gold fever had already surged through this area of the Basin Range. Harry showed up late and made out in spite of the expert opinion. He never got aggravated that he received no credit for his success. He got the gold.

"Why should I care what they think?" Leaning forward to make his point, Harry had smiled his irrepressible smile at Jake. "To hell with 'em, I say!" A fella couldn't help but give that smile back to Harry in equal measure.

Harmon made his follow-up strikes twice Jake knew of. He got rich the first time picking pockets of passed over plunder right around Sutter's Mill in the original strike area, finding gold among the rocks of an ancient stream bed, long grown over with forest. Quite by accident, he found color shoulder high in a little flat-topped hill with absolutely no promise, near no mountain, slope or water course, and it started him thinking about other less likely opportunities. The back door turned out to be Harry's strength. Using his talent and intuition, he worked best once the crowds had moved on to easier pickings.

In the time before the big rush, everybody who wanted gold had found it. Every lad who could walk or ride dropped what he was doing, made it up to the old Grist Mill and staked out his own ground. Washing dirt, in those days, was a full time concern. Nobody worried much about thieves and bandits. Those were tranquil times in the Mother Lode country. Later on, as pickings thinned out and the population flourished, mining became a far more dangerous occupation.

Jake had come west with his brother Travis about that time and had made a good living protecting those who pulled treasure from the rocks and streams. He helped Harry leave the territory with his first fortune intact and reach St. Louis, where he could enjoy it. Not everyone survived the adventure so easily. Harry remembered the help, and the misery Jake's help had saved him, so Jake was the first person he telegraphed when staking his new claim at the western edge of the Great Basin, right up against the Sierras.

Why Jake? This was not a career he grew up with or something his father did that he was trained for. It had to do with choice.

After surviving the brutal killing of his foster family, at the tender age of sixteen Jake began making decisions that shaped the remainder of his life, forever denying him the occupations held by normal men. Hard work didn't bother Jake. It's just that someone had to stand strong against the lawless. It's not like he stood taller or broader than other men or was divinely chosen. His height and size were deceptive, amplified it seemed by his quickness, strength and measured rage. And though guns were a necessity in the trade that had become his life, Jake didn't like guns all that much because they should be the very last resort in any dispute. Guns were too final.

Jake threw the barrow handles into the air as the steel-shod wheel thumped solidly against the heavy stop-board at the end of the sloping path. Almost half-a-yard of glistening gravel spilled down the wooden chute onto a broad slab of nearly level bedrock beside the stream. They used the long flat surface to break the bigger chunks before sluicing. Warped and stained backboards surrounded the area on three sides, catching flying fragments as the rocks shattered under the impact of swung steel.

Standing shirtless and hip deep in the pit beside the rock, Jarred did most of the ore crushing. Each man among this small company had found his favorite task and this was Jarred's.

With a single jack the young Appleby worked at breaking what Jake dumped. Even as Jake stood watching, hands on hips, the hammer rose and fell, again and again. A ten-pound sledge with a short handle built power in a man's arms, not that the youngster was lacking to begin with. Jarred was bull-strong. And as he was short in years and didn't know any better, work was still a pleasure. Turning a wide, toothy smile up at Jake, Jarred reflected the joy they all felt at the sudden richness of Harry Harmon's strike.

Jake nodded his head in wordless understanding at Jarred. They'd all been called fools and worse for digging in such worked-over ground. Only a rusty tinge to one eight-foot section of granite and a lonely, incredibly thin line of gray material, probably lead, had hinted at mineral anywhere in the area.

After weeks of walking up and down the mountains, sitting, staring into space for long periods with chin on fist, Harry walked to the base of this cliff and proclaimed the location of precious metal fifteen feet into a blind, L-shaped crevasse, barely twenty foot wide but shooting all the way to the top of the cliffs above. Gold was there all right but only after digging through tons of worthless rock.

Barren, exploratory shafts dotted the hills around them, like the dark holes of sightless eyes scattered among the trees, haunting the landscape, marking the unschooled and overly optimistic efforts of those who came before.

Weather-rotted timbers collapsed slowly but certainly under the relentless, oppressive weight of the mountain and of time. In a dozen years or fifty, nothing would remain to mark those failed labors.

Others who condemned Harry spoke out of turn. They didn't believe in him as Jake did, who had seen him make good his brag once before.

"Why don't you clean the sluice, Jarred?" Jake suggested to the boy. "Let's pack up all the dust we have and go to town with Harry. It's time to kick up our heels some."

"I was hoping you'd say so Mister Tallon." Jarred flashed his broad, white smile at Jake.

"When you gonna stop that nonsense, Jarred, and call me Jake or Tallon like the others? I'm not so much older than you." Jarred always did as he was asked but would never change this respectful manner of speaking to Jake without it were a cold day in Hell. Before Jake finished talking about it, the boy picked up and stored his tools under canvas above the water line.

Jake nodded approvingly. Walking around Jarred, he stood for a moment above the foaming white waters of the little creek, deciding whether to change all his clothes or just wash up. In the end he loosened the throat lacing, stripped the dirty work shirt over his head and knelt near the edge of the stream. Scooping the cold water up in both hands, he splashed it liberally over his head and shoulders. Jake felt the dirt and dried salt dissolve away under his hands as he scrubbed at the filth. Soap would be nice but that would wait 'til they reached town.

Picking up his shirt, he pushed it forcefully beneath the surface of the clear water and used the heavy wad to scrub at the caked-on dirt and sweat on his neck where it accumulated under the collar. Mining is filthy work but more so today, Jake decided, thinking about the twelve-by-twelve timbers he'd used to shore the walls of the vertical shaft.

Satisfied he would get no cleaner without hot water, Jake rinsed the shirt itself with both hands, watching the dirt emerge downstream like a brown shadow drifting in the current. No time for a full washing of its heavy fabric, he twisted it dry and threw it over a nearby bush to air overnight. For a fresh going-to-town shirt he bent to his saddlebags, lifted the leather flap and pulled out the last clean, button-up, store bought shirt he owned. That's the story of my life, right there, he thought. I'm always using my last shirt.

Deep inside himself with such private thoughts, Jake fastened the buttons, starting at the collar and working down his shirtfront. He looked up in time to find young Jarred starring with open-mouthed amazement.

"Watch it son, you'll be killing flies if you don't get that mouth of yours shut." Jake smiled to take the sting from his words. "'Course, you won't be nearly so hungry when you get to town."

Looking down, he saw a button hooked out of sequence and refastened it. "How many flies you figure it takes to ruin your appetite?" Of course, Jake knew what bothered the boy. There was no cure but to endure his questions and answer them.

"W-W-What happened to you?" the young man stammered.

"Nothing you'll suffer if you stay clear of gun trouble," Jake answered wryly, looking away, resigned and embarrassed. If he didn't put stock in this youngster, he'd have stopped there but Jake felt he should answer more completely out of courtesy to Jarred as a friend.

"Mostly these scars are near misses 'cept for the one down here." Jake lifted the corner of his shirt and pointed to the obvious puckered scar of a bullet exit wound between the lower ribs on the right side, not looking the boy in the eye while he explained. "This was given me by a piece of back-shootin', Sante Fe scum, near put me down. My Sarah cut the man up for bear bait with my boot knife before I hit the ground."

Everybody knew about Sarah. For her spunk and beauty she had as much a reputation as Jake. Thinking of Sarah distracted Jake from his explanation of old wounds. This trip was the first time they'd been apart since hitchin' up last fall.

Thankfully, at that moment Manuel stepped up beside Jake.

"Showing off again, eh amigo?" Manuel flashed his big smile and swaggered between Jake and Jarred to get his own gear from the rough lean-to they all shared for personal storage. He knew how very shy Jake could be and prodded him cruelly whenever opportunity presented itself. In some mysterious, Latin way, the stocky Mexican understood the limits of good fun, always avoiding Jake's real anger.

Jake had no doubts Manuel broke up the little soiree just to save him additional embarrassment. Like all of José Altimera's kin, Manuel shared a wealth of tact that went hand in glove with his superb horsemanship. He looked, however, nothing like José. Manuel was short and heavy while his cousin José stretched the same weight over a much taller frame.

As Jake finished tucking in his shirt Manuel said, "José will be here soon, mi amigo. His letter waits at the Post Office, I know."

"How can you know that, Manuel?" Jake questioned, voice heavily laced with doubt.

"It calls out to me from the little box where it sits waiting," Manuel smiled, unflustered. "How is it that you Gringos cannot understand these simple things?" he asked, palms up, his hands shouting his quiet but sincere frustration at Jake's stupidity.

"Because such things are given only to the special among us," Jake mocked the Mexican's speech and his accent in the spirit of good fun. "Only you are so anointed in this company of friends."

"Ha, ha, ha," Manuel laughed his hearty laugh and put his weight behind a vicious punch, aimed at Jake's solar plexus.

By pure reflex Jake rotated his left forearm at the elbow and brushed Manuel's punch effortlessly to the outside, then patted Manuel's unprotected face twice, affectionately but firmly with his right hand. They never stopped trying and never had they landed a punch. By this time it was only ritual. Manuel only tried because he knew he could not succeed.

The Mexican smiled and slapped Jake's shoulder. That one did not get blocked. That was ever the final step of the ritual.

"Mail is as good a reason as any I know to go to town," Jake agreed. "You got something to read, you won't need any of that nasty cactus juice," he referred to the mescal Manuel liked so much.

He finished tucking in his shirt. "That must be an acquired taste, Manuel. I sure 'nough can't drink that foul stuff, myself." Holding his elbows close to his ribs, Jake shuddered theatrically.

Jake decided he liked being around people with schooling. People like Manuel.

There were some things about growing older that set well with a man. Older, he thought. I'm not even thirty yet but sometimes I feel like a hundred. I've had enough life for two men. Why can't I just settle down and be Sarah's husband? "What am I doing here, anyway?" he mumbled half out loud.

"Wait till you have niños, Señor Jake, then you like to travel."

"What did your parents ever do to you that made you such a mean man, Manuel?" Jake scowled at his Mexican friend. "I like kids. I don't know for sure that I like babies, but I know I like kids. Sarah tells me she likes babies. Maybe that's enough to get us through that part," Jake mused.

Manuel had come west with Jake from Sante Fe, when José Altimera had stayed. As far as he or Manuel knew, José remained there still. "You miss your cousin?" Jake asked Manuel.

"Si," Manuel said. "He is more like a brother than a cousin. Both our families shared one roof in Texas."

Jake smiled at the splendid exaggeration. "It was a very big roof my friend. Folks all over the country talk about the size of your hacienda."

"Si, it was a big roof but still both families lived closely together. Good times, bad times. We shared everything."

"There's the problem," Jake pointed a finger at his friend. "You had to grow up with that scoundrel." Dropping the accusing finger, he looked away and within. "Truth is that I miss him also, though I hardly got a chance to know him well. Even I don't have to be a genius to spot such an honorable man."

Heck, Jake realized, he knew Manuel better than José, even though José had been the one to save his life. He swung the gun belts around his waist one after the other, buckling them each in their turn. "No fancy tie-downs for cross draw," he remarked to no one in particular as he cinched up the belts, allowing the right holster to hang lower, off the hip to favor an old injury. "Some things never change and some things do."

"You talk much to yourself, Señor Jake." Manuel had drifted once again to his side, comfortable in their friendship.

"Maybe that's because no one else will listen," Jake replied. "You know I gave up my '51 Colt Navies for the newer Remington pistol on the say-so of your cousin, José? 'Course, it's still cap'n ball. Maybe I should jus' get a cartridge-fed pistol if I'm gonna change?"

"So why do you change if you don't like it?"

"I'm not sure, Manuel." Jake raised the hammer on one pistol to half-cock and spun the cylinder, checking the loads. "I used those Navies for a full eight years. Your cousin caught me when I was getting married and couldn't think properly."

"Maybe he was right, Señor Jake. He always say a real man carries a forty-four. No more sissy thirty-six caliber Navy for my friend Jake Tallon." Manuel's eyes twinkled with his gentle humor. "But not so pretty maybe?"

"Yeah, but he said the barrel was a full eight inches long instead of a measly seven-and-a-half. What I do like is how the frame cants forward. Favors the natural shooter in me." Jake hefted the piece and pointed it off across the stream to illustrate the point. "Balances better. Damn near aims itself." Jake looked sideways at Manuel. "Maybe it was a good trade after all."

Talking about José Altimera brought back conflicting feelings from the year previous and fooling with the guns gave Jake an excuse to avoid Manuel's searching gaze. Carefully wiping each gun in its turn, he holstered them with a flourish, and reached down to grab his black, flat brimmed, going-to-town hat.

"Your cousin gave me this as a wedding present. I had the Gunsmith over to Bodie drill out buttonholes on some Mexican Dollars and sewed them onto the band myself. Think he'll like 'em?"

"Si," said the short Mexican, reaching for the hat to better appreciate it. He ran his heavy, callused fingers along the sweatband inside the crown, savoring the weight of the bright silver coins fastened on the outside. "He will like them ver' much Señor Jake."

Nobody enjoyed showy attire more than these fancy Mexican cowboys.

"Muy Vaquero!" Manuel exclaimed, handing the hat back and nodding his head in exaggerated, smiling approval.

Seating the hat carefully over his short brown hair, Jake patted it into place and reached for the scuffed leather saddlebags, heavy with the dust and nuggets from a week's work in the hole. Eighty pounds he figured. A good haul.

Fifteen thousand plus dollars would create quite a stir in their little town. Nazareth hadn't seen this much gold in a year. Jake didn't know exactly how he felt about that. It made him vaguely uneasy. They didn't need the extra attention.

He wasn't so worried about folks crowding the claim. The five of them had either bought up or filed on any ground close to it before they got dirt under their nails. He just didn't like the notice all this new gold brought them. No excitement was always better when gold was concerned. Excitement got people killed.

Jarred showed up with the last small buckskin bag from the sluice box, and lifting a leather flap, added it to the rest, then buckled the worn straps into place for Jake.

Shouldering the heavy bags, Jake stepped off toward the corral at the base of the hill and everyone naturally dropped in behind, single file, like some kind of parade. He waved at Harry as the big man looked up from saddling the broncs. Harry believed that they should come to town all together. It was only fitting that they celebrate. A bath, a woman-cooked meal and a good time waited in Nazareth and they could still get there before dark.

Harry's smile crowded his face for space, standing his big yellowing teeth side by side, from one ear to the other.

Catching the excitement of the men, the horses made mounting difficult with their frisky behavior. They spun and bumped each other, stirring up dust on every side. Harry's line-back bay mustang, Rascal, reached out to nip at the flanks of the other horses. Harry was a hell of a miner but a middling horseman. That horse needed a firmer hand, thought Jake, scowling momentarily at his friend.

Finally, with everyone in the saddle and Jake in front, the contained excitement of an entire week brimmed over. They burst through the gate at a dead run, whooping and slapping the flanks of their mounts to let off steam. With their big grins flashing back and forth, they shared the conviction they had not a pocket of ore but a true strike that would run long and heavy.

South of the mountain the happy group of friends hit the sagebrush plain, circled east for two miles avoiding a sea of broken rock and changed direction as the road doubled back on itself and turned into the setting sun. The horses settled into a distance-eating lope and finally a rapid walk after bleeding off their excess energy.

Jake reached down to pat the neck of his spotted mare when his world turned violently upside down. No pain, just a glimpse of sky and a brilliant light that faded, tunneling quickly to the darkest night.

Spirit Lodge

fter a spell, who knows how long, Jake's vision returned. He was standing now, not riding.

Very slowly, objects came into focus.

He stood at the edge of a circle of dim light that seemed like a clearing in the forest or an island of light on a dark sea. Looking to each side, Jake sought a large fire to explain the light at the center but there was nothing of the sort. In fact, he recalled, when last they rode, they were in the middle of a broad, flat plain, at or about sundown with plenty of sunlight.

This new quality of light bloomed exceedingly strange, kinda silver, getting brighter. The action within the illuminated area captured and held Jake's attention.

He figured he'd been shot, so he should be hurting, only he wasn't. He didn't even seem to care. In fact, this was the best Jake had felt, that he could remember.

Gradually, the action in the center became clearer as three other figures drifted in close to stand with him on the edge of the circle. He recognized Manuel, Manuel's brother Esteban, and Jarred, all pale, silent and unsmiling.

Together, they turned inward toward the stage of light where some drama played itself out without their participation. Horses stood nervously around the edges of the activity, reins trailing, while six men moved among the four forms that lay motionless like piles of wrinkled, abandoned clothing.

Those are bodies, Jake suddenly realized. Our bodies!

A standing man had Harry by the shirtfront, holding him up partially off the ground where he lay, one leg bent crookedly under him. Standing man's lips moved as he shouted at Harry. Face thrust forward, contorted, the veins bulged on his neck. Harry held both hands palms up in a confused shrug. A look of terror flashed across Harry's face as the standing man shoved a gun into Harry's chest and pulled the trigger.

Jake saw the recoil, the smoke, but heard no sound as Harry sagged back limply against his clothing. The standing man dropped the empty husk of their friend into the bone-dry dirt.

Still Jake heard nothing.

He felt nothing. No, this did not quite ring true. Jake felt a profound relief from fatigue and worry. A sort of anticipation grew in him as the weight of the World lifted from his shoulders.

The brightness dimmed before them like a theater shutting down the gaslights. The friends turned as one and walked into another, brighter light that 'minded Jake more of a rising sun. He thought in a distracted way of a new day. Vaguely, Jake became aware as Harry fell in at their rear, hesitant at first, but following.

Jake had feelings again but not the ones he expected. He felt warm and happy. A kind of excitement surged through him as they stepped forward on a smoothly cobbled pathway angling gently upward. Now they walked a country lane under a canopy of interwoven maple limbs and leaves, gentle light filtering down and around them. From the corner of his eyes Jake saw the others smiling and realized he must wear a similar expression.

He felt joy, the same feeling that Sarah gave to him with the announcement of her pregnancy. Given the nature of his death, it must certainly be wrong to feel this good. Oh, he thought, I could say it and it wasn't that hard. With the life he lived, it was only a matter of time. "I'm dead," he uttered his first words since entering upon the path. Death was a friend after all. It only surprised him that it was so easy to die. He'd been close before. Serious injuries didn't hurt that much until sometime after-wards, once the shock had worn off.

"Dead." He let the word roll around in his head. As he realized Sarah would not be with him, Jake looked around in a sudden panic. At the very thought, a window opened to his left. Jake saw her below and far away at some happy task. He peered closely at her, as though through a telescope, loving her for perhaps the last time.

She froze under his gaze. Fear rose up in her eyes. Looking at her, Jake almost felt the breath catch in her throat as she raised a hand to her mouth. Sarah looked in Jake's direction. Intuitively, he knew that Sarah couldn't see him, but somehow she knew that he watched.

He tried to speak, to reach out. Nothing worked. "I love you darling," he shouted. "I love you, Dear Heart." Jake felt himself swept away from his love as though on the strong current of a rushing river. Her image dwindled, becoming ever smaller.

Intense sadness colored the moment. Sarah carried their child. Where was she now? Back at the ranch already? Or was that only his wishful thinking? Probably she remained back East, Jake knew.

When Harry had collected Jake for this enterprise in the spring, Sarah was already talking about riding the Iron Horse east, to Baltimore, to say good-bye to her childhood before she got tied down with youngsters of her own. She loved the West and the fragrance of Wild Country as much as did Jake. It only made sense for her to visit, one last time, the museums and galleries that were her world before Jake Tallon.

Still the good-byes were tearful and exciting all at the same time. Dying wasn't Jake's idea of how this trip should end. He just didn't see it coming. Didn't even suspect it.

"I'm sorry sweetheart," he tried one last time as the window blinked shut with finality.

Anguished, Jake struggled to remember the events bringing him to this moment. When he first filed the claim, Harry had some substantial trouble from Vernon Laszlo, the town Sheriff. That's why Jake had asked Manuel to come also. Once they all showed up together, there was nary a peep from anyone. Strength in numbers was good defense against unfriendly authority.

I was too happy, thought Jake. Once married, the brawling, riding and sleeping-out lost all the shine. The love that he and Sarah shared was a treasure that shined brighter than all his gold. Away from her, Jake could think of nothing else.

That was trouble.

When the hair-raising premonitions of danger presented themselves, he did not listen or did not notice. That failing had now robbed him of the love of his life, his child and his future. What would she do without him? What would she do alone?

Only half aware, in this misery Jake watched as a vaguely familiar figure passed those ahead of him onward with a grand open gesture and beaming expression. As Jake moved also to pass, the old man placed a restraining hand gently upon his chest saying, "No Jacob, it is not yet your time."

"What?" Jake asked puzzled. "Of course it is. I died back there, along with everyone else."

"Do not be too quick, my young friend," the old man cautioned. "You are right as far as you know, but you do not understand everything yet."

He had Jake flatfooted there. He didn't know everything, especially now, when he felt like a baby just starting out. "Okay," Jake allowed doubtfully, "but who are you to say who stays and who goes?"

"I am Shantee," the old man said. "I am so named by the Ones Who Came Before. Also the Anasazi, though I am much older than they," he said wistfully, "old beyond time. I have many names in many cultures. We will smoke and talk together in the lodge."

Mutely, Jake nodded agreement, when Shantee gestured with his open hand to an adobe structure on the right that Jake had not seen before. Jake pushed aside the material hanging over the entrance, and stepped forward, seating himself to one side of the fire as Indian custom dictated.

As the host, Shantee walked around the fire and sat facing the door. The cloth lifted again and several other figures entered. Jake had no idea where they came from but he was now beyond surprise. Among them was Rudy Barnette, his foster Father.

This shocked Jake profoundly. Rudy was long dead. What was he doing here? Seeming to read his thoughts, Rudy seated himself opposite Jake and addressed him after a brief nod and smile to Shantee.

"Now, Jacob," Rudy said, "you know from what you just went through that dying is easy. Very easy, indeed. Not at all what a fella might expect. I know now that it's the living of life that's so hard. I speak for the whole family," he went on, "when I say we are proud about the way you stopped the ugliness that ended our time with you. You couldn't have saved us, no matter what you did …

"Life is not hard here but it is very much a life. We do many of the same things we did in Missouri but we are free from care and from pain. Now and again we visit with you around the fire but I'm not sure you are always aware." Looking away, Rudy seemed to laugh at Jake from the vantage of some secret knowledge.

Jake felt dense with his inability to understand the deeper meaning of Rudy's revelations. He was profoundly distracted by the gratitude he had for this man who had opened his home and family to him as a young boy. "I'm sorry, Rudy," Jake choked. "I couldn't do no more." At that moment he felt again like the child who watched the killing of this family.

"We know, Jacob," Rudy said with a renewed expression of under-standing. "Some people will always abuse their free will, but even young as you were, you stood up and fought back. You did not lose your spirit to that tragedy, Jacob. In its own way, this was your test, your opportunity." He seemed to reach out to Jake across the fire in a fashion that brought peace upon Jake's heart. "You learned much that day and please us greatly that you continue to grow and change."

Tears stung at Jake's eyes. Concealing his reaction, he swung his gaze from Rudy to Shantee. This old man struck some chord in Jake's memory but Jake was unsure just how he knew him. He blinked. Before Jake's eyes, Shantee's robe changed from glistening white to the gray-white cotton of the Mexican farmer and finally to the decorated buckskins of a High Shaman.

Nice trick there, Jake thought, smiling.

With a twig from the fire, Shantee lit a fine clay pipe, puffed at it briefly and passed it on to Jake. "When last we met, Jacob," he said conversationally, "I gave you the Red Stone of Friendship. A Lightning Jasper, I think. Do you have it still?" His smiling eyes pierced Jake's heart like a thrown lance.

At a loss for words, Jake reached inside his open shirt, his hand closing upon the warm stone. The Jasper pulsed and glowed as he brought it forth and in that moment he remembered the kind eyes of the old man, the Mexican with the perfect English he had met in the desert that blazing hot day coming out of Sante Fe. Understanding started as a rolling tremor at the base of his spine, flashing up his back and exploding behind his eyes like a fourth of July rocket.

"Ahh," Jake uttered an involuntary exclamation. "I stopped at your beautiful farm in the middle of the arid lands," Jake said, transfixed. Like a dream, Jake revisited the memory and once again felt himself sitting before the old man, the simple but wise old farmer, talking and drinking sweet water in the shade of his adobe walls.

With a start, Jake remembered the Medicine Pipe in his hands, and puffing the coals again into life, passed it to his left. Not all faces in the room were familiar though there existed an overwhelming sense of oneness. Jake was among friends.

"When you return to your life, Jacob, you will find you no longer have the Friendship Stone," said Shantee. "It has been taken from you in death and one of your first tasks will be to recover that talisman. In short, you cannot die yet, Jacob." With the commanding tone of his voice, Shantee drew attention once more in his direction. "There is much yet for you to do, much that is required of you beyond the simple task of vengeance."

Pictures flashed before Jake's eyes, once again like scenes through a speeding train window. He didn't know how long it lasted because the passage of time in this Spirit Lodge was obviously notional.

"These visions," said Shantee as Jake returned to awareness of the present, "you will remember later in pieces as they become appropriate."

"I'm not sure that I want to go back," Jake admitted honestly, "meaning no disrespect." His comment reflected the need for a better reason.

Shantee gestured to the doorway where stood a young man of upright posture and collar length golden hair. The spirit of the youngster was so strong the room dimmed around him, leaving his radiant face floating bright against the velvet blackness.

He looked upon Jake without speaking, giving him a strong feeling of connection for which Jake could imagine no good reason.

"This is Julius Tallon," said Shantee out of the darkness, "your son to be. You have an agreement with and an obligation to his spirit that may not be lightly set aside."

A natural affinity for this young person moved Jake deeply. He heard Shantee again from the darkness to his right, "Julius needs your help growing up Jacob, as does Sarah. You cannot leave them." Jake felt the correctness of Shantee's words.

"There are many other reasons," the old man said, "these are the easiest to understand."

Deep in his heart, Jake heard Sarah at some far distance, confused, wondering, praying and crying out in her misery. "Okay," he said. No room existed for a different response.

Awareness of the lodge returned to Jake. Shantee smiled his gentle, calming smile. "I am with you more than you know, Jacob," he said. "During those moments of peace as you watch the fire or look to the stars, you hear my voice and think it your own. This is my own sorrow," he sighed. "I feel frustrated when you do not recognize me as we talk or when we walk together. Survival is sometimes such a challenge for the living that there is little room for a more spiritual consciousness. Now that you have been to the Spirit Lodge and returned to the living, you will have time to listen for me and to learn."

He reached within a belt pouch saying, "I have something else for you, for your journey home."

As he extended his hand palm upwards, Jake saw a bright, semi-spherical golden ornament against the dark skin, flat on one side, domed surface facing up, like a shimmering over a large drop of water. Apart from the unusual light pulsing from within, the ornament might have been an ordinary broach or decorative pin.

As Jake's fingers closed around the brilliant gift he felt over-whelming pain blossom in his head. He shouted out in agony but knew this cry to be the most pitiful kind of mewing, like a wounded kitten. Yet his attempted scream made him breathe and the breathing hurt his lungs.

He knew he lived.

Missing Friends

North out of Sante Fe is some of the prettiest country a man can see. pine shrouded mountains of all sizes run down to the pale green sagebrush plains. Most times a horseman is only two or three hours of hard riding from the opposite extreme of geography.

That understanding did not pleasure José Altimera as it might many others. Some nagging misery deep within the heart of this Spanish-bred Mexican ate away at him. He hungered unreasonably for the old ways, open plains, grand haciendas, long lazy days tending stock, respect for the Church and those attitudes that made a man honorable.

As a youngster he had watched with side-glancing eyes as bearded Americanos came and went from his beautiful Sante Fe. At that time the white-skinned intruders were few and the law of Spain forbade them trade within the territory. Yet some lingered overlong.

Still, they thought, these brawling, cunning, often disrespectful strangers were no real threat to the Mexico he knew. But the eventual defeat of President Santa Anna and the Treaty of Guadeloupe Hidalgo changed all that, forever. Now the hated Yankees and Tejanos were themselves the law. Their hated ways became the very way of the land he loved so much.

Living in these times reminded José of struggling for firm footing on the sandy bottom of a fast running stream. The sand beneath the foot ran away first here and next there as the water found a way to push the tiny grains of rock. The weight of the body shifted out of control creating a windmilling embarrassment for the cruel amusement of someone watching from the shore.

So it was in New Mexico and California. A man had little to hang onto that he might trust. He had a horse, a gun, maybe a job and even more rarely a friend. A friend. Altimera let the word roll around in his consciousness, savoring the taste of it. Jakc Tallon was a true friend, tested by their mutual adversity, and bound by their mutual honor.

His head nodded once, soberly, while he rode, to punctuate the feelings held so strongly in his heart. Friendship is nothing without loyalty, without integrity. It was the way he was raised. It was the way he lived.

Sitting astride a big, blood-red sorrel, plodding packhorse in tow, José Altimera cantered uneasily toward the distant peaks of the northern Sierras, with the furnace-orange sun approaching mid-sky overhead. The breakfast eaten in the town of Nazareth did not set well in his stomach. It rumbled and gurgled unhealthily behind his belt like a living thing in the throes of agony.

Certainly, the food itself was fine. Some calamity waited beyond his control, beyond his knowledge. It upset him and he could find no reason nor cure, no matter how he tried. José had not slept well for days as he hurried north to find his friends.

Rushing his journey for reasons beyond explanation, José rose early, ate little and rode hard. When he arrived in Nazareth he found his letters unclaimed. He asked around for directions to the diggings of Harry Harmon. That simple request created more interest than it warranted and did little to dampen his concern. He became even more concerned.

As the day grew hotter, José removed the waist-length embroidered Spanish jacket and rode simply in his snow white shirt, string tie, and black flat-brimmed hat, looking more like a Spanish gentleman than a Vaquero. The contrast of bright white against his dark skin brought out overtones of copper that spoke of Indian blood to which he would never admit.

He had more dinero than a hundred Vaqueros but retained the callused hands and horsemanship that branded him as a man who worked stock proudly.

Rising waves of heat made the trail shimmer before him. A lonely drop of sweat trickled into the corner of his eye and then on down his cheek. José did not feel well. Unscrewing the canteen cap, he sipped at the warm contents, seeking relief. The bouncing of the horse under him surely did not help.

Almost doubling over the saddle horn with a sudden violent stomach spasm, he let himself slide abruptly from his seat atop the horse to stand beside the patient animal. With his hands on his knees, his stomach emptied itself onto an unoffending trailside bush. The cramps eased off. José tried experimentally to stand straight. It worked and he noted with relief that now he really felt pretty good. He inhaled deeply, lifted the canteen again to his lips, rinsed his mouth and spit to one side.

"Ahh, that is better," he announced to no one in particular.

Pulling a folded white cotton handkerchief from his pocket, he wet it with more water from the canteen and used it to clean his face and lips. Then looping the canteen strap once more over the horn, José bent to retrieve his hat from a rock where he'd dropped it … when his eye was drawn to a short, straight line. There are few straight lines in nature.

A boot, he realized. Only a dusty cast-off boot. A curiosity. No more.

Not fifteen feet away, he saw only the pointed toe with the sole toward him. Mildly interested, he stepped between two hip-high sage bushes for a better look. The Mexican-style boot did not appear badly worn. In this land people did not throw away useful things. He found the second boot a dozen feet deeper into the sage.

Holding one in each hand, he wondered how such a thing had transpired. Somebody bought new boots in town and changed them way out here? Es loco! Estupido! These boots are worn, certainly, thought José as he turned one over in his hands, but they did not deserve to be so lightly cast aside. Angling his head slightly upwards, looking thoughtfully into a cloudless portion of Sierra Blue sky, he weighed the possibilities in his mind. Nothing added up.

Dropping both boots where he stood, José walked back to the trail. Looking into the dust, he saw that his tracks were the only ones showing. That made no sense either, since this was a significant trail between several small towns. There should be many tracks at any one time.

He hitched his packhorse to the bare branch of a stunted tree at the base of a small hill on the turn of the trail. Climbing aboard Big Red, he rode down the trail a ways and dismounted, examining the dust once again. Many tracks. Why should these tracks disappear like magic, José wondered. He smiled knowingly to himself at the thought. No magic here, mischief perhaps. Only mischief.

Intrigued, Altimera mounted once again and rode directly away from the trail on the east side. He found nothing unusual. Circling back he cut the trail again below the small hill where his pack animal waited, then headed off to the west circling back toward his starting point. The answer to this mystery must be close, the patient man thought, peering first to one side of his horse then the other.

Before completing a full circle, he found the tracks of more than a dozen horses coming and going. A regular crowd, he thought. The makings of a great riddle confronted the dapper Mexican, previously Segundo to a large Ranchero and a very capable man.

Now truly interested, José rode back to collect the other horse. With the burdened animal at the end of a taut rope, he followed the tracks as they led off toward a series of lightly forested hills that walked toward the even more distant mountains.

As the ground rose under him, he flushed a pair of coyotes from the brush to one side. They glanced resentfully toward him as they ran for cover, moist tongues lolling over small, sharp teeth.

Raising his eyes, José saw a buzzard pecking intently at the soil near the base of a sandy slide no more than a hundred yards off. Looking abruptly to the sky, he noticed several more birds circling tightly in a descending pattern. Had he not been searching for tracks, their presence by itself would have led him here immediately.

"Oh-h," he groaned, a bad feeling eating again at his stomach, making him miserable once more.

Digging his spurs into the flanks of Big Red, leaning forward in the saddle, he charged suddenly ahead, putting the bird to flight. As his horse skidded to a stiff-legged halt, his eyes found that thing he most dreaded, a human hand protruding forlornly from the sandy soil - showing only a short length of cuff! Blessedly the buzzard had only begun his gristly meal.

"Madre Dios!" he breathed, crossing himself, for José Altimera was a religious man.

Heart racing, José picketed the horses and returned to the hand. It was dead but fresh. Grasping it in both of his own, he dug in his heels and pulled with all of his great strength. The sand gave way, exposing the entire body and parts of yet another man as it spilled outwards to where he stood!

Now down on his hands and knees, José dug furiously at the loose soil. Next to the second man, he found another, placed head to feet in a shallow trench. Obviously, a sandy bank had been collapsed over several corpses, covering them, but not well. Blessed Virgin, he believed he knew one of these men! Cursing, he ran to search his equipment. The only digging tools he possessed were a heavy bladed knife and a metal dinner plate!

His frantic, sweaty work produced five bodies and no more. Yes, it was true! The sand-filled eyes of his cousin Manuel stared sightlessly above a shattered countenance, where a heavy rifle bullet had smashed the front teeth and jaw to sever the spine at the base of the skull. "Aiii!" groaned the heartsick Mexican, throwing his face to the sky like a wounded animal, sudden tears cutting dusty tracks down his face as he rocked and sobbed.

"What can I tell your mother? What can I tell your sisters, Manuel?" Recovering his composure, he wiped a sleeve across his freely running nose, then tenderly touched the shoulder of his dead cousin, almost a brother. As José sat grieving over Manuel a giant dread crept upon his heart like a storm cloud over the wide plains.

Fearfully, his eyes strayed to the other still forms lined head to heel against the sand bank. Manuel was one of many friends working with Harry Harmon. And Manuel's brother? Yes, there was his brother! Recognition was difficult as death is the ultimate disguise, stealing both animation and mannerism. And there was Jake! His great friend, Jacob Tallon, face caked in gore. Some part of José died at the very thought of Jake losing anything in a contest of arms, much less his life. Impossible!

"Spawn of Satan!" he cried, mourning the corpses, his arms stretched wide, as though to embrace them all. "Who could have done this terrible thing to you?"

They will pay, José Altimera promised in his heart. Bitter tears streamed down his face as he struck his thigh with a clenched fist again and again. He did not yet know how, or even who, but they would pay. There would be no stopping until this obligation was satisfied.

Laboring as the sun slid toward the mountains in the west, José dug another, deeper trench and arranged the bodies with dignity along the bottom. Altimera looked up frequently, scanning the horizon all around, unwilling to be surprised at his work as had the carrion eaters before him.

Each man had been shot one or more times through the face or chest. Were it a real fight, the wounds would be more varied from one man to the next. When, finally, he got to his great friend, Jake Tallon, he saw the gruesome death wound but was surprised when the body remained supple though chilled. The legs could be easily straightened and rearranged as could those of the living.

The chest did not rise and fall no matter how hard he watched, yet the body was not truly cold. Carefully, he brushed the sand from the face of his good friend. "Aiii!" he shouted, grasping Jake's shoulders and shaking the whole body. "You cannot die, my friend! I have lost my cousin, my brother, so you must live!"

When his agitation produced no response, Altimera sat back on his heels, bringing a single finger thoughtfully to his chin. After a moment, he bent to another corpse to compare the warmth. The one was definitely warmer than the others. Still uncertain, he took a moment to say good-bye and speak the Rosary over each of the others. He asked his God to welcome these friends into his house. It was all he knew to do.

When he turned again to Jake, he found upon close examination that though his friend did not breathe, he also did not seem completely dead. The body had more color than the others and tiny specks of fresh blood welled up from the edges of the torn flesh on the forehead and temple, even through the dirt yet covering his face.

The wound looked as ugly as any José had ever seen. Was there still a chance for his friend? More importantly, could he afford not to try? Rising, disbelief heavy upon his shoulders, he forced himself to return to the Sorrel, and in a daze of grief and impetuous hope, retrieved his half-empty canteen and a few first aid supplies that might inconceivably help him challenge fate.

"Please, give me guidance," the usually confident Mexican pled as he rushed back to the body of his friend and stared thoughtfully for a moment before kneeling at Jake's shoulder. Carefully, yet with renewed intensity, José washed at the damage, removing the obvious dirt, and found himself pulling a slender, inch-long bone fragment from among the torn flesh, then another. A long shudder rolled down the Mexican's spine.

This is not so good after all, he thought. It appeared that an area as big as his hand above Jake's temple had been crushed into his brain. No man can recover from so serious an injury, but Jake Tallon is my friend and for him I will try everything, anything. The Mexican pulled back the torn flesh from each edge and sloshed tequila from a fresh bottle into the wound.

Having been buried, there was much dirt and many small rocks to remove from the wound. Soon the wound bled more freely, carrying away many impurities with the new volume. He dressed Jake's temple to stem the flow, taking the necessary time as the sun nestled in earnest among the peaks of the Basin Range. Soon it would be dark, he realized.

Sitting back upon his heels, José appraised his work. Obviously, many people had been required in order to kill his friends so quickly. His interference, if noticed, would be little appreciated and would certainly represent a threat to those involved. He must soon find a safer place for his injured friend if Jake was to have any chance at all. The two of them would need more water, wood, concealment and a great deal of luck.

As the shadows of the distant peaks raced across the desert floor, José Altimera had his solution. Mountains will ever provide the refuge for the pursued, he thought, as he devoutly hoped for something more than just protection.

Sleeping Beauty Wakes

"**H**ola, Amigo!" Jake heard dimly as though from a far distance. A dream? No! No dream feels this bad.

No longer in the Spirit Lodge, he found himself on a rough woolen blanket spread across the hard ground - hurting. Good Lord did he hurt! He hurt all over, but mostly his head was afire.

Painfully bright light lanced sharply beneath closed eyelids. Jake covered his face with weak, shaking hands, trying to salvage the peaceful dark but managing only to accidentally bump the injured forehead. "Arrghh!" he yelled involuntarily, tears springing from his eyes. Waves of surging scarlet and yellow agony washed through his head. Groggily, Jake noticed that his right eye refused to open at all, and then became immediately afraid that his left eye might not open either.

What a weakling I am, he accused himself.

"I thought you might never awaken," the worried Latin voice sounded close now, clearer than before. Jake knew that voice from somewhere, but his mind was saddled with an incredible weight that made thinking so difficult, remembering so slow. Fighting the lethargy, he struggled for clarity with all of his might, but from his lips rolled only inarticulate moans.

"You looked dead, like the others," spoke the voice gently, "but when you didn't start stinking right away, I washed you up a bit and pretended you might live. So here we are!"

Still, Jake could not speak. Moving a hand cautiously away from his face, he cracked the left eye open just a bit. Even the little light made his head ache beyond belief. Thankfully, between him and the brightness of the fire crouched the blurred but dapper figure of José Altimera. Oh, yes. Now he recalled the proud Mexican. The memory seemed so distant, a lifetime away.

Beyond the physical pain, Jake was sick with a sense of loss he could not define. The Mexican was speaking again.

"Always I find you like this, amigo," José scolded, "shot up and dying. I think maybe this is the last miracle, the last extra life you carry on that sorry carcass. I worry for you."

"You talk too much, you Mex bastard," Jake groaned with harshness totally unlike his normal self. He could never say such a thing to his good friend, but Jake was confused and hurt. "Sorry," he mumbled contritely.

In spite of the rudeness, José smiled broadly, his face lighting from the inside. "Good," he said. "Not all your brains got spilled, you recognized my true nature." He paused, reflecting, and with some hesitation began thoughtfully, "You could be very much more respectful, however, to the person who climbed down off his horse, pulled you from beneath the ground, drug your dirty carcass to a place of safety and cared for you all of two weeks without a single syllable of thanks in either language." Alternate waves of relief and outrage washed through the Mexican. He found the level of his voice rising beyond control at the end of the short speech.

Taking one slow, deep breath José continued more reasonably, "Not to mention, I have the blood of Spanish Nobility in my veins." He nodded his head vigorously to reinforce the point. "Perhaps you can call me the Honorable Mexican Bastard."

"I guess I offended you after all," Jake slurred, able to keep his eyes open no longer. He faded into a superficial sleep troubled by the intense pain of his wound. Occasionally he became aware of somebody, likely José, tending the injury and patiently trickling water between his lips.

Sometime later Jake felt a warm soup or a broth poured into his mouth. This was the critical nourishment he knew his eventual recovery required. With effort, he managed to regain wakefulness long enough to choke energetically and force down a few deliberate swallows of the thin liquid before passing into unconsciousness once again.

Many hours, perhaps days passed, while Jake inhabited his own world, dreaming very real dreams he could not fully explain. Neither could he write them off entirely as the tortured fantasies of a wounded man. They were too real. One in particular, a very important dream, kept returning to him again and again. He felt himself slipping toward sleep with a certain anticipation.

Reality faded away. Soft pastel mists thickened, swirled and dispersed. Jake saw himself again dressed in a suit of black broadcloth with thin vertical stripes of cream color. Wearing the stiff white collar, black silk ribbon tie and ruffled shirt with a joy that defied his usual disdain of formal dress, he descended the steps of a freshly painted white building beneath the spires of a Denver church. Methodist, a voice seemed to say.

Grace and loveliness, clothed in white lace, graced his right arm. Jake felt consumed by a boundless love from and for this beautiful stranger. Sarah, he slowly understood. This was the life he must remember. A life started someplace else, at an earlier time.

One hand already on his arm above the elbow, she circled his biceps with her free hand, locking her fingers together around the hardness of that muscle.

Jake felt the softness of her breast against his elbow and dizziness threatened to overwhelm him. Sissy, he scolded himself, to let a woman make you so weak. He saw the mischief in her upturned, smiling face. "You know what you're doing, don't you?" he accused.

"Yes," she replied breathily, "and it makes me feel like a terrible hussy." She squeezed the firmness of his arm again. "But I like it."

Releasing his arm and hooking her fingers delicately over his larger sun-browned hand, she let him help her into a lacquered coach drawn by a team of matched bays with blaze faces. They danced prettily as the coachman released the brake and the scene faded and bloomed into an entirely different setting.

Before him Jake saw an outdoor reception tent with a peaked roof and open sides. Scores of well-dressed people drifted aimlessly but all eyes focused instantly on Sarah as Jake guided her past the pavilion with its tables of crystal and china.

Down the gentle slope of a sandy, winding path, Jake heard a stream of some kind beyond a screen of aspen. They had been married, he knew, yet they stepped eagerly to another kind of ceremony.

Why can't I remember everything, Jake chided himself, standing outside the dream, watching.

The couple stepped from under the canopies of pine and aspen, into a clearing with a single occupant. The biggest Indian Jake had ever seen stood resplendent in immaculate, beaded buckskins, his long black hair dressed with seven perfect eagle feathers.

The Cherokee Shaman, Night Walker, remembered Jake. That man's big as God himself!

Guests from the White Man's wedding gathered round as they descended the trail behind Jake and Sarah. Scanning their faces, Jake saw in their eyes the uncertainty and fear at the prospect of this strange and unusual event. Still holding Sarah's hand, Jake stepped forward across the mossy carpet of the clearing to gently disengage the Indian's left hand from among his folded arms across the massive chest.

Jake turned to the assemblage, holding the big Indian's hand aloft in his own, as a referee might hold the hand of a champion at the end of a boxing contest. "This is my friend, Night Walker," he proclaimed, "the Cherokee. He has taught me many things and only because of him, am I here today. He is a true man and a true friend. There is a world of learning outside the wooden frames of our White Man's way. I am happy you chose to share this experience with Sarah and me and our friend and brother. May you also feel his friendship."

As the crowd relaxed, a collective sigh rose from many throats. Smiling, they drew closer to the three friends.

When Jake and Sarah turned again toward the Shaman, he extended a bowl of crushed herbs in either hand. Each took a fistful of the fragrant mixture and trickled it into small fires on either side of the Cherokee.

Walker used hawk wings, hanging on cords about his neck, to swirl the rising fragrance around them in the otherwise still air.

"Earth, air, fire and water," he intoned with the confidence of his ancient understanding. Jake lost his hearing as he took both of Sarah's hands in his. The world was beautiful. Only fragments of Night Walker's speech could he hear above the hammering of his heart. Something about the great blessings of the Circle of Life and the will of Can Lun Lun Ti Ah Ni, Man Above.

Faces of the guests swirled about them with dizzying speed, holding and reflecting the happiness Jake felt in joining his life forever with Sarah's.

"Jacob! Jacob!" Night Walker brought Jake's focus back to the ceremony. "Do you bring this woman to your lodge as your first and only wife?"

Jake's eyes would not be torn from the face of his beloved. "She is mistress of my life and all my concerns," he promised, "For all time."

Sarah melted up against Jake, speaking her promises with the warmth and softness of her body.

"Not yet, not yet!" Night Walker restrained her with a firm but gentle hand.

Caught in the moment, the crowd laughed along with the admonition of the smiling Indian. Tears ran freely from the eyes of Sarah's father, across his normally stern countenance and into his bushy, gray mutton-chops. He scrubbed futility at the offending fountains to no avail.

Mr. O'Connell was not the only one to cry, Jake noticed as he scanned the faces of Sarah's mother and their friends. Every man and woman around the circle shared the magic equally, leaving not a single dry eye. The women wept openly and without shame as they leaned against their own husbands.

"Do you Sarah, accept the word of this man, Jacob, in all things? Will you give him sons?"

Sarah knew that "sons" really meant "children" - and in an even greater way it meant "life" - so she beamed as she answered, "Because he multiplies my life, I will multiply his."

With her response, Walker swirled the free end of a colorful woolen blanket around the couple, catching the opposite end skillfully in his free hand. Jake had never seen this blanket before but he recognized the symbols: leaping deer, growing corn and family.

Walker spoke the meaning of the symbols in his best booming voice, "You will walk together always in plenty and always in beauty. You begin as one and become many." As he finished he drew the blanket tightly about them, allowing no option but the close embrace they both so desired. Jake's mouth sought Sarah's with unabashed hunger. For that moment he forgot that anyone but the two of them existed.

Beyond the circle of family, at the very edges of the gathering, José Altimera and other of Jake's friends from across the wild lands of a young America recaptured their attention with a loud cheer, joined by even the most timid of the group. In the joy of the moment strangers hugged strangers and hats flew into the air.

No man Jake knew ever had a finer wedding. His heart swelled with remembered gratitude for his friends and his Sarah … his wife. This is the real dream, the dream that draws me back, Jake realized, eyes still closed, content to revisit the good life he had and still could have. This memory reawakens my purpose. I am a part of the great Circle of Life, of which my friend Night Walker speaks, and my absence affects many.

Man Above, return me to this dream, Jake prayed. Make it real! Make it mine! … I will get well, he pledged. I must.

With that thought, Jake slowly climbed the long winding staircase to consciousness. He felt refreshed knowing the ultimate purpose of his recovery. When he opened his eyes the camp was empty.

Jake closed his eyes again to doze, this time peacefully.

His good friend, Night Walker, the Cherokee Shaman had explained dream life to Jake while they camped together at Big Mesa the year before. That now seemed like a lifetime away. Forever ago.

The Cherokee Shaman explained that dreams mostly spoke to the Dreamer about what transpired every day and told him more how he felt about those events. There was plenty of that for Jake. The suffering from his injured forehead put a painful cast on everything that entertained him in the never-ending dream of recovery.

Dreams were also about other things, Jake knew. Through dreams the Dreamer reexamined the past until unresolved issues were put to rest or he could jump ahead to forewarnings of future events. It was difficult for an untutored person to determine the difference. Indian boys returning from vision quests talked of their dreams with the Shaman to learn that difference.

The Shaman, in this wonderful position as counselor, receives a great education in dreams himself, interpreting the dreams of others. Long conversations with Night Walker gave Jake some of that same perspective during their time together.

Jake had asked dumb questions at first, gradually becoming more sophisticated. Of the dreams he experienced now, several important dreams reoccurred. He knew they had significance, but being barely conscious, he lacked the wherewithal to unravel them all as he had the wedding dream. That would come later.

In the days that followed, light and dark alternated in a blur of dim awareness. All he could do was heal. It was enough. Altimera fed him several times of which he was aware. José showed great care and persistence in these simple tasks. Without him, Jake knew he surely would have died.

Finally he woke long enough to have another short conversation with José. At first Jake heard only the chirping of birds. Not dream birds this time. Hesitantly, he drew a shuddering breath deeply into his lungs. Oh, that felt good. The pain remained, only not as severely.

"Hola amigo," Jake ventured weakly. It seemed like late afternoon. No one answered his greeting. He dozed and when he awoke, José dumped wood next to the fire. The logs fell, bumping and banging loudly against each other onto the ground.

Jake thought his head might explode with the noise. "Ouch! Stop all that racket," he moaned. "Please." His hands waved uselessly in the air before his face as if they could defeat the sound and prevent the torture of pain. Jake resolved never to give this man a job at a hotel where the rest of the guests was important.

"Jacob," Altimera almost shouted in his surprise. To Jake that hurt as bad as the banging of the logs. "The Dead One, he lives." Hastily the Mexican bent to Jake's side and helped him sip water from a tin cup nearby. He knew Jake needed water at every conscious opportunity.

"Golly, that's good," Jake mumbled between gulps. Cool relief washed through him with each drink. His stomach must have shrunk, because he found he could hold only so much.

"That's enough water for now," José propped Jake against a saddle, so he could see a little of what transpired around him. Jake's head fell back limply against the polished leather as he stared into the concerned face of his friend.

I'm weaker than a rag doll, Jake thought, a dirty and worn rag doll.

"How long?" Jake asked, "And where are we?" Nothing looked familiar. Dense forest blocked his view on every side. He was, he realized, just thankful to be alive.

Cocking an eyebrow at Jake, José said, "If you stay awake long enough, I will tell you." He paused, "To start with we are in the mountains not far from Harry Harmon's claim, I think. We have been here for three weeks or so."

Jake remembered Sarah and something else that nagged at him. What was it? To his frustration, the memory remained tantalizingly out of reach.

Jake's inner conflict caused the Mexican to regard him with a strange expression. Dismissing his obvious concern with studied effort, José relaxed and sat back on his heels. Eyes losing focus in his effort to address detail, the Mexican massaged his stubbly chin with the fingers of his right hand and launched into the story.

"Whoever shot you tried to bury the bodies but did not do so good a job. Like I tell you before," José said, "you were the only one without the odor of death, so I figured you must live. That was about the only thing going for you all this time. In the beginning you breathed not at all. Not even once!" José paused and reconsidered. "That is not quite the whole truth," he corrected himself, "your skin was not so very cold as the others."

Altimera paused thoughtfully, tapping his cheek with an extended forefinger, then continued, "This confused me. At first, I consider that because you do everything you do so well, it must be that you find a better way to die. You become the first man not to go to the grave stone cold and stinking, except for perhaps the Son of God." José glanced briefly toward the heavens, crossing himself hastily.

The Mexican's eyes twinkled a bit at this last exaggeration. Either Altimera did his best to entertain Jake or he had been so long without conversation that he made up for lost time with creative storytelling. Jake found himself smiling in spite of his intense discomfort.

"It required almost a whole day to get you up here from where I found you," he went on. "I'm not sure how you endured all the rough travel but I believed it the best thing and still do, considering I did not want someone coming back to finish the job and put holes in me also."

"The others?" Jake slurred. "What about the others? Who else died?"

Placing his right palm on the ground and shifting his weight, Altimera crossed his legs, Indian-fashion. More of the concern reappeared on his face as he leaned back and used a long thick stick to push a middling-sized black kettle toward the hotter part of the fire. "You do not remember, Amigo? Harry Harmon, my cousins Manuel and Esteban, and the others with whom you worked the claim?"

"They're all dead?" gasped Jake as memory flooded back into his awareness.

"No one was left alive. It appeared as though you were shot from ambush at the turn of the trail. The older White Man, Harry Harmon I think, was shot close up. I believe that because of powder burns on his shirt."

"I thought that was just a bad dream," Jake's eyes drifted away as he relived the events that transpired in the island of light.

"Si, amigo. In any case it was a bad dream," José could not help remembering the corpses he unearthed when he found Jake.

Turning his attention once more to the living Jake Tallon, Altimera spoke again, "After I got you safely set up in this camp I had to leave several times. One time I doubled back to pick up the packsaddle and supplies I left when I used the horses to carry your stretcher. Another time

I went into town to get medical supplies and more food. I never knew what I would find when I returned, but there was no choice in the matter.

"Somebody wanted you real dead, amigo, and was willing to kill everyone else to get it done."

At the moment Jake was too tired to change his friend's thinking. José thought the whole world revolved around Jake. All the plots and counterplots featured Jake Tallon as the central character. In reality the world revolved around gold and this time as in many times previous, Jake was merely in the way.

I've been here before, he thought with some resignation. "This is the life I've chosen," he spoke aloud before fading out. Jake didn't wake up again 'til the following morning.

"I gotta go," Jake announced to no one in particular.

Raising his head proved much too painful, but he managed to part the blankets and relieve himself to one side of his pallet. To Jake's great relief the dirt quickly soaked up the tell-tale moisture. "Better there than the blankets," he breathed gratefully. Thank goodness no evidence remained of this weakness.

Jake realized he felt wonderful. He had actually done something for himself but still remained weak as a new puppy. A full cup of water rested where José set it down after the last drink. At first the cup could not be lifted, as Jake had no energy even to raise his arm.

Pulling the cup across the blanket and tilting it toward him, he drank from the lip until the cup was dry. More strength came with each swallow. Finished, Jake dropped the cup and fell back, gasping from the simple exertion.

Not an auspicious beginning for a man bent on regaining considerable strength.

Jake may have been foolhardy in his ambition, but still his eyes darted back and forth across the campsite seeking the next challenge. It leaned against the firewood pile, a walking stick, five or six feet of sturdy Hickory, maybe three inches in diameter at the top.

Under the blankets, he lay nearly naked but because the camp was deserted Jake knew nobody was going to notice. He threw the blankets aside and rested, taking great, deep breaths. After some moments, he rolled to his left side and pulled himself slowly forward, one determined elbow after the other, resting his chin upon the pine needle covered dust between efforts. His head throbbed in time with each heartbeat. Maybe this wasn't such a good idea, he allowed. Still he would not stop without completing the goal. He could not stop!

Consciousness dimmed and blinked once and again, but finally he arrived. Jake opened his eyes enough to see the pointed end of the stick dimpling the dust just a foot short of his face. He stretched out one filthy arm and grabbed the end of his new staff with a profound sense of victory.

"Hey!" exploded Altimera in outrage from beyond the edge of Jake's vision, "What in the name of the Holy Mother do you think you do? You should not be out from under those blankets!" As Jake heard him crunching forward, José said, "It is much too early. You are badly wounded amigo, more serious than you know."

"You want me to just lay there and die?" Jake gasped weakly, his face beaded with sweat from the recent exertion. With effort, he rolled over to better watch the Mexican, who strode purposely toward Jake with a brace of birds in one hand and a muzzle-loading shotgun in the other.

"You could die!" José confirmed, "If you do too much, too soon, and this is way too soon." He set down the birds and the gun by the fire and moved toward the pallet side of the firewood where Jake lay.

"I take a lot of killing, amigo," Jake's voice croaked and rasped. "I survived getting shot, buried, dug up and then carried into the mountains on two slab-footed horses and now suffer the attentions of a ham-handed nurse. I'm not about to expire while I retrain my legs to carry my own weight." The absence of strength and control in his voice made Jake's case weak.

"That's what you think Compadre," José said with hands on hips, now towering over Jake. "When I cleaned you up after digging you from that hillside, I pulled pieces of bone from your head. The only reason you're still alive is your head was so messed up, it never occurred to the estupido killers that you could possibly live. Your head is still messed up," he said angrily, jabbing his finger in Jake's direction, "but it is more your thinking, this time, that is at fault, not so much your skull."

Crouching down, he faced Jake on Jake's level, arms across his thighs, "One of those big silver pieces on your hat got pushed into your forehead, amigo. The impact tore a lot of skin loose and there was much blood. Much blood!" he emphasized. Spittle flew from José's mouth in his excitement; eyes bulged from his face with his intensity.

Sucking in a long deep breath, Altimera sat back on his heels and spoke more quietly again, while looking helplessly into his hands. Jake could hardly hear him. He said, "It seemed like the whole side of your head was blown open. It looked ver' bad!"

This description shocked Jake as José had intended it should.

José looked directly at him for emphasis. "I was and remain ver' afraid for you my frien'. I'm still not sure how bad you were hurt. I think maybe the bone of your head split all the way to the top."

"Sure feels like it," Jake agreed. Indeed, his head felt like it was splitting still. He rolled face down onto the ground and levered himself laboriously hand over hand up the long shaft of his intended walking stick, until he stood nearly upright. "Are you gonna watch me do this all by myself?" Jake asked the concerned Mexican pointedly.

"No amigo." Altimera mumbled contritely as he rushed to lend support. "Though you ignore my great concern, and treat me like dirt, I will help." Jake held the staff with both hands under his chin, smiling over his friend's intended guilt, as José held him under the armpit and helped him turn. Blood pounded painfully in Jake's head. His vision blurred and his breath came in sharp gasps.

"I had to do this small thing, José. Some little things first. Later I will do bigger things," Jake pledged.

Shaking his head with intense frustration, Altimera guided Jake back to the pallet and helped him slip between the blankets. Sweat mixed with dirt covered the front of Jake's legs and chest. Before lifting the blankets over him again, José roughly wiped the dust from him with the moist cloth from the bowl beside the pallet.

"See you only make more work for me! Why do you do this, amigo?" he asked rhetorically.

"I don't know," Jake answered himself honestly, fresh cold sweat popping out all over his body. "That could be the stupidest thing I've ever done. I guess I just had to see what I could manage, José."

The staff lay beside him now under the blanket, comforting him, proving by its very existence that he could do for himself. If he ever wanted to make his way back to Sarah his ability to overcome obstacles was very important. Jake held the staff close and slipped swiftly into the waiting blackness.

He awoke the next morning with José crouching over him, patiently dripping water onto the dressing. Jake felt almost human as long as he didn't move. He watched José's intensity as he worked, seeing sincere concern in the dark eyes. But as José pulled away the final bloodstained cloth he brightened.

"Bueno!" Altimera said. "This is better than I hope. The swelling, it is almost gone."

"Still hurts like hell," Jake confirmed. "If it's not gonna bleed anymore, let the air at it." He brushed away Altimera's hands with clumsy irritation.

Unsure of himself, Altimera picked up the soiled cloth in one hand, the basin in the other and backed toward the fire.

"I can eat some if ya got anything," Jake offered hopefully, seeking to assuage his friend's obviously hurt feelings. After a brief pause, he added, "Por favor, Señor Segundo. I beg of you, something to eat please."

José smiled broadly, "Now I know you get better when you speak polite to me, mi amigo. I deserve your respect." He bent over a steaming pot and dipped a wooden bowl into it for Jake and handed it over to him.

Sitting against the wood by the fire, José wrapped his arms around his knees and watched his friend eat. Jake spooned his own soup but had no strength to lift the bowl. It rested upon his chest.

"You 'mind me of a Heifer I saw one time," Jake said between spoonfuls, "watching her baby chew his first grass."

"Si! And I'm real proud of you also, Jacob."

Food gave Jake strength. He breathed deeply and carefully lifted the bowl to one side only half empty. Altimera still hadn't moved from where he sat.

After another moment the Mexican asked quietly, "Who shot you, amigo?" seeking an answer to the mystery from Jake for the first time.

"I don't know," Jake answered, also in a subdued voice. "We didn't have a chance. I must've been the first man hit because I never even heard a shot."

"Then someone knew what they were doing to shoot you first. Do you know why?" Answering his own question with a touch of humor, he said, "Could've been someone to whom you spoke rudely. I could shoot you myself, at times, you have such a bad mouth." He was laughing now. The Mexican's moist eyes would've given him away if his chest wasn't already shaking with strangled guffaws.

"Are you finished with your fun?" Jake was unable to restrain his own smile. Golly, the head hurt. He grimaced. But it was better than yesterday. Or was that the day before?

"Probably had something to do with the claim," Jake said as the Mexican's laughter tapered off some. "It started paying really good the last few days. If someone were watching, they could tell how rich it was by the time we spent picking dust out of the sluice box." Jake had Altimera's complete attention now. "Anyway, whoever shot us got about fifteen thousand dollars in dust and nuggets."

"Chihuahua! Repay your rudeness and get rich also. What a deal!" The Mexican's mustache twitched and danced as he struggled for control.

"This is really funny to you?" Jake asked, smiling again in spite of the pain and in spite of himself.

"No, amigo. I laugh, I think more because of my great relief." Exhaling loudly, Altimera released the pent-up tension of the past days and weeks and continued, "I could not tell you before, but now that I am sure you are okay, I can. I saw you lost some of your brains through the wound. I never saw such a bad wound in the head, where the man lived." He looked at Jake steady to see how his friend took the new information.

"Are you sure?" Jake asked with wide-eyed amazement. "How can that be and I yet survive? How can that be and I still have thoughts and dreams and memories?" He could only shrug helplessly.

Looking deep inside himself, Jake examined his own feelings and reflected that he didn't really care that brains of his were spilled. What difference did it make as long as he was okay. "I had too many in there anyway," Jake said with a nonchalance he actually felt.

José paused, still looking at Jake with a distrustful intensity, "You a strange Hombre, Tallon."

"You don't know strange until you hear the rest of it José. I stood off to the side when it was over, looked at my own body and watched 'em finish Harry when he didn't answer what they wanted of him. There were seven of 'em, that I saw. I'll remember each one when I see 'em. I promise I'll remember, 'cause I'll find every mother's son of them before I'm done. They'll each answer for the deed."

"I have heard of such things before," muttered the Mexican, unable to meet Jake's eyes.

"I was dead, José. Don't quite know why my body didn't stink 'cause I surely walked that Starry Path and sat in the Spirit Lodge with Man Above."

Eyes hooded, Altimera fidgeted, patiently dismembering a living twig.

Jake thought over what he had said and waited for his friend's reaction. He sure as heck didn't think about it before he'd said it. Jake had spoken as the memory replayed itself upon his inner eye without considering the particular beliefs of his friend.

This must challenge the Mexican's Catholicism. Jake knew how José felt about the Mother Church. For some heartbeats, he held his breath, not knowing how many of these Indian beliefs his friend might allow.

"Si," the Mexican said finally. "I believe you, Señor Jacob. There are many wonders the padres cannot explain, or maybe, will not explain." Altimera narrowed his eyes as he reexamined past memories. "When I found you, a smiling man dressed as a Peon told me to care for you, and that he would look after Esteban and Manuel. What could I think about that?

"Then he was gone like he was never there at all. Vanished! I believed it could only be my imagination." José looked up at Jake, finally meeting his eyes for the first time since Jake began discussing his apparent death. "That is so?"

"They found the Light, amigo. They are with Man Above just as I was for a short time in that better place. They might also be with Mother Mary. I just didn't see her during my short time in the Spirit Lodge.

"I saw a lot of folks who I knew, many who I didn't but who somehow knew me." Long seconds ticked off the clock in Jake's mind before he spoke again. "I got the feeling there were an awful lot of folks up there looking out for us."

"Huh." José grunted. "Angels." He stood and walked away from Jake to the edge of the forest, brooding. The Mexican needed to be alone with this strange new information, Jake understood.

"We can talk more later, José. I'll sleep now," Jake said. That was not an idle threat. He slept immediately. During his rest, he dreamt that strangers in glowing robes worked over his head wound, two or three of them at a time. The little clearing in the forest was sure crowded, he thought in some remote part of his mind.

When he woke, Altimera brought him more water and food. Jake didn't need to sleep again right away so José helped him to his feet and they staggered and swayed around the camp a couple of times in a good imitation of a Saturday night drunk.

Jake rested, ate again and began fantasizing his recovery. He remembered another Jacob Tallon in another life who lived with full strength and agility. Sadly, he thought, that was not the current state of affairs. It will be so once again, he pledged, some time soon!

Walking close by on some mission of his own, José did a double take on Jake's forehead. "Jacob," he said, "it looks like your wound is healing very well indeed. Looking at it now I couldn't guess it was that bad unless I saw it for myself right after it happened."

"Yeah, it doesn't hurt so much at all anymore. I'm mostly tired and weak as a new dropped foal." Jake remembered the dream about the healing angels but kept that part to himself.

Before the week was out, Jake began pushing his body slowly toward increased strength, beginning with his usual regimen of light daily exercise. Stretching each muscle, he began the slow motion positioning of each strike and defense move he remembered so well. In this way, Jake drew his strength from the air and the sun and the very fact of his determination.

Altimera watched Jake fight, close up and in slow motion with the same fascination he'd enjoyed in dismantling an old pocket watch in his youth. Like everyone else, he had mostly heard the stories of Jake's fights and saw the results after the fact. Now he saw how all the pieces went together like those of the watch and how a good fight was built from a series of small moves, strung together. Both the watch and Jake's fighting moves made more sense when you saw the pieces.

Teaching Jake the art of Chinese combat, after all, was how his brother Travis had saved Jake's life and his mind the first time.

Healing

ach day Jake improved, becoming stronger, faster and tougher. Nowhere near his old self yet, he reflected how hard it was to undo the damage that more than three weeks of near-death does to a person. And it made him different in ways he found difficult to explain.

He had gained some things and lost others. No surprise to anyone that he had lost plenty of muscle bulk and energy. That should return with time, he knew. He'd been wounded before and had gone through a recovery process before. As far as he could tell he was right in the head, although significant worries haunted him after hearing José's fearful description of bone fragments and spilled brains.

To begin with, Jake's vision was different. He saw lights where none should be and that worried him. Had the wound permanently affected him? In what way? What did he lose? Was he less a man now? Would he ever regain what he'd lost?

This worry refocused his attention inward as he examined his attitudes and actions, comparing himself to José. Did José believe that he'd been permanently changed by the injury?

Jake felt adrift without sails until he realized with a single, clear dramatic insight, that he could only be himself, good or bad. In some ways he'd always been a little crazy. That understanding brought a whimsical smile to his lips.

Snatches of memory from the Spirit Lodge returned to him in unguarded moments but remained tantalizingly out of reach whenever he sought a complete version of what had transpired. This search for a fuller memory inspired Jake to think about an escape into the woods that he might be more on his own and away from the distractions of José's mother-henning.

Folding his hands carefully in his lap, Altimera regarded him through worried eyes. "You're going hunting with a staff?" he asked skeptically when Jake announced his intentions.

"You're damned tootin'," Jake laughed back at him. "Even if I get nothing, I'll come back stronger." The bravado masked his silent but substantial doubts on the enterprise.

Sparks of color seemed to drift and flash around his Mexican friend. As Jake beheld them, he somehow felt José's warm concern emanating from the color itself like a different form of speech. Jake blinked his eyes, hoping his vision would improve, but the colors failed to disappear.

More and brighter sparks danced around his friend's torso. Happy sparks, Jake thought distractedly. Could be something there after all, though I don't know what.

Quickly Jake glanced to the horses. No sparks there. He looked to the darkness under the trees, thinking sparks might show up as a contrast against the gloom if his eyes were the problem. Not there either.

Yet the colors still danced around his friend as though they came from inside the man himself. There was nothing wrong with his eyes though that might have been the simpler solution.

These things disturbed Jake deeply. What did the colorful sparks mean if it wasn't his eyes? He continued to worry they may be due to his injury, yet before his foster father, Rudy, was killed he'd talked about how each person had their own lights. Jake always thought he used that as a manner of speaking. Now he was not so certain.

"Watch your back trail, José," Jake said on impulse. "I'm worried that we may not be totally safe, especially if someone remembers you asking directions to the claim, finds the burial place disturbed and makes a connection between the two."

"Si, amigo," José brightened. "I will be careful." This was more the Jake Tallon he remembered.

Picking up his staff and forcing the colors from his mind, Jake turned and ran smoothly into the woods with no particular plan. In fact Jake knew absolutely nothing of the area in which they camped. He just wanted some distance from his troubles and a chance to clear his head of the doubts and negatives that accumulate with inactivity.

Still weak and feeling a little clumsy, silence eluded him as branches slapped and pulled noisily at his clothing. He remembered a time when he could run like an Indian, but right now he sounded like a battalion of cavalry. Worse, Jake didn't know for sure from what he ran. Maybe he ran just to be tired but after a few minutes uphill Jake got all of that.

Slowing to a walk, he gradually cooled and finally stopped, leaning back limply against the rough bark of a pine to rest and better get his breath. Jake closed his eyes.

When he opened them again, there stood Man Above, Shantee or whatever he called himself, impeccable in loose white cotton clothing. Jake sensed his own inner conflict between the concept of Man Above and the reality of Shantee. Shantee seemed like a friend with whom he could visit, not at all as unapproachable as the most powerful entity in the universe.

"Why do you run, Jacob?" the very solid-looking being asked curiously, with the harmony of the wind through grass in his voice.

"I'm afraid," Jake answered truthfully, between still ragged breaths. His eyes refused to fully focus on his new mentor and friend. Sweat ran freely down his face.

"Why are you afraid?" Shantee smiled gently.

"I don't know," Jake wiped at the sweat with a forearm, noticing with mild surprise that Shantee stood six inches above the debris of the forest floor.

"Surely you know, Jacob. Think for a moment. Be as honest with yourself as you were in your first response," Shantee instructed.

Seconds passed as Jake's heart slowed and his thoughts turned inward. "Hah," he said with resignation, "Maybe I'm afraid my head got hurt in a way that time won't fix. I'm afraid I'll be addled, a misfit to be taken lightly among my equals, a freak." Suddenly, he felt lighter, as if this simple admission lifted a burden of rocks from his heart. Jake stood straighter against the tree. "Ah," he breathed, "that's better."

"You are more perfect," Shantee smiled brightly again, "than you have ever been, because now you know what waits beyond death."

"Ah," said Jake again, his breathing now fully recovered, eyes brightening at Shantee's encouragement.

"Knowing that, you see life more clearly than ever before. You see a purpose for life that others do not share." The Old Man's smile bridged the distance between the heart and the eyes.

Jake felt the gentleness of Shantee wash over him, shaking him, moving him with the force of a rolling, breaking wave. Shantee faded gradually away.

Extending his hand in panic, Jake reached out to him. "Don't go!" he yelled. "Please don't go!"

Dimly he heard, "I'm always here, Jacob. Do not be afraid. I am always near. Always here. Always in your heart."

Jake looked at the forest around him, as if seeing it for the first time. He saw how the wind loved the trees and how it reached up to caress the face of the mountains in the distance. He saw each creature of the forest as a child, innocent at its own task.

In that flickering instant, Jake fully understood his friend Night Walker and the unique reverence he held for every animal that gave its life for their food and warmth. He understood the Indian of every tribe. Jake understood both the ignorance and the glory of the White invaders. He understood both cultures and the part they played in the larger plan.

The brilliance of the understanding faded but Jake knew of it now. He also knew he did not need to be burdened with it for every moment.

Forgetting his fatigue, Jake started running again with new joy, slowly, following a vague path between trees, an opening in the brush that wound among the hills. He now ran soundlessly, evading branches and clinging brambles with eerie precision. Jake ran in harmony with the forest.

The wind carried a musky scent of short fur. Without seeing the animal, Jake knew it to be deer. His stomach spoke to him of uneaten meals and reminded him of his boast to Altimera.

Knees rising and falling tirelessly beneath him, Jake quickly covered a hundred yards and more. He tucked the staff under one arm as he ran, pumping the other arm in time with his confident strides. The sun was high so Jake knew that somewhere ahead the deer lay abed resting between meals of tender leaves and grass. The wind in his face promised him that the animal could not smell him coming.

Jake ran only by instinct, drifting first in one direction then another. Driven by that unseen hand, he sprinted between trees, up a hill, across a wash and along the other side. Without warning, a deer broke cover at his passage, running beside him, startled but ever graceful.

This was the only upwind path from its bed. Jake knew the deer would spring away the instant it realized the threat from which it ran matched it stride for stride on the same path. Of its own volition, the staff under Jake's arm unlimbered in a wide roundhouse swing that brought its solid length across the base of the proud animal's skull.

The deer collapsed with Jake on top, his knife instantly out and across the warm, pulsing throat before they stopped tumbling. Chest heaving, hands on knees, bloody knife on the pine needles before him, Jake knelt beside the cooling animal, startled at his own spontaneous violence. Never had he killed an animal in this manner before, like a panther or a wolf.

"This is all part of Life's Circle, Jacob," whispered the trees around him.

"Why did you show me this?" Jake yelled, head turning every way at once, seeking the source of the voice. "Why did you do this to me, Shantee?" he yelled. "I did not wish to kill!"

"Because it is so written here on Earth," came the gentle reply. "The life this animal offers is precious. May it make you strong, Jacob. Let yourself feel the gratitude this animal deserves for the gift of its life. Do it like the Indians, Jacob."

Gradually the rage drained from Jake's body just as the blood drained from the deer at his feet. Kneeling, then slumping against the still form of the deer, Jake embraced the quiet. He stroked the short fur reverently, giving the deer his full-hearted thanks, as a measure of calm slowly suffused Jake's spirit, lifting him up in a new way.

"You are my gift from Man Above, friend Deer, yet I do not take your life lightly." He paused, "I can never be the same as I was. And because of that I will never forget what you have done for me today."

With the hunter's ritual, he hung, bled and gutted the animal. As the sun descended in the sky, Jake built a fire and roasted fresh cuts of meat. This day gave him much to consider.

Sleep evaded him as he sat before the small fire through the night, wishing to remember, to savor this closeness with Shantee. Jake heated water in a bark cup and drank. Pieces of memory from the Spirit Lodge revisited him until he felt he had most of it in place.

Stars circled slowly over his head. With a start, he realized that the glowing, golden ornament given him by Shantee that hurt so much was the precious gift of life itself. That memory, circling ever in the back of his mind, had come suddenly to the fore. Jake smiled inwardly. Life captured beauty and pain at the same time, he realized. This was yet another profound truth.

Glancing up, he saw a coyote sitting on its haunches just beyond the light of the fire, staring at Jake with luminous eyes. It was husky for its kind, looking nearly as big as a wolf and just as sleek. Tongue hanging from its mouth, it sat courteously, waiting.

Jake felt a closeness with the creature difficult to explain. "I am like you," he told the Coyote. Jake marveled when the animal did not bolt at the sound of his voice. Such boldness in a wild thing was beyond his experience. Could this be a spirit animal, he wondered? "What do you have to tell me, friend Coyote? Do you ask for my generosity?"

To the side of Jake rested meat of the deer, cut and ready for breakfast. Selecting the largest piece, he tossed it to this new friend. Celebrating Jake's gift with prolonged eye contact, the large gray animal picked up its treasure slowly, almost delicately, and left without a backward glance.

The regal poise of the Coyote left Jake with much to ponder. Gradually he came to see the visit as not an isolated incident but part of his larger experience. Shantee speaks with many voices, he realized.

As the stars lost their brilliance, light from the rising sun stabbed across the eastern horizon and between the trees. Although he had not slept and was not tired, Jake's rear end ached from sitting so long in one position. Dry, sharp needles on the ground beneath him poked through his thin clothing. Trees and bushes released their perfumes to rise and swirl in the still atmosphere, speaking to the new sun in the only way they could.

Smoke from his rekindled fire added a touch of civilization to the riot of aromas, making Jake smile. When the fireside rocks reached an appropriate temperature, he seared the two remaining cuts of venison from the night before and turned them until the juices stopped flowing from knife cuts in the center of each piece.

Not so much remained after giving the best cut to the Coyote but Jake made the most of it, lingering over each sliver of meat as he cut it and brought it to his lips in a kind of ceremony.

Finished, he stood slowly, unkinked his limbs, eased through a few stretching exercises and swung the staff around and about experimentally, cutting the air with a sharp, distinctive whistle. Jake bent, parried, dodged and slashed, the staff becoming a natural extension of his ability. He felt truly alive for the first time since waking in José's camp. Revitalizing strength surged through his veins.

Bending to retrieve the heavy deer carcass, Jake threw it effortlessly across his shoulders and began jogging casually toward the distant camp. Must be a good five miles off, he thought, lengthening his stride. Running felt good, even with the added weight. He felt stronger, more confident of his ability, more certain of a future that finally seemed to stretch out before him, spanning numerous years, like rolling prairie hills seen from a high vantage. A future with Sarah and Julius Michael.

Longing for more civilized pleasures, Jake thought about the coffee that reposed within José's canvas bag waiting for the boiling water that would bring it life and purpose. Jake wondered idly what his friend might be doing at that moment.

The smell of the fire smoke reached him well before he saw the camp. It didn't surprise him to find José crouched above a small blaze as, still running, he rounded the last bend of the trail. Slowing to a walk, Jake saw his friend bent over an open white cloth sack, unpacking the contents. The Mexican seemed to be coming rather than going, he thought.

Altimera looked up when Jake stepped from the shadows under the trees. A smile of greeting lit his brown face from ear to ear.

"Hey, amigo!" he shouted happily, "I never expected to see you carrying anything heavier than a cup of coffee." José rushed solicitously forward to help Jake lower his burden to the ground.

The deer must have weighed a hundred thirty pounds were it an ounce. It never occurred to Jake it might be hard to do. He just did it. Altimera still worried on his behalf.

"Now that you mention it, José," Jake sighed, "I'm right tickled to set it down." Grunting loudly, he heaved it into José's arms. Jake's head throbbed, but briefly, as he shrugged off the weight. "I wouldn't have invited this deer back if I didn't think he'd make it on his own. His legs gave out five miles back."

"You should have known better, amigo," said Altimera, "Even I can see this deer has no guts." He laughed uproariously at his own humor.

As José carried the carcass into the cleared area near the fire, Jake stripped off his bloody shirt and retrieved the staff from the moss where he'd dropped it. Altimera stood up from his task, and looking back in Jake's direction, went suddenly white in the face. "Look what followed me home!" He thrust his chin at an area behind Jake.

Twisting around, Jake saw two strangers, silent and threatening, standing within the cleared circle of their camp. One positioned himself slightly forward of the other with his thumbs in his belt and guns tied low to both legs. He wore a heavy buckskin jacket with a three-inch fringe and a black felt hat with the brim pulled down to shadow the front of his face. The eyes gleamed like sparks of evil light in a pool of inky darkness.

His neatly trimmed black beard and the way he cocked his head fairly shouted bully at Jake. Plainly, he was more confident and more dangerous than the Hombre behind him with the drawn six-shooter.

"The name's Bingo Mackinaw," spoke the cocky gunslinger with an insolent smile. "I followed your friend here hoping to find me a grave robber at the end of the trail."

Jake stood half-naked with a blue cotton bandanna tied around his head like a Barbary Coast Pirate, and a five-foot length of seasoned wood in his left hand. He knew perfectly well whom Bingo sought. His need to make big talk might well cost Bingo something he wasn't prepared to pay, thought Jake.

"If you come for grave robbers," Jake said, stepping two steps forward as if to shake his hand, "you've come to the wrong place, friend."

The aggressive behavior caused the second gunman to stumble back a step and push his pistol forward nervously saying, "Stay right where you are, partner."

Thumbs still in his belt but now a little more off balance, Mackinaw stammered, "Wu-why don't you take off that bandanna and show us what you got there on yur forehead."

"Sure I will," Jake said, moving the stick to his right hand and using his left to comply without hesitation. Anybody could see the big black shadows around his eyes. Looking at the fresh wound would remove any doubt that yet remained.

Jake's hand continued smoothly past the bandanna to the butt end of the staff. "By the way … I'm not your partner," he spat, stepping forward again and snapping the smaller end of the staff up from the ground with lightning speed, catching the gunman solidly under the wrist behind the extended pistol.

The gun discharged with a loud bang as it leapt from the man's hand and cartwheeled, smoking, through the dappled light beneath the trees! As both the gunman's and Bingo Mackinaw's eyes flew open, wide with shock, Jake cross-stepped to his left. The striking point of the staff rotated upward, leaving the blunt butt-end forward.

In the blink of an eye, Bingo put a slug through the space where Jake had stood only an instant before. Absolutely certain that everything hinged upon his own boldness and accuracy, Jake thrust the staff forward with all his strength, aiming at the point where the wide ends of Bingo's mustache met together under his nose. Simultaneously, Bingo's second shot heated Jake's bare ribs under the arm as the bully went over backwards.

From behind, Jake heard two quick shots. Crouching defensively, he turned in time to watch the man he'd disarmed fall dead on his face in the pine needles. Altimera slipped his irons back into leather with a flourish and strode forward in his hand-tooled boots, cutting the layered gunsmoke in the clearing with his passage, like the prow of a proud China Clipper.

Stopping as he came even with Jake, they stood together peering down at the garbage littering their campsite. After a moment of silence, still looking downward, José asked with a note of awe in his voice, "That deer didn't stand a chance, did it, amigo?"

Saddened by this latest violence, Jake answered slowly and with some distraction, "No my friend. And like the deer, these two misguided souls go to a better place. Whether they deserve it or no, they go to Glory."

José bent to turn over the man he had shot. The two bullets had struck high in the chest bone and could be covered by a silver peso. "Not bad at thirty feet," Jake complimented him.

"That Mackinaw was snake quick," the Mexican said with a tardy mixture of fear and awe as he looked to his friend. "Had I any idea he was that fast, I never would have let you try anything so foolish."

"Had I not done something, we would be on the ground now, 'stead of them." Jake knelt beside the fallen Bingo Mackinaw, pulling the still warm pistol from his right hand and shoving it into his own belt. Bingo would have no need of that or any gun again. Likewise Jake unbuckled the belts and untied the holsters from the fallen man's legs.

Dying, the gunslinger did himself a favor. No one would've believed he'd been bested by a man with a stick. At the last moment he arched away from the staff, saving his teeth but taking a fatal blow between the eyes. He might have saved himself even then if he wasn't trying so hard to get lead into me, Jake thought. And he almost made it.

Still looking at the fallen gunman, Jake shivered with premonition, "There will be others. What I can't figure is why these Buckaroos weren't in the group that tried to kill me the first time. I never saw these fellows before. It was other men I saw kill Harry. I'm thinking there is a larger interest afoot. A much bigger fish swims in this pond."

"You may be more right than you know, amigo," said Altimera. "In Nazareth yesterday, people there were ver' uncomfortable in speaking with me. Even among the Californios, my own people, was I made to feel uncomfortable. The Yankee gunsmith, Eliza Crombe, he warned me not to stay too long in town, but would say no more." José avoided Jake's eyes.

His interest suddenly alive, Jake asked, "What did you do with the gunsmith?"

"Look at this," Altimera commanded. He held his Model '61 Army Remington barrel skyward with the breach over his cupped right hand. He turned the cylinder with the thumb of the left. An empty brass cartridge fell shining against the olive tones of his palm. Pulling two new cartridges from a vest pocket, he pointed the barrel downward, and dropped one into the back of the cylinder with a neat metallic click. He repeated the process with the other pistol.

"W-What's this?" Jake asked, now totally fascinated, "Cartridge-fed Remingtons?" Like most other folks, he was aware of the seven-shot, rim fire, twenty-two caliber pistol made by Smith and Wesson, introduced during the War, and the S & W Russian that came out later. "What's the story here?" Jake asked with sincere interest, reaching for the forty-four caliber Army.

Altimera handed him the piece to look at. As Jake accepted it, he brought it close to his face and flipped open the loading gate as he had seen José do. He found himself looking at the rear end of a modified, forty-four caliber rim fire Henry Rifle cartridge. To get the feel of it, he let it slide into his own hand and replaced it.

"Slick," Jake observed, "How does it shoot?"

"Muy bien," José replied, watching Jake closely. "Only difference is, it loads better, much better. You can load it on the back of a running horse or in the dark. Doesn't make any difference."

Jake lifted the hammer to half cock and spun the cylinder experimentally. He opened and closed the loading gate and spun the pistol with his finger hooked in the trigger guard. "I like it," he pronounced finally.

"He tools his own cylinders," said Altimera, "bores them straight through to chamber them for this cartridge. Cost me thirty-six dollar apiece."

"That's twice as much as a regular Colt."

"You're absolutely right," José answered, "But money is no object, since I wired your account in Sante Fe."

"My account?" Jake was instantly outraged, "Isn't that stealing?"

"It would be if I didn't buy you guns with it also," he humphed with a straight face. "This way you can make me a present of two from the original four I ordered from your generous allocation of cash." He was sailing now. "What the heck, Compadre, I'll buy you a drink with the money left over."

"So how did you get money from my account, without my permission?"

"I know many important people in banking."

"You mean you have many cousins and uncles."

"Same thing." José couldn't stop smiling.

"Pretty proud of those pearly-whites, aren't you?" Jake asked. "I know you are because you just can't stop showing 'em to me."

While Jake raged good-naturedly, Altimera dragged the gunslingers out of the area by their feet, arms trailing bonelessly above their heads.

"Think you pulled one over on ol' Jake, do you amigo? Just because someone shoots me and steals my pistols, you figure you can palm off some new-fangled idea on me. Huh?" Jake prodded.

José walked back from the circle of trees with his hand out. "If you don't like it, Señor Tallon, give the Remington back. I won't have my perfect intentions sullied by your ungenerous disrespect." He was only half kidding but Jake realized he had hurt his Mexican friend with his slow gratitude.

Jake didn't want to give the gun up, and slow to admit it, looked to the trees, the dirt - anywhere but his friend's demanding face.

Increasingly stern, José gestured impatiently once again with his open palm. "Give it to me, ungrateful one!"

Reluctantly Jake handed over the reworked Remington.

"Come," José said. "You can't have this one anyway, it is mine." Striding to his horse, he pulled two more pistols in handsomely polished, hand-tooled holsters from his bulging saddlebags.

"Oh, muchas gracias," Jake blubbered like a ten year old kid at Christmas. Now he was truly pleased. José handed them over with a broad smile.

Jake felt whipsawed and wanted to explain but knew the reasons were still beyond him.

"It's a big change," was the best he could manage.

"I understand, Señor Tallon," José replied with mock seriousness. "Though these pistols are exciting, giving up on your old guns is like putting down a favorite saddle horse."

"Exactly," Jake brightened. "Please tell me you went through the same thing."

"Si, I did," replied the Mexican without hesitation. "Once you get used to the idea, you'll wonder why anyone would want to hang onto those old cap'n balls."

Jake hardly heard him, so absorbed was he with the new hardware. As the first belt circled his waist he felt complete again.

"Before you buckle the next one, amigo, you may want to put this on the belt also." In his hand lay a small, heavy belt pouch similar to ones Jake previously owned for the replacement cylinders used by his cap'n ball guns. "Even with cartridges," José said, "this is still a good idea." Opening the pouch, he showed Jake two extra cylinders, already loaded.

Carefully, Jake threaded the second belt through the loops on the back of the pouch and slung the belt around his waist. Settling the belt firmly on his hips, Jake sobered.

"The game is up now, José. The appearance of Bingo Mackinaw tells us someone is suspicious and suspects I may not be dead. Until we learn their identities, they will have the advantage of surprise. We will always be guessing."

"It is time to move," agreed the Mexican, with equal seriousness. "This has also been much on my mind and you are now well enough to travel."

"That's what I'm thinking. Let's go down to Bodie town and find us a room where we can lay up in comfort. Three days travel ought to be enough distance."

"Those banditos will know you anywhere you go, Señor Jake. The advantage is they may not look for you so far away." José gestured toward the shadows under the trees. "You can see that Bingo was not all bad. He was kind enough to bring us extra horses and saddles. We should not ignore this gift, eh?"

With that, Altimera slapped Jake on the shoulder and walked back toward the fire to finish fixing breakfast. As he did, Jake began to pick up the camp and pack away what he could. It was only then he realized that after the ambush, the Bushwhackers on the road to Nazareth had taken almost everything he owned, even the Friendship Stone.

All he retained were his boots and the clothes he wore. If those had not been worn they might also have been taken. Manuel was buried without boots because they were his pride, worn only for the special occasion of going into town, prime loot for the killers. In a flash of memory, he saw a cruel Latin face bent over his own body after the killings.

With José's help, he must build another outfit.

Sitting on a rough log, Jake stripped off the moccasins borrowed from his friend and replaced them with his own worn work boots. Once finished, he returned to the fire, sat down across from his Mexican friend and poured them both coffee into battered tin cups.

José loaded up a pair of tin plates with beans, bacon and biscuits. They ate quietly, each consumed with their own thoughts. For his part, Jake felt damned good. He ran his left hand tentatively over the fresh bullet burn, appreciating the pain as a reaffirmation of his life.

Reflecting, he repeated Altimera's earlier concern, "If I had known he was near that fast, I never would have tried what I did with those Yahoos. That was sure stupid."

"Sure amigo," Altimera reminded him, adopting Jake's previous reasoning, "and if you had been that much smarter, one or both of us would surely be dead right now. Here we have a real argument for ignorance." The Mexican gave Jake a broad wink.

José threw the last of his coffee into the fire and stood, kicking it apart.

Choosing his own tasks, Jake scrubbed the plates in a bucket of water and drowned the coals remaining from the fire with it as he finished. No point of disguising the camp. He was armed now. Let 'em come.

Bodie Town

Hidden within the hills and forest-carpeted mountains to the west, and now behind them, lay vast cool lakes and bubbling streams of clear water. By contrast, the Great Basin presented fields of blasted, broken rock and unmarked vistas of arid sand under a fierce yellow-orange sun.

"Looks like the Devil's front yard, don't it, José?"

"Smells like it too," responded the Mexican, squinting his eyes against the brightness.

"What you're smellin' is likely the mineral in the rock," Jake commented. "And I expect that if this place were covered over in forest, it would smell a lot better, but the gold in Bodie Butte would never have been discovered. Desolation is a double-edged sword."

"I jus' make the smell part up to emphasize my point." Altimera narrowed his eyes resentfully in Jake's direction. "Sometimes you are very agreeable for all the wrong reasons."

"You can taste it too."

"Now you go too far my friend. I will not lick the rocks!"

"It might come to that," teased Jake, "if we endure much more of your cooking."

After endless sun, and heat that left them parched, they finally reached their destination. Pulling up under some rare tall trees, Jake and Altimera sat their horses, looking down a long straight stretch of false-fronted stores and saloons. Several intersections interrupted the march of construction. Jake had visited this town several times before joining Harry Harmon at his proposed mine site. People down there knew him by sight. That's the reason he and José sat looking instead of riding, at least in Jake's mind.

"I don't know I'm up to this, amigo," Jake moved his gaze from the town before them to his friend, Altimera. "A few more days of rest appeal greatly to me but now that we're here, this town worries me."

"Do you speak to amuse yourself, Jacob?" The Mexican gestured in helpless frustration. "Seems like we've been down this trail at least once already."

51

Grunting with the agony of a stiffened body, Jake hooked a knee around the saddle horn, unwilling to be pushed into any fast decision. His horse turned its head, casting him a weary eye. "It's more than my weakness, José. Something changes inside me. I'm not who I used to be. I'm afraid if I ride down that street, folks will expect the old me and I might end up giving them what they want before I know enough about who I am now to react honestly."

"You're loco, amigo," Altimera spat. "I don' understand you sometimes. First you want to be here and now we are here, you are not so sure anymore, even who you are. Maybe I just kick you under a rock and cover you up again like I foun' you."

José made more sense than he knew.

"Not bad thinking for such a broken down Vaquero," Jake complimented him with a solemn nod of his head.

Altimera bristled instantly at the words, turning in his saddle. "You want to see broken-down?" he asked pointedly.

"I'm serious," said Jake, secretly pleased to get the Mexican's goat so easily. "Let's find a rock to hide under for a while so I can sort things out. You must know some folks down there in Old Town. Let's rent us somebody's back room or a couple of horse stalls. After living under a sand hill, I have fewer fancy notions."

"Si, this we can do, amigo. Ha!" he commanded, spurring Big Red energetically back onto the trail.

Jake unwound his leg from around the saddle horn, worked his foot back into the stirrup after a couple of tries and followed the Mexican out from under the shade of the cottonwoods. Together they skirted the sparsely populated edges of Bodie Town, angling to the south.

"I'm glad, amigo," said the dapper Mexican, "that you choose to humor me. I do not want to fight you in your current weakened condition. I might never forgive myself for hurting you badly."

They both smiled at this shared humor.

Outside of an old man dumping trash behind a saloon, no one paid them much attention as they entered town. With the bandanna headgear and one set of tattered clothes, Jake knew he made less than a memorable impression. Being remembered was the one thing he wished to avoid.

Away from the hubbub of Main Street, Altimera guided them to a collection of more humble adobe buildings. He inquired of a youngster for Señora Dolores Ferdinand Hernanda Garcia. Happily the boy chattered away in Spanish with a speed that defied Jake's meager understanding. He got the yes part of what the boy said before he saw the soles of his bare feet throwing little clouds of dust in the air behind him down the street.

Jake's eyes would not remain focused. Three days in the saddle had eaten away at his reserves of strength, leaving him uncommonly weak. He

felt poorly, something he was slow to admit. Fear teased at his consciousness. He wished to see Sarah again, hold their boy, Julius Michael, after
his birth. At this moment he feared that death might rob him of his future
and his family. "Please, Shantee," he breathed through gritted teeth, "Help
me. Give me the strength I need to go on." Vividly, Jake saw himself
sitting across the fire from Shantee in the Spirit Lodge. In an instant
replay, he saw how he had resisted his own return to life! "You were right,
after all," he mumbled, smiling ruefully in spite of his weakness.

Jake returned reluctantly to the present as José slowed his horse in
front of a slightly more imposing two-story adobe. The Mexican jumped
from his horse as the youth ran ahead. Deep shadows imprisoned within
the doorframe of the adobe structure hungrily consumed the youngster as
he crossed the threshold.

With barely energy enough to remain in the saddle, Jake fidgeted
with the impatience born of fatigue. His clothing itched and chaffed
against his skin as he watched his Mexican friend lift his hat and carefully
run his fingers through his black wavy hair and then stand quietly with his
hat held before him in both hands.

Wobbling nearly out of control, Jake clutched suddenly at the
pommel before him for support. Waves of heat and icy chill surged
through his body, causing him to sweat and freeze alternately. What a
weakling, he thought, hoping nobody noticed. Certainly José paid him no
attention. Jake saw only the Mexican's back during the entire silent
ordeal.

Even as that thought formed, a young woman and a regally
beautiful matron with glowing skin appeared in the doorway through
which the boy had vanished. Both of the women conversed with José in
rapid Spanish, punctuated with warm smiles and dramatic gestures as the
Mexican stepped from the saddle.

Spinning 'round Jake like a slow-motion carousel, the world tilted
perilously, causing a low moan to escape his throat involuntarily. How can
it spin like that, Jake wondered abstractly, feeling increasingly unwell,
looking to the ground beside his horse with longing. When José finally
turned to Jake, he barely caught Jake as he flowed liquidly from the
saddle toward the waiting ground.

No matter what that Mexican went through, thought Jake, he
always looked good. On the other hand, Jake knew that tattered, dirty and
unshaven as he was, he looked like hell. Of course, he'd just recently been
shot, so maybe he had an excuse.

Pulling Jake's arm over his sturdy shoulders to better support his
sagging weight, Altimera looked up as the matron excused herself from the
conversation and hurried into the house with urgency. Jake noticed that
José watched the disappearing form longer than ordinary interest required.

"Something special?" commented Jake pointedly, though weakly.

"The Señora must return to her dinner party," José answered, continuing to stare and pointedly ignoring the question around which Jake's words were wrapped.

Jake's head rolled loosely on his shoulders. "Ahh," he groaned. With some help from the younger woman, José moved him inside where they pulled off his boots and shirt and got him under a blanket. This is an improvement, thought Jake with relief, already feeling better. The Mexican continued to talk but Jake was unable to comprehend, closing his eyes, focusing instead on the pleasant drone of his friend's voice.

After a bit the young woman reappeared to help Jake into a bath, prepared in the next room while he dozed. Jake looked wildly around. Where did Altimera go, just when he was needed most?

Simultaneously, Jake realized he was alone with the girl and she was quickly getting him naked. "No," he protested weakly. "I'm married. This is not decent!"

"No comprendo," the girl insisted sweetly, showing him her beautiful, mischievous smile. Jake found no strength to resist. Nor, he realized, did he have the strength to remain long embarrassed. Fortunately, the young woman demonstrated only honorable intentions.

Soapy water soon swirled warmly around Jake's tired muscles, draining away the accumulated aches and fatigue. He let his head sag wearily against the arching metal end of the tub as the young woman scrubbed at his arms and shoulders with a rough chunk of soap, bigger than her hand. Energy flowed into his tired body directly from the sudsy water. She pushed him forward so she could scrub at his back and, once finished, left him to relax with every inch of his skin feeling fresh and new. Jake soaked, blissfully dozing once again, until the girl returned with an evil looking straight razor to remove his beard and trim his hair. Water sloshed over the edges of the tub as Jake sat abruptly straighter. So many times had the blade been sharpened, that less than half the original width remained.

Jake relaxed while she worked on his hair, her slender fingers building a neat pile of trimmings on the polished floorboards next to the tub. Some part of him noticed a light sprinkling of gray in the mound of brown. "No wonder in that, after all I been through," he mumbled.

The girl ignored his murmurings or accepted them as natural for a man in his condition and worked industriously until, before he knew it, Jake found himself clean and trimmed. Heck, he thought, this is where I was headed more than a month ago when Johnny Lobo blew me off my horse.

Shocked, as though splashed by a torrent of cold water, Jake wondered, where did that name come from? The West is a small place, he mused. He'd heard of Lobo before but in no particular connection to himself. The skin tingled electrically across his body. As bizarre as it seemed, this was a certainty that Jake could not ignore.

But why Johnny Lobo? He did this to me? Who paid him? He must've been paid. Jake vaguely remembered Johnny Lobo referred to as an easy-going killer with few personal grudges.

Receiving that name felt strange, like someone whispering in his ear, but the girl Teresa had long since left the room. Teresa? She looked like a Teresa but again he seemed to know without being told. The water went suddenly cold. The goose bumps popping up across his skin had nothing to do with the temperature of the bath or the room.

He wanted to share this new information with José. No! Though a trusted friend, Altimera might be too quick to judge such a personal revelation. Mostly he wanted to tell Night Walker, because Jake knew Night Walker would understand. Night Walker would help him. But Walker would be far away in the Territories among his own people, not here.

Standing now, Jake dripped into the soapy water lapping about his knees. He realized he was on his own. Toweling off, he slipped into the fresh long handles left him for that purpose.

Strangely agitated, Jake felt a powerful urge to get away, anywhere, but certainly someplace else. There was someone, he thought, with whom he might share! Dressing quickly and pulling on his heavy, worn boots, Jake pushed open the back door and headed toward the stables, savoring the rush of new energy.

Several horses milled aimlessly about the dusty corral, swishing at the clinging flies with their long tails. Wading into the crowd of animals with a loosely coiled rope, he cut out a long-maned, gray stallion with a heavily muscled chest and bright eyes, then dropped a loop over his head.

Reeling him in hand over hand, Jake looped and tied the other end of the rope into a makeshift halter and slipped it over the animal's nose. Leading him out of the gate, he closed it carefully behind them and straddled the long bare back of this fast looking horse.

Riding an unsaddled horse out of the yard, Jake felt the probing stares of many eyes on his disappearing back. Without guilt, he rode directly out of town and toward the looming mountains, ones he hadn't yet explored. Could be, they thought he was stealing this horse but Jake knew he'd left extra horses behind him and he knew he'd be back in any case.

He didn't have to ride far and he didn't need a trail. Water wasn't that important. Even food wasn't important to him at the moment.

Right now, disturbed on a very deep level, Jake needed open country to cure what ailed him.

Signs of civilization dropped away as he rode into the lower hills. No farms or houses perched on the sagebrush-dotted slopes before him.

Only the wind and the sun or an occasional bleary-eyed prospector visited such places.

Long shadows of the mountain pines reached down across the rolling slopes to greet Jake as he climbed upward. The horse slowed to a walk and finally stopped of its own volition to blow after the long run. Already Jake began to feel Man Above's peace settle upon and into him. He slid from the side of the horse, and using the makeshift bridle, led him forward among large, weather-rounded, granite boulders. Lifting his eyes, Jake searched for a high place where he might wait out the visitation he believed was coming.

Man Above had appeared and had spoken to him several times since his injury. Having been to the Spirit Lodge, Jake understood and accepted his talks with Shantee during those times Shantee chose to be seen. Perhaps he'd been weakened and more open because of it. Now Jake deeply desired the counsel of Can Lun Lun Ti Ah Ni out of his own choice. He needed it!

As the sun disappeared beyond the western ridges, Jake mounted the last of a series of long hills. Before full dark he picketed the stallion at the end of a climbing canyon and made his way upward among short, thirsty trees, onto a flat stone outcropping thirty yards across that looked over the yellow-green, sage covered valley below. Man Above was out there somewhere, he knew. How should Jake call out to him? What name should he use?

Crossing his legs, Jake settled down for the evening on the hard, bare, time-tested rock and watched the world below. While his eyes remained active, the breath entering and leaving his lungs slowed to an imperceptible rate. Each muscle assumed a perfect state of rest.

A small breeze caressed Jake's face as he gazed upward into the sky going lavender to purple. A hunting owl coasted downward, slanting across the mountain in front of him, cutting the fabric of darkness on silent, searching wings. The very sight of the beautiful predator kindled the wild song in his heart. Breathing deeply in the free, cold air of the star scattered night, Jake let the land soak into his bones.

For the first time since regaining consciousness he felt at peace. Most of the fear and pain were behind him now. No task demanded his attention. Each breath possessed its own value. He tasted the pure air as he drew it in again and felt it warm against his face as he let it slowly go, to swirl on the wind and wash back across his skin, his tension draining away.

Much of the night passed in this fashion. Small sounds of nature came to Jake as he sat unmoving in the dark. Stars whirled around the sky above his head. Dozing for a short period, Jake awoke to a brittle clarity before sunrise, its brilliant gold leaking like liquid fire across the horizon before him.

Life was enough, all by itself. Jake knew that this must be the affirmation he sought.

So thinking, he rose evenly from the seated posture of the long night and stood, arms at his side to face a rising sun. Each young man of the Nations took a vision quest on his passage to manhood. Alone in nature he waited without food or water for the vision or the life totem that would shape his days of maturity.

In a small way Jake felt cheated. Man Above had never appeared. Nor had he seen a glorious bear, or even the clever Coyote of a few nights ago. No grand vision presented itself to him, but he understood his difference in a big way. Whoever Jake Tallon was before his death experience did not count for spit. He felt his newness like a just-purchased set of store-bought clothes.

Consciously setting aside the nagging disappointment, Jake affirmed that if Man Above had chosen him at his advanced age of twenty-seven to start again, he would do it with determination and dignity. Jake remembered Shantee telling him he was more perfect simply because he understood more now than before. Maybe I can be a better person, because I know what waits beyond death, he thought. Maybe some of this feels uncomfortable but I never met a man made me back water. I'll not run from ideas either.

Let's see what happens.

His stepfather, Rudy Barnette, had said one time that dignity and determination were the only real clothes a man needed. It stuck with Jake then and he remembered it now.

The new rays of the sun warmed his face and slowly moved downward until his entire, lightly clothed body was awash in the orange light of the new day. Jake felt finally and fully at peace.

Shoulder the Burden

Turning on his heels, Jake retraced his steps down the steep path to where the Gray was picketed. Spending the whole night without a friend or a fire, the horse was glad at Jake's return. Jake heard his wicker long before he could see the lonely animal.

The Gray pulled at his tether as Jake came into view, calming only at his touch. First stroking his shoulder in appreciation, Jake untied the picket and hobbled him to better graze the lush green grass below the seep. As the horse dined, Jake washed and drank from the small gravel-bottomed pool. His own stomach began speaking to him. "This horse could eat better back at the barn and so could you," it said.

With the spontaneous enthusiasm of his new optimism, Jake slipped the hobble from the legs of the horse and swung a foot over his bare back. He kicked him into a gallop out the long end of the canyon and ran the horse for all he was worth until they neared the outskirts of town. Slowing to a walk, Jake picked his way among the scattered shanties that housed the town's exiles until he again spotted the white Spanish dwellings of his lovely and courteous host, Señora Delores.

Jake stepped from the back of the Gray, and holding the halter close to the chin of the horse, put his own face near so he was certain the animal could hear. "You did good, boy," Jake said, stroking the side of his long face. "You run like a colt. Your heart is as big as the sky!"

The big gray horse blew through his nostrils in acknowledgment, shaking his head. It occurred to Jake that because the horse belonged to his host, Jake did not know the name of this beautiful animal and had not given him a new one. Stepping close, he stroked the long, muscled neck affectionately and sadly.

In return the horse bumped Jake a little with his shoulder and whickered gently back at him. It reawakened memories of Sam, the big Grulla he'd ridden all last year, now at the Colorado homestead. The Gray was a good horse also, Jake decided, like Sam.

He soon found himself in front of the barn behind the adobes where he'd started. Waiting at the door of the family quarters was the dignified older woman he had seen before. Jake assumed her to be Señora Dolores.

The doorway in which the proud and gentle woman stood was awash with a soft blue light that swirled around her like a billowing cloak, easy to see against the darkness of the hallway behind her. This was more of what he'd been through before with Altimera so Jake was halfway prepared for the phenomena. The feelings he received from her were of deep kindness and great wisdom. Jake reached to take off his hat in polite respect.

When his hand met only empty air where his hat should have been, they both laughed at the mistake. "Welcome back, Señor Tallon," she said. Wrinkles fanning outward from the corner of each eye spoke of a life filled with laughter. "I hope your evening on the mountain was pleasant."

"Very pleasant, Señora," Jake answered, smiling back at her generous understanding. "The lovely fragrances of your kitchen reached out to me in invitation, even on the mountain." They both smiled again as Jake finished asking himself to breakfast. "I could not long ignore them."

In her late thirties, Señora Dolores retained her great beauty. An ornately carved wooden comb held her shining ebony hair in a bun, high on the back of her head. She wore a black, open necked, lace-trimmed dress that seemed far too grand for the dwelling and the town.

Yesterday's barefoot boy ran from the shadows of the stable to take the gray stallion from Jake and care for him. "Muchas gracias," Jake smiled as he handed over the halter rope to the well-scrubbed young man.

Señora Delores stepped aside so Jake might enter, then she followed behind as he passed her. "Go to the right," she instructed with the music of laughter in her voice, "or you can just follow your nose."

Walking over the rug-covered wooden floors Jake took the right turn she had indicated and then an immediate left. At the end of a short hallway he saw an elaborate, formal dining area with a lace covered, highly polished dark wood table. Teak, he guessed, as he let his fingers brush across the satiny surface. He'd seen such furniture in Sarah's home in Sante Fe.

Halfway down the hall he saw a large, ornately paneled, heavy wooden door set strongly into a plain wall. Through this he stepped onto the broad shining tiles of the home's kitchen. The high-ceilinged room took Jake's breath away, both with smells of cooking and the enormous display of copper and iron food preparation equipment hanging from racks and walls.

"Hola," he said in sincere awe, "I've been long on the trail. This must be cooking heaven."

Señora Delores laughed with a crystalline tinkle that warmed his heart. "Food is so important," she said. "Food makes a family strong, it brings them together over the table and can do the same for people of different cultures. It is a tool. My home is the truce-ground for the Whites and the Mexicans of this town."

Dressed in a billowing work-skirt with rolled up sleeves, the cook heaped big plates for Jake at a side table under a window in the thick adobe wall of the kitchen. He could see steam rising from at least three interesting dishes. Being all night and most of yesterday without nourishment he required no further invitation.

"I can see how that might happen," Jake said to her over his shoulder. The kitchen woman smiled at Jake's obvious enthusiasm and pulled out a chair for him as he approached. As Jake sat she spread clean white linen across his knees.

"Daddy always said that hunger is the best cook but it always helps to set a fine table." Evidently, Señora Dolores let no one down in that regard. Jake was to learn later, the esteem in which folks held her famous meals. An invitation to the table of Señora Dolores was highly valued throughout Bodie.

Jake hoped his obvious relish pleased the Señora's cook because he did not do a very good job of thanking either of them at that time. His only attention was for the food itself. Hopefully, they understood.

Before Jake finished eating, Altimera came clattering into the kitchen, spurs across the tiles. A short-haired dog yapped playfully at his heels. The cook chased it off good-naturedly with mild curses and a big wooden spoon.

"I found a friend of yours, Jacob," José announced.

"The dog?"

"No, not the dog, you loco Gringo."

"Didn't know I had any here." Even as he chewed, Jake scooped pieces of steaming, spiced meat and fried vegetables into another twelve-inch corn tortilla and rolled it up that he might hold it with his hands. The thing dripped like crazy out the open end but the meat, herbs and peppers were a celebration after the weeks with José in the mountains.

"You like watching me eat?" Jake asked him as José stood with a silly smile spread over his face.

"I never saw anyone eat like you eat."

"Maybe, if you were half a cook, you could have seen this before," Jake responded with an accusing eyebrow.

"Maybe I didn't want to see it before. I was just protecting myself," Altimera slapped his leg with his hat, laughing. "Just protecting myself," he repeated. "Now I don't know if I can watch you eat again. It would be too awful." He leaned back against a heavy butcher block for support. Finally he slumped into a chair exhausted by his own laughing.

"I like for my friends to have a good time," Jake said, genuinely pleased with him. "Just puzzles me how you can have such a good time over something so stupid." He grabbed the hat from José's hand and rose from his chair, beating José soundly on the head and shoulders with it. The Mexican howled in loud protest.

"Niños, niños," shouted the cook approaching rapidly from the opposite side of the kitchen. "You grown men act your age or go outside," she admonished sternly with hands on her ample hips, her face screwed up in serious disapproval.

Sitting down again in his chair with a contented sigh, Jake pushed the empty plate away and looked up at her contritely. She had neither moved nor changed her stern expression. "I apologize, Consuela, can you bring my friend a cup for your good coffee, por favor."

Startled, the cook froze in her tracks. "How is it you know my name, Señor Jake," she asked, eyes wide with surprise, "when nobody toll you."

"You must have told me," Jake winked broadly at her.

She turned away for the coffee then turned sharply back to Jake again. "No, I did not tell you," she asserted.

"Must've been a little bird, then," Jake said. Secretly he shrugged, knowing in fact that she had never told him and this was one more instance of the mysterious "knowing" that had settled upon him.

I must learn more discretion, he cautioned himself. This is a strange gift and I cannot fully understand it. Until I do, I must be more careful.

Altimera witnessed the exchange quietly with serious eyes.

Consuela returned with black steaming coffee in two handsome ceramic mugs. Jake took a minute absorbing the quiet, comfortable surroundings with his friend and the coffee. He appreciated the comfort of four thick walls and the protection they offered. He could rest. Another moment or two passed.

"You said you found a friend of mine."

"He found me," said Altimera. "Man name of Colt McKenzie, says he knows you real well. He asks me if you still fight with trees."

"So what did you tell him?" Jake sipped at the coffee.

"I could not lie," Altimera shrugged expressively. "I tell him you still muy loco, only more now. He only laugh. Colt McKenzie is the Town Marshal here in Bodie."

The conversation lapsed and silence stretched out between the two friends. The weight of unasked questions made even Jake uncomfortable. Altimera studiously watched his cup as he rotated it in a pool of moisture on the table.

"To where did you rush off, yesterday?" the concerned Vaquero asked finally.

Jake exhaled in great relief. That question could be comfortably answered. Other questions he asked of himself did not yet have clear answers.

Pushing his legs out straight under the table, Jake slouched in the chair and looked up at José from where his chin rested upon his chest. "Another Vision Quest," Jake told him. "This head injury changed a lot of things for me that I still need to think about. Finding time alone in the forest or on the mountain is important to me right now. Yesterday it became a need I could no longer ignore."

"Si, amigo," Altimera nodded with real understanding.

"After I got cleaned up, things kinda came down on me all at once. Didn't even feel like I had time to explain. Didn't even take a saddle," Jake finished, smiling uncomfortably at the apparent stupidity.

"I watched you go," José said with his own smile. "I knew you must eventually return. You left your pistols on the wash stand."

"I didn't get much sleep on the mountain but I'm happy I went. Now I'm glad to be back." Jake rubbed an open hand appreciatively across a full belly.

"Come amigo," said the Mexican, abruptly standing, "Let's go get you into some decent clothing."

In pure reflex, Jake stood and followed José's long, thumping, spur-jangling strides out of the room into another wing of the building that Jake had not noticed from the outside of the structure. They found themselves in a wide hallway with heavy doors set deeply into the walls on either side. Built just like a fortress, Jake thought.

The building was not old. No man-made structure existed anywhere near Bodie Butte until the recent discovery of gold. Before the mining, there were only rocks and lizards. This hacienda was architectural custom transplanted from southern California and New Mexico.

Three doors down on the left, José levered an ornately curved, six-inch bar that served as a handle. The wide, heavy door swung quietly open, revealing a bedchamber with long curtained windows looking onto an enclosed garden. Seeking the open door, the warm breeze billowed the gossamer curtains into the room, bringing with it the smells of fresh watered soil and growing plants in the courtyard beyond.

Heart singing, Jake rejoiced in the beauty, the very peacefulness of this simple room, drinking it in, absorbing it.

Never hesitating, José walked straight across the room to the bed and began energetically unwrapping paper packages, setting the tightly wound hemp twine to one side.

"The Señora will want to save this," he said when he saw Jake watching curiously. "Simple things are sometimes difficult to obtain."

"You're a very considerate man. The Señora must appreciate your attention," commented Jake dryly.

Altimera acted as though he had heard nothing and continued unwrapping parcels, of which there were many. Jake saw two pair of denim pants, another set of long handles, plus shirts, handkerchiefs and personal items like soap and a brand spanking new straight razor.

"What's all this?" Jake asked stupidly, swinging an arm wide to encompass all the new supplies.

"Yours," José said. "While you took a holiday in the mountains, I shopped for you in Bodie." Stepping back from the bed, thumbs in his belt, he asked, "Do you approve?"

"Si, amigo," Jake answered, deeply touched as he surveyed the bounty. Everything he would think to buy lay before him. Jake looked up at his friend.

Seeing the question in Jake's eyes, José added, "It was your dinero, mi amigo. But wait, I have more."

Altimera reached into his pocket and extracted a soft leather pouch full of dully clinking coins. Handing it to Jake he added, "It will be enough for some time."

The bag caused Jake's hand to sag heavily toward the floor. He could tell just by the weight that it contained several hundred dollars. With clean shirts and money in his pocket, Jake felt even more like a complete man.

"Muchas gracias, Compadre," he said sincerely while slipping into a new blue shirt with thin vertical stripes. "You are too good to me." He put on a pair of new pants and when Jake reached again for his old work boots, Altimera placed a restraining hand on his arm.

"Try these," he said pointing to a handsome pair of brown, hand-tooled boots with silver toes and inlaid silver on the heel.

"Whew," Jake said, "look at those boots! You must've sent all the way to Sonora for those, my friend."

"No such luck," José ignored Jake's sarcasm. "But when I found them I think of you. I know you prefer softer foot gear, but these are better for riding and will do until you can kill an elk."

Absently nodding agreement, Jake's eyes were drawn to the reworked Remingtons across the room. They occupied a place of honor in the middle of a low chest of drawers, the only furniture other than a chair and the bed. Their wide belts were wrapped snugly around the long tapered holsters, forming identical bundles with the curved handles facing outward in opposite directions.

Between them set a small vase with a short-stemmed cluster of bright golden daffodils. "Gunflowers," muttered Jake, smiling at the contradiction of terms and remembering another time on a bright green hillside where the term first came to mind when he watched puffs of smoke rise from his gun in an eerily beautiful way.

Stepping forward he lifted the pair of pistols almost reverently and held them briefly in either hand, thinking about the recurring pain in his right hip from last year's bullet wound.

Jarred came to mind and Jake wished for an instant he could tell him of the pain, that he might understand why there is no romance in old scars. They hurt. But it was too late for Jarred.

Like an echo in the back of his mind a distant voice said, "Maybe next time."

Jake looked up startled. "What does that mean, next time? There is no next time, once you're dead. Never heard of such a thing." Simultaneously Jake felt the smile of the distant voice and the sideways glance of his Mexican friend.

"Of what do you speak?" asked Altimera.

"Nothing," replied a perplexed Jake Tallon. "Just talkin' to myself."

"Jésus Cristo said he would come again," volunteered a hesitant Altimera. "Does that help?"

Embarrassed by the incident, Jake ignored his friend. He reversed the first holster on its belt so it could hang conventionally and dropped it lower on his right hip so it wouldn't irritate the sensitive area. He replaced the second pistol where he found it on the bureau. He wanted no more conversation on such confusing topics.

José watched Jake's deliberations quietly. Finally he observed, "Without two cross draw pistols, no one will recognize Jake Tallon."

"Couldn't have said it better myself," Jake felt relieved at the change of topic and clapped his friend warmly on the shoulder as they turned toward the door.

"You can come again and maybe no one will notice."

"Maybe once is enough." At the moment Jake felt like being irritated with the dapper Mexican and scowled meaningfully in his direction.

Soon both were out on the street headed into the business section of Bodie. Like many boomtowns on the east slope of the Sierras, Bodie was a bustling hive of activity. They were soon lost among the throngs of miners crowding the boardwalk from every corner of the world, even a Celestial, a venerable Chinese elder, in a dark silken robe.

Jake surprised the bent old man with a greeting in his own language. "Have you eaten today?" he translated for José when the Mexican asked. For his part the old man stumbled, lost his composure, and stood speechless, watching the two well-dressed men disappear into the throng.

"Barbarians," he muttered, "But sometimes surprising."

Who would speak to someone so low on the ladder, he must be thinking, much less in his own language? Chinese worked the tailings and leftovers of the Caucasians and counted even less than Indians and Mexicans. Free slaves had more stature than these lowly Chinese. They were allowed to own nothing, Jake knew, much less a claim of their own. Yet they accumulated wealth as they cleaned up after others. Slowly they earned enough to buy passage for their families.

Jake lived among them briefly during his first visit to the gold fields near Sacramento. He learned from them and learned to like them and their rice and noodles. Perhaps there would be time apart from his chores of vengeance to revisit these humble people.

Reclaiming the present, Jake had time only to see José duck into a doorway some yards ahead. The Marshal's Office nestled comfortably among the burgeoning sixty-five saloons of Bodie Town. Stepping across the threshold, Jake did a double take. The inside of the office could not have been more different from the town itself.

If the town was a mass of rollicking disorganization, the office of the Marshal was neat as a pin and you could bet that Colt McKenzie did his best to impose this neatness on the town around him. Visitors to this office gained a new understanding of law and order.

"Jake Tallon," came the booming authoritative voice. "Why the hell aren't you in somebody's jail?"

"And what's wrong with hello?" Jake boomed back at him. "If you don't put this guy in his place right away," he told José in a staged whisper, "he'll run you ragged."

Shoulders wide as a door, Colt stood up from behind his desk. Jake stifled an urge to whistle when he saw this good-looking Marshal dressed in broadcloth trousers, bright white shirt, with a black thin bow tie and fancy tailored black and gold brocaded vest. A huge toothy smile painted itself across his young, fair face. The two fourteen-inch Colt pistols looked out of place on this roughneck in gentleman's clothes.

"Pretty fancy dressin' for a lawman," Altimera said to Jake, as if Colt weren't even in the room.

"He needs all the edge he can get my friend. If he can't clear a room with his looks, he'll start swinging chairs."

While Jake said this to José, Colt moved swiftly around his desk and wrapped a heavy forearm playfully under Jake's chin from behind. Knowing it remained playful only as long as he could stop him, Jake cross-stepped right foot over the left, exposing Colt's solar plexus to the piston-like, backward jab of his right elbow. Jake hit him just hard enough to drive the air explosively from Colt's lungs.

"Hufff," Colt sagged limply back against the corner of the desk. "Never could get the drop on you raggedy Missouri ne'er do well." Of course, Colt knew Jake was rich twice over from his own prospecting and mining.

"If you would start talking to your Chinese citizens and treatin' 'em decent they might teach you how to fight a lick or two," Jake lectured. This was an ongoing argument between them. Big and strong was always good enough for Colt.

"You're just so bull-headed, you think a gun is the only way to deal with riffraff," Jake continued without encouragement. "Lucky for you, you're good at it."

Colt McKenzie assumed his full height, pasted on a chicken-stealing grin and swaggered around the desk and back to his chair. As he sat himself down he said, "I heard tell from your friend here that you tried to stop a rifle ball with your head and you go calling me bull-headed? Least I know how to duck."

"No tried about it," Jake boasted, "and I lived to walk away. So I've got the bragging rights."

"Don't you get carried away, amigo," chimed in Altimera. "You got dug up long before you walked away. Without divine intervention from me and the Holy Mother, you still be buried under that sand hill."

"The truth will out," quoted Colt McKenzie, squinting up his eyes and nodding sagely.

"You really know how to take the wind out of a man's sails, don't you amigo?" Jake shook his finger at a grinning Mexican.

"Somebody has to do it," shrugged a consternated Altimera, "because we'll never get down to business or beer with you two parading around and flashing your feathers at each other."

"Okay, I'll buy," Jake and Colt said together, laughing uproariously.

"Damn strutting game cocks," sputtered the Mexican in frustration. "I knew this was a big mistake. Nothing good could come of getting the two of you back together."

"Took the words out of my mouth," Colt said, ignoring the mumbling Mexican. He pummeled Jake's shoulder in his good-natured way.

"No, you took mine," Jake accused him. "No way I'm gonna let a fancy-dressed Hay Seed get one up on me. Everyone will know your true origins before we're done here." They turned as one and walked toward the door. Jake shouldered his way through first.

"That's okay, Jacob. Everyone here 'bouts figured I crawled out from under a rock anyway. Anything you tell 'em gonna be a step up in the world for me." Colt followed Jake out onto the boardwalk, with one hand companionably upon his shoulder.

"Good to have you around, Jake," he said sincerely. "I've missed you and Travis."

Altimera rolled his eyes in disgust and shut the door behind them. "Caramba," he pronounced. "What a couple of mixed-up Hombres."

As they strolled down the boardwalk, Jake reflected how good it was to have friends like Colt. His hand went to his own collar, seeking the comfort of the square Lightning Jasper on the cord around his neck, the Friendship Stone given him so long ago. With a start Jake remembered it no longer hung in its familiar position and hadn't since he was unhorsed by Johnny Lobo.

Jake's temporary shock caused him to miss a step and Colt looked over curiously. "What's wrong, Jake?" he asked. "You just lost two shades of color."

"Let's get a beer and I'll tell you," Jake promised.

Hunter's Cafe

McKenzie led the way up the boardwalk and took an abrupt turn into the first wide alley on the right. Nearly free of garbage, it slanted slightly uphill to connect with the next higher thoroughfare.

The three men mounted a series of four long steps paved into the far end, bringing them even with the street above. Though they had never been really close, Jake trusted Colt. Unlike many lawmen of the time, McKenzie was compulsively honest. He would always do what he thought was right. That was a trait Jake admired even if the big man was too competitive to allow real friendship.

Jake shook his head pensively as he puzzled over Colt McKenzie. Any man that big and smart should be more confident. Should be! It made no more sense now than ever before. For some reason Jake didn't understand, Colt acted as if he had to prove himself constantly in every relationship. Jake accepted that shortcoming but found it difficult to endure for long periods of time. That explained why he never spent long in this friend's company. But given the difficulties facing Jake and Altimera, even a flawed friend in the Marshal's Office was an asset. Jake was enormously grateful to find Colt in Bodie Town.

Jake emerged from his reverie as they stepped out of the alley and onto the boardwalk. Most of the boomtown was flat as a poker table with the far end terraced into the side of Bodie Butte. The downhill streets had a gutter in the middle to accommodate runoff from the infrequent heavy rains and melting snows, since Bodie was one of those towns where winter snows got twenty feet deep or more.

Bending their direction left, they soon saw a sign reading "Hunter's Bar and Cafe" over the bobbing, weaving heads of other pedestrians. Jake squinted. The way in which the intense sun struck the white wooden frame made it seem as though the rectangular sign was cut brightly out of the hazy blue Butte in the distance beyond the end of the street.

The broad storefront itself featured lace curtains in the windows and covered tables just inside. McKenzie pushed his way through the half-glass double doors, left hand on the knob. Loudly protesting brass hinges announced the smallest movement of the door, making stealth impossible. The Marshal seemed not to notice.

"They have no oil here?" complained Altimera to no one in particular.

Colt smiled at the Mexican without comment.

Angling between the chairs, they found a table against the back wall and seated themselves as a natty man with a small mustache and a clean apron showed up to take their orders. Jake could smell the heavy pomade the man used to slick back his hair. The civilized fragrance confused Jake briefly and he found himself wondering if he were in a barbershop or an eatery.

"What's on the menu today, Zack?" McKenzie asked the man.

The sound of conversation seemed to center Jake once again. His mind cleared.

"We got pronghorn and taters today," he reported enthusiastically. "Tommorry it'll likely be mule deer and taters. The taters is standard and the meat changes 'cording to what we got."

"Bring us a platter of lunch," McKenzie told him, "and beer all around."

Turning back to Jake, Colt explained, "Hunter isn't the owner's name, it's what he does. He owns the place and shows up every couple of days with an animal carcass. Speak of the devil," McKenzie interrupted himself, looking toward the street out front. "Look what the cat drug in."

Everyone turned toward the doors in time to see a buckskin clad figure with a long gun in one hand set down a cougar carcass as he reached for the handle. "You mean, look who drug in el Gato," said Altimera unnecessarily.

With a whoop the apron-clad waiter rushed from the back room to relieve the Hunter of the big cat as he stepped across the threshold. He fairly scampered back to the kitchen with the heavy carcass across his own shoulder.

"There's another on the horse outside," Hunter raised his voice to reach Zack through a door already swinging closed behind him. Looking up from his instructions to the waiter, he spotted Colt sitting against the wall. McKenzie waved him over.

"José, Jake, this is Virgil Carson," Colt made the introductions. "Virgil, this is Jacob Tallon and his friend José Altimera."

"No relative," Virgil intoned flatly, referring to the famous scout, Kit Carson, and fidgeting with mild embarrassment. Eyes twinkling, the Hunter took in Jake's headgear with a lingering stare as he quietly shook hands all around. Pulling up a chair, scraping the legs across the scarred boards of the softwood floor, Hunter tossed his hat with a plop on the table next to them, then rested the rifle across his knees like another appendage as he seated himself.

Jake knew his kind and it made him glad. "Mind if I call you Hunter?"

"Many do. Always did like to share my meat," Virgil told them. "Only trouble is, there's no money in it. So I partnered up with Fancy Dan, I call 'em, an' he runs this place for a right smart profit. Buys me all the powder and ball I want with some left over."

I'll bet, Jake thought quietly to himself.

"Truth be known," Colt said, reading Jake's mind, "there's more money in food than mining." He winked at Virgil, whose eyes crinkled up at the corners as he smiled his agreement.

This man found a way to get in on the strike that let him do what he enjoyed, Jake understood. He himself liked the sun overhead, far more than living underground in the tunnels.

"I don't much like town life," Virgil said. "Sometimes I just show up and drop the animal on the step. 'Cept ever once and awhile it's nice to taste someone else's cooking."

The platter arrived with a tray of foamy beer glasses. Jake could see where Indian herbs had been used in the cooking. Salt and pepper had their own containers on the table. Mighty savvy cook, he thought.

"Got us an ice house, dug deep, downstairs," Virgil was saying. "Gets so cold here come winter, we make our own ice blocks and store them against the heat of summer. Real handy for beer," he observed.

"Not as good as the Oro Fino," Colt observed. "You did a good job on yours, Virgil, but it's just too hard to dig one that big."

"Yeah, I know an' you're a mean man for even bringin' that up," Virgil huffed. "Iffn you like it so much, why don't you buy your lunch there?"

"Food's better here, even if the beer is warm late in the season. Where you been huntin'?" Colt changed the subject with studied lack of concern. He glanced away to further allay any suspicion of interrogation.

"Canyons up north of here, Nazareth way. Miners have kilt most the deer. Cats prowl the camps at night makin' mischief. Miners get a mite uncomfortable so they pay me a bounty on every one I bring down and I get to keep every other one I shoot."

Jake liked listening to Virgil talk. Lonely by choice, and a good friend to have when your back's against the wall, he thought. In spite of his rough and trail-grimed exterior, a gentle light danced around the man. Jake was not fooled. This was no man to cross, just like Ed Schouter, the soft-spoken trapper who died in the mountain ambush on the way to Big Mesa. Maybe he was luckier than Ed.

Jake put an arm across the back of his chair, chewed antelope tidbits and listened to Colt and Virgil catch up on gossip. A big part of the law business is just accumulating little pieces of information, Jake knew. McKenzie was uncommonly good at it.

Jake's mind drifted as the talking fell into the background when something Virgil said got his full attention.

"No good sons-of-bitches. Damn dog-spawn," Virgil cursed, "Shot an old miner for his outfit and sold it for whiskey money, they did."

"Who'd you say they were? Who are they?" Jake asked urgently, somewhat shrilly, his hand suddenly bunched in the material of Virgil's sleeve.

The intensity of Jake's query shocked Virgil such that the Hunter's mouth sagged open in mute surprise.

"Sorry," Jake apologized abjectly and just as quickly let go of the stunned man's shirtsleeve. Everybody stared at him as he patted the material back into place. Even José showed alarm. "I have an interest here," Jake explained lamely, still dealing with the anger he felt over the two desperados in question.

Hesitating only briefly, Jake lifted the corner of the bandanna over his right temple, showing the crosshatch of new scars. "They did this to me," he pointed unnecessarily. "Them and four others bushwhacked me and killed my friends. They've still got something of mine and I want it back. I want it back real bad."

Colt reached over and carefully lifted the bandanna an inch higher, looking critically at the scars with his eyes squinted. "Good thing you're already married, Jacob," he said. "You won't be so pretty no more."

"That's not the point, McKenzie," Jake scowled humorlessly, focusing his intense emotion on his friend. Urgency flavored his tone. "Who are those buzzards, dammit? I want to know."

"Cruz Brothers," Virgil said without hesitation. "Nasty scum. The camps draw all kinds and they're the worst of the lot." The Hunter started to spit the distaste from his mouth but realized he was indoors and stopped himself short.

"Miguelito and Lopez Cruz," added Colt helpfully. "I got circulars on 'em back at the office."

Taking a deep breath, Jake nodded his thanks. He knew one of those two had robbed his body of the Friendship Stone while he visited with Shantee in the Spirit Lodge.

Still looking with interest at Jake's scars, Colt added, "Wondered why the change in head gear. You've always dressed after your own notions. I just figured you were being ec-centric." He delivered the last word slowly for emphasis.

Colt and Jake grew up together in Missouri. Jake could tell when Colt pulled his leg. Likely he waited all week to use a fifty-cent word like that.

Lunch finished, the three of them said their good-byes to Virgil and pointed their boot toes toward the street and the Marshal's office. As they walked Jake explained to Colt in more detail, "On the way over, I realized that I was missing a polished stone given me by an old man in the desert last year. It was stolen from me after I got shot. I mean to get it back."

Jake thought to tell him more about Man Above but knew another, more relaxed time would serve that subject better.

"I realized when I reached for the stone back there," Jake said, pointing with his thumb over his shoulder, "that I no longer had it. I've been too busy healing and frankly I'm not all here yet." Jake tapped the uninjured side of his head meaningfully with a left forefinger. "Things are coming back to me in pieces and I'm gonna have to take them on one at a time. I know there are a lot more pieces to the puzzle than just the Cruz Brothers. Maybe somehow they'll supply a few more of the answers."

"You know why you were shot?" questioned the Marshal.

"Gold. It's always about the gold."

"You know who did it, Jake?"

"Well I know about the Cruz Brothers and I believe Johnny Lobo was in on it."

"Never heard of Lobo before," commented McKenzie thoughtfully.

"Not much of a bad man but he has a name in some circles. He's a low profile killer."

"Anything I can do to help?" asked Colt.

"You already are," Jake clasped the back of Colt's upper arm as they walked. Hard as a young tree, thought Jake.

By the time Jake turned his attention back to their destination, Jake found they had already arrived outside the Marshal's office. Colt led the way inside, marched to the back of the single room and began banging around in the cupboard.

"Want some coffee?" he asked.

José and Jake both answered, "Sí," in unison and sat down at different tables to leaf through stacks of dried and curling wanted posters. They found the Cruz Brothers in short order, with a five hundred dollar price for the both of them.

Arriving with a steaming pot and tin cups, Colt looked down at the pair of posters in Jake's hands, "Not nearly enough for those two. I count my blessings they don't hang around Bodie much." He served the coffee without sugar and sat down to drink it with them as they worked.

After looking at a dozen more he didn't recognize, Jake found a flyer on a hard case named Jeff Toppen, wanted for murder in the Arizona Territory.

Colt bent toward Jake out of his own chair. "There's a bad 'n," he said, tapping a corner of the yellowing page with his unlit pipe. "He runs with French Pete and Randy Quern. You'd be doing everyone a big favor if you took care of that back-shootin' scum. They never done anything here I can pin on 'em but they're always around when trouble's afoot."

"Trouble is surely afoot, my friend." From the description on the flyer, Jake recognized Toppen as the one who shot Harry at the very end. The face was not that clear to Jake but Jake's whole body trembled with a rage that signaled the certainty of Jeff Toppen's involvement in his injury. He didn't know how he knew, but he surely knew.

Two for Trouble

ossing and turning on the fine bed provided by his host, sleep eluded Jake as he waited for the rising sun. For most of a month his body had known nothing softer than pine boughs. Beyond frustration, he pulled the blankets from his mattress and curled up on a colorful, oval rag rug for a few minutes of good rest.

Dawn found Jake and José dressed for travel and headed north. For the moment Jake cared about only one thing. Find the Cruz Brothers and bring them to account for their actions. Recovering the red stone on its soft leather thong added a sense of urgency to the hunt for these Owlhoots. Given its pivotal role in Jake's personal history, the Friendship Stone was beyond price. He didn't want some two-bit Bushwhacker losing it for all time or destroying it by some thoughtless act.

Sundown on the fourth day found the two of them on the canyon trails leading to the next boomtown, one in a string of temporary settlements that marked the discovery of mineral through the Basin Range and not the first they had visited in search of the Cruz Brothers.

Small campfires dotted the Sierra hillsides as prospectors and claim-holders cooked their meals with scavenged wood. Plenty of miners crowded the small watercourse, washing dirt in the last available light.

Using a pine board flume, one enterprising miner brought his own water down from some spring higher up on the mountain. His work and ingenuity gave him all the water he needed and more. By the look of his outfit, Jake thought, he must do real well with it.

Cold wind swept like icy death down from the snow covered peaks and glaciers up above. Jake shivered and Altimera cried out in dismay, "Hah, it is so cold."

Stopping without dismounting, they untied their heavy sheepskin coats from bedrolls behind the saddles and then continued their journey with single-minded focus. After a few moments within the warmth of the coat, Jake realized just how cold he had become without knowing. Warmth returned slowly to the numb flesh only after he turned the fleecy collar up to shield his neck and cheeks.

74

"Warm is good, my friend," he said absently to the shivering Mexican.

"Si! Such cold is unnatural," groused Altimera. "Man was never intended to live in such forbidding circumstances. Perhaps only snowbirds or the white bears of which I have heard."

"Sweating your life out through your skin is better?"

"Si!" the Mexican responded with certainty.

A full mile down the road Jake saw a rider going hell bent for leather, flogging his horse, moving quickly away from them and toward the main camp. This was not a rider who'd passed them earlier. The trail up which they rode was little more than a hundred feet from steep hills on either side. No one could get by them on a horse without their notice.

All the evidence suggested that those for whom they searched were just ahead. Did the rider hurry to tell the Cruz Brothers just how closely they were pursued? Jake could have no certainty of exactly where they waited or if they ran until that final moment when he faced them across a smoking pistol. His life was kinda like that.

Rain drizzled down more intensely from a graying sky. Darkness closed in with the clouds that crowded between the peaks on either side of them.

Jake pulled the pistol from his right hip, checked the loads front and back and wiped it down good with his new kerchief. He smiled, remembering this habit of checking loads was necessary only for cap'n ball pistols when the ball could fall from the front of the chamber or just loosen up and jam the cylinder by falling partially forward, preventing rotation. That didn't happen with cartridges because the open end of the brass was crimped around the lead to hold it solidly in place. A good idea, he allowed.

Jake repeated the operation with the second pistol, which he now wore openly on his left hip. He omitted the front-end check on that piece, trusting the cartridges not to lose their lead.

The Cruz Brothers would never allow him closer than pistol range. Most who knew of Jake at all, knew better. And the Cruz Brothers knew someone was after them. They may or may not know for sure that it was Jake pursuing them but they would know in short order and they wouldn't go easy in any case.

With pistols, Jake liked longer range because he was only middling fast but a good shot once he got the piece out of the holster. At closer ranges he enjoyed going hands on with his opposition. Physical combat appealed to him because he didn't lose much and a person has more choices than killing or maiming, which is pretty much what happened with six guns.

The trail dipped and they could no longer see the camp, only the smoke that rose above it like a grimy finger pointing downward, slanting across the sky, to mark their eventual destination. By the time they topped out again it had become full dark. José said nothing nor did Jake, each of them absorbed in their own private thoughts. They knew why they were here and knew what to expect. Trouble. Lots of trouble.

By the time both men climbed stiffly from their saddles, the camp buzzed with the frenetic energy of the newly rich working desperately to throw away their hard won wealth. Leading the way through the jostling crowd, Jake walked his horses toward a rope corral, stopping in front of a seated man with a rifle across his lap.

Wire held together the old Captain's chair upon which the guard sat, tilting back. Suspicion and insolence warred for dominance on the upward angled face. Where did he get a chair like that in a place like this, Jake wondered? A fragile looking construction of ornately carved wood, it fought a losing battle with the elements. Jake marveled that it supported the man's considerable weight as it did without an even base and the legs a full three inches deep into the evil-looking muck outside the corral.

When Jake glanced to the rifle, the guard said cryptically, "Horses are much sought after."

"How much for the night?" asked Jake.

"Three dollars if you expect to find them here in the morning." When they didn't flinch at the price he added, "Each!"

"I'll pay your six bucks," Jake said, feeling gouged but understanding that the money bought the alertness of the guard throughout the long night. He saw no need to warn him against failure. The work-worn rifle across his knees showed Jake all he needed to know about the man.

Before handing over the mounts, Jake lifted the flap on a saddlebag and extracted an extra Calvary Colt. A cap'n ball, it lacked the top strap over the cylinder that made the Remington such a desirable pistol. After checking that the hammer rested on an empty chamber, he pushed it down behind his belt and slapped the horse affectionately on the flank. It was the big Gray loaned to him by Señora Delores, a bright aspect to a bleak enterprise.

The saloons, cafes and hotels of this town were little more than tents. Fancy ones had wooden side walls. The mud paths between them sucked at the shoes of animated miners looking for an evening of revelry. There were two kinds, miners already working rich ground and others excited because tomorrow they knew they would find theirs.

Few did. Gold has value because it is rare and hard to come by.

The rain fell intensely now. Turning into the first tent, they found a cafe and a chance to chase the cold from their bones with hot coffee. Jake and José sat down to a table of rude planks with empty whiskey kegs for chairs. They ordered a full pot and warmed their hands on the hot, thick ceramic mugs.

José regained his voice first. "They hide from us, Jacob. Somewhere they cower. I can feel it."

"You are wrong, José," Jake said, placing one hand on José's arm, "They wait." Deep inside him the conviction welled up as words. "They will not run now. They know I come and they will not run. These are very bad people, amigo."

"Give them time to fear in that case, mi amigo," José said. "Let's have another cup of coffee."

They chatted back and forth, ignoring the pressure of the task before them. Three different camps they had searched, frequently finding some calling card of the Cruz Brothers in Boot Hill. People to whom they spoke feared the pair greatly.

Now they had the two outlaws cornered. Or maybe vice versa, thought Jake.

As one, the two men set their empty cups upon the table and turned for the door. The paths outside were crowded but when they stepped from the tent, men moved quietly aside, staring, always staring. The tinny notes of a lone piano bravely fought the silence. It seemed as though there was one in every boomtown.

Passing from tent to tent, word got around. A cloud of apprehension gradually settled down upon the whole camp, muting all sound and life. As the eyes followed them, Jake heard only his and José's boots in the mud, splashing as they stepped down and sucking as the mud released them.

The first saloon held only white faces, all staring at the soon-to-be-dead men who searched for the Cruz Brothers. The desperados, Jake thought, must be in the next saloon, for there remained no other choices. Pushing back through the canvas flaps, the two of them found the muddy street once again.

All around them, Jake smelled death. In his mind he saw the Bushwhackers, picking over the silent, crumpled bundles of clothes on the desert floor, out of Nazareth. Standing aside from the others, he saw a spare man of medium build with a long gun in his left hand. Johnny Lobo. The name came to him as mysteriously as it had before. Two others picked over a body like coyotes. Mine, Jake realized. Anger rose up in him, filling his throat with bile, as he remembered the Jayhawkers who murdered his foster family, the Barnettes.

"This is wrong," said Lobo to the two in Jake's inner vision. "You were paid enough. Don't steal from the dead!"

"Shut your filthy face, Gringo," Miguelito Cruz snapped viciously at Johnny. "Your squirrel popper ain't gonna bring me down because I don't turn my back on you."

Lobo bristled but held his peace.

The images of murder's aftermath faded away. Off Jake's right hand walked Man Above, hands clasped serenely before him. "These are outlaw souls, Jacob," he said.

"I'm torn," said Jake. "I want the stone but I'm not sure that I can kill. I do not want to kill again! Even them."

"They have chosen to abandon the light … and learning. Their path has been one of constant pain and violence. Only their base needs have any notice in their thinking, yet there is always a chance." Sadness flavored the words of the old man. "Should they give you no choice, Jacob, send them to me. I will be close."

Jake blinked. Man Above was gone as if he was never there. Did I imagine that, he wondered? "Outlaw souls," he repeated aloud, in a hushed and awed voice.

"Si," agreed José nervously, oblivious to Jake's vision. "These are bad Hombres."

Jake smiled wryly. Maybe it's best he doesn't know I'm seeing things, he thought. Coming through the flaps, a clear aisle opened for them, from the tent entrance all the way to the rough plank bar top. Miners crowded to either side, faces tense as stone statues. No one breathed.

Two long-muscled men with serapes and drawn brown faces shadowed beneath big hats leaned against the barrels that supported the warped plank. Silent as those who watched, they stood out from the crowd, only because no one would stand near them.

Rainwater ran from the brim of Jake's hat in a steady stream right in front of his face, then slowed to individual drips during the time he took to absorb the scene before him. These were the Cruz Brothers who faced him!

With tired, nervous eyes the bartender looked first left, then right, searching for cover. He'd been through this before. With nowhere to go he threw his towel to the bar top and dropped behind the meager cover of empty whiskey barrels upon which the bar top planks were laid. Jake sincerely hoped he had the good sense to lie flat on his face.

Patrons crowding up against the wooden walls shared one thing in common. They all prayed for a tight shot pattern. Beyond that, their reactions were as varied as their origins. Some showed the eager antici-pation born of boredom and others wore the dread of previous experience. Gunfight drama was still new to many of them.

The packed earth of the floor ran freely with the mud and water flowing in from under the walls to mix with the beer and spilled liquor. Jake rested his hands almost comfortably on the butts of his cross draw pistols and watched the brothers for a sign of fear or recognition. As a result of the recent vision, he recognized each Cruz brother clearly.

Without changing their posture, they watched intently through hooded eyes as Jake and José walked away from the door, toward either side of a four-inch post supporting the canvas roof, Altimera on Jake's left. Until he and his Mexican friend came more forward, Jake realized they remained in the shadows away from the main light while the Cruz Brothers were fully bathed in the glow of many overhead lanterns, their big mistake. They could not clearly see Jake and José as they themselves could be seen!

Obviously they waited. The Cruz Brothers had been warned of pursuit and had decided to stop running. Lopez Cruz broke the silence with his nervous, heavily accented English. "What trick do you pull, Gringo?" he almost shouted. "Jake Tallon is dead of a rifle bullet in de head. You are not heem."

The growing silence writhed like a living thing until it seemed that only the roar of pistol shots could interrupt its progress. "Can't you believe your own eyes, Lopez?" Jake asked smugly, pleased to find the renegades so upset. This bonus swung the odds even more in Jake's favor. Nervous gunmen make mistakes, snap their shots. "I stand here before you."

"Si," the bandito paused significantly, uncertainly shifting his weight from one leg to the other, "I believe only my eyes, Gringo." Cheek twitching now, he ran a sleeve across his face nervously, accidentally opening a sore, causing it to bleed. "I also saw you … heem … with his brains spilling in the sand and I saw heem in the ground and I laughed."

He shook his head slowly and wiped at the fresh trickle of blood. "You are not the same man. You cannot be the same man." A boastful smile hung below the eyes, but the smile was empty.

"I saw you cold in the ground," Lopez said again as if to reassure himself of a private truth.

While the Mexican spoke, Jake's eyes swept the room, seeking a back shooter at a side table, expecting it. Seeing nothing, he returned his attention to the pair before him.

"You cannot be Jake Tallon," sneered Miguelito, who had been silent until now. "Maybe you are only a brother to Jake Tallon … or an impostor!"

"Is this what you saw?" Jake asked calmly, ignoring Miguelito and folding back the edge of the blue bandanna with his left hand, exposing the still livid scar tissue.

A gasp went up around the room as the significance of the injury could be easily seen. It still looked like a killing wound. The eyes of the Cruz Brothers showed white all the way around, as they stared in stark amazement. Both recoiled against the plank bar in fear, upsetting glasses along the length of the splintery surface.

Smiling with the effect of his revelation, Jake allowed the blue cloth to fall back into place and dropped his hand once more to the pistol at his hip.

Miguelito recovered first. "I will dance again on your grave!" he hissed, spittle flying from his bearded mouth, as both of them straightened from their slouch.

Without another warning, the fronts of their colorful serapes ballooned outward, blossoming smoke and flame as the two desperados fired hidden weapons from where they stood against the bar. Jake's left hand was thrown from his pistol grip by the slamming impact of a large caliber ball, his arm suddenly numbed to the elbow.

From beside him, José grunted with the awful sound of bullet striking flesh, as he dropped to one knee, nearly toppling to the side. Jake stepped to the right and palmed his Remington with a reverse grip, thumbing back the hammer and thrusting the six-shooter out before him.

Wincing, he felt a bullet tug at his shirt seam near the armpit. Jake fired, looking down the barrel into the face of Lopez Cruz, then thumbed back the hammer and fired again! Glass shattered behind him. With relief, Jake heard both of José's guns thundering to his left as the good Mexican fired from one knee. Lopez Cruz dropped abruptly into an awkward sitting posture with a small splash, uttered a spectral sigh, and rising slightly, toppled sideways onto his face.

Desperately, Miguelito struggled to free the big gun from his smoking serape, as José fired and Jake fired again. Jake saw all three bullets strike the upper chest of Miguelito Cruz, slamming him back against the bar, breaking bottles and glasses with his flailing arms. Eyes rolling upwards, upper torso twisting in pain, dying reluctantly, the cold-blooded killer dropped his iron and melted into the ground. Beside his fallen brother.

Jake could see nothing, hear nothing except the deafening silence that follows gun thunder. Neither he nor Altimera could chance another surprise from a surviving Cruz Brother. Ducking quickly beneath the gunsmoke drifting thickly between them and their antagonists, Jake extended his pistol before him, looking for some final challenge from the treacherous pair.

With some last reserve of determination, Lopez Cruz struggled vainly to rise from the muck, reached futility for his fallen pistol, but failed, coughed and fell face first once again with a final splash into the mud of the floor. A ripple of tension moving from the gunman's feet forward signaled the exit of life from the body. A single fragile bubble formed against the cheek and burst with a small but audible pop in a room full of stunned and deathly silent onlookers.

Looking away from the death scene, Jake glanced downward at his useless left hand, expecting the worst. Blood ran in slow drops from the webbing between the thumb and forefinger. Otherwise all the fingers were still there. He flexed them unbelievingly in front of his face as the feeling gradually returned. Sighing with profound relief, he mumbled, "How lucky can one guy get?"

Looking down again, Jake saw that his pistol, positioned for the cross draw, had taken a slug on the bottom of the handle, shattering the maple grips, peeling the steel all the way back to the frame and cutting his thumb with the jagged end as it curled away. Had the bullet struck a quarter inch one way or another, he would've lost fingers. Only the cylinder and the barrel remained undamaged. The frame was shot, literally. The thought produced a brief ironic smile.

"What was he shooting," Jake asked no one in particular, "could peel back steel that way?"

Returning Jake to the present, the voice beside him asked, "Hey amigo. When you have a moment, perhaps you can help me not bleed to death."

Quickly, Jake looked once again to ensure the Cruz Bothers had not moved, and holstering his smoking gun, bent to help his injured friend.

Altimera cradled a damaged thigh in both hands, blood welling up from a wound in the center of the big muscle.

Gently but firmly, Jake removed the Mexican's hands so he might view the wound unobstructed. "I was worried for you, José. I didn't know where you'd been hit at first." He sought his friend's belt knife with a free hand and began cutting at the fabric of his trousers above the wound. "Could'a been a lot worse than this."

"Some friend you are," José groused, "You think this is not bad."

With concern and sincere compassion, Jake observed, "Bad enough, José. I wish you'd not been hit at all. The bullet is still in there, Compadre. You want it out now or later?"

"Now I think is okay," the Mexican gritted his teeth together and moved to cover the wound with his wadded bandanna. "I think it can hurt no worse than it hurts already."

Except for José and the Cruz Brothers, no one else caught lead, a miracle all by itself. Relieved miners helped Jake carry the wounded Vaquero to the bar, where they laid him on the plank over the barrels after sweeping aside the cups and bottles with a racket of crashing tin and glass onto the floor. The bartender collected additional lanterns and hung them close overhead, while Jake cut away more of the heavy material of José's pants. Altimera's leg trembled under his hands.

"Here, let me look at that," the bartender gently shoved Jake aside, "I've done some doctorin' before this," he offered reassuringly, without looking up from his task. "Some dentist work too."

Reluctantly, Jake stepped back and let him examine the wound.

Pouring tequila with one hand, the bartender swabbed gently at the oozing hole with a clean towel.

"Ohh!! I was wrong," howled José, sitting up in agony, "It hurts more! Too much more!"

"Don't be a baby!" snapped the bartender-doctor, pushing José flat against the plank on which he lay. "You'll only make it harder to help you. You fellas," he glanced to either side, "help me hold him down." Several burly miners jumped to the task at the request.

By their smiles, Jake felt, they almost enjoy watching José suffer. Maybe some of them had been in the same position before.

For the most part, the men in the room had stopped watching. The struggle had ended. Life went on all around them, ignoring the drama playing out on the bar surface. One of the holders on José's shoulders grinned at Jake. "He's in good hands partner," he promised. "I've seen this Doc work before."

The bartender inserted a thin double-bladed knife into the wound and quickly cut upwards one inch and downward one inch from the wound.

"Argggh, ohhh," screamed José, "Why don't you chop up some chili peppers and mix them around in there while you're at it!"

"Shut up," ordered the bartender, "and let me find that lead." He probed downward, tapping with the knifepoint. His efforts were immediately rewarded with a dull thump. "There it is," he said, "right up against the bone."

"How do you know that's not really the bone?" Jake asked, genuinely curious.

"You're so chatty," gritted Altimera, squirming against restraining hands.

"A bullet at close range will pass right through muscle if it hit no bone and if that was the bone, he would've screamed again, is how I know," the bartender glared sternly at Jake as reward for his ignorance. Reaching behind him into a drawer under the mirror, he found a pair of long nosed pliers, an evil looking instrument.

"Tooth pliers," he smiled at Jake, grimly. He up-ended the tequila bottle over the instrument then jammed it nose first and without warning into the bleeding wound. José stiffened briefly and went limp.

"Got it," the bartender said after poking and prodding unmercifully. He showed Jake a misshapen ball locked in the jaws of his instrument.

"Now," he said, dousing the wound again with the bottle, "wrap it up good and tight and he'll be fine, if he don't get the gangrene. Should be okay though. There are no big veins or arteries on the front of the leg like that. Mostly on the inside."

"You know that, do you?" questioned Jake skeptically.

"Sure. And you would too if you had to cut a leg off yourself!"

Jake swallowed back his nausea at the very thought.

The bartender-doctor thrust a roll of linen toward Jake and busied himself serving drinks, saying over his shoulder, "That doctoring will cost you fifty bucks, my friend. The bottle is free and so should the doctoring but I lost too much money while he was on top of my bar. Can't thank you enough, by the way partner, for taking care of those no-goods."

"Thanks yourself," Jake paid him happily with three double eagles and a nod. They shared the understanding that the life of a friend is without price.

The party surged around them as the room all but forgot the recent pistol drama. Men resumed the arguments and enthusiasms in progress before the confrontation and the sound level returned to a normal roar. Only an occasional side-glance at the figure on the bar betrayed any recognition of the event.

Jake tied off the dressing as Altimera regained consciousness. "We better find you a place to sleep it off, my friend," Jake told him, "You smell like the town drunk. Seems like we can't go anywhere you don't fall down and get whiskey all over you."

"Here," José reached to the bar behind him and grabbed the half empty bottle, "If I'm gonna smell like it I want a little inside me also. I earned it."

Swinging his legs off the edge of the bar and sliding gently to the floor, the Mexican continued to lean weakly against the bar top. His space was happily appropriated by relieved miners jostling for a refill.

While José fought for balance on his uninjured leg, Jake bent to the floor behind him and rolled Miguelito onto his back. To his great relief, Jake found he was still dead.

Ignoring the sightless eyes, Jake ripped open the assassin's shirt collar with a jerk and searched for the red stone beneath the serape. His hand came away with the severed thong and a fistful of clotting blood. The cord had been clipped by a bullet.

Suddenly desperate, Jake pulled his big knife from the sheath in the small of his back and slashed upwards at the coarsely woven blanket material with a force that lifted the cooling body from the floor. He dropped the heavy knife with a clatter, and grabbing either side, tore the serape all the way to Miguelito's belt. Buttons flew every which way as he did the same for his shirt.

The commotion around them came briefly to a halt as miners turned curiously at the noise and commotion created by Jake's intensity.

As the layers of material came apart, Jake saw that Miguelito had a big Walker Colt tangled in the folds of his serape. Don't see them too much any more, he thought abstractly. That sure explained the damage to his own pistol. That cannon could pack a double charge for each ball. Could've been a lot worse.

Miguelito had been hit in a star pattern as big as Jake's hand. In the center lay the Stone of Friendship, dull and without luster. Somewhere near Jake's ear a voice said, "These poor men could not be friends even to themselves. The possession of the stone was wasted upon them." The words, Jake knew, were for him alone to hear and understand.

Wiping the stone on a clean portion of Miguelito's shirt, he felt the red Lightning Jasper warm in his hand with a life of its own. Until he could get a new cord, Jake dropped it into his vest pocket for safekeeping.

Crouching there with his forearm across his thigh, Jake slowly let out his breath. It felt as though he'd been holding it since walking through the flaps of this squalid, noisy tent. What had he accomplished by killing the Cruz Brothers? He got the stone back for one. Two … what? He rid the world of two more conscienceless killers? There were enough of those to keep him occupied forever if that were his only concern.

Jake glanced down into the expressionless face of Miguelito Cruz, the sightless eyes no more animated than glass marbles, the jaw hanging open as though on the verge of some important utterance destined never to come. Wiping his stained hand on a relatively clean portion of the serape, Jake tried bunching the material under the chin of Miguelito Cruz, only to have it sag open again to spite his best efforts.

As stupid in death as in life, Jake reflected. He was no closer to answers now than he was after confronting Bingo Mackinaw, and with frustration he realized no closer to justice.

Slowly, Jake allowed a number of coins to roll from his soft leather pouch onto the bar top. "Drinks all around Doc. I've got to help my friend, José, find a better place to rest."

Certainly, José would have preferred no movement at all.

With a miner under José's other arm, they made their lurching, staggering way through the tent flap and next door to what passed for a mining camp hotel, two rows of cots facing each other across a dirt floor, roofed over with canvas. The owner found him an extra cot, which he set up in his own small room at one end. Once José was comfortable, Jake brought the saddles and gear down from the corral to keep them out of the rain.

He threw the damaged gun into his bags. Not much of that Navy could be salvaged except maybe the cylinder. It would wait for the Yankee Gunsmith at Nazareth. Removing an extra Calvary Colt from behind his belt, Jake dropped it into the empty holster.

That Gunsmith would be worth meeting anyway, Jake thought, just because he'd warned José. Not that he'd provided that much information, true, but certainly more than anyone else in that poisonous little berg was willing to offer. Maybe there was additional information he was anxious to divulge.

Keeping José company all night, Jake sat on the damp ground beside the cot, flexing his own bruised hand and thanking his lucky stars. In any case there was no use trying to sleep. The rest of the evening was a boomtown nightmare of shouting and laughing drunkenness punctuated by an occasional gunshot. The world moved on around them ignorant of their need for sleep.

Come morning, everyone finally went back to work and José could rest a little. And two days later they said their silent good-byes to a town that had named them dead men, and headed back to Bodie.

José was strong enough now to travel and he complained too much to stay. He got on everyone's nerves.

Thankfully, their return trip was empty of the same drama experienced on the way out. Even the skies had cleared. Camping early and sleeping late, they retraced their previous three-day trip in nearly a week. During the course of the journey, clean living and the high mountain air performed their healing miracles. José's pant's leg looked pretty shabby but outside of a small limp, folks couldn't tell he had a recent wound unless he walked uneven ground or was forced to say something nice.

He sat a horse right proper. Knowing José, most of that was Vaquero pride. The earlier complaining was likely for bragging rights later.

Quarro

efore heading directly into Bodie, Jake insisted on a side trip into the mountains for elk. Jake's feet hankered for their customary footgear, and the tough hide of the elk would provide the leather. The respite would be good for José, allowing him a time to heal out of the saddle and off his feet.

Virgil, the Restaurant owner, had been right, of course. The hills close by were all hunted out or the animals were deep in hiding. Gold did that to a countryside. With the lure of a new strike, more people flooded into an area than the game could support. In the beginning there were hungry times for miners and anyone else in the area.

Experience had shown Jake that food and supplies didn't always follow so soon after a big gold discovery. It took a long time to develop a system of delivery since most of the early arrivals were interested only in the gold itself. Merchants and freighters came later. The land required even longer to recover from the reckless over-hunting.

Looking down upon the barren countryside, Jake was deeply disheartened.

They sat atop a rocky prominence, horses tethered out of sight, behind them in the trees. All afternoon they had watched a pair of treeless hillsides and the watercourse that wound around their base and on down the mountain. The hills had been stripped of timber to provide shoring for the hard rock mines down below. The grass and brush that sprung up in the absence of timber provided excellent browse, but neither elk nor deer appeared while they watched. In a pinch I'll settle for a deer hide, thought Jake.

"Ughh," Altimera grunted, screwing up his face in pain. Slowly, with a long sigh, he extended his injured leg out in front of him. The hot air from below drifted up the hillside toward them, touching and moving around their still figures as it passed.

Watching the silent terrain below, Altimera spoke lazily, "This is not such a bad place to take a bullet, you know." He bent his leg at the knee again to stretch out the big muscle on the front of the leg. "But the bone is very painful," he added sorrowfully.

"I'm not surprised," Jake told him. "I'm just glad that bullet didn't break the bone, though you could have a crack there. It feels about the same as a break but doesn't lame you up so bad. Most doctors just cut a broken leg off. Setting the bone or even splinting a break is a new idea."

"Why?"

"'Cause a bad break often leads to infection and gangrene. Surgeons don't want to take a chance, so they just cut off the leg. That's why there are so many one-legged soldiers left over from the war."

Altimera shook his head dismally. "I really needed that information, amigo. You know how to cheer up a wounded Vaquero alright."

Going silent for a moment, Jake allowed his eyes to drift across the landscape. "I haven't thanked you for standing with me, José. It's a rare thing you did and I want you to know I'm grateful." Jake smiled to lighten the moment and looked back at the Mexican, "Just be glad you didn't take a ball from that Walker Colt! You wouldn't even need to amputate that leg."

"You're right about that, amigo. Gun fighting is a risky business even when God is on your side."

Startled, Jake looked at his Mexican friend. "What do you mean by that?"

"Oh, nothing," answered Altimera without apparent concern. "I was just thinking about others who end up on the wrong path and," he smiled at some inner joke, "on the wrong side of your anger. I meant to tell you earlier but forgot when I foun' you dead under all that sand. It is only now I remember."

The Mexican paused, massaging the injured leg. "When I returned to Texas last fall, I foun' Angelo. We called him Knife Angel from when he was just a leetle boy."

Struggling vainly to catch up to the Mexican's line of thinking, Jake looked blankly at his friend.

"He worked for Señor Longer," the Vaquero explained, "You must remember because you took a knife from him at Mission Gap during that big bar fight you had there."

Still Jake did not remember.

"You broke his right elbow when you took his knife from him."

"Oh!" Jake brightened. "Yeah, I remember," Jake replayed the scene on his inner eye. "I bear him no animus."

"That soun's ver' dignified but there are no bears here. No other animus either. Not even elk," joked the Mexican.

"I mean I don't hate him just because he tried to gut me."

"I know what you mean," said Altimera. "It's just that sometimes you sound like that big Indian you used to hang 'round with, Night Walker. He has more Gringo in him than you do!"

Jake smiled, still staring into the tree line below. "You mean he's educated."

"Sure! But I speak to you about Angelo. He sends thanks to you."

Now Jake was truly interested. "I broke his elbow, amigo! Why is he thanking me?"

"Exactly! He went home and married a nice girl. There was little future for a one-armed knife fighter and besides, he sees what you do to the others. He knows he got off lucky. He's ver' grateful. Tell him, thank you, Angelo says."

"Huh," Jake grunted noncommittally. Both returned to watching the hill below, but Jake was happy inside. A kind of sorrow surrounded each violent act, even in self-defense. This news gladdened him. Something worthy had come of the hard life he lived. This one victory with Angelo outweighed a dozen disappointments. Closing his eyes, Jake thought of the man as he was crouched with a knife growing from his right fist, and then imagined him as a changed man, courteous and respectful. The image worked.

"I must see him sometime."

Altimera nodded.

Soon, Jake had his own boot off, massaging his stockinged foot with his right hand. The boots José had bought were handsome, but chaffed and blistered his feet in awkward places. Jake longed for his moccasins. He knew where to find the elk up around Nazareth but that did him little good now.

"Looks like another frijoles dinner tonight, eh amigo?" Jake mourned out loud.

"What do we do up here anyway, Jacob? Oh, yes," José reminded himself, "The elk hide moccasins. My expensive boots are not good enough for you."

This Mexican made Jake smile. He complained to entertain. With the octagonal barrel pointed into the sky, Jake placed the butt of the Henry rifle next to his stockinged foot and levered himself to his feet, using it for support. The sun had disappeared behind the rim of the Sierras to their rear, throwing the hillside upon which they sat into deep shadow. Jake knew that darkness comes quickly in the mountains.

"Maybe we better build a fire while we can still see to find the horses," Jake suggested.

"Si, amigo," said the Mexican, now standing also and favoring his injured leg.

Hopping on one leg for balance, Jake slipped his foot into the boot with the fancy inlaid silver on the heel and joined José, casting one last look down the barren hillside.

As he held José's arm, Jake helped him hop from rock to rock on his good leg. The horses waited seventy-five yards back into the trees toward which they labored. Bored beyond the usual wilderness caution, the two friends stepped into the welcome shelter of the pines, hobbling with painful slowness toward their camp.

Looking up, suddenly Jake gaped in amazement and stopped dead in his tracks. Not ten steps from the horses stood the most magnificent elk he had ever seen, all black-hooded head and neck with a tan body. Its heavily muscled torso was every bit as big as that of a horse, and without the wide rack of horns and unique coloring, would have blended perfectly with the grazing stock.

Also wide-eyed, Altimera slowly raised his rifle. Jake stopped him, placing his hand on the long barrel as it came up. Still holding the rifle, Altimera turned to look at Jake in wide-eyed disbelief.

"This one we do not shoot," Jake told him. "This is Quarro, King of all Elk, a totem. I know him from my dreams. And in my heart, I believe he brings something but I have no idea what."

Altimera gagged and stuttered, stumbling over his tongue in a frantic search for the right word. He had difficulty deciding whether he was more amazed by the elk or by Jake's speech. His mouth moved soundlessly before he could talk. "Now you sound just like that crazy Cherokee, Night Walker," he sputtered finally. "You spend too much time with that Indian, amigo. It twists your thinking."

Turning to the denser foliage of the forest behind him, Quarro raised his head in a stately manner and walked forward, undisturbed and unhurried. Just seeing the noble animal filled Jake with irrational pride. Before vanishing among the foliage, the regally racked animal turned to regard them one last time, gracing them with a full view of his huge seven point antlers.

For their part, Jake and José moved not an inch. It was a spectacle well worth the watching. Jake's heart felt big enough to burst. "Just look at that, will you?"

José looked from him to where Quarro had vanished and back again, saying, "Es loco." One more time, together they turned to look where the big animal had entered the woods, blinked and blinked again.

Within spitting distance of where the elk had passed, stood three Indians among the deep shadows between the trees, watching them, unmoving and impassive.

With arms at their sides, they appeared peaceful enough. Naked to the waist, dressed in leggings and breach clout, the young boy in the center held a brace of handsomely feathered birds. Kneeling, he silently spread them out across the ground before them, much like an offering.

"Don't shoot them either," Jake instructed Altimera needlessly.

The two standing Indians now held their right hands up, palms out and empty, showing peaceful intent. Jake shifted his rifle to the left hand and also signed for peace. Having lived his life fighting the less peaceful Comanche and Apache, Altimera was leery. But out of respect for his friend, he also lowered his rifle, allowing himself only narrowed eyes and a few muttered apprehensive curses in his native Spanish.

Ignoring his friend, Jake knew that when an Indian brought food some serious eating was gonna happen. Only bland frijoles waited for their dinner and he thanked Man Above for these thoughtful guests.

Picking up the birds again, the boy and the pair of braves walked forward as one.

A bright curiosity danced within Jake. With their short bows across their backs, long braided hair, and regal bearing, these Indians were no locals. They looked like Horse Indians out of the Rockies. Maybe Utes or Shoshones. Many Indians were unpredictable, but these measured up. Could be wishful thinking, Jake allowed, but he was so tired of fighting it seemed appropriate to accept them on the face of their peaceful declaration.

They made signs for palaver and Jake made signs for food. It looked to him as if that's what they had in mind anyway but the similarity in the hand sign caused laughter among them, breaking the ice as they chattered between themselves in their own language.

The big one sent the youngster scampering into the timber and, with the remaining brave, stepped forward toward the obvious campsite. Everyone, except José, soon pitched in, gutting the birds and pulling feathers in great handfuls. With an untrusting eye aimed toward the new guests, José built a roaring fire for a nice bed of coals, his rifle never far from his hand.

Before they were nearly finished stripping the birds, the youngster showed up, towing five fine horses close behind. They were good-looking animals that could not be the property of a poor warrior.

Meaningful glances passed between the braves as they noticed Jake's appraisal.

Eating is a serious business often requiring both hands. The youngster, Wind Running as he introduced himself, spoke passable Spanish so he and Altimera held a lively conversation as the birds broiled, dripping fat, hissing into the coals. While they talked, Jake heated beans and coffee as their contribution to the meal.

Wind Running introduced the largest brave among them, a huge man with the broad shoulders and the trim waist of a natural athlete, as

Broken Fire, their leader. The second warrior he introduced as Thunder Maker, the quietest of the three. The Indians were Colorado Utes who roamed an area not far from where Sarah and Jake ranched and who'd trailed the Cruz Brothers for some mischief inflicted upon their families. José didn't press for details, nor could he and Jake help but notice how their eyes flashed with outrage when they spoke of the Brothers.

The conversation flowed around Jake as he wondered why the Cruz Brothers were in that territory anyway. That was more than a thousand miles from the Mother Lode Country, where they would normally be found. The two killers must have come to Colorado immediately following the bushwhacking. Why? None of the possible answers felt good to him. Jake's only consolation was that Sarah was back East, out of harm's way. But his ranch and his stock were not.

As Jake's attention returned to the present, he noticed Wind Running engaged in a reenactment of the shoot-out in the tent saloon. The boy was good. He pantomimed Miguelito's death throes down to the last bullet strikes when he fell face down next to the fire with a realistic thump, raising dust all around him in small eight-inch clouds. Jake found himself laughing in spite of his personal worries.

Lifting himself from the dirt and needles, Wind Running related that he, in fact, was there watching the fight. Vengeance on the Cruz Brothers explained their presence. The fact that Jake and José beat them to that task did not seem to greatly disappoint. If they were smart, as Jake supposed they were, they dreaded doing the chore.

Lopez and Miguelito were mean as snakes and far more dangerous. Had these Red Men managed to avenge their families, the miners would have quickly strung them up for their trouble. No White Man would have taken a moment to understand, as the times pitted White against Red at every possible turn.

It could only have been lose-lose, thought Jake sadly. *Only by my unplanned intervention were they vindicated.* He glanced up and found the attention focused upon himself. *What did they expect of him now?* Sitting up straight, Jake waited.

In his turn, each of the braves pronounced a sincere *Muchas Gracias*, affecting even the stalwart José. Jake watched his Mexican friend's suspicion of these Red Men gradually lose its hold, as he saw his friend's dark face slowly relax from its former expression of stern mistrust.

With surety, Broken Fire stood and pointed directly at Jake, motioning that he should stand also. Leading the way beyond the circle of firelight to where their horses were tethered, the big Indian stepped confidently among them and reached for the bridle reins of a huge sorrel stallion, easily a hand taller than Altimera's red horse and even heavier. This just had to be his number one warhorse, Jake thought. Maybe it was the best horse belonging to the tribe. He could not imagine the cost of such an animal at auction. No man in his right mind would part with him. Jake could barely comprehend what followed.

Reaching for Jake's hand, Broken Fire placed it confidently upon the bridle. "Muchas gracias," he said again, looking directly into Jake's eyes and patting his hand as he held the rope.

The implication was obvious. The Ute's eyes went to Jake and back to the horse. Jake nodded mutely, knowing better than to refuse the gift of this wonderful horse, a deadly insult to the proud warrior.

Once certain that Jake understood, Broken Fire gave him a tour of the animal, pointing out his strength and wind, patting or slapping the horse here and there to make a point. For his own part, Jake could not take his eyes off those of the horse. This was a knowing creature, which not only tolerated Broken Fire but also seemed to understand the big Indian's intent, blowing and whickering gently in the way of horses.

Jake stepped close-up to get better acquainted. The Sorrel dropped his proud head, placing a sleek nose against Jake's belt buckle, then raised it abruptly, throwing Jake four feet backward. Picking himself up off the ground, Jake grinned, knowing this was the horse's way of telling him he preferred being a partner and not a servant.

The Indians smiled widely at this antic and chattered in the Ute tongue. This wonderful beast reminded Jake of another great horse, Sam, who waited for him down at the ranch, his ranch in Colorado. The pleasure of the moment was lost to Jake in a surge of concern over the presence of the Cruz Brothers on his home range.

Fine horseman that he was, Altimera hobbled up behind Jake to watch the show. His eyes sparkled as he beheld the big red horse. Taking the halter gently from Jake's grasp, the Vaquero ran an open hand appreciatively across the animal's neck and shoulder.

Slipping away, Jake returned to the camp where he found the last two potatoes at the bottom of a nearly empty grub sack. He cut one in halves and, returning, offered it to the horse, which snatched at it eagerly. "Ahh, the beginning of a beautiful friendship," Jake said, smiling once again.

Taking Broken Fire by the arm, Jake led the curious Indian back to the camp gear and saddles, from which he pulled two rifles previously belonging to the Cruz Brothers. Having received such a wonderful gift, it was important to Jake that he honor it with one of his own of at least equal value.

As Jake presented Broken Fire with a Henry Repeater and a breach loading Sharp's carbine, the eyes of the Indian came alive. He reached out to accept the Henry for such repeaters made the owner an important man among the tribes. When Jake continued to hold the Sharps, Thunder Maker stepped forward and accepted the piece as his due. In truth, the horse they gave Jake was worth every possession he had with him and a sizable bag of coins to boot. The rifles of the Cruz Brothers were a very small price.

Face impassive, Wind Running stood quietly in the background.

Jake could not be fooled by the lad's expressionless exterior. To ignore the youngster diminished his standing in the tribe. Jake understood he was part of the venture and an important part of the present Jake had received. Momentarily, Jake was at a loss. The rifles just presented were the last extra long guns they carried.

Walking resolutely to his gear, Jake lifted a pair of saddlebags belonging to Lopez and Miguelito. Ammunition for the two rifles filled one side and the other held both Miguelito's Walker Colt and a Confederate version of the model '51 Navy Colt with a brass frame and trigger guard. The brass made it a showpiece that any Indian would enjoy.

So when Jake showed the pistols to Wind Running, the young Indian's face exploded in joy. Holding them above his head, he whooped and danced, stamping his feet rapidly, in a circle of jubilation. Everyone laughed along with him.

Jake received a small nod of appreciation from José for his diplomacy and realized with a start that José liked these Indians, in spite of his long-standing mistrust. What a turn-around for the Mexican! Friends count for a lot in wild country and Jake never knew friends more loyal than those he had among the tribes. Their loyalty had always affected him deeply.

In a general good mood, they all returned to the fire and finished the birds and almost anything else that could be eaten. Only the dry beans were spared. José put those in water to soak overnight and the cleaned bones of the birds went into the fire. It was bound to be a hungry trip back to Bodie, Jake realized.

Maybe not, he reflected. All my needs have been met in the most unexpected ways. And I have seen Quarro. Perhaps I will never see him again, but I will always remember this day.

Colorado on My Mind

The next morning they ate a light breakfast of coffee and seasoned beans. Jake gave the last of the coffee to the three Indians. Fresh supply, he knew, waited barely a day away.

Before the good-byes, Jake gathered everyone in a cleared space of sandy ground near the fire. With a long stick and crude marks in the dirt he illustrated the Colorado Rockies and then, by showing local rivers, pointed to the general area where the ranch lay. Of course they knew the land. Much head nodding and shared glances indicated their understanding. Wind Running rattled off some Spanish to Altimera, who frowned, sobering.

"He say, amigo, they back-track the Cruz Brothers to this area. He is worried for you and for your home."

This had been Jake's worst fear. Briefly, panic flickered through his eyes, driving him to his feet before he mastered the impulse. No, he thought, I'll surrender to my personal fears at a later time. I'll save my worries for when I can be alone with them!

As Jake focused on the present, Altimera helped him communicate his appreciation to Wind Running and the others for sharing this news, and also his desire to see them again in the short days of winter at their home in Colorado. The snow was bound to be too deep for Jake, or anyone else anywhere near Harry's claim in the mountains west of Nazareth. Even in Bodie the snow piled deep and miners often abandoned their diggings until the thaw if they could not be worked.

Before mounting, Broken Fire stepped before Jake and held Jake's hand and forearm solemnly in his own two strong hands. "You will always have friends nearby," José and Wind Running translated.

Departing with many grunts and smiles, the Indians rode single file down the mountain with a last wave of friendship over bare, bronzed shoulders.

Standing as they were for some moments, Jake and José watched the Indians work their way through the trees and out onto the far desert, headed east, away from the foothills of the Sierras. Quiet surrounded them, interrupted only by the intermittent mouse-like squeaks of little gray and black birds that played happily in the lush undergrowth. Watching, Jake noticed many young birds among the adults. A good year for birds, he thought. A good year for me, too.

Jake lived and others did not. The robed figures had visited him again the night before, even with the Utes sleeping nearby. For some reason Jake was confident they would be seen by no one but himself. Memory of the event reminded him that healing continued. His head still hurt enough so that it was difficult to wear a hat.

As he gently touched the wound, Altimera turned to Jake, "Here amigo, let me have a look at your head again." Jake pulled the blue bandanna all the way off so his friend could see the wound and the healing clearly.

"Looks good," he said. "Let's wash it up a bit." Turning away again, Altimera filled a small pot with canteen water and set it on flat rocks to overhang the energetic little flames of their fire.

Once steam began rising from the surface, José removed it from the fire and dipped the end of Jake's bandanna into the pot. Jake let the tension flow from his body with a long, deep sigh and prepared for the discomfort sure to accompany his friend's untutored attentions.

"This is payback for that nice doctor who dug the bullet from my leg with a spoon," José teased. "Don't worry. I will not hurt you nearly so bad." He wiped gently at the salt scale and loose skin, coming at the new patch of skin patiently from each side. His earnestness made Jake smile.

"Are you laughing at me?" the Mexican asked indignantly.

"If you tire of being a fancy cowboy, you could get good wages as a healing angel," Jake told him jokingly.

"If only I had a mirror," the Vaquero said, ignoring the humor, "you would witness a great miracle."

He raised a hand to Jake's forehead and gently probed at the center of the wound. Jake flinched away with pain, though he tried to remain still.

"Ow!" Jake complained, "That's still pretty sensitive."

"Interesting, amigo," Altimera mused, obviously deep in thought. "You no longer have a dimple in your forehead and the red edges of scar have all but vanished. The center is still soft but it is more like bone now than skin. The skin itself is new. That's about the only proof to say you took a bullet there."

Still staring at the wound, José put his chin in his hand and his elbow on his knee. "Never have I seen anything like this before. First you are killed but you do not die, and now you are disfigured but it shows no longer. What angel watches over you, amigo?"

"You are closer to the truth than you imagine," Jake told him obliquely, but chose not to pursue the explanation any more precisely.

Uncomfortable with his staring, Jake recovered the wound with the wet blue bandanna. "It all sounds like good news to me." Standing abruptly, he walked purposefully away from the close scrutiny of his good friend.

Altimera reached over his own shoulder and caught the brim of his hat where it hung by its chinstrap, put it square on top of his head and patted it into place. Casting his eyes along the path they had traversed the evening before, he saw the brightly lit promontory from which they had searched for game only yesterday. The rising sun told him the morning was history.

Heat reached Jake even in the shade of the forest. Suddenly Jake shuddered. The emotion he had held inside in the presence of the Utes came flooding back. A sense of urgency flooded across his awareness. Again and again in his mind he replayed the image of Wind Running, speaking of the Cruz Brothers in Colorado.

Why? Why were they there at all? Did they have business of their own? Was it coincidence or did they seek some vengeance against Jake's family? There would be no rest until he found out. Jake understood that he must retrace their steps and visit the ranch for himself.

But now that he had officially returned from the dead, he felt he had to see to the claim and the ranch both. He was conflicted between the two. Chances were, he would find the rest of the Bushwhackers and whoever put them up to it back at the diggings. Yet the vengeance did not claim as big a part of his heart as did his home and his wife. Jake needed to see Sarah. He ached for her and feared for her safety.

Colorado lay hundreds of miles eastward across some of the harshest country the West could offer. Were he to get there anytime soon, he had best be off.

They had no food to pack and the extra weapons were already on their way to Colorado with his friendly Indians. Looking at the big Sorrel, Jake decided to put off saddle-training the animal for the time being, so he put the saddle and baggage on the gray stallion and saved the saddle blanket for his new horse. Broken Fire had left Jake a fine bridle of carefully braided hair for his new horse.

By the time Jake grabbed a double handful of mane and figured out how to mount the animal, his spirit was halfway down the trail.

"José! Can you make it back to Bodie on your own?"

"Why do I think this is not a question?" José smiled. "I heard the same things you heard and share the same worries! You need to go, Compadre!"

He tossed Jake the Henry from his saddle scabbard and put the saddlebags on the horse behind Jake as the Sorrel danced impatiently in a tight circle.

"When you return," he waved, "look for me in Bodie at the casa of the Señora. I pay an old debt in your absence." The Mexican smiled mysteriously.

Who's Boss?

Johnny Lobo leaned his chair backwards against the white-washed, plastered wall of the office, knowing exactly how much it would irritate the Mayor. Uninvited as Johnny was, any insolent action of his was bound to stretch the Mayor's patience thin. He watched the man get hot from the collar up, finally sinking his several chins into his vest and glowering at Johnny from under unruly black brows.

God didn't short the Mayor none on eyebrows, Johnny thought to himself while the Mayor stewed.

"What do you want, Johnny?" Big Bill Zachary queried impatiently. "State your business or get out."

"What I want Mr. Mayor," Johnny said, shifting his matchstick lazily from one side of his mouth to the other under a short brown mustache, "is for you to own up to your part in this shindig."

"This what?" Big Bill responded with a poker face. "I don't know what you're talking about."

"Let me draw you a picture then, Mr. Mayor," began Johnny Lobo, rocking the chair forward, settling it squarely onto the floor again with a thump. "Some loafer no one has seen since, paid me fifteen hundred dollars to kill Jake Tallon and his friends. Plain for me to see he never put together that much money on his own and cheap enough considering the risk involved."

No point in mentioning, Johnny thought to himself, the fifteen thousand dollars worth of gold in the saddlebags, though he suspected the Mayor knew there would be some.

"I had nothing to do with that," Zachary waved a hand limply in dismissal and looked into the far corner of the room, hoping by some magic that Johnny would disappear by the time he looked back.

"I might believe that," Johnny narrowed his eyes shrewdly, "if you weren't the one moved into the mine to pick up where Harmon and Tallon left off, immediately after their demise." Johnny leaned back in the chair again, waiting for the Mayor's reaction.

Pointedly, Zachary relaxed in his high-backed, swivel-seated leather throne, sticking his fat thumbs into the armholes of the heavily brocaded vest he wore to make himself look important. The desired effect was totally undone by the excessive weight that threatened to overwhelm his belt and buttons.

"That had nothing to do with anything," Big Bill denied. "We had a long dispute over that ground. When those claim jumpers disappeared, I stepped in to take what was rightfully mine. Got all the legalities in line to prove it! They deserted the diggin's anyhow!"

The Mayor was on solid ground now. He'd worked months to build this fiction and it was well documented all the way down to the Land Office in Bodie.

"You can't prove anything to the contrary, Lobo. Around here," Bill Zachary pointed out, "you're just another hanger-on with no apparent source for your substantial resources and a bad reputation to boot."

"Ouch," said Johnny. "You surely know how to wound a man's pride." Pausing, he slowly allowed his hurt expression to become more serious.

"Point is, Mayor," Johnny put his chair down square on the floor again, "you've got more to worry about than just me. Just for a minute, let's assume you had nothing to do with anything." Johnny leaned forward on the front edge of his chair with his elbows on his knees, looking up toward the Mayor. "Five men died on the trail into town and got buried under a sand hill. A couple of days later, someone visits that sand hill and finds four proper graves, not five.

"Now I'm not gonna dig 'em all up to find out who's missing. I don't have to." Johnny paused meaningfully, "Things have happened that paint me a real good picture." The tip of Johnny's tongue caressed the end of the matchstick thoughtfully, causing it to move up and down between his lips.

"Several weeks ago," he went on, "a local low-life, Bingo Mackinaw, and his partner go looking to find out more about who messed with the graves and both of them show up again, layin' straight-out in the back of a rancher's buckboard under a blanket. Bingo's got his face caved in and his partner is ventilated a couple o' times."

Johnny paused to let the information soak in, although he very much suspected Big Bill Zachary knew it all anyway.

"I don't understand …" protested Zachary before Johnny waved him silent.

"A short time later," Johnny continued, "The Cruz Brothers died in a saloon shoot-out near the side hill diggings above Connery. They were part of that shindig on the trail, as you may know. The shooters sounded like Jake Tallon and that Mexican who was knockin' around here asking questions of Harry Harmon before the fact."

During this monologue, Johnny had not been watching the Mayor. Bad manners to stare, he thought. When he turned back, he found he had the Mayor's entire attention.

"Ah," Johnny said, "apparently something you haven't heard yet!"

"No," the Mayor replied nervously, "nothing at all. Fact is," he dissembled, "I've heard of the Cruz Brothers and they're a pretty mean pair."

"They're filthy animals is what they were," Johnny replied, spitting on the floor beside the chair leg. "Sorry Mayor, they just leave a bad taste in the mouth. Even sayin' their name tastes bad." Lobo made a sour face.

"What's the rest of it?" Zachary prompted impatiently, his snake eyes narrowing, "Not that I'm interested."

"Oh no," Johnny said, "not that you are at all, but the pair who nailed Lopez and Miguelito Cruz came away mostly standing up, which means that sooner or later they're gonna be showing up here and asking how come you got the mine. I've got me a hunch Mr. Mayor that they'll take issue with your story and all the phony d... all the deeds," he corrected himself with obvious pleasure, deliberately needling the big man across from him. "It'll take more than a bought Judge and a crooked Sheriff to save your mean rear end when you finally answer up to Jake Tallon."

Now if the Mayor didn't scare a man, thought Johnny, his hired help, Dutch Honniker, surely would. Dutch wasn't the brains. Would never be the brains behind anything, but he could run the mine. But even Dutch might not be enough to stop Tallon.

No matter how much he disliked the Mayor, Johnny held a kind of grudging respect for the man. Maybe caution was a better word. He knew Big Bill Zachary was behind every little thing that happened in Nazareth. If Johnny wanted in the game, it would be with the help of this man or over his dead body, and Johnny simply didn't have that much ambition.

The Mayor was speaking. "Johnny, how come Tallon isn't in one of those graves?" he leaned intently forward over his desk once again.

"I don't know why," Johnny said sincerely, "all I know is the evidence says he isn't. There on the trail, Tallon was as dead as any man I ever seen. The whole side of his head was blowed open," Johnny exaggerated, using his hands to demonstrate. "He didn't breathe and he cooled down right proper. So you tell me why he isn't in one of those graves!"

"Maybe his brother is behind all this," suggested Zachary hopefully.

"Could be Travis, if I didn't know for certain he was still back Missouri way. So I don't think so. Besides that, there are differences between the two brothers. Jake has a way of messing a man up, goes way beyond even what his brother, Travis, does. He really finished a fight! You can track Jake Tallon across the country inquiring of newly crippled men. Bingo Mackinaw is a prime example."

"Why didn't you kill him for sure, if you were paid to do so in the first place?" persisted the Mayor.

"I killed him right enough but I wasn't paid to Comanche him up in little pieces afterwards. Some Indians do that to make sure their enemies can't get even with them in the hereafter. Looks like whoever kills him the next time might have to do just that," Lobo finished, pulling the matchstick from his mouth and studiously examining the frayed end, while the silence dragged on.

Irritated beyond measure, Zachary slapped the desktop explosively, yelling, "Are you going to kill him, Lobo?"

"Only paid to kill him once," Johnny answered matter-of-factly. "I can just leave the territory now and he can come find me if he wants. Maybe he'll do that, maybe he won't. But I do know for sure he's coming here. Count on that," Johnny gestured, pointing with the matchstick.

Johnny Lobo needed only to be quietly known by a few to make a living in the way that he did. Those familiar with him at all would not come looking for any reason, were they half smart. Most figured it was like sneaking up on a brush fire. A man could find it right enough but was sure to get burnt in the process. Any other half dozen men would be easier to deal with than Johnny Lobo.

"You expect me to pay you again?" Zachary asked, eyes widened disbelievingly.

Johnny's eyes twinkled. He had whatever confirmation he needed, which was half the reason why he came to visit anyway.

"I expect if you want it done, Mr. Mayor, you'll hire it," Johnny said, nodding his head up and down once to make his point. "Only this time, it'll be five thousand dollars. That's the amount you should've paid in the first place and I know since you're doing the buying that you can afford it. If you think that's too high, you go find someone else can get it done," he challenged.

Johnny Lobo had a point, Zachary thought. Now that he managed to backtrack the buyer himself, Lobo made a fair proposal. But Zachary truly resented being found out. Inside he silently burned with intense humiliation over being tricked by Johnny. Maybe he could find a way to get even with Lobo in the process, he mused to himself, showing only a small secret smile to the outside world.

"Maybe you got a deal, Lobo," he said. "I'm gonna think on it some. Get out now," he commanded, abruptly turning away. "We'll talk later."

"Don't beat around the bush, Mayor," Lobo sneered as he bent over at the waist to pick up his newly purchased hat. "Be seeing ya."

Headgear in hand, Johnny walked casually to the door and opened it without looking back. Listening as the lock snicked neatly into place behind him, Johnny stepped quickly to the side and stood listening. He didn't trust the Mayor but was now satisfied he remained safe, at least for the moment. Maybe when you kill from ambush yourself, he thought, nothing feels safe.

Lobo looked down the street from the vantage of the second floor landing where he stood, before descending the stairs that ran down the outside of the building. Seeing nothing to arouse additional suspicion, Johnny rolled the side brims of his hat in both hands before placing it on his blonde brown curls, then descended the stairs. Reaching the bottom, he stopped again and rested his left hand on the carved ball that topped the lowest post of the banister. Idly his fingers explored the crack that split the sphere halfway to the base.

During the war Johnny Lobo shot others, but wasn't paid nearly so much to do it. He came from an area of Missouri not far from where Jake Tallon lived, but enlisted for the Confederacy, while Jake went West. Always a good shot, Johnny's skill took some lives and saved others but more as a matter of duty and pride. It was different now and Johnny was uncertain he could tolerate it much longer.

Unable to defend himself against the onslaught of a healthy conscience, Johnny Lobo writhed uncomfortably inside his shirt. That man, he thought, makes me want to change the clothes I wore into that office. If this don't work out I won't be losing no sleep over it. I already got paid and I bought the new outfit I wanted. I got a lot of money in the bank and frankly I get no more respect than I got before.

That's all I ever really wanted, anyway.

Pa held back his respect, Johnny remembered, 'til I learned to shoot as good as him. He made me earn it! After that it just seemed easier to get noticed once people knew I could shoot well. Right now I don't 'specially like where it brought me. I feel so empty an' I know food won't fill me up.

Sad truth is, Johnny reflected sourly as he looked around him, if I want more respect, I gotta change who I am and stop dealing with slime bottled in a shirt like that dirty Mayor upstairs. The thought creased his face into the first heartfelt smile he'd experienced in a month.

Johnny stepped away from the painted side of the building and turned the corner without looking.

Chance Encounter

"**O**h, my," the startled feminine cry exploded under his chin with the impact.

Johnny Lobo fell backwards off the step and the attractive young woman who'd struck him rebounded against the windows set into the face of the building. All eighteen panes rattled dangerously. She brought a hand to her mouth, her eyes wide with surprise.

Like a startled rabbit, Johnny thought, finding himself suddenly speechless. A real good-looking rabbit!

"Goodness," the young beauty said breathlessly. "Don't you ever watch where you're going Sir, or are you in the habit of bowling folks over?" She brushed imaginary dust and wrinkles from the front of her dress in her embarrassment.

Suddenly in uncharted waters, Johnny could not muster even an articulate stammer. He'd never seen a woman this pretty. The blue fairly spilled from her eyes, toward him from under her corn-colored hair. All he could do was smile stupidly. He held his low-crowned hat in two hands, shifting his weight uncomfortably from one foot to another.

Deep within himself, Johnny wished desperately that he were indeed someone else, someone better. A voice inside him queried provocatively, "Do you want to change, Johnny? If you had the right reason, could you change?"

Oh yes, he thought earnestly, looking at the blonde goddess in the blue sunbonnet before him, you bet I can.

Out loud he said happily, "Please excuse me Miss. I should be more careful." I hope she's a Miss, he thought desperately, but she had white gloves covering her fingers and Johnny could see no ring.

"Yes," she said a little flustered, "And we have not yet been properly introduced, so for that reason I can't even speak with you." She turned to go.

In the grips of a beautiful dream, Johnny spoke quickly to arrest her step. "Certainly that's the case! But the good Lord would never allow that

102

situation to continue for long. How is it that we have not been introduced?" he challenged. "Who can I blame for that shortcoming?"

Stopped cold by Johnny's engaging question, she turned yet again to face him. "My," she said, "you're truly bold once you have your tongue back." The color rose in her cheeks. She was charmed but would die before admitting it.

"Bold but courteous," she modified, now a trifle coquettish. "I'm just off the coach to meet my married sister, Sarah. Not that you're entitled to know, Mister …" She paused, head tilted to one side, waiting for Johnny to fill in the blank.

"L- Lobo, Lobo," Johnny stuttered, cursing himself for slowness, but he just couldn't stop staring.

"Your shyness becomes you, Mr. Lobo," the young woman continued, standing even more straightly as she felt the advantage moving in her direction. "My name is Tia, or," she corrected, "Althea Rebecca O'Connell. I'm looking for respectable accommodations. Perhaps you can assist me?" Her eyes said please. She smiled sweetly.

Johnny knew what she saw and was glad he'd shaved the beard.

Althea saw a trim, yet muscular young man in his mid twenties, dressed in a ribbon tie, white shirt, broadcloth vest and trousers. He wore a gun but so did everyone else. What she couldn't see was his history and that worked in Johnny's favor.

If she comes to know me before she knows my history, he thought, thoroughly smitten, maybe I'll have a chance to change after all. She's more worth it than any other reason I've ever seen.

"Mother Flannagan's Boarding House down the street," he offered. "She's not really a mother but she likes to act as though she's a mother. Her name's Molly. When I'm in town, I stay there for the meals."

Truth is, Johnny thought, not many people this far west know much about me, and my disreputable profession has not yet made my face hard. At least, he corrected, no more than anyone else who lived through the war. Polite folks never discuss that anyway.

He gallantly offered his arm to Althea O'Connell.

With a crisp rustle she swept her skirts aside to show him a large ivory print bag resplendent with red roses in needlepoint resting beside her on the dusty boards of the walk. Beauty likes beauty, he thought, pleased at the thought of getting to know her. Bending, he snatched it up with his free hand and again offered her his arm. Taking it with a comfortable smile, she allowed him to guide her south along the sunny street in Nazareth.

Johnny showed little on his face but felt like his heart might tear a hole in his shirt, it hammered so hard.

For her part Tia was profoundly surprised at herself for her inattention to popular convention. Good girls were not so familiar with strangers as this. She wasn't a good girl, she reminded herself, she was an O'Connell. O'Connell girls found and married strong men who were comfortable with strong women.

She looked at her Mr. Lobo from the side of her eye and saw a man like her sister married - strong, confident and competent. Her father taught her to judge character in men and she liked what she saw.

More than a few eyes noticed them, as they made such an attractive couple strolling together on the boardwalk, fairly radiating happiness. No one save the Mayor, who watched from above, had any reason to think them out of the ordinary. He had not yet decided whether to kill or to use Johnny Lobo. If Lobo disappeared, would the woman care? Would that create a new problem for me, he wondered?

For all of his obesity, the Mayor was immensely strong. This man consistently got what he wanted because he understood strength. Idly, his thumb caressed the hammer of his deadly but blocky-looking Smith and Wesson Russian revolver where it rested in its holster, the only such gun in town.

Homecoming

Too long coming home, thought Jake. Each set of hills looked exactly like the last, casting their shadows far ahead of him down the slopes before his slow stepping horses. He began to think he'd missed some landmark in the fading light.

That was certainly possible. Jake had ridden the last four days nonstop, trading for fresh horses down to Cortez. Buck, the fast gray horse belonging to Señora Delores, would wait for him in Bodie Town on the return trip. Even that big red stallion, given him by the Utes, had a limit and the closer Jake got to home, to the ranch he loved, the more important getting there became. Food and rest were poor seconds. Jake felt like a bearded scarecrow sitting this strange new horse, a winter-raggedy Appaloosa. What a pair they made. Jake needed a shave and a bath and the Appaloosa needed a haircut.

The animal was uneasy with him for more than Jake's looks or his unwashed condition. Jake hadn't taken the time to know the horse before running the wind out of him. That, he berated himself, was flat unfriendly. The Appaloosa trembled in exhaustion under Jake, even as they moved forward.

Leaving the saddle in place, Jake slid to the ground and traded back to his mouse-colored companion to ride bareback for a while. He wasn't much more rested than the Appaloosa but at least it had traveled for a spell without the additional weight of a rider.

Shadows waiting under nearby trees rushed outwards across open ground as the sun sank behind the Rockies. Without sufficient light to see, the swish of grass against the legs of his horses and the sound of hooves striking moist earth dominated Jake's world.

Jake's restless eyes probed the deepening darkness on either side. Moonlight through the overcast didn't show him much more than the grass around them and the vague shapes of hills and trees, yet it reassured Jake that the land continued to descend. He knew his spread lay somewhere close to the base of these hills. But seldom having approached his ranch from the west, he remained uncertain.

Should he start to climb, he'd know for sure he'd overshot the buildings and corrals he called home. Just keep going, he told himself, you'll find it.

Final darkness closed down upon him like a blanket. Just when Jake figured he could go no further, the glow of an outdoor fire, flickering spectrally between the pines a hundred yards ahead caught his attention. Shadows danced like hundreds of moving figures in between. Jake scrubbed at his eyes.

Overwhelming fatigue seemed to swell from every muscle. Sagging suddenly against the neck of his horse, he felt incredibly tired and dirty. No matter how close he was, this would be as far as he went tonight, Jake knew. His git-up-and-go, had got up and went. He couldn't stay atop the horse a moment longer.

The trees became thicker and the ground leveled out as he aimed the stumbling horses toward the glowing beacon of light and the suggested shelter of the trees. Some puzzle clamored for Jake's attention that his foggy mind failed to grasp. The fire glowed from a jumble of river rock with a single small figure crouched unmoving before it. Back almost out of the light were the vague outlines of a rented buggy. The paint threw back the light with a polish too good for any kind of ranch wagon.

"Ho, the fire," Jake huffed, struggling valiantly to rise from his miasma of fatigue.

The small figure sprang erect and stepped away from the fire, pointing a steady arm perfectly in his direction. No doubt in Jake's mind what adorned the fist at the end of that small arm. Ratcheting clicks of a drawn gunhammer rewarded his guess.

Jake smiled wryly.

"Get down off that horse, Mister, and state your business or die where you sit," the sharp feminine command cut through the night.

"Whoops," Jake said. "Don't be shooting something you can't see, lady," he said. "It might be a friend." Amusement and anger warred within Jake as he slid off the horse and walked unsteadily forward, stumbling, almost falling. "I'd hate to come this far and be shot by a woman. If Sarah found out she'd finish the job herself."

"Oh, I just knew you weren't dead!" the woman shouted with delight.

"Me too," Jake thought, confused, as he was hit chest high with a rushing tangle of enthusiastic arms and legs. "Uh-h! Golly, what's going on here?" he protested.

"Wahoo!" she yelled.

Bang! The gun discharged with a sharp report behind his head and the bolting horses pulled Jake over flat on his back, with her on top! Jake struggled just to keep hold of the reins and got dragged some for his trouble in spite of the added weight of his friendly attacker.

This woman had used his name - Jacob - he realized. The voice sounded remarkably familiar. A smile washed tardily across his face as Jake realized that this was his very own Sarah, the woman he'd traveled so far and so very hard to find. "I've been here before," he said into her hair.

"You rogue," she shrieked. "You nasty man." She aimed a pretend roundhouse slap at his unprotected face. Blocking it out of habit, Jake noticed she still had the smoking pistol in that hand.

They both fell together laughing hysterically. Sarah smothered her head against his unwashed neck in a careless flurry of wet kisses. Jake felt the child in her against his stomach as she sobbed and laughed alternately, saying, "Jake, Jake, Jacob," over and over again.

Entwining the fingers of one hand in the hair at the back of her head, he raised her hungry lips to his own and drank deeply and longly of their sweetness. After some moments, he gently grasped her shoulders and pushed her slowly up, so he might sit also. She stayed on his lap, desperately wrapped around him, trying vainly to assure herself of his actual presence. The horses calmed to nervous prancing at the end of their taut reins. Jake stroked Sarah's hair, slowly comforting her. This is about the nicest thing ever happened to me, he thought. No, he corrected himself, she is the nicest thing that ever happened to me. As long as Sarah is healthy and alive, the whole trip was worthwhile.

"You gonna be okay, Darlin'?" he asked, pulling her hair away from her face and bending to look deeply into her eyes as she leaned into his manly chest.

"I love you, Sweetheart." This habit of her's, cuddling up against him, had the affect of making him feel uncommonly strong and protective. His fatigue melted away in the rush of his joy. Jake had his love back! Now, he could breath again.

"Oh, yeah. I mean yes," she said as another sob wracked her. "It's been a terrible month, Jacob, but it just got a whole bunch better." The air rushed from her lungs in an extended sigh. "I had this awful feeling you were dead. I hurried so to leave Baltimore, and when I got out here, all I found were bodies and ashes. It was too terrible!"

"Where's here?" Jake asked stupidly, failing to register the entire substance of her short speech.

"Home," she said emptily. "This is all that's left of our home, Jacob, our beautiful ranch. There is nothing left but ashes!"

"Let's move over to the fire, Sweetheart," he suggested, gently disentangling himself, as reality intruded upon his initial delight at seeing his wife. Suddenly Jake felt cold inside, as he realized his suspicion had proved correct after all. "Let me put up the horses," he requested distantly.

Sarah sat for a moment in the dust, watching her Jacob move away from her into the darkness. Across the widening gap she felt the growing coldness in his heart. Part of her chore, she knew, would be to heal that hurt even as she struggled to heal her own.

The corral was still standing, Jake saw.

By the look of it, the only horses inside were the ones that came with the buggy. Swinging the long gate open, Jake led his own two horses inside without letting go their reins. He wrapped them around a rail so he might strip the gear from their backs and properly but swiftly wipe them down.

As he finished with each in turn, he stripped off the bridle and gave them an affectionate swat on the rear. They needed whatever rest they could get. Whenever they felt like it, there was plenty of hay still piled loosely near what remained of the barn.

Pausing just beyond the gate, Jake saw five fresh graves on the far side of the corral, just barely visible by the flickering light of the fire. Only three hired hands and the housekeeper stayed behind when they left, Jake thought. The numbers weren't right. As he turned toward the fire itself, he was knocked sprawling by a tremendous blow from behind.

It felt like the last time he was shot in the back only not quite so bad. Jake heard Sarah yelling his name urgently, "Jacob, Jacob?"

Lying on the ground felt so good, he wanted neither to answer nor to get up. He just lay there struggling to fill his lungs. Next thing Jake knew he had horse breath washing across his face.

He opened one eye and witnessed the biggest horse he'd ever seen standing directly over him, like a tree grown beyond years, towering far into the sky, blocking out the stars. A lot of it, he knew, was only because he was face down on the ground, looking upward over his shoulder. Jake rolled onto his back.

That horse looked awful familiar but it sure wasn't the Appaloosa he'd ridden the last legs of this journey. He sucked in a deep breath born of his surprise.

"Sam! Sam, my best old friend," Jake shouted happily. There had been no time to sort out all the details but obviously the horse was only now returning, since he wasn't already inside the corral. Sarah always felt Jake was too permissive with the big Grulla.

So I'm not shot after all, Jake realized with relief, letting out another deep breath. I've just been knocked flat by my over-affec-tionate horse.

"Hi would do just fine," Jake complained, struggling to sit erect. He would've managed but Sam kept bowling him over with his enthusiasm.

In frustration, Jake rolled over, scrambled to his hands and knees, and turned, grabbing the big mouse-colored stallion full around the neck before the happy horse finally calmed down.

"I'm here to stay, Sam," Jake soothed the horse, tousling his full mane vigorously and fussing over him. "You're such a fine, big horse. Where in Heaven's name have you been, anyway?"

With one hand always on him to maintain the contact Sam craved, Jake looked him over as best he could in the dark. The big horse seemed to have no injuries, he noted with relief.

Jake turned to see Sarah watching with her hands clasped before her, smiling benevolently.

"I like seeing the two of you together again," she said. "In fact, I just like seeing you, Jake, any old way."

Crossing the distance between them at a run, she leapt again into Jake's arms. Using her momentum, Jake spun her, flipped her upward, and landed her comfortably astride Sam's back in a blink. "Whoa," she exclaimed, dizzy from the move, then laughed with abandon.

Leading his happy friends toward the fire, Jake's face relaxed into the first smile he'd worn in a while. Fatigue, though still deep within him, seemed to retreat into the distance. He needed food but Sam continued to require his attention.

Sarah understood. Looking once to her husband and his horse, she turned to the task with a satisfied smile. Before long, smells of meat frying and biscuits baking made Jake dizzy as he waited. While he traveled, food had not been important. Just like always, Sarah had changed his priorities. Jake's belt rattled around his waist like an old tire hoop and he realized that his personal experience with food was little more than a memory.

Finally comfortable that Jake was home to stay, Sam ambled over toward the other horses. The big animal wasn't going anywhere, Jake knew, there was no need to pen him up at all. He would wander the area all night like a watchful dog.

Sarah pointed her man toward a pan of hot water and soap. He pulled the stiff and sticky shirt off over his head, feeling the luxury of fresh air wash against his skin. As he bent over the basin, Jake realized this was the first time he'd seen water outside of a canteen in a week.

With relish, Jake scrubbed away at the accumulation of dust, sweat and debris that had crusted against his flesh, under his clothing. Toweling down his chest and arms, he searched amongst his kit, and found the new razor José had bought for him back in Bodie.

Picking up the soap again, he built a lather between his hands and spread it generously across his jaw and neck. Sitting astride the old stump before a hanging piece of mirror, he shaved by the dim light of the fire.

"Ahh," he moaned as his flesh came clean under the loudly scraping blade.

Common things, with Sarah near, felt like Heaven. He found that his eyes strayed constantly to where she worked by the fire as he cleaned the stubble from his face. Sarah felt his glance and knew his hungers. She brought him a piece of steaming meat on the end of a fork and sat next to his knee as he took it from her.

"I pulled some things from the ashes," she said matter-of-factly, her eyes dancing across his upper torso. "Wasn't that much left that was worth the trouble. I'm sure glad I'm here though." She smiled up at him.

Biting off a chunk of hot, seasoned meat, Jake asked her as he chewed, "When did you get out here?" Deep inside he cursed the mouth that muttered such mundane words. He yearned for the words that spoke his pent-up feelings for her.

"Three or four days ago," she answered, placing one of her hands over the other, atop his knee. "I just cried for one whole day and then I got mad." Sarah realized they needed to wade through these common matters before she got really close to this man again. Her man. She felt herself warming to the task and anticipating his touch. Her body sagged toward him as though drawn by a magnet. With conscious effort she restored some measure of distance and her upright posture.

"That mad part scares me," he told her, laughing too much. "I've been around when you get mad and generally some man gets maimed."

That memory put a bright smile on Sarah's face. Giving into impulse, she reached for him now, snuggling up to Jake's arm, while he continued shaving. Talking into his biceps as if hiding from the memory, she lowered her voice and said, "I found what the coyotes and birds left of four bodies in the yard. There wasn't much left to bury and sometimes little to tell me who they were." Her voice went to a new, quieter level, difficult to hear even in the stillness of the night. "I found a fifth body in the ashes of the house, that I'm sure was Josephina." Unconsciously her fingers tightened about Jake's arm. This memory saddened her in spite of his nearness.

"Many brass rifle casings surrounded the body. I could tell she took her own life at the end but I'm sure she died before whoever they were burned the house. I found no metal rifle parts near the body to show her Henry had been burned. They took it from her body then set fire to the house."

Wordlessly, Jake hugged her, sharing her grief, comforting her, wishing intently that he could make her pain go away.

Sarah paused as though personally reliving what Josephine must have experienced, "I've picked up and salvaged what I could. I found kitchen things, bedding and clothes scattered all over."

"Probably not Indians in that case," Jake surmised. "They would've taken more than they left. I've already got a notion who it was and maybe what they wanted." Jake felt her face shift provocatively into his shoulder. Carefully, he put down the razor and wiped his jaws clean on a towel. Breath staggered in his throat as the tension of desire caught at his chest.

"Come on Cowboy," she whispered breathily. "There's been enough jawing. Let's get you some rest."

"I ain't no cowboy," Jake objected.

"That's okay, I don't plan on you resting much!"

Morning arrived much too early. Light flooded the clearing where the buildings of a young family once stood. Sarah sat in front of the fire on a chair with no back, making coffee and cakes. Jake felt better physically than he had in days, but looking at the ruins around them would take the shine off the Mardi Gras. Every building was burned down to the stone foundations. Trees surrounding the compound were singed by the great heat of the many fires. Even the chimneys were toppled.

He cowered in his blankets, trying to absorb the enormous loss. Work involved in the buildings was the least of it. He had friends here he would never see again. At play and at work, he saw them as he remembered them. The death of the Cruz Brothers was small consolation.

Looking up, Jake saw Sarah had walked up and sat down on crossed legs near his head. She wore jeans and a shirt like she did last night. Her beautiful, dark auburn hair was tied behind her head, out of her eyes. She reached out, at first touching his arm and then placing her delicate white hand over Jake's large darker hand.

Her eyes danced around the wide-open area between the trees, absorbing what she knew he saw for the first time in the light of day. "Seeing it like this kinda takes your breath away, doesn't it?" she asked soberly.

He nodded mutely. "I don't think they found what they wanted. They burnt the place to destroy it, just in case they overlooked it."

"What were they after?" Sarah looked to Jake.

"I'm sure they were after the deed to Harry's mine. They just figured I had it for some reason. I never did. They killed four people for something that was never here." Jake looked out toward the graves of his friends, clenching his fist so hard that his arm trembled.

Sarah spoke to fill the silence. "Almost two months ago," she began again, "I was having a good time with my older sister Lillian, in Baltimore. We went places, enjoyed ourselves and just caught up on things. I played with her children and I helped out with chores like I did for Momma when we were kids."

Sarah stared vacantly into space, thinking back. "Then one day," she began again, eyes tearing, darting back and forth in inner agitation, " I felt the most dreadful sorrow. It was as if you were close to me, then gradually drifted farther away. I became crazy because there seemed nothing for me to do." Her voice had risen. Breathing unsteadily, Sarah tried for a measure of calm, "I soon made everyone so miserable that I had to come home with my other sister, Tia. I got off the train at Cumberland Crossings and Tia went on to Nazareth," Sarah finished. "If I go into town, I'm sure I'll find a wire from her waiting for me. There was just so much to do here." She gestured helplessly, with her hands palms up as she looked all around them. "I don't know anymore. What more … I can do."

Jake watched the tears overflow Sarah's eyes as the remembered pain and frustration became too much for her. It was time for her to hear as much as he could tell her of what had actually happened.

"I know you go to church regular, Honey," Jake began thoughtfully. "Your family raised you to believe in the Lord. As for us, we haven't really talked about religion much. The only time we've been to church together was for the wedding. Ha!" Jake exclaimed, remembering the ceremony Night Walker held for them afterwards.

Jake looked into her face, seeing how she hung on his every word, holding her breath. "There's hardly a way to tell you how it really works, Sarah." Jake's face contorted in his search for words. Finally he blurted, "I think that I did die, Sarah. I've been there and I've come back again."

She looked at him, confusion washing across her face. Even Jake was confused. He'd never tried to explain the experience fully to anyone before.

"Where?" Sarah was mystified.

"Heaven … I think. At least the Spirit Lodge part of it. I never saw any angels or clouds like the great painters seem to think. It's more like the green meadows and still waters of the 23rd Psalm. All peaceful, like."

Jake went quiet. His eyes searched everywhere for the words he wanted. Not finding them, he settled his gaze on Sarah and took her hands in his. "You remember when I told you about the Friendship Stone?" He squeezed her fingers in his larger hand.

"The Old Man on his farm in the desert!" Sarah smiled warmly at the memory, squeezing back.

"His name is Shantee, or at least that's what he calls himself now. He never told me before."

"Now? You mean you met the Old Man again? How?" she asked with sudden interest.

"I met him after I got this," he pointed to the fresh scars on his forehead. "I met him in the Spirit Lodge."

Reaching to touch it, she said, "Looks like you took an awful spill, Honey."

"No Sweetheart, I was shot," Jake understated. "I was killed in the ambush, where Harry and my other friends also died."

Sarah gasped sharply, bringing her hand suddenly to her mouth, eyes wide with worry. "It doesn't look that bad, Jacob," she protested, reaching out again, touching the area ever so gently. "And if you were killed, how is it that you're still alive, still with me?"

"There's more to it than I have words for yet, Sarah. Memory from my time in the Spirit Lodge comes back to me in bits and pieces and the images are sometimes hard to understand. I'm still trying to sort it out," Jake fidgeted in his frustration. "I can tell you I've already met our son. I remember that part very clearly." He put his hand on her warm, growing belly.

"Oh, Jacob," she said, tearing up again. Sarah spent enough time with the Cherokee Shaman, Night Walker, that she understood more than most White folks might, given the same information. She also had the good grace not to push a full explanation right away. She asked only, "What's his name? What's our son's name?"

"Julius, Julius Michael Tallon," Jake answered smiling. "Shantee or Man Above or whoever he is, and you know I mean no disrespect, said that you and Julius needed me too much for me to depart my life on Earth. That was the main reason that I couldn't stay on the other side. Coming back was very painful," Jake said, touching the scars on his forehead, "I can tell you that for sure, right up until last night. Then it got fun again."

She whacked him playfully across the shoulder, thankfully without a heavy object in her fist. He covered his face and she rolled him over with the weight of her whole body.

"You just want your way with me again," Jake mocked playfully. That only increased the playful punches and lightweight slaps until she ran out of wind and plopped down beside him on the ground.

"Of course, I do," Sarah admitted. "Only I also want whoever did this … whoever killed our friends … to pay."

"They already have," Jake told her soberly. "They paid for this because when they killed me the first time they took the Friendship Stone and I went after them to get it back."

"Don't say it like that, Jake. Don't say they killed you at all," she interrupted. "It sounds so final! So ugly!" Sarah made a face.

"I can learn to forgive a lot," Jake said, thinking of Man Above, "but they can't have this." He held the Red Jasper in his fist. "It was his gift to me. Altimera and I found the Cruz Brothers in a little mining camp up into the Sierras north of Bodie. He took a ball in the leg," Jake pointed to the middle of his left thigh, "and I didn't think him up to traveling as fast as I wanted to get here to find you. I rode like the doggone Pony Express." Jake embraced her fiercely.

"Tell me more about this," pulling away, she pointed timidly to Jake's head.

"It scares me some," Jake admitted. "José told me it looked awfully bad when he pulled me out from under a sand hill, where they left me and my friends as a final resting place. You can imagine I was pretty dirty. José said I wasn't smelling too bad so he thought to move me to nicer accommodations." Jake didn't think she needed to hear about the shards of bone.

"Buried!" she exclaimed. "How long?"

"Maybe a day," he guessed, "not long. The wound has healed more than anyone had a right to expect. Seeing you again, Sarah, nearly puts me back to normal." Jake stretched out and lay his head down in her lap. He looked up at her, locking his fingers together across his belt buckle.

"Why is all this happening?" Sarah asked, genuinely puzzled.

"Well, the mine worked out better than Harry hoped it might. The rest is simple. There's always someone else wants wealth without working for it. It's an old story. My trouble is that I was having such a good time finding the gold and working the gold, that I forgot to be careful and didn't see trouble coming down on us. My friends paid the price of my carelessness." Jake's shoulders sagged under his burden of sadness.

"You can't blame yourself, Jacob," she admonished, her face all furrowed with her earnestness. "It's not possible to foresee every ambush."

That's so true, Jake thought as he remembered being struck by the bullet on the trail into Nazareth. "If it's not a surprise, after all, it's not much of an ambush."

She leaned away from Jake and pulled a five shot, nickel-plated Remington Special Model from her clothes somewhere. It looked like a thirty-six caliber version of the model '61 New Army with the frame closed over the top of the cylinder, ivory grips and a shortened barrel.

"I want you to help me with this, Jake," she said with the pistol laying flat in her open palm. "It belonged to Daddy. I can shoot it, but I want to shoot it well."

His eyes were poised to leap from his face, so surprised was he. This woman defied every convention. "Why bother with sewing," Jake teased, "if you can shoot?"

Sarah smiled indulgently at his wit. "Teach me," she insisted, ignoring his argument.

"When have I ever said no to you, Sweetheart?" Jake placed his hand over hers and the pistol, squeezing them gently.

After some breakfast he collected old tin cans from the dump behind the cabin and set them atop a log down the trail from the house.

"Guess it don't matter where we shoot," he gestured helplessly toward the blackened foundation. "It's just habit."

Sarah showed serious all around the eyes, ready to accept everything Jake had to say about her new toy. Ladies didn't do pistols back East but they both knew the West was more dangerous, and anything to do with gold was deadly. Proof of that fact lay all around them.

"Teaching you how to defend yourself is the smartest thing to do, Honey," said an equally serious Jake. "Marrying me was a dangerous proposition in the first place. Trouble's goin' to follow me and I can't run from it. I'm not built that way."

"I know all that Jake," Sarah protested, "but I want to carry my own weight."

Taking the piece from her hands and pointing it carefully away from them, he showed her how the hammer could be raised only partially to half-cock. Spinning the cylinder, he showed her how to check the loads front and back.

"Uh-oh," he observed, touching a finger to fresh powder residue on the cylinder face. "You seem to have an empty chamber in this fine handgun."

"So?" Sarah felt embarrassed but remained uncertain why she should be so concerned. "Why is that a problem?"

"If you don't clean it right away," Jake explained, "the barrel rusts up from the spent powder. That's the first important thing to learn. If you don't care for it, pretty soon you have a gun that won't work."

"That's no good, I guess?" Now she was embarrassed for missing something so obvious.

"Go ahead," Jake told her, "Spend these last four shots on those cans."

Holding the gun with both hands, Sarah banged away with calm deliberation, hitting one in four at fifteen yards. "Not half bad," he admired. "I know plenty of men don't do that good." This woman got his approval for anything she did just 'cause she tried so hard.

"Now reload it," Jake requested patiently.

"Do I have to?" she pouted cutely. "Why don't you do it for me?" She cuddled up provocatively into his shoulder.

"That won't work this time," said Jake. "You have to do it yourself or you don't learn!"

"Oh, all right," she pouted, pulling away. Out of her bag she pulled an embossed silver powder flask, a coin-sized tin of percussion caps and a soft leather pouch of lead balls and patches. This woman was fully prepared, Jake admired.

With thumb and forefinger he selected a lead ball and held it up to his face for a close examination. He could see the seam running cleanly around the middle where the mold split. The doggone thing was perfectly round as it could be. Store bought! Had to be store bought. Personal experience taught him how hard it was to mold perfect balls. It all had to do with the mold and it was hard as heck to find a good one.

While Jake daydreamed, she tilted the powder flask upside down with a finger over the open spout. Releasing the spring-loaded gate, she turned it right side up and emptied the powder in the long brass snout into each chamber perfectly in turn. Then one at a time she picked up a waxed patch, waded it over the load and, centered a ball over the mouth of the chamber, rotated it under the loading lever and cranked it into place, flush with the front of the cylinder. It all took her a little over a minute. Reversing the pistol with business-like efficiency, she used a little penknife to pop a spent cap off one of the firing nipples and place bright new number ten caps from her enameled tin over each of the five snouts.

Damn, Jake thought. This woman could load! Plainly, she'd done it before.

He stepped to the side as she cocked and raised the piece. "This time," he said, "don't aim. Look over the barrel of your pistol and concentrate on the one specific part of the can that you want to hit," he coached.

"Part of the can?" She questioned.

"Yeah. Concentrate on the top edge of the can 'cause the ball will drop some between here and there, anyway. Now go ahead and bang away!"

And so she did, this time hitting two out of five but getting consistently close every time.

"It helps," Jake showed her, "if the webbing of your thumb is tight against the base of the hammer. Make sure the pistol fits deeply into your hand. That way the weight of the gun pushes against your palm instead of being held by the fingers. When you pull the trigger, it's more of a squeeze and it doesn't jerk the barrel off target so much."

Holding her hands to show her the correct positions as he talked, Jake realized how uncommonly strong were her hands and wrists. But then most women didn't enjoy chopping wood like Sarah or spend as much time in the saddle. These simple things toughen a person a little at a time, almost imperceptibly. This woman was beautiful but no muffin!

Sarah reloaded quickly and shot again. This time she scored four hits and a wobble. "You just can't do much better than that," Jake told her. "More practice will make it instinctive."

For the first time since shooting instruction started, she spoke, "That makes such a difference, Jacob. I almost know what I'm doing now. It's a big relief. Thank you." She hugged him warmly.

Putting the ammunition back in her purse, she turned with Jake to walk away from the targets. Palming his gun, Jake spun and popped five more of the cans off the long log, one after another.

"Oh Darling," she clapped her hands together as the echoes died away and the smoke cleared, "you're so good!"

Jake couldn't help but puff up under her praise. "Right enough, Honey Dew," he replied proudly. Blowing smoke from the end of the barrel, he spun the gun for affect and dropped it backwards into the tooled leather for the reverse draw.

"Oh," she said, placing a hand to the base of her throat in mock horror. "Aren't you going to reload it?"

"Of course, I am." Jake stammered, realizing that this was Sarah's payback. "That, my dear, was only a test and you passed." Knowing a lame response when he heard one, Jake pulled the gun again and opened the loading gate, dumping five rim fire empties onto the ground.

"Isn't that just slick!" Sarah observed soberly, staring down at the shiny cartridges half-buried in the dust at their feet. "When do I get a nice pistol like that?" she pointed at Jake's Remington as he thumbed in fresh loads from his vest pocket.

When he failed to respond right away, she went on the attack.

"That was a nasty little trick," she scolded, "making me reload my dirty old gun when yours is so tidy. Is this the way our marriage will proceed? You get all the nice guns and I get the hand-me-downs and the obsolete?"

"Now, I know what obsolete means," Jake said. "I never thought of it as mean," Jake tried to explain as they walked together back to camp. "In fact, I never thought about it much at all. I'm just getting used to cartridge-fed pistols myself."

He paused thoughtfully, "I do have an idea. Why don't you take my big, tidy gun and I'll trade it for your little dirty gun? That way you'll have what you want."

She frowned at him as they walked. A small smile reformed her sweet, heart-shaped lips. "I know what you're doing, Jacob. That big forty-four is at least twice as heavy as my pretty little thirty-six caliber custom model. I couldn't carry that weight all day and be comfortable. You're making fun of me is what you're doing," she pouted again. "That's just as bad as giving me the crummy guns like you did in the first place."

"Okay," he reasoned, "until we get yours converted, it's what you have, so it's good for you to learn to do it right."

"Was that a lecture?" she asked innocently. "Sounded like a lecture to me."

"If I'm going to lecture," Jake responded, "the lecture would concern the proper choice of women. On that one I'm an authority." With his hand on her far shoulder, he pulled her close against him as they walked. She warmed to him all over again.

"Dodged that bullet, didn't I?" he asked.

"Oh, you're a charmer all right!" Sarah felt a stupid schoolgirl smile overwhelm her face. This is my Jake, she thought fondly. He helps me be the best I can be, but he still makes me weak in the knees.

Mayor of Nazareth

Big Bill Zachary watched as Johnny Lobo and Tia O'Connell disappeared down the street toward Molly's Boarding House, Mother Flannagan's as it was called. Molly still owed him for part of that property, he remembered. Distance and shadow made the couple indistinct but he could still identify them by the way they walked arm in arm, already deep in conversation.

Smitten, he thought. Johnny Lobo was smitten. The Mayor smiled, shaking his head ruefully as he watched. How could a woman grab a man like that, fresh off the street and involve him so totally? Must be weak-minded.

No, Lobo was not a weak man, Zachary corrected himself. Lobo was a certain killer. That was the whole reason Zachary hired him in the first place. Men like Jake Tallon allowed only one chance and sometimes not even one.

The apparent failure of his primary strategy left the Mayor angry and frustrated. He felt trapped into hiring the Bushwhacker again but intensely resented that need. He hated Lobo for tricking him into owning his part in it. Sometime down the road, Lobo would pay for that.

Everything Johnny Lobo had to say about the death of the Cruz Brothers and the unfortunate demise of Bingo Mackinaw, the Mayor had heard before. The difference was that previously he could shrug it all off as mere coincidence. Bad people met untimely death. It was all in the way they lived.

But when Johnny drew the more than obvious conclusion that Jake Tallon yet survived, he could no longer deny it. Hearing it from Johnny, in that way, made him cold all over despite the warm day.

Jake Tallon, riled, was an unstoppable machine of incredible destruction and though Zachary had never met the man, he'd heard the stories. Now it seemed he was living one of those stories and he didn't want to hear how it ended unless he had control of that ending. And at the moment, control eluded him.

Normally Big Bill Zachary feared no one. Over six foot two inches, he'd allowed himself to go to fat but remained mentally tough and shrewd. Behind him stood an army of hired riffraff. In time of trouble he called upon them for muscle. He'd done so many times before and that had always been enough.

That's what he intended to do this time. Not even Jake Tallon could defeat a whole town, his town. Turning to the oak coat tree in the corner of his office by the glass-faced bookshelves, the Mayor repositioned his shoulder holster for more comfort and reached for the heavy broadcloth coat, hanging from an upper hook. A sweltering heat waited on the streets outside but that coat was his symbol of power, besides hiding his Smith & Wesson. Slipping into the coat right arm first, he placed a floppy brimmed, high crowned, white hat on his intensely black curls.

In bright sun, that hat cast his face in a pool of shadow where his cold eyes seemed to float, balanced menacingly above his big mustache. Given his height and size, the effect was threatening and the Mayor used it all to project strength and create fear.

Shrugging his clothing into position, Zachary crossed the threshold onto the landing and closed the door behind him without locking it. No one in all of Nazareth had the nerve to disturb his personal property, he thought with no small arrogance. The outside stairs creaked threateningly under him as he made his way down to street level. Much as he had seen Johnny Lobo do, the Mayor stopped to survey the main street of Nazareth in both directions.

Who knew or cared what occupied the mind of Johnny Lobo, thought the Mayor. Who cared if he was infatuated? Lobo was the outsider. This was Big Bill's town and he felt pride when he viewed the dusty thoroughfare. Staking out the whole thing himself, he had sold lots during the first strike in '66, keeping the best sites for himself. Like the boarding house, many still belonged to him, in part or wholly. Most of the property he saw, looking up and down the street, was still his.

With a destination in mind, he stepped up to the boardwalk a good twelve to fourteen inches above the dust of the street. For the moment he had the street entirely to himself. It was his street anyway, he thought. He'd built it.

When the placer gold petered out, Zachary mused, he'd found other ways to keep the town going, though not nearly so busy. The new strike by Harry Harmon, now his, would put Nazareth on the map once again. From the beginning, Zachary knew that this time he could have the town and the gold from the mine as well, if he played his cards right. That had always been the plan.

The newly arrived miner had talked too much, like some men do, when he first came to town. An incautious man. The talk sounded crazy but the fellow could not be shaken of his conviction. Zachary noticed the miner spent several days in the hills and came down after a spell to wire his friends, including Jacob Tallon. This time, Harmon kept to himself. He kept quiet.

That fact all by itself got Big Bill's attention. Silence translated as success for the ambitious prospector. Tallon in the mix made the play more risky but added credibility for Harry Harmon. The man must know what he was doing, after all.

Zachary could only conclude that the prospector bore watching. Eventually the watching paid off. Even from a distance, a man with a glass can tell when a miner is cleaning dust and nuggets from a sluice box.

Moving right on the boardwalk, the Mayor turned his back on the reputable part of town and headed for the Oro Fino Saloon. Even strong men sometimes need conspirators. That would be Judge Hoagland and the chambers of the jurist were locked this day because the Judge had an appointment with a bottle at the Oro Fino.

Hoagland wasn't a real judge. He held a position as Justice of the Peace.

Zachary had a fine appreciation for the law as long as it was his, so he controlled the Judge by his bar tab. Whiskey was always free for the Judge but carefully doled out. He could not be allowed to drink himself to death. Permanent numbness was all that Hoagland desired anyway.

Zachary didn't have far to walk. Passing only three buildings down on the right he turned into the Oro Fino, painted brightly white on the outside with gold leafed signage in the windows and mahogany dark on the inside. Once this had been the finest saloon east of the Sierras. That was before the strike in Bodie and others that followed over the years all up and down the Basin Range. Now it was just a nice place to buy a drunk.

Pushing through the bat wings, Zachary saw the Jurist halfway back in the room, just beyond the range of sunlight but close enough to appreciate the artfully carved, single-piece bar brought around the horn from Milan, Italy. The Judge created a dark silhouette as he sat alone with a tall brown bottle and a full glass of amber liquid before him. Big Bill watched him with interest.

He'd heard the Judge talk about feeling numb but Bill suspected smugly that the Judge spent his time feeling sorry for himself, not numb. It was all in the choice of words. Semantics. Thin but not wasting, the Judge sat staring at the glass, unmoving and surprisingly elegant in a St. Louis suit. The damage alcohol inflicted on this man did not become apparent until a person looked into the rheumy, deeply circled eyes.

Big Bill allowed each step to fall heavily as he approached the table, that he might not surprise the Judge unnecessarily. Despite the Mayor's careful consideration, one half of the Judge's mouth cranked upwards in a non-smile, announcing his annoyance to the world in general.

Arrogantly inviting himself to sit, Bill tossed his hat down beside the bottle and turned the chair so he could straddle it, resting his heavy arms along the curving back. His jacket sagged open, revealing the smooth brown handle of the Russian revolver. Its presence and the implications were not lost upon the Judge. He just didn't care.

As the Mayor arranged himself, he saw the ever-weary Hoagland wobble where he sat, then snatch the full glass of whiskey and toss it off at a gulp. Zachary understood suddenly what the Judge's ceremony with the glass most reminded him of, a cat and a captured mouse. When the cat tires of the game, he breaks the spine of the mouse and eats it. Zachary allowed himself a tiny smile at this understanding. That drink couldn't put up much of a fight, smiled Zachary. Couldn't even run.

While the Mayor was busy thinking, the Judge picked up the bottle and prepared to fill his glass once again. Big Bill covered the glass with a meaty hand and looked him full in the eyes. "I didn't come down here to watch you drink, Hoagland. We need to talk first, then you can return to your drinking."

Judge Hoagland buried his chin into his stiff, white collar, looked ruefully at the Mayor and back to the bottle, still mostly full. Plenty of time for drinking, he thought. "Okay," he said bitterly, noting that his words had not yet begun to slur.

Arne Carlson inched his nervous way up to the table, wanting desperately to bask in the glow of power represented by these two august figures. Seeing the man with his peripheral vision, the Mayor remembered Arne as an odd-job laborer, a man of little personal ambition.

"Arne," snapped the Mayor without looking up, "go find Laszlo!"

"Shore, Mr. Mayor," Arne groveled, wringing his shabby hat in both hands, "I know right war he is." Moving quickly on uneven heels, Carlson hit the bat wings at an uncoordinated run.

"What a fool," complained Zachary to no one in particular.

"Look closely, Mayor," said the Judge acidly, "they're all around you." Big Bill Zachary usually got on his nerves and he was hard pressed to conceal it, especially when the Mayor interrupted his drinking.

The words had no apparent effect on Big Bill Zachary, who warred internally with the unaccustomed fear surrounding the return of Jake Tallon. Fear! He couldn't use that word to explain his presence to the Judge or even tell the man what he wanted from him. He didn't know for sure what he did want. He was scared.

"Drink some coffee," he told the Jurist testily, "and try to be more civil." He snapped his fingers at the Barkeep who, seeing the two men together, knew exactly what was required.

Judge Hoagland hated the coffee because it took the edge off the drunk he tried so hard to cultivate, but it amused him to be lectured by the Mayor. Who was the Mayor to lecture him, anyway? A better person? Hah!

The same ritual repeated itself on these occasions, with little variation. He knew it so well, he could almost repeat the next lines from memory. So he did.

"That bottle's gonna eat you alive," said the Judge.

The abrupt change in roles shocked the Mayor so badly, he would have swallowed his cigar if he smoked one. It broke his mood. He looked up at the Jurist, speechless. After only a heartbeat, he guffawed loudly and, bending over the table, slapped the Judge heartily on the shoulder, the impact causing the frail Judge to rock again in his chair. This time he had an excuse.

Coffee and the Sheriff arrived at the same time. The Barkeep went back for an extra cup as Vernon Laszlo pulled up a chair backwards like he saw the Mayor doing. "What's up Boss?" he opened, pushing his dirty, battered hat further up on his forehead to expose a sweating bald spot. Childhood smallpox had battled across the man's gaunt cheeks, leaving them pitted and scarred.

Distracted by his own troubles, the Mayor watched Laszlo lazily shifting a matchstick in his teeth and wondered briefly if he and Johnny Lobo were related. No, he decided, Johnny Lobo wasn't ugly enough.

"What's up," said Big Bill Zachary, leaning forward conspiratorially, "is that Jake Tallon isn't dead and we've got some problems we hadn't planned on."

Laszlo's busy matchstick came to an instant halt. The Judge's eyes widened perceptibly as he slowly leaned forward in his chair. Seconds ticked by as the Mayor allowed them to absorb his information.

"How do ya know that?" the seedy Sheriff wanted to know.

"Lobo was in my office this morning, putting two and two together. He says one grave is empty, that Bingo Mackinaw was messed up in a way that reminded him of Jake Tallon, and the Cruz Brothers may have been killed by Tallon and that Mexican fella been nosing 'round here of late."

"Why not just kill 'em again?" Laszlo volunteered.

"Seems like we already tried that," the Judge had even less patience with Laszlo than with Zachary. The Judge was a drunk but he wasn't stupid.

"Two problems," the Mayor reasoned. "One is, I'm still not totally convinced that it is Jake Tallon. Even if one body disappeared, I can't imagine Tallon surviving a head wound like everyone says he received. The second problem is that Harmon and his friends disappearing can cause loose talk but as long as there's no body, no one really knows for sure.

"If we try killing Tallon again, it may not stay so secret as we managed the first time," the Judge warned. "The blame could come home to roost and we could lose our hold on this town, not to mention the mine."

"Or our freedom," mumbled Laszlo, matchstick teetering on the edge of his lower lip.

"The claim is all in order," said Judge Hoagland, now thoroughly sobered by the alarming topic under discussion. "There's no problem at all without the original deed to contest the matter."

But somewhere deep inside, untouched by all the booze, lived an active conscience. The Judge had an increasingly difficult time containing it. He did the Mayor's bidding but he didn't like it.

"That can be a real problem," said the Sheriff, ignoring the obvious discomfort of the Jurist, "because we never did find them deeds of Harmon's."

"You finishing off Harmon before he told you, didn't help us any there," accused Big Bill.

"I wasn't the one done it, first place. Second, he wasn't about to tell us no-how, anyway," Laszlo heated up. The matchstick fell unnoticed from his mouth to the floor.

"Hush-up," cautioned the Mayor, a silencing hand stretched over the table between the three men.

"Hold on a minute here." Slapping both hands down sharply on the table top, Judge Hoagland got everyone's attention, "Aren't both of you worried," he struggled to control the level of his voice, "that we're talking about someone who was dead one minute and who's now alive?" He pierced each man in turn with a long hard look.

"We don't know that for sure," growled an irritated Zachary, pointedly ignoring eye contact with the Judge.

"No we don't, but I'm scared to death," said an agitated Jurist. "And who is this man, who sounds like Tallon, looks like Tallon and kills like Tallon?"

"Might be his brother, Travis," said the Sheriff, idly making a series of rings on the table top with the bottom of his coffee cup.

"I thought so too," the Mayor acknowledged the shortcoming of his own argument. "But Johnny Lobo is convinced the brother is still back East in Missouri somewhere."

"Well, hold on here, again," said the Judge, fairly spitting, "We were all assured that Tallon took a rifle ball in the head, and was buried cold and blue under a sand hill."

Big Bill Zachary saw years of control unraveling because of a cowardly and over-imaginative Judge. "Sounds like we have the makings of a good spook story," he smiled, forgetting his own fear for the moment, smoothly deflecting Hoagland's agitation. "Stranger things have happened during the war. Men shot dead, got to their feet and lived again. You heard as many stories as me, Hoagland."

This subtle manipulation was not lost upon the Judge. Smiling, he simultaneously admired and hated the man before him. He felt the evil but found himself wishing he felt so strongly as the Mayor, about something, about anything at all. Until the time that changes, thought the Judge, he can control me. Right now I just don't care. He shrugged in resignation and reached for the bottle. This time Big Bill Zachary did not stop him. Hoagland filled the glass only half full and quickly tossed it down. Only the next installment on slow death, he realized, but the spreading warmth felt so good.

"Them two Jaspers what shot up the Cruz Brothers is mighty curious," said Laszlo thoughtfully as he twisted at the ends of his tattered salt and pepper mustache. "Friends of the Brothers tracked 'em back toward Bodie and ended up in a brush with some Injuns coming back down the same trail they followed. These fellas got shot up considerable. Said they never ran into Redskins packing that much hardware before.

"Long story short," Laszlo concluded, "is that them Injuns slipped away in the dark, these fellas patched themselves up, what survived, and picked up the trail again in the morning. The Mexican and Tallon, if it were him, split up. One rider and two horses made it back to Bodie ahead of these friends of Miguelito's. They looked around town and found no trace of either the Mex or Tallon. But then Bodie's a big town. Bigger 'n here, anyway. A second rider on one big horse and towing another took out of the mountains and across the Great Basin," Laszlo summed up the facts as he knew them. "Figger that 'n out."

"Let's see if we can put this all together," Zachary scrubbed at his chins and leaned forward, steepling his fingers in front of his face, elbows on the table. "The fellas that shot the Cruz Brothers left the diggings above Connery and headed back toward Bodie." Leaning back in his chair, Zachary fished in his pocket for one of the brown-papered Cigarillos he seldom smoked. "Before they got to Bodie," he went on, finding a match in another pocket, "they split up and one of them headed over Tahoe way." Big Bill struck the match on the table and brought it deliberately to the end of the wrapped tobacco between his lips. "Maybe toward Colorado. That about it?" He inhaled deeply and sagged backward again into his chair, lost in thought.

"Sure 'nough," Laszlo said, "that's the way I see it Mr. Mayor."

"You say these friends of Miguelito's were in the camp when the Cruz Brothers were killed?" questioned the Mayor, leaning forward once again.

"Yep," nodded Laszlo, wondering just exactly what the Mayor wanted.

"Did they ever say how bad Tallon and the Mex were shot up?" Big Bill squinted his eyes quizzically. Something Johnny Lobo had said about when they healed, they'd head this way, made him increasingly uneasy.

"Yep, they did at that," affirmed the seedy looking Sheriff, fishing for a fresh matchstick in his own pocket. "The Mexican took a ball in the leg. He was back on his horse two days later."

"Why didn't these friends of the Brothers just take care of the pair before they left the camp?" asked the Mayor, stabbing his Cigarillo across the table at the corrupt lawman.

A general lapse in the conversation ensued as Laszlo sipped from his cup and the Mayor studiously brushed the ash from his Mexican cigarette and relit the ragged end.

The Judge watched both without drinking or even blinking. These two were real performers, he thought. This was the best show he'd seen all week.

"See Mr. Mayor," began Laszlo, talking into his cup as he sipped at the coffee, "the Cruz Brothers were both no account bullies." He paused to run a sleeve across his lips. "Nobody liked 'em." Laszlo groomed his mustaches again. "When this fella and the Mexican took 'em down, everyone was real happy."

The Sheriff shifted his gaze pointedly from his cup to the Mayor. "On top of everything, the fella with the bandanna bought everybody drinks. That did nothin' to turn sentiment against 'em either." Laszlo paused to watch a couple of miners walk through the door and sit at a table near the bar before starting again. "These fellas was in no mood to take on the whole town in order to avenge the Cruz Brothers. They preferred to take their chances on the trail."

"Sounds like a dead end," offered the Judge, now sipping cautiously at his whiskey. He no longer wanted to get drunk. The thrill was gone.

The Mayor ignored the Judge and studied the raggedly burning end of his Cigarillo for some moments before asking, "How far is Colorado on the other side of Tahoe?"

Visitor in the Night

J ake's eyes blinked suddenly open. Something sure wasn't right. Looking straight forward, he could see Sarah, snuggled up in her blankets next to him on the ground. Firelight danced among the low branches of the pine trees standing around the edge of the camp. The stars in their multitudes shone between the higher branches. At least three or four hours remained until dawn. The fire was down to coals when they had turned in and he knew that only fresh fuel would account for the current blaze. The little hairs on his neck and arms danced crazily in agitation.

"I can hear you thinking, White Man," a voice rumbled quietly behind him. "Must be someone by the fire, your thoughts say. You wonder, if I turn real fast, can I surprise this visitor?"

"Only one Indian I know can carry on a lop-sided conversation all by himself," Jake said casually, relaxing back into his blankets and quietly uncocking the pistol held before his body. Like Night Walker, Jake spoke no louder than the passage of wind through the grass so as not to wake Sarah.

Carefully, Jake peeled back his blankets and sat up straight, reaching for his boots. He saw the big Indian for the first time directly across a good sized fire. As Jake moved to pull on a boot, the Cherokee tossed Jake a tightly wrapped package through the reaching yellow flames, nearly striking Jake in the chest before he could raise his hands to catch it.

"Try those on first," the big Indian said.

Puzzled, Jake undid the knot on the soft, compact package bound by the tied corners of a large kerchief. As it came open he found a pair of knee-high, elk hide moccasins.

"Haven't worn any of these since I saw you last year," Jake said with genuine pleasure.

"Beware of Red Man bearing gifts," mumbled Night Walker cynically around a mouthful of food.

"Why?" Jake asked, pulling on the welcome footwear.

"Because I'm here for an important reason," the Cherokee said, "Sadly, not for a holiday with my friend in the Shining Mountains."

Jake's skin went goose-bumpy with apprehension. "Oh, oh," he said. "Are you going to tell me you dreamed of trouble?"

"You got that right, Pale Face," Night Walker chewed steadily, calmly, studiously examining a fresh piece of dried meat.

Jake relaxed just as suddenly as he'd tensed when he realized Night Walker likely dreamed of what had already transpired. "You're late by several weeks," he said with relief and disgust, "trouble has come and gone."

Unperturbed, Night Walker pronounced, "Not this trouble. You got a double handful of trouble headed this way, chasing you out of California." Reaching for the ground on either side, the big Cherokee steadied himself. "Oh, I'm not feeling well at all Jacob. I have traveled non-stop for a week. I need rest right now. I can talk no more."

That was about all the big Indian had energy to tell him. Jumping up, Jake rapidly circled the fire. Jake took the roll of skins with which the Cherokee struggled and laid them across an open area of needle-carpeted ground, half a dozen feet from the fire. Night Walker crawled between the furs and was immediately beyond consciousness.

This was not the first time Night Walker had performed such a feat on his behalf and for that reason Jake worried. Even a person of Walker's great physical endurance cannot be so drained physically. Everyone has his limit. Walker obviously thought the impending threat important enough to make such a big sacrifice on Jake's behalf.

It's not over, Jake realized, shivering as a cold draft moved across the back of his neck and down his shirt. Finding Sarah had moved trouble to second place in his mind. The whole week with her had been another honeymoon as they celebrated their reunion and a fresh chance at life together.

Events moved forward in ignorance of their bliss and caught up with him once again as surely as a skull-busting headache following all-night revelry. The difference now was that Sarah was vulnerable to the same dangers that confronted him.

Before long the sun cleared the Rockies behind them. The long shadow of the mountains always allowed a late sunrise near their base. Night Walker lay long in his skins. His message gave Jake much to consider. Certainly he was days getting here, thought Jake and required many hours of sleep to catch up.

Fixing fresh coffee, Jake waited patiently to greet Sarah as she stirred and stretched. The sight of that woman gladdens my heart, thought Jake. The worry of Walker's warning slipped to the background once again as he poured her a cup of Arbuckle's and carried it to her blankets.

"Where did you get the moccasins?" she asked, staring at his skin-clad feet.

"The little Fairies visited in the night," Jake teased her, sitting close and speaking softly to protect the sleep of his friend. Setting her coffee to one side, he slid into the blankets behind her and wrapped his arms around her, holding her close, savoring her warmth.

"I dreamed that you spoke with someone," she mused, sleepy-eyed, turning to cuddle against his chest. "But the voices were so soft, I could neither understand nor bring myself completely awake."

"Is that a question?" he whispered into her ear, building a slow fire under her curiosity.

Shaking herself awake and suddenly shedding Jake's embrace, Sarah craned her neck around her husband, eyes seeking the still form of the big Indian across the fire. "Not dead, is he?" she was fully alert now.

"No Honey, it's the Cherokee, our friend Night Walker. He showed up late last night with something on his mind and woke me with the light of a larger fire."

Jake slowly shook his head in wonder. "The man moves like a shadow whenever he wants, without sounding a footfall. Never heard his horse. Never heard him build the fire. Never heard a thing and I'm a light sleeper."

Jake wished Sarah to wake up fully before he told her the whole story. She pushed herself to a sitting position and rubbed her knuckles into her eyes, clearing them of sleep.

Over among the picketed horses, Sam tossed his head and whickered a double warning at them. Jake knew that tone of his horse as surely as if the animal had yelled in alarm.

Turning where he sat, Jake looked along the winding, indistinct trail running down the mountain west of them, into the mist-shrouded trees three or four hundred yards off. Making their unhurried way among the early shadows of scattered pines, rode a pair of nondescript horsemen.

They didn't appear to be the trouble of which Night Walker warned, out in the open and as unhurried as they came.

Jake looked on down the trail behind them for a long moment and saw nothing to excite additional concern. He wondered for only a moment why they had no packhorse, but then, neither did he and Sarah.

Sarah saw him looking and followed the direction of his stare. Trusting as she was and unburdened with Night Walker's warning, Sarah presumed an innocent visit. Given his own extensive experience, Jake remained somewhat more suspicious. Regarding the two strangers with narrowed eyes, he cursed his lack of caution in not better shielding his morning fire. Those two riders certainly knew they were here more than an hour ago.

"Excuse me, Jacob," Sarah said, "I think I'll go tidy up for company." Grabbing a brush and a canteen she scampered for the bushes. Jake sat patiently, watching the two travelers work their slow way up the hill, following the natural switchbacks of the climbing trail.

"Trouble's the visitor you never see 'til he sticks a gun in your face," Jake recalled the musing of his brother Travis. These Jaspers looked innocent enough.

The Killing Chore

"**H**o, the camp," came the cry from first of the two horsemen.

Jake stood and waved a borrowed hat in a wide, relaxed arch to signal his permission. "Come on in," he yelled, watching them take their hands from saddle horns and kick their horses into forward motion.

Somehow they reminded Jake of light cavalry in the way they rode their long-legged mounts. Chances are they partnered during the war and stayed together coming west. Good horses, Jake confirmed as they drew close.

The larger of the two smiled with a nod before dismounting and stood, reins in hand to make the howdy-do's.

"The name is Buster Stanley," he announced. "My friend here," he motioned toward his partner with a handful of leather, "is Slim Packard. When we turned out this morning, we saw your fire like a signal against the mountain and thought to share some fresh elk that stumbled across us yesterday."

"Betcha the elk was more surprised than you," Jake smiled at his own humor, without volunteering his own name. Night Walker slept on undisturbed by the intrusion. "My friend here has been travelin' and is all done in," he excused the Cherokee Shaman. "Step up to the fire, you're welcome to share what we have."

Buster looked across the camp at the five horses tied under the trees, doubtless doing mental arithmetic. Maybe he saw Sarah, maybe not. Willing to let his partner carry the conversation, Slim pulled meat from his bags, wrapped in the partial hide of the animal.

"Been a while since we tasted elk," Jake offered, ignoring Buster's puzzled expression.

"Not much different than beef," said Slim, speaking for the first time. "Makes me feel like I never left home."

"Where's home?" It seemed the right thing to say. Jake smiled in a friendly way.

"Louisiana, mostly," Slim answered, "after the war, every place else."

Trouble was, Jake heard none of the slow, wide Mississippi in the man's voice. There was more Kansas in the inflection than Southern, he decided. Why would the man lie?

Sarah came back into camp all smiles and ready for visiting. "This is my wife, Sarah," Jake introduced her.

She stepped forward with an energetically outstretched hand saying, "O'Connell, Sarah O'Connell." From wherever she was, she had listened. Sarah knew Jake had not yet offered names and for some reason she cautiously gave only her maiden name. "You met Randall, already," she gave Jake a brand new name. "He's sometimes not very forthcoming in his manner."

This woman is a marvel, Jake thought, looking at her fondly, a little faster upstairs than me, sometimes. Busy now about the fire she wasted no time emptying the old coffee and starting a new pot. While the meat roasted on green skewers hung over the flames, they passed around day old biscuits. Buster and Slim thanked Sarah like they were fresh. No one talked much while eating.

"Your friend is sure a sound sleeper," commented Buster as Sarah collected breakfast dishes.

"Walker likes his sleep at times," Jake said noncommittally. He decided he didn't like Buster's eyes; they were too close and didn't look at a person straight on, flicking here and there nervously. The man just seemed too nosy. He put Jake on edge.

Picking his teeth with a thin green twig, Buster asked casually, "You haven't seen someone pass you one way or the other wearing a blue kerchief tied over his head, have you?"

There it was!

Jake felt gut shot with shock at the question and prayed desperately that it hadn't shown outwardly. The inquiry spoke volumes on everything he most dreaded hearing. These two were after him all right. His true identity was saved by the hat he had only started wearing after meeting up with Sarah. The addition of her and Night Walker added fresh confusion to his identification but Jake's pause registered on Buster, who shifted his weight subtly. Slim appeared to pay no attention but Jake knew better.

Sarah also sensed trouble coming. Jake's guns were halfway across camp and much too distant to be of any use. His hands were equally lethal but a fire separated him from his new enemy.

Even as Jake thought it, Buster spun to his feet and whipped out a Confederate model Army, Colt forty-four. Jake stiffened in surprise. The brass trigger guard was a give away for that model, Jake reflected, and told him which set of principles Buster supported. The Confederates didn't have enough steel during the war and used brass whenever they found an opportunity for compromise.

He noticed the piece had seen a great deal of use. Both metals were flash scarred and corroded all around the chamber openings. Easy for me to tell, Jake thought, looking right into the business end of that pistol. He saw also the dull glint of five lead balls all snug in their beds. This fella was no pilgrim. Buster's friend Slim followed his lead, looking sideways to Buster for the next move.

Completely unprepared, Jake sat blinking, his legs stretched straight out in front of him. This was not the double handful of horsemen of whom Night Walker warned, yet might prove just as fatal.

"Maybe you can explain," Jake asked innocently. "Those six shooters make you look right unfriendly. Helluva way to repay the kindness of a free meal."

"You'll pardon the hardware, Mr. O'Connell," Buster said with exaggerated courtesy, "If I'm wrong, you certainly have my apologies. I need to find out if you're the man I'm seeking. Please lift your hat so I can have a look at your forehead."

Jake knew what they wanted to see. Given that they had the guns, he was in no position to refuse. The only question was how long he would live once Buster knew he was Jake Tallon.

"Ahh," said the two of them almost together as Jake lifted his hat. "You weren't so tough after all Mr. Tallon."

"Why don't you put down that iron and we'll revisit that issue, Buster," Jake suggested mischievously.

Jake never got an answer because Night Walker's sleeping skins exploded into the air and his big knife cut the air in front of the two ex-Confederates with a terrifying whistle, sinking nearly hilt-deep in the solid wood of the tree just beside Slim's suddenly ashen face. As they shifted their aim to cover his Indian friend, concussion from a close-by pistol discharge slapped the right side of Jake's face with physical force.

Dumbstruck, Buster looked downward at a small stain in the middle of his chest bone. "How'd that woman ... get a pistol?" he muttered, his gun-arm suddenly sodden with fatigue.

Starting from a tiny hole, the stain spread rapidly, then spurted crimson fluid into the fire between them with a hiss of billowing rose-tinted steam. The pupils of his eyes rolling into his eyelids, Buster toppled over backward without loosing the grip on his piece. Jake experienced a brief moment of unease as Buster's gun muzzle swept across his position.

Just that fast, Slim's status as captor changed to captured and he found himself looking into the smoking bore of Sarah's pretty little, five-shot pistol. She ratcheted back the hammer for another shot and stared, steely-eyed, over the barrel at him. Wisely, Slim decided to set his gun down before him, uncocked and unfired.

Jake couldn't hear right then because of the muzzle blast so close to his ear. He shook his head to clear it. Looking quickly around the fire, it took another second for him to understand that Sarah was speaking. She reached up and touched the right side of his face apologetically.

At the moment, other things were more important. Rising, Jake circled the fire and looked downward at Buster who was gone, already, on his last journey up the Starry Path.

Losing no time, Jake picked up his gun and Slim's as well.

Tired as he was and content to leave things in Jake's' hands, Night Walker rolled over, to sleep once again. Jake looked in time to see him pull the last skin over his face.

"Been partner's long?" Jake asked coldly, standing above the stunned and speechless Slim.

At first the man moved his lips soundlessly, fumbling for words. "Since First Bull Run," Slim said finally. "Most the time we rode with General Stuart 'til he got all full of hisself toward the end of the war. After that, we sorta 'tached ourselves to Longstreet's staff, like his private scouts."

Standing silent, Jake let Slim talk it out.

"Kinda takes a man's breath away," the gaunt partner ruminated. "Him leaving so fast as that. All that ridin' and all them battles and he lost a fight to a woman. Jus' seems so hard to believe."

Slim paused for some moments, his eyes distant. "No good-bye or nothing." He cast his gaze toward the departed Buster as though looking for the friend that no longer inhabited the body next to him on the ground.

Jake couldn't help feeling sorry for the man, but his friend Buster was in the process of taking away all their choices. "Find somewhere to plant him," Jake said more brusquely than he intended. "He's in a better place now, Slim. Man Above will likely show him more mercy than he's earned here on Earth. We'll have to decide what we're gonna do with you … next." Jake delivered the last word with just the right note of malice.

Sarah came up from behind with a short-handled shovel, rescued from the ruins of their ranch and thrust it toward Slim in a small white fist. Slim took it with thanks and Jake helped him roll Buster's body in a blanket and carry it over into a grove of tall, delicate aspens with a clear space at their feet that looked like it had more soil and less rocks.

Stained as it was by blood, the blanket was a lost proposition. Jake had never seen a man bleed that much all at once. The bullet striking him in the chest bone, piercing the heart and busting the spine on its way out exhibited more power than any handgun he'd seen, other than the Walker Colt, only the caliber was wrong. It was too small.

He remembered holding the piece, showing Sarah how to shoot and noticing the lack of side flash. More power straight down the barrel.

That gun was a marvel of modern machine tooling, certainly customized by one of those big Baltimore Gunsmiths for a wealthy client like her father.

Slim likely didn't notice how well Sarah's gun shot, thought Jake, eyeing the man as he cleared rocks from the grass, looking for a place to dig. He just lost his partner. Without a gun in his hand, Slim looked just like any other tattered traveler, not nearly so threatening as he'd been in the company of his deceased friend, Buster.

Sarah brought Jake another cup of coffee and sat with him in silence, watching Slim work. After a bit, Jake turned his attention to his wife. Setting the coffee aside, he took her hands in his and studied her troubled face with concern. "How ya doing, Babe?"

Sarah seemed to struggle with her feelings, returning from a distant place to the present. "I took away a man's life," she said desolately.

"So, how does that make you feel?" he questioned tentatively. She needed to talk and Jake wanted to give her that chance.

"Like a thief," she said. "He was so animated, even though his actions were evil. He was so alive, right up until the time I pulled that trigger."

Plain to Jake she felt pretty down about the shooting. "You blame yourself for his death?"

"Yes, Jake! I do." She buried her face into Jake's shoulder and wept without restraint. Jake stroked her hair softly, staring at Slim as he labored over his hole. "So what do you think would have happened to us, had he lived? What would his friends have done with us?" he asked. "If we even lived that long? You can't be blaming yourself over this, Honey, though I know just how very bad killing a man can make a person feel."

"His friends?" asked Sarah, puzzled. "What part of this don't I know yet?"

"That's what Night Walker came so fast and so hard to tell us." Jake looked over to see the Indian's knife, still firmly buried in the pine tree with a trickle of sap glistening in a downward dribble under the blade. Unlike him to leave his knife lying about, Jake thought humorously.

"It's also why I didn't take these two Jaspers seriously," he turned again, facing Sarah squarely. "According to the Cherokee, there are supposed to be a dozen or more in a group, headed our way. I wasn't looking for only two."

"More trouble is what you're thinking?" Sarah stated bleakly, distracted by the whole idea.

"Night Walker sure believes that. These people would have got us without his warning and his being here. I'm sure he's right about it. I'm so sure, because he's never been wrong. Never!"

Recovering somewhat from her funk, she smiled a tiny smile up into Jake's face and wiped away at her tears with her knuckles. "You're sounding more Indian all the time, Jacob."

Jake brushed a hand under his nose to hide the smile she brought him. "Did you reload that gun?"

"Sure did," she said smiling brightly. "I wouldn't let you hold that one over my head again." Her nose had started to drip in the last stages of her grief, so he handed her a clean kerchief from his pocket.

Jake knew the killing of Buster had put its mark on her soul, like any decent person, but at least she was smiling. Seeing the light in her face once again, he pulled her close. Sarah took comfort in Jake's arms and apparently felt no immediate inclination to move. As the sun swept slowly across the sky, however, Jake got uneasy with the passage of time.

"Hurry it up," he yelled at Slim over Sarah's shoulder, "or we'll just leave the grave open." The man redoubled his efforts.

Sarah had pulled away after Jake's outburst, but was looking greatly recovered. He stroked her hair by way of apology and asked, "Why don't you see how much of that elk is left. Let's cook it up and be ready to move. We can't stay here any longer! We might not get much warning when his friends arrive."

Jake strapped on his pistols and walked over to Slim as he sweated to fill in Buster's hole. He'd done a good job for his friend but Jake had a nagging suspicion he stalled for time. "You can finish later," Jake said, "if there is a later. Leave the shovel in the hole and come with me."

Taking a canteen from his horse as they passed, Slim drank deeply and then used more of the water to rinse off his face and hands. Jake finished the contents of the canteen himself, then tossed it aside and took the rope from his saddle. "Climb up into that birch tree, Slim." Jake indicated a cluster of four or five white trunks, sprouting from common roots, each of them maybe a foot in diameter, with ample space between them for a person to stand. The lowest branches were easily a dozen feet off the ground.

When Packard cast him a questioning look, Jake gave him an impatient shove and climbed in after him. "Put your hands together behind the bole," he commanded.

"What ya doing?" Slim protested, fear causing his eyes to dance.

After looping his wrists securely, Jake used the balance of the rope to bind Slim's legs and body firmly against the tree.

"If you have to stay here a couple of days," Jake told him, "you can sleep without the worry of a fall."

"A couple of days?" Slim gasped.

"Sure, that long anyway. How far are your friends behind you?" Jake asked innocently.

"A day maybe," the words tumbled out of Slim's mouth before he stopped himself. His eyes went sly.

"Well, now," Jake drawled, "that's most of what I wish to know. How many are there?"

Slim set his jaw, determined not to answer. In a wink Jake palmed a forty-four and shot the tree trunk near the inside of the silent man's thigh and barked his crotch. Sarah let out a little shriek of surprise. Jake eared back the hammer for another shot. The effect on Slim was like magic.

"What ya want to know Tallon? You been right with me all along. I'll tell ya anything I can." The man couldn't be more helpful.

"Aren't you worried about waking Night Walker?" asked Sarah, looking to his pile of skins, which now lay empty.

"He's out scouting, I imagine." Jake turned his attention to Slim again. "How many?" he gestured with the gun.

"Maybe a dozen more," Slim said, feeling shamed. "The Mackinaw Brothers is riding to the head of that column. They got some kind of grudge on you."

"I didn't know about the Mackinaw Brothers," Jake said. "I knew about Bingo Mackinaw but he deserved to die. The man was cruel and careless."

"I know what ya mean," said Slim, eyes dancing to the ground and back. "But I'm not sure that makes so much difference to them. They're his kin. They're gonna kill you iffen they can."

"What they going to think," Jake asked, "when they find you tied in a tree?"

"Not so much over me," said Slim, "until they find you've also killed Buster. He had many friends among them hooligans. They'll be as angry as a nest of kicked mud wasps."

"Why these fellas come after me, Slim? Why are you after me?" Jake asked. "I don't know them or you."

"Money is all," Slim answered regretfully. "Money and the Mackinaws. They hired everyone on, but I don't imagine they came up with all that cash they-selves. They had them a bunch of gold money. A bunch!"

Sarah walked up and handed Jake a plate of steaming meat. Taking a chunk in her fingers she stepped nimbly into the tree and finger fed it to the tied-up man.

"Thank you, Ma'am," he said humbly, chewing wetly. "I don't have a right to expect much after offending your hospitality the way we did." Slim swallowed part of the mouthful and tucked the rest into a cheek while he talked. "I'm sorry you had to be the one killed Buster, Ma'am. We sure had it coming." He fell silent while he finished chewing the meat.

"A woman shouldn't have to handle no gun." His eyes twinkled suddenly, "But you did it right proper, ma'am. Buster always did enjoy a job well done. He was a colonel of cavalry and mostly a good man."

Turning abruptly away, Sarah wiped at her eyes, uttering a muffled sob.

That explained a lot, thought Jake. As he turned to face Sarah, he saw her take a deep breath and square her shoulders. She moved up closer into the tree to talk more with the man named Slim.

Jake didn't stay to hear what was said between them. He walked down the path a bit thinking about what to do with the crowd coming up the trail. There were too many. He couldn't risk Sarah in a standing fight. Hell, he'd had enough of stand-up fights to last a lifetime.

Money by itself wasn't enough of a reason, he knew, for those men to risk their lives in a real live-or-die confrontation. Their numbers make them too bold, by far. There had to be a way to separate the hangers-on from the angry and deal with them a few at a time. Maybe talk some sense into those that were less resolved and destroy the Brothers only if there was no other way.

How? That was the hard part.

They Went
Thata Way

"**Y**ou wanna come down from that tree and eat with us or you gettin' 'tatched to your perch, up there?" Jake stood below the bound man with his hands on his hips.

"Be obliged, Tallon," Slim's eager smile betrayed his abject gratitude as Jake worked at the knots binding the man's wrists.

"We'll let you sleep on the ground after you bury Buster, Slim, but tomorrow you go back into the tree."

"Fair enough Mr. Tallon. I won't trouble ya none. It's been a long hungry day."

Sarah served the two men through the silent meal, her eyes flicking constantly to the prisoner with a mixture of regret and distrust.

Night Walker showed up before they turned in and confirmed Jake's best guess. Slim and Buster had been the vanguard of a dozen more men following their lead up into the Shining Mountains and eventually to the Tallon homestead near Cumberland Crossings.

"This is the danger of which I came to warn," Night Walker pronounced with certainty, standing humbly before Jake and Sarah.

"I always believed you, Walker." Jake's knuckles whitened in anger around a stick of firewood. Unable to bear such stress, the stick exploded in a cloud of dry splinters above their cheery fire, each separate splinter bursting into its own sparkling flare of light and energy.

"Wow! Lookit the fireworks," smiled Sarah, pointing like a little girl and destroying the seriousness of the moment.

The two men grinned involuntarily at her comment. "Yeah," admitted Jake, "I guess this situation makes me more than a little mad. Gettin' burned out wasn't enough. Those boys came a long way huntin' trouble and now I feel obliged to give them some."

"They'll get their share," the Cherokee echoed.

Come morning, after they all had coffee, Slim was returned, grumbling, to the tree. Walker built the fire up nice and big so the gang down below could see it as they came along. "No sense in them getting lost," he looked meaningfully to Slim, "Unless you wish to spend more time where you are."

"No thank you, Cherokee."

Come full light, the big Cherokee took a bunch of horses and headed north along the mountains, while Sarah and Jake headed south with a couple of others. At the end of each trail was a box canyon of one kind or another. Off the entrance to the southern canyon, Jake built a hunting blind from piled rocks and brush arranged in a head-high barrier. He and Sarah waited patiently for Walker to appear, their horses hidden in a cul-de-sac of weathered beige stone behind them.

An hour passed, and then two. Preceded by a racketing of hooves on naked rock, the big Indian arrived, his face dressed in obvious delight.

"Slim sure did his job well," Night Walker reported, sliding from the back of his Sorrel. "They're all fired up. Some are coming this way and some are following my false trail in the other direction, just like you figured. Given Buster's death, I'm thinking that anything they do will be more angry than smart."

Hiding the Sorrel with the other horses, they sat down to wait. Sarah brooded quietly off to the side. Jake stuck a piece of grass in his mouth and let his eyes wander across the approaches to their position. He knew Sarah continued to deal with Buster's killing but sensed she needed room to work it out herself. He understood there was no more he might say without repeating himself or appearing to impose an easy and thoughtless solution upon her before her time.

The sun inched across the azure sky. By mutual agreement no one spoke. In some remote part of his mind Jake wondered how his Cherokee friend had so outdistanced his pursuers that the three of them were required to wait so long for their arrival. Why was that?

One more Cherokee mystery!

Soon on the tail of that thought came the thunder of many hooves. Leaves and branches jumped and rattled around them with growing intensity as the group of horsemen approached. The ground shook like a taut drumhead.

Rising carefully, Jake peered through the leafy top of their cover to see five intent men bent over the necks of sweating horses, riding pell-mell, unknowingly into the box canyon. When they reached the blind end, they were sure to be upset and he wanted to be there when that happened.

Sarah, Jake and the Shaman mounted and charged after the would-be killers, into the narrow entrance to the canyon. Though he had no plan to speak of, it couldn't have turned out better. With Sam under him, and Sarah on Buck, all three of them rode horses considerably heavier than the mustangs and Indian ponies they followed into the canyon.

The opposition understood their predicament more quickly than Jake imagined and had already turned around. Riding knee to knee, Sarah, Jake and the Cherokee met them coming out through their own dust in a tremendous, head-on crash of horses and riders. Slim Packard's friends didn't stand a chance against the bigger mounts.

The lead horse was knocked from his feet and run over, the rider barely dancing from harm's way. Jake hated to see a good horse lost simply because of his unprincipled rider but there was nothing to be done for it. No choice at all.

The next two horses bounced backward, pawing air and dumping their riders in the terror of their pain and confusion. Amid the screaming horses and swirling dust, Jake saw three men standing, stumbling, arms outstretched, frantically looking for any protection from the deadly dancing hooves, and three more men still mounted, but barely.

One went for his gun. Jake holed him through the chest. The others simply put their hands in the air while the horses continued to mill and stomp, raising clouds of choking dust. "Get off those horses," Jake yelled to the remaining riders.

It was over that quick!

Sam danced and snorted as Jake worked to calm the big horse. Confident that Sarah was safely behind him, Jake slid from the saddle. Gun drawn, he walked to where the two remaining men helped their partners. One looked simply stunned. Jake saw that another had a broken arm, the bloody end of jagged bone poking through the shirtsleeve.

The man Jake shot had been hit in the neck and the slug exited below the rib cage. His eyes went fixed even as Jake watched.

"You played hell, you did," a hatless man accused Jake, bitterly scrubbing at the dust and sweat covering his face with a wadded kerchief.

"You want my condolences?" growled Jake into his face, bending close. "Seems to me, you sorry sons came here after my hide. You only got what you deserved and you know it. You tell me if you see it any different than that. And just speak up if you want more of the same."

A second man, snarling suddenly, went for his gun and Jake back-handed him smartly across the face with the barrel of his Remington. The unlucky antagonist, an uncommonly big man, collapsed into a disorganized heap, writhed for a moment, then went completely limp.

"Who was that?" Jake asked jumping from Sam's back, "Who wanted me so bad he'd make a try against a drawn gun?"

"That were Charles Mackinaw," said the other, meekly handing Jake his own gun, handle first, to ensure no misunderstanding with such a volatile antagonist.

Jake turned abruptly in a deadly sweeping blow that captured his full strength, and broke the bones of the big man's right hand with the butt end of his buddy's just-surrendered gun. "You tell Mackinaw when he comes to, that if I see him again, I'll kill him as soon as look at him. The broken hand will be his reminder."

Jake allowed his rage to dissipate as he collected all the guns he could find and loaded them upon the horse of the dead man. Two of their other horses were lamed as well as two of the men. Looking intently at each man in turn, Jake said, "Don't let me see you again. Ever!"

With particular emphasis Jake told the last standing man. "Any of you. If I see him," he pointed at Charles, "and you're with him, I'll kill you first. You understand that?"

The man stood before Jake, nodding mutely, bone white, shocked by the violence of an irate Jake Tallon. He understood. "We plainly didn't know what we was gettin' into, Mr. Tallon," the would-be-badman whimpered.

Jake knew it would be tomorrow before they came out of that canyon and months before they got their confidence back. The longer it took, the better for them all.

As they walked from the canyon, leading their restive mounts, Sarah found her voice again. "What do you call that, Jacob?"

"I hammered 'em! I hammered 'em good," Jake responded, "because I wanted to make sure they understood exactly what they were up against. It was that or kill 'em. I didn't want to do that, yet I can't afford to leave any doubt in the matter or they'll pick up and come after me again. I've made that mistake one too many times."

Soberly accepting Jake's assessment, Sarah nodded, then observed, "That's only half of them, Jacob. What about the others?"

"We're gonna pester the others," he told her optimistically, "until they get tired and go home."

"Is that what you did to these men? Pester them?"

"Didn't get much of a chance to think it through before it happened. Next time, I'll do better. I take my pesterin' seriously." Jake couldn't help but smile at her sarcasm, yet he knew the source of her bad feeling. He knew it wasn't him Sarah was upset with, so he didn't take it personally. Sarah was still consumed by the guilt of her own violence and she had to learn to deal with it. Every life has its share of trouble, he knew.

Night Walker handed him Sam's reins and they mounted again in unison. Riding back toward the original camp, the big Cherokee chose a track leading higher up the mountain. Before long they had a good view of the little clearing below and watched Slim, now free from the birch, moving about at one task or another.

Just before sundown the rest of the posse showed up with Jake's extra horses in tow. Obviously frustrated, they had no choice but to wait where they were for the return of the other group. They had no way of knowing just how long they were to wait.

As the sun edged below more mountains further west, Sarah retreated again to her brooding, hugging her knees to her chest and staring blankly into the distance, nodding with the throb of some inner rhythm. A fire sprang up among the group below. Jake watched, chewing on cold elk meat, mostly not talking. Sarah glanced at him when she thought he would not notice but he always did.

The woman was a magnet to Jake that he was powerless to ignore at any time, much less during her suffering. Sarah certainly understood the seriousness of the task before them. If they didn't stop these men now, they would be hounded into the ground. It wasn't like her Jake to run and Sarah knew it.

The violence of the last encounter gave her something else to think about and helped put Buster's killing into clear perspective. There was no ambivalence about those men below, she knew. They had come to kill. They would kill Jake if they could and everyone with him, her included. And Julius. They would kill Julius also. As she realized that her child was at risk, the rest of her priorities clicked neatly into place. She would be okay.

With full dark, Jake, Sarah and the Cherokee mounted up again and picked their way carefully down the trail they'd used earlier. Night Walker led the way for he had eyes that pierced the dark. Even with the Cherokee in the lead, it required a good two hours to travel the mile and a half required by the roundabout path down the mountain. Still three hundred yards shy of the outlaw camp, the three companions pulled up and tied the horses.

Weighed down with her own apprehension, Sarah could offer little verbal support. "Where are you, Sarah?" Jake found her by her subtly shifting shadow against the darkness of the trees and her delicate scent. The woman always smelled like flowers. "You have your gun, Sarah?" he asked. Jake saw her head bob up and down in the darkness. "Take this also," he handed her up a Henry rifle. Only when she took it, did he know for sure the shadow was his wife.

"I'm scared, Jacob. I don't know what we're going to do."

"We don't either, Sweetheart," Jake chuckled grimly, "but you won't have to do anything this time. It was only my lack of foresight that put you in the middle of that last shindig. I'm sorry for that, more than you know!"

"I know you are, Jacob," Sarah reached to touch his arm as they rode.

"We'll have to improvise," said Jake, "but we've done this before, Night Walker and me. We know where they are and they aren't sure where we are or what we're up to. They don't know what happened to the other bunch yet. The advantage is ours at this moment."

In his heart, Jake was not nearly so confident as he wished her to believe. "Just remember to stay here and stay off the trail. If our raid works out right, their horses will all be headed back for California, right over this ground, where you're standing." That part sounded good even in Jake's ears.

"Okay, Jacob. Be careful, will you? Take care of him, Night Walker," Sarah pleaded in a hushed voice, "He's all I have. He's my best part."

Hearing his wife speak such a sentiment gave Jake pause. Hesitating in mid-motion he allowed himself time to digest her sweet words.

"Hmmm," he said, almost like a cat purring. Though deeply affected, he was distracted by the danger they faced and could find no words of his own with which to respond.

With Sarah and the horses in the shadows behind them, Jake and the Cherokee crept cautiously along either side of a section of open starlit trail. Putting his failure to respond out of his mind, Jake marshaled every sense, focusing on the dangerous work before them. Gradually the trees closed in and shut off even the meager starlight. They moved so slowly now, staying close together, that Jake and the Cherokee touched occasionally.

Horses of the outfit could be heard, shuffling at picket, long before Jake smelled the wood smoke in the night air. The wind must have been wrong for the outlaw horses not to hear or scent them.

"They just figured us to run," Jake whispered. The horse guard was already asleep, the sounds of his gentle snores echoed back at them from surrounding trees and shrubs.

Moving slowly, they found him by the smell of the cooking fire on his clothes. Slipping silently to the guard's side, Jake slammed his right hand over the man's mouth and shoved his pistol up under his ribs for shock value. Moving swiftly beside Jake, Night Walker relieved the stunned guard of his pistol and rifle.

As it turned out, the enterprising Buckaroo was neither shocked nor intimidated. He found a big bladed knife with his free hand and might have skewered Jake had not Night Walker blocked the thrust with a vicious downward stroke of the rifle butt. Jake slammed the guard alongside the head with his pistol barrel before he could make a second effort.

"All this training in Chinese combat," Jake protested to his Indian friend in a tense whisper, "and I'm reduced to pistol whipping these Yahoos. Anyone can do that!" He was badly shaken by the near fatal lapse. Too much riding and not enough practice, he thought. "Thanks Walker!"

"What's happening, Luke?" a voice of authority asked from only a few feet away in the dark.

Instantly, Night Walker lashed out with the borrowed rifle, clubbing and slashing at the spot from which the voice issued. The impact of wood on bone and flesh resounded clearly back from the trees. A single futile protest and the intruder lay quiet, crumpled in deepest shadow at their feet.

This wasn't nearly so soundless as Jake had planned during their approach and got only noisier as more sounds and excited voices issued from the camp not fifty yards away. The enemy fire flung shadows in every direction as suddenly excited men rose from their bed rolls dashing here and there. "Damn it," Jake said, "We've done it now!"

Together, they disarmed the fellow Night Walker had clubbed and turned to the nervous horses. "Hurry," Jake hissed, "Cut them loose!" He slashed desperately at his end of the picket rope as horses reared and bolted.

A shot rang out. "Don't shoot the horses!" came a furious cry.

Incredibly, the man that Night Walker had clubbed got up and lunged growling in Jake's direction. Jake shot him once, twice, point-blank, gun flashes illuminating bared teeth and a fierce visage. Anyone that tough can't be stopped with half measures, Jake thought. After a bare moment of reflection, he shot him a third time, just for insurance.

More running men could be heard. A passing horse slammed Jake headfirst into the brush. A figure passed him on the trail dashing pell-mell behind the galloping horses. Jake heard the steps and saw the fleet shadow eclipse the stars from where he lay momentarily stunned under the branches and leaves.

Pulling himself painfully erect next to the cover of a large pine, Jake emptied both captured pistols in the direction of the camp - all with his eyes closed to protect his precious night vision. Firing the last shot, he spun to the far side of the thick pine for cover against return fire that never came. More shouting and a single curse rewarded his single-handed barrage. Maybe one of those slugs found a home, he hoped.

When he opened his eyes, Jake could still see. Quickly changing position, he ran doubled over for a low profile. The stygian darkness made vision beneath the trees difficult and anything close to the ground harder still. His last wish was to present one of those Yahoos with an easy target against the sky.

He was one against many. Who knew where the Cherokee was? Probably with the horses, he answered his own question as quickly as he posed it. The occasional shout to his rear and the sounds of men crashing through the brush on either side underscored his loneliness, making him feel exceedingly vulnerable.

The empty pistols he still held tightly in his hands.

Maybe it was just because he was low that he saw a darker shadow in the gloom under the trees, just ahead. Somehow Jake knew by his size and the way he stood, it wasn't Walker. Must be the man who ran up the trail after the horses.

Still running, Jake reversed grips on the borrowed pistols and hurled them end-over-end into the chest of the threatening shadow. A Remington pistol weighs almost three pounds and striking butt first or barrel first does a lot of damage on impact.

As they struck, the Bushwhacker's own guns discharged harmlessly into the air as he pitched over backwards. Had Jake waited only another moment, that man could have fired directly into him as he passed.

"Thank you, Shantee," Jake mumbled, "for giving me eyes to see in the dark." Somehow he had felt the helping hand of the gentle old man. Jake knew, more than heard, his acknowledgment.

Yes.

He's always there, wishing me the best in all my concerns, thought Jake, and I don't always recognize his effort. Even pursued as he was, Jake felt a measure of peace thinking of Man Above.

Standing astride the fallen Bushwhacker, he found himself searching the ground around the body for more weapons. The man's breathing sputtered as he regained consciousness. Holding two of the found guns in one hand, Jake brought the third one down sharply on the collarbone. He felt it separate with a brittle snap under the impact.

The man cried out in pain and drew his knees up into his chest to better protect himself.

"Little late for that now, don't you think?" Jake's question was rewarded by a long drawn-out groan. Now Jake knew for sure there was one less to challenge him when it came to a final reckoning. Well, two less, counting the man he had just shot three times. That man was no longer a threat if he yet lived.

Before running after Night Walker, Jake looked down at the man on the ground and kicked him hard in the ribs to get his attention. "I know that hurts but it's less than you would've done to me, given the chance." Bitterness filled Jake's words. "If I see you come morning, I won't be near' so thoughtful."

Jake kicked him again for good measure. Kindness he reserved for those who understood enough to pass it on or give it back. Not so here. These folks deserved any bad thing that befell them for what they were wishing and planning.

Except for Night Walker and the rear ends of many horses, the trail lay empty before him. Jake ran easily in that direction, quickly covering a mile or more, passing the spot where he had left his wife an hour before. As he came even with the point where the trail bent to ascend their mountain, Jake found Sarah, Night Walker, and many of the excited outlaw horses strung together against their will, snorting and stamping restively.

"Jacob," Sarah shouted with concern and happy excitement, "over here!"

"Let me cool down from my run," he sputtered, "I'm all out of breath."

Jake walked up the trail and back with his hands on his hips. If we keep the horses with us, he thought, we keep control. A good idea. "You do good work," he complimented Walker. "This is more organized than the time we spooked Longer's mounts at the pass out of Santa Fe."

"These are fewer," the Cherokee observed, "and easier for one, or two people to control." He looked meaningfully in Sarah's direction.

Jake paused, stunned. "Ah," he said, "My sweetheart, the wild horse wrangler, gave you a hand, did she?"

"Don't make trouble for me, my friend," said Sarah, pointing a fist full of coiled rope at Jake. Her pale face was stern in the moonlight. "I worked horses at our family ranch back east when no one else had the time!" Her mount danced under her with a combination of their mutual pent-up energy.

"What about the baby?" Jake asked stupidly without considering how much trouble that question might create for him.

"He did his share," she snapped back. "What do you know about women and babies? I'll do what I must to protect my man and my children. That's what I do. It's not always for you to say, Jake, though you are my husband. I shot Buster, when I saw it had to be done, and now I did this!" Sarah fairly spit the last words at Jake.

"Scuse me for meddlin'," Jake kicked at the silvery, starlit dust beneath his feet, so embarrassed. Everything that escaped his lips sounded so lame. He loved her so much. This was no sitting room posy. This was a real woman, his woman. "I was just out beatin' up bad men in the dark. Pregnant women riding string are new to me. 'Honey knows best' is my new policy." Now lit by a rising moon, slanting beams of light lanced through the trees around them. Jake shook his head in mock wonder.

Sarah collapsed in a fit of nervous laughter over the saddle horn. "Oh, Jake," she said, "you're so full of bull and I love you for it." She took several breaths, finally calming herself and sliding out of leather to land beside him for a sweaty, full body hug.

"We're in this together, Cowboy," she whispered, "for better or worse, is what the Preacher Man says, so don't you be counting me out of any ruckus." Reaching out to Jake, placing a hand on each of his arms, she gave him a prim little kiss on the mouth and looked upward into his face for one long meaningful moment.

"You take my breath away, woman," Jake told her, his head spinning. "I think we're paired up right proper. No man I know can stand up to you, including me. That says a lot!"

Looking up at his Indian friend, Jake said, "That lets you off the hook, amigo."

"She scared me," Walker said loud enough for Sarah to hear. "She looked so determined and ornery, I wasn't about to tell her no."

Walking down the line of broncs, Jake counted eleven head, which was about what all of them put together should total. Still he had no real plan, but the three of them had control as long as they kept these horses.

"Seems to me, those Owlhoots should be ready to talk this over in the morning," Jake said. "They aren't going anywhere unless they walk. Several won't be in any condition to walk anywhere."

"Let's find a place to hole up," suggested Night Walker, "I'm still missing some serious sleep."

Sam came to Jake out of the dark and put a nose under his hand. "If you could only talk, Sam, the four of us would have a right festive chat." He grabbed a handful of mane and jumped, without touching a stirrup, into the high saddle. Sam rose upon his hind legs and pawed air with a sense of joy both he and Jake felt whenever they joined together in adventure. "Wahoo," Jake exclaimed, barely seated on the plunging horse.

Pulling the extra mounts behind them at a gallop, the three friends retraced their steps up the switchbacks to the overlook they'd used before sundown. They repicketed the stock except for Sam and threw out the bedrolls for an evening of overdue rest.

Sleep came slowly to Jake Tallon, listening to Sarah's regular breathing beside him. He thought of the boy, Julius, he'd met in the Spirit Lodge. Who will you become, he wondered, when you have me for a father and such a lovely, strong-minded mother like you do?

You bought into quite an adventure, son. Can't wait to see you again, Jake thought, remembering the clear blue eyes and blond hair. Finally, he slept.

When Jake awoke, Sarah's blankets were already rolled and tied to her saddle where it lay on the ground. Looking through the trees toward the prominence, he saw her crouched among the rocks, gazing intently on the party of men below with a Henry rifle across her lap.

Firewood lay all around the campsite. Jake pulled his feet under himself and reached out from his blankets to collect the larger pieces. A small pile lay near his feet, where he had kicked them to make a smooth place to sleep the night before. After pouring a small measure of powder from an extra pistol flask into the pile, he tossed in a match.

Whoosh! Instant flame rewarded his efforts without the inconvenience of kindling.

"Why not just yell at them?" Sarah hissed urgently from the rocks where she crouched. "Look at that cloud of smoke."

True! Looking over his shoulder Jake watched a tidy little mushroom cloud created by the powder explosion boil twenty feet into the air above his fire.

"They'll know soon enough anyway, Sweetheart," Jake didn't even look back to Sarah. "Were I them, I'd figure I was being watched right off. Only makes sense."

Their camp had no running water, nor did it have any pooled water. The horses would have moved to it by now, had there been any. All the water they carried with them combined to barely fill the coffee pot. After performing that chore, Jake sat it next to the fire to heat.

Only then did he relax, taking a moment to sink onto the rocky ground beside the small blaze, drinking in a full measure of its unrepentant cheerfulness. "Ain't life grand," he announced to no one in particular.

Sarah regarded her husband with a quizzical smile and returned to her watching.

Strapping the heavy guns around his waist, Jake walked out to keep her company. She heard his steps and turned to watch him cross the last fifty feet. Speaking in a whisper, Sarah gestured toward the camp with her chin, "They found the last man only after sunrise," and then turned to look at Jake intently. "There are so many injured among them," she said, "What did you do last night?"

"Pistol whipped one of 'em," Jake said, "Shot another one pretty good, couple o' times, maybe a third one got hit. Mostly I just tried to get the horses and get out with my skin."

"Whatever happened," Sarah said, "they had it coming. What were they thinking, coming all this way with only fourteen men? That was sure stupid!"

"Their problem, Honey," Jake responded, "is that they thought to find me alone. If they figured a Mama Bear like you into the mix, they would 'a brought twice that many."

Forgetting her previous efforts at silence, Sarah laughed with hearty abandon. It seemed to Jake as though she was over the worst part of what happened with Buster the other day. When he knew she wasn't looking, he regarded her fondly. "Quite a package," he mumbled.

They sat companionably, soaking up each other's good company with the early sun. From out of the blue, Sarah asked, "Is this our honeymoon, Jacob?"

What do women think about, Jake wondered briefly. Here we are, scrapping for our lives and she's thinking about honeymoons. Knowing the perils of too much silence behind a question, he responded, "If you're having a good time, it is."

"As long as we're winning, it's good," Sarah said thoughtfully. "But mostly, I'm scared, Jacob. I don't know what's going to happen next."

He put one hand over hers as she held the rifle. "You haven't met Travis yet," he reminded her. "Travis spoke to me a great deal about military philosophy he'd learned from his Chinese teacher, who claimed that his people had more than three thousand years of written history."

Jake sorted through his memory. "I don't remember all the names of the men he quoted. Much of it is just common sense if you think about how people behave. Most are cautious, if only because they wish to protect their own skin. Too much caution cripples their ability to be effective. So I figure a little initiative keeps most folks off balance. I don't wait for something to happen. I make it happen.

"They'll do the reacting and it's them that has to wonder what will happen next. Last night was a serious loss for them all around. They lost their horses and half their effective number."

In his earnestness to make her understand, Jake squeezed her hand too hard and she squeaked, "Ow, Honey!"

"I'm sorry Sweetheart," Jake apologized as they both looked to his offending hand.

"I like how you think, Jake. I feel better knowing that you act from some kind of knowledge. What are you going to make happen now?" She put her free hand over his.

Looking again at the piled hands, he knew she asked only for reassurance. He wanted to tell her about the Spirit Lodge and dying wasn't so bad but he knew she didn't want to hear that now. She carried life within her, and focused only on bringing it whole and happy into the world. Everything was about living for Sarah, not dying.

For his own benefit as well as hers, Jake summarized, "With your surprise help, we took care of Slim and Buster. That situation held the most danger for us because we had no control at all."

A pair of crows floated between the trees higher on the side of the mountain. "We didn't know they were part of the people that Night Walker came all that way to warn me about."

Past events replayed themselves in Jake's mind. Possible future outcomes rapidly rearranged themselves in fresh combinations, seeking the best solutions.

"We split their main force and took five of them out of the action altogether, including one of the Mackinaws, a main player." Jake experienced a twinge of misgiving, thinking about the crippled but still living

Mackinaw. "He was a really big man I might not have taken on had I time to think on it. Maybe I got another of the Mackinaw Brothers last night. I'm pretty certain that three of the seven in this last group were badly hurt."

"Wow, all that, huh!" she gave him an admiringly, wide-eyed look.

"I'm happy you're proud of me," Jake smiled with irony, "but in spite of what people say about me, I don't enjoy hurting even those that have it coming. It's just the better alternative than you or me getting hurt.

"After a while, I'm gonna go down and see how determined they are to nail my hide to the wall. If the other brothers are anything like Bingo, they got sand. They're tough! We may have more trouble before this is over. Unless we go stomp 'em some more, I expect they'll just think we got lucky, get up and come after us again. They are all very tough men."

Sarah liked an honest assessment, Jake knew. She wanted to know what he had in mind and would become a valuable part of his plans if he included her.

Sitting two inches taller on her rock, doubt drained from Sarah's eyes and she laughed a little nervously as she found herself leaning forward more aggressively. "You make it sound too simple, Jake. I know there's more to it than that."

"I'll watch them for a while, Honey," Jake smiled back at her, "if you want to unpack a little food for us."

Jake took the Henry from her and assumed her position, watching as men moved around in the camp below. Slim tended the fire. If he didn't pick up a gun again, Jake had no quarrel with him.

Even at this distance, he saw two men in arm slings, one with his shirt off and a fourth man binding his chest. Still another had his head swathed in bandages while a sixth man lay unmoving to the side, with his face covered by a blanket.

Instinctively Jake knew the man wasn't sleeping. That must be the one Night Walker clubbed and I shot, he thought. If that had to happen, I hope it was one of the Brothers.

Deep in thought as he was, Sarah surprised him, walking up with steaming coffee and a chunk of elk meat. "Biscuits are on," she smiled reassuringly. "What's happening down there?"

"Not much, but it does seem like we did well last night. I'm counting four down or injured already. That's about half of them."

"Only three left?" she asked hopefully.

"Three and Slim," Jake confirmed. "I hope he stays out of it but there's no telling until he has the chance to declare himself one way or the other. A person always takes a chance when he leaves an enemy standing." Again Jake thought of the Mackinaw with the busted hand.

Reaching out to take the cup from his hand after he'd sipped, she shared his coffee. Back in their own camp, Night Walker threw aside his sleeping skins. Another minute or two, and the yawning Indian stood beside them looking down into the camp below. Certainly he saw everything Jake did. His sharp eyes missed nothing.

"When we going down?" he asked, reaching the same conclusions Jake had.

"Anytime now," Jake said. "We wait too long, they get their confidence back."

"I agree with you, Jake. Back on the left quarter of the clearing," he pointed, "there's cover halfway up the hill. You give me a head start and I can back up almost anything you do."

No better or smarter friend had any man, yet on this trip, they had shared so little. Walker showed up out of the night and picked up his share of danger like he was here all along.

Jake had seen no smile from this normally happy man since their reunion only yesterday. They were fighting Owlhoots almost constantly with no time to smile, yet Jake longed for the lighter side of his friend. He longed for the companionable banter they both enjoyed so much.

"Are you having fun yet, Night Walker?"

"This is not fun, Jacob," the Cherokee glared accusingly. "I do it because I enjoy your company and I want you around tomorrow and the day after."

"You picked yourself a mean task, Partner." Jake was getting stiff sitting on the hard rocks so he stood to stretch out his back muscles and get some circulation back into his limbs. Even as he rose, a puff of smoke blossomed at the edge of the clearing below. The bullet twanged off the rock parapet in front of him, knocking his hat backward on its chinstrap and sending him sprawling on his rear, the misshapen slug having cut a small but decisive path neatly through his hair!

Standing again instantly, Jake emptied the magazine of the Henry, arching shots into the camp below as fast as he could crank the lever and fire. Night Walker did the same. Too far to be truly effective, the return fire sent every Owlhoot who could run scrambling for cover.

Sarah's cheek bled from a rock chip. Other than that and Jake's holed hat, they were fine. Looking at the rock and the hole in his hat, Jake figured at least a fifty-caliber slug with a lot of powder behind it. Maybe a Sharp's rifle. Without the rock to deflect it, the bullet would have nailed him square in the chest. The shot needed only half an inch of elevation. Without that deadly inch, Jake, Sarah and the Cherokee remained in control.

We live by such a narrow measure of chance, Jake thought somberly. Recovering from the shock of her wound, Sarah dug frantically for her pistol. He put a restraining hand on her arm and bent close to examine the rock cut.

"Bring tears to your eyes, a cut like that," he observed. "Looks like we both made out pretty good, Honey Pie."

She choked back tears of rage, and gulping once, stood tiptoed to examine Jake's scalp, forgetting all the time they were still exposed to fire from below. Jake figured the Owlhoots were too shocked by the volume of return fire to try again.

"Cut a regular plow furrow through the hair up here," she said.

"No Honey, that's the part in my hair," he corrected her out of ignorance.

"Then you're balding," she scolded, showing Jake a handful of loose, light brown hair. "No blood though."

She smiled and kissed him quick on the cheek.

"You've got company," Night Walker reminded them, "and kissing so publicly, embarrasses him."

Sarah stepped away from Jake, wiped at her eyes and wiped her hands on her shirtfront.

"I've had it up to here with those back-shootin', no good vermin," she said. "They ain't had enough yet but they will soon." Still breathless with her rage, she grabbed the empty repeater from Jake's hands, pulled back the spring-loaded follower into its hinged receptacle and rotated it away from the front of the magazine tube. Methodically she fed in a handful of forty-four caliber cartridges.

"Mad is good," Jake observed. "Pretty soon you'll have a reputation and no one will mess with you."

"Just like you, huh, Mr. Target-on-his-forehead Tallon? What I've noticed is that any Owlhoot sees you, he automatically cranks off a couple of shots for good measure."

Night Walker turned away diplomatically, but Jake could see his shoulders shaking with laughter.

"Hey," Jake said, "we're still on the same side last time I checked."

Standing to the open again, Sarah commenced to crank off measured shots that landed first by the fire and once she got the range, walked them around the brush at the edge of the camp. When she finished, Night Walker handed her his reloaded rifle and she repeated the process in as fine an exhibition of distance shooting as Jake had ever seen.

When she finished, her anger had dissipated. A white flag sprouted on the near side of the clearing among the logs and bushes. "That's our signal," Jake announced, "They've had enough!

"I do believe," he told Sarah, "you could've defeated these Jaspers all by yourself."

Night Walker caught the smoking Henry as she dropped it and flung herself into Jake's arms.

"Shooting at people makes me so tired," she sobbed. "I'd rather be doing something else."

"Don't forget the getting shot at part," Jake reminded her. Pulling up on her chin with a couple of fingers to raise her face from his shirt, he said, "We still have to care for that cheek, you get my shirt all bloody every time you get up against me."

"No," she said, wiping at the blood with a sleeve and examining it critically. "I want something to prove I shared the danger, so I won't have to talk about it. People will know."

"What are you saying?" Jake asked.

"It's my dueling scar," eyes still brimming, she pointed emphatically at her cheek. "You told me once."

"Yeah, I know. Proof of manliness," he said, "but you're a woman!"

"I noticed," she yelled back, sticking out her belly at Jake. Turning, she stalked off toward the fire.

"Boy am I dumb," Jake said, defeated. "I can almost understand, just not quite."

Night Walker collapsed against a tree in as near a fit of comical hysteria as Jake had ever seen. Still he managed to suppress his outright laughter so Sarah might not think he failed to take her seriously.

Tears of laughter streaming down his cheeks, the Cherokee turned, leaned back against the pine and started feeding shells into his Henry again, shoulders shaking. "Well, I think I'm finally having fun. The two of you really put on a show. Whew," the big Indian exhaled. "I think most of those Owlhoots are down for the count," he gasped, still trying for final control of his voice.

Jake watched the Cherokee take two deliberate breaths and stand up straight from the tree. Though his eyes continued to twinkle, he now had control of his face and his voice. "It is time."

Jake felt all shot at and whipsawed first by his wife, then by his friend. Those Owlhoots gotta be simpler to deal with than this, he thought. Anything should be easier!

Sarah had her own mount saddled and sat watching them put leather on their horses. Meeting her eyes briefly, Jake shoved an extra rifle into her scabbard to compliment the one she carried over her saddlebow.

Mounting, they reined around and put their broncs on the trail leading down the mountain and around the long loop into the camp below. Jake wanted to arrive before their mood changed. If they had more time to think about it, the shock of Sarah's barrage might wear off and they could choose more resistance than less.

Well within rifle range but around a bend in the trail, the three pulled up and dismounted. Jake made sure each of them carried extra guns and ammunition. Night Walker faded soundlessly into the brush on Jake's left. He directed Sarah up the safer hillside to his right, where she could look down into the camp from above without great risk.

Jake counted slowly to a hundred and stepped around the corner into the open. A hundred yards separated him from their camp. Before ten steps fell underfoot, a bearded man in a filthy striped shirt stumbled from the brush on the left to fall limply, face first into the dust of the trail. Night Walker never showed himself but Jake knew with certainty it was he, who had discovered this back-shooter. No other reason for this man to be this far out from camp, hiding in the bushes.

Jake trotted forward a half-dozen strides and bending, slung him over his shoulder, partly as protection and also as a potential object lesson. Looking up, Jake saw the back-shooter's friends peering anxiously around trees and above bushes to his front.

"I'm Jake Tallon," he shouted. "Who the hell is this back-shootin' scum who dishonors your white flag?"

No answer came back so he threw the man onto the trail with a thump, where he could be easily seen by the watchers, pulled a gun and shot him through the outside of his thigh. Purely a flesh wound but enough for drama, and a sober reminder on cold days, if he lived to get old.

He came to, doubled-up around the injured leg, shouting his surprise and pain.

"One more time," Jake yelled, ratcheting back the hammer of his Remington Army for another shot.

"What's the question, damn it!" shouted the stricken back-shooter in wild-eyed desperation.

"What's your name, gutter-scum?"

Tears streamed down his cheeks as the injured man gasped, "Jeff Toppen's ma name. Please don't shoot me again!"

Shocked beyond belief, Jake looked dumbly down into the man's terrified countenance. "Couldn't do the job the first time?" he hissed through clenched teeth. Jake crouched now with his face close to the Bushwhacker's. This, he now recalled vividly, was one of the crew with Johnny Lobo and the Cruz Brothers, who ambushed him on the trail to Nazareth. This was the man who shot Harry, the same one on the yellow and curling poster in McKenzie's office.

"You like shooting from cover, don't you, Toppen!" It was an accusation. "Where are your friends, French Pete and Randy Quern?"

Jeff Toppen sobbed as he saw his death standing above him with a pistol in his hand. "I don't know," he whimpered. "I don't know where they are."

"Ha!" Jake yelled, striking him suddenly across the bridge of the nose with eight inches of rifled steel. Toppen's head snapped to the side with the impact.

"All those years," Jake shouted, "you terrorized those you figured less than you!"

Vengeance is yours if you wish it, Jake heard from the air before him, but you have a chance to change the heart of this man with his own fear. In this moment he sees the entirety of his life parading before his inner eye and he doesn't like it!

Standing, Jake stretched the man out with a series of four or five vicious kicks that lifted the prostrate figure off the ground, shocking the watchers wide-eyed with the brutality of his actions. Through his foot and leg, Jake could tell the man was uncommonly solid, so he knew the kicks hurt less than it appeared.

Once more face-to-face, his hand bunched in Toppen's shirt front, Jake told him, "I'll leave you alive by the will of Man Above but if I hear your name again in an uncomplimentary way, I'll track you down, gut you with a shovel. I'll kill everyone you ever knew as a friend. Do you understand? I'm gonna tell them also that their fate is tied to your good behavior so they'll help you stay straight. Do we have an understanding, Toppen?"

Jake stared at him until the man nodded sickly, stunned beyond response, blood streaming into his long dirty hair from his damaged face. The watchers heard everything that passed between the two of them.

"You ain't dead yet," standing, Jake yelled at the hiding men, "but you could be! Give up your guns forever and live like peaceable men." Feet spread shoulder wide, Jake reached down once again and grabbed Toppen by the shirt, tossing him from his path like a straw doll. As he started toward the camp, pistols and rifles came arching over the bushes to land more or less in a pile before him.

That's what reputation and a little demonstration can do for a man, Jake thought. Slowly, those who were able made their way to the center of the cleared area, careful to keep their hands in plain sight.

Dropping his own pistol into leather, Jake put his thumbs in his belt and faced them all with the calm attitude of a Greek Colossus, an aura of casual power filling the space around him. Sadness colored his words. "You had to come looking for me?" he said, eyes moving around the group. "Why?

"Why?" he barked a second time, making them jump in unison. Each man looked to the others in confusion.

"I already told you, Mr. Tallon," Slim spoke for them. "It were the money."

"Was it enough?" Jake scanned each face in turn.

"No," they answered nearly as one, terrified.

"If you don't already see this as a losing proposition," Jake lectured, "we're gonna make a point. Slim, put your hat down on the ground in front of me."

"Oh, crimminy," Slim said. Surely he saw Jake's purpose before the others. As he put the hat down, he carefully emptied his pockets of all gold and silver. Drawing a pistol again, Jake motioned with a gun barrel for everyone else to do the same.

"Don't hold nothin' back," he instructed. No one moved.

"This is robbery," one man complained.

"Were you law-abiding citizens," Jake spoke woodenly, "it might be robbery. But you aren't and it ain't. I'd be within my rights to string you all up, shootin' at a pregnant woman like you did."

They looked guiltily one to another. "Pregnant? We didn't know nuthin' of the kind."

"Which way would you rather have it?" Jake asked. The men followed Slim's lead, emptying their pockets, one after another, falling over each other in their eagerness to comply.

"Now," Jake asked as they stepped away from the bulging hat, "which one of you is the last Mackinaw?" Several in the front row pointed mutely to the blanket-covered form behind them.

"You already shot him full of holes," Slim said, "only he ain't the last. The two youngest Mackinaws be back at Nazareth."

"There's more? Are they from Salt Lake?" Jake could hardly believe it, thinking of the Mormon penchant for plural marriages.

"Naw," Slim answered for the group. "Their dad hitched up with a younger woman after his first wife died bearin' the middle son."

Jake shook his head in disbelief. "Why ain't they here?"

"They thought chasing you were foolish," Slim said, sitting again, hugging his knees. "When they hear about this they may have no choice but to toss their hat in the ring after their brothers. They won't have any brothers left."

Night Walker materialized from the bushes and picked up hardware scattered in the dirt. With her rifle at the ready, Sarah appeared from between the bushes on the hillside.

"It'd be best if you boys didn't find your way back to California," Jake advised.

"Why's that?" one startled man asked.

"Number one, if I see you, I'll kill you myself. Number two is, by the time you get back, everyone will know you tried to gun a pregnant woman," Jake reminded them, nodding toward Sarah, who knowing Jake's mind, patted a slightly swollen stomach.

Stricken, they recoiled at the idea, looking quickly up to the woman at the base of the hill. Like Slim, many of these men were decent at heart.

One of the men, sad and long of face, tattered hat in hand, stepped forward, saying, "We could kill you fair enough, Tallon." He smiled brokenly and shuffled uncomfortably, "But we never meant harm to any woman, yours or any other. For my part, I hope I never see you again."

"Me too. Crime don't pay," bending, Jake picked up the loaded hat. "Remember that part too." Pursing his lips, he glared menacingly at the defeated men one last time before turning his back and walking away under the cover of Sarah's rifle.

Trouble Downtown

Not so very long ago, Jake had sat astride a horse looking over the town of Bodie before entering. This time Night Walker rode off one knee and Sarah off the other as they looked into the same town.

"Nothing more we can do here in Bodie," said the Cherokee, "when your real trouble waits you elsewhere."

"We have not spoken of Nazareth," said Jake.

"It is not necessary, when I know all things."

Jake regarded the big Indian with a wary eye, not knowing just how much he knew, guessed or had heard from Sarah, who was more talkative than he. Jake figured Walker's sense of humor required him to play-act the mystic, although Walker usually seemed to know things and achieve feats denied ordinary mortals.

"Okay, amigo. Let's leave the extra horses in Bodie. There are too many of them to drag around the country and some are sure to be recognized in Nazareth as belonging to the Mackinaws and their friends and raise questions we don't want to answer right away."

"Good thinking, Jacob. And we will surely find Altimera at the house of Señora Delores. Perhaps she will feed us a fine meal before you return to Nazareth tomorrow morning." The hint of a smile touched the Cherokee's lips.

"You enjoy this, don't you?" Jake pierced him with an accusing gaze before kicking Sam once more into the lead, determined to find José and get the four of them to Nazareth, a much smaller settlement, a days ride north and west of Bodie.

The horse, Buck, given Jake by Broken Fire, had developed an immediate affinity for Sarah. Since Jake's horse, Sam, had found him again at the ranch, Jake had no need of Buck and was pleased that Sarah should choose to ride the fine animal, kind of keep him in the family.

158

Since they'd reunited with Altimera, that put all four of them astride horseflesh that would stand out anywhere in the world, one at a time. Four together like that, folks came outdoors to watch as though the circus had come to Nazareth. They lacked only the colorful tents and clowns of a truly major attraction.

Jake glanced to the storefront under the Gunsmith's sign as they passed, thinking about his damaged second gun. This was the man who'd made them in the first place, Eliza Crombe. The door remained shut, curtains drawn.

"Hey Compadre," Altimera spoke across the concave surface of his polished saddle after dismounting in front of the Livery, "did you see a friendly smile on the way through town? Any smile at all?"

"Not my side of the street," Jake answered.

"Nor mine," Night Walker chimed in.

"We aren't here for a popularity contest," Jake said. "We're looking for the other boot."

"You're muy loco!" Walking around the hitch rail, a frustrated Mexican confronted Jake, placing hands upon his hips, "What do you mean, other boot? You don't wear boots no more. Never did you like boots."

"It's only a figure of speech, amigo," Jake enlightened him with an indulgent smile as he loosened Sam's cinch strap. "Waiting for the other boot to drop is the way folks say it. A man can't climb into bed until the second boot has hit the floor. So we're here to find the other boot."

"Oh," said the Mexican, smiling proudly, "to unravel the mystery is what you say? Find out what happens."

"Do you boys talk like this all the time?" asked a much-perplexed Sarah, "Or do you only talk to entertain me?"

"Si, we entertain," said Altimera, hitching up his belt, "and also we keep your crazy husband in line. But there is no stopping him," the Mexican complained, "He brings us here just to be shot and I have been down this road one too many times with him."

"You complain like an old woman, José," Jake smiled at his friend's mischief. "If I didn't know you are a true Vaquero, who fears nothing, I might listen seriously."

"Of course, you are right," Altimera said, "but we must use care and much common sense."

"That's right, amigo," Jake said, "and I have a plan."

Of course, Jake had less of a plan than his boast implied. He knew that whoever killed his friends had a great deal to worry about and more to cover up. They hid behind money and the greed of others trying desperately to finish a job that started at the jog of the trail, near a small hill, just outside of town.

Given enough rope, they would hang themselves. Jake had confidence in that outcome. The problem was that Jake must stay alive long enough for the entire mystery to unravel. He needed all of his friends and more. Just beneath his shirt, the Red Jasper warmed against his chest at the thought. Already, he had many friends but the weight of numbers arrayed against them seemed daunting. Would Jake have enough friends and where could he find the additional help he needed?

Down the street, Sheriff Vernon Laszlo slouched in the shade of a wooden awning, watching the group's arrival in Nazareth with a sharpened interest. They might be any dust-covered strangers except that he recognized José Altimera right off as the nosy Mexican, who now walked with a noticeable limp. Laszlo had trouble placing the others, though he certainly had his suspicions.

Even under the trail grime and plain clothing, the woman was gorgeous. She easily drew attention from the men to herself, her sultry posture shouting sexuality. This was no doily-knitting, starched-petticoat Priss from back east. Made a man like Laszlo wonder why he never married, why he could never find a woman like that himself.

The big dark man with the group might well be the Indian who rode with Tallon last year out of Sante Fe. Difficult to tell with his short hair and regular clothes. Didn't look like any Indian Laszlo knew. So big, he looked like a mountain dumped upon the flat floor of a broad, smooth valley.

He'd look out of place on any street, in any town. Other than Dutch Honniker, the Mayor's bullyboy, this man was the biggest hombre Vernon had ever seen. Ever!

The fourth man puzzled Laszlo in the extreme. He wanted to say he was Jake Tallon, the man they so feared, but he saw neither scar nor bandanna to identify him as the fella who done in the Cruz Brothers and Bingo Mackinaw. He was easily the least impressive of the group.

Nothing added up. He'd never met the legend and Tallon was reported to be about average until you pissed him off. Laszlo sure wasn't in the market to get maimed. Standing away from the pool of shade, he aimed himself in the opposite direction of the group he watched. Should he curse his cowardice or compliment his discretion? The Sheriff smiled secretly. Not getting paid enough to get dead before my time, he reasoned.

The Mayor should be told but he wasn't in his office. When Zachary's in, a man can see his big white hat on the rack by the window, like a sign reading "open for business." Laszlo saw no hat so he didn't need to climb the stairs to find out. Nor was the Mayor with the Judge at the Oro Fino. For that matter, the Judge was also gone. Together, he wondered? Where could they have got off to?

Walking back to his hole-in-the-wall office, Laszlo lifted the latch and let himself inside. He wrinkled his nose at the dusty smell. The Mayor's strong-arm tactics made the law unpopular in Nazareth, so the only visitors he ever had were behind bars in the back room, and it smelled worse in the cells than it did in here. Especially, he thought, with that man, Lobo, back there. Why couldn't he die anyway? Laszlo asked himself. I'd shoot him again, if I thought no one would notice.

Living, Lobo was proof of the Sheriff's momentary lapse of judgment.

Vernon poured himself a cup of cold coffee that he didn't want and walked back to his desk. Pushing all the paperwork to one side of the surface, he made space for his coffee and his boots.

As he leaned back in his loudly squeaking chair, Laszlo thought bitterly of the new woman in town, Tia O'Connell. She's just as exciting as the woman with Tallon! Without her inflammatory presence, he would not have the complication of a new trial. But she had pulled in from Sacramento and stirred things up, and stirred Laszlo up.

Johnny got the wrong idea, or, he corrected himself, distractedly tracing the dusty surface of the desktop with a forefinger, maybe I did let my mouth get away from me. Johnny grabbed my arm and I shot him. I would've shot him again if the woman hadn't stepped in between. That would'a been a whole lot easier.

Whole damn thing got out of hand. Now we gotta kill him legal.

Laszlo smiled his crooked, lonely smile. He ran both hands down his face, accenting the sagging flesh on his cheeks and beneath each eye. It all had a bad feeling about it, he thought. How'd I get here? My daddy taught me better. He'd be sad if he saw the mess I made of this.

Beyond the dirty windows of the crooked Sheriff's office, the sun moved slowly west overhead and three men and two women talked over an early dinner in another part of town. It was a reunion for Sarah and Tia, who hugged and whispered intensely between themselves, but the whole thing had gone south for Jake, who fumed quietly and played with the food on his plate. The women were oblivious to him, as were José and Night Walker, who came to eat.

Making a noisy clatter, José dropped his fork with sudden understanding. "Chihuahua," he said reaching over to put his hand compassionately upon Jake's arm.

The women stopped talking, drawn by Altimera's intensity.

"What?" they said almost together.

"I almost forget," said Altimera, looking back to the women even as he held his friend's arm. "Jacob toll me some time ago about Johnny Lobo and we have not talked about it since. Johnny Lobo is the man who shot your sister's husband, Miss Althea! Now you say Johnny Lobo is your hero?"

"Jake?" asked Tia dumbfounded, "Johnny shot Jake?"

"She has another husband?" José gestured to Sarah with an open hand.

"Oh, my God!" said Tia, "This surely can't be true."

"I'm afraid it is," said Jake bleakly, "It complicates absolutely everything. A person just can't let something like that go. It's not like we had some kind of misunderstanding. He shot me from ambush." Jake ran his hand somberly over his healing forehead.

"We can't possibly be talking about the same man," said Tia pleadingly. "If anything, he's more like you than anyone I've ever met. Johnny's hurt and in jail now because he tried to do the right thing, protecting me."

"That's something," Jake admitted, spooning food into his mouth and chewing deliberately, "but I've gotta work this out for myself, Tia. Maybe I'll talk with him after a bit."

Setting his spoon carefully beside his plate, Jake wiped his lips on the heavy fabric of his napkin. Privately, as he balled up the linen and stood from the table, he thought, maybe that bushwhacker will just die of his wounds and I won't have to do anything at all. No, that would be too easy, some inner voice argued, too easy for you, Jacob.

The women watched in silence as Jake turned toward the door, seeking the counsel of the night.

Disconsolately, Sarah watched Jake leave, knowing she could do nothing to help her husband with his dilemma. She trusted him to reach a sound judgment but knew he needed solitude.

Jake was still unaccustomed to spending lots of time with other people and didn't get so much time to think on his own as he did before the marriage. Sarah understood that about Jake.

Outside the restaurant, dusty streets began to cool, releasing the oppressive heat of midday to a serpentine breeze sliding down from the distant slopes. The mountains of the Basin range appeared as a glowing haze in the west by the light of the rising moon.

Jake remembered José's lady friend, the Señora in Bodie, from whose house he rode to find the spirit of the mountain and maybe Man Above. I know what I'm doing this time, Jake thought, turning resolutely toward the stable to find the old man, Seth, who cared for Sam at the Livery.

I'll find some peace away from this town where I can think and come back to the Livery and bed down. Sarah will certainly want to be with Tia at the Boarding House. José will stay at the Casa of the Señora and Night Walker will find his own way as he always does. Just myself and Sam and the night, right now. Perhaps Man Above will counsel me, he thought, casting his eyes along the rooftops and into the growing darkness of the California sky.

Approaching the Livery, Jake saw two unshaven, disreputable looking characters lounging against the outer corral rails, talking quietly between themselves in the late light. One wore leather chaps. The other was distinguished by a plaid shirt covered with a shabby vest. With interest Jake noted their tied down guns and shortened, five inch barrels, for the faster draw. Fast draw doesn't make much difference if you can't keep your gun on target once you have it out. Good for close work or people who can't shoot back. Maybe I'm just too cynical, Jake thought. He felt tired. Spiritually tired.

As he passed, one stared, nodded briefly, but said nothing. Jake said nothing in return. He needed no conversation with such obvious trouble. These characters were unpleasant fixtures in his world, like poorly matching furniture in a familiar room.

Jake noticed the old man, Seth, under his lantern near the office door smoking a pipe. Smelled like fancy pipe tobacco. On any other evening Jake might stop to jaw with him some. Tonight he wanted only open air and open country.

"Your horse been askin' after you," the old man said as Jake approached.

"Just like him," Jake replied. "Thought I might take him out for a spell if you don't mind."

"He's your horse, and you know where to find him."

"He always knows how to find me, it seems." Jake heard a low wicker from the side of the long building.

"That critter's confused. Thinks it's a dog, the way it follers you around. Cries when you leave and carries on. I think you otta learn that horse proper!"

"If you don't stop talking so mean, old man, I won't leave my animals here no more. They're too good for a rundown stable like this anyhow." Jake smiled in spite of his mood. He walked past Seth and found Sam at the gate waiting for him, glossy neck stretched out over the top bar. The big horse tossed his head, conversing in a constant wicker that went in degrees from soft to loud and back again. Lowering his long face, Sam let Jake briefly wrap his arms around his jaw and stroke his hide.

"Let's go see what the moon does to the desert. What do ya say, Fella?" Jake unwrapped himself from the big animal and strode toward the nearby door. Stepping high with anticipation, Sam paced him on the opposite side of the fence.

Finding his gear in the tack room, Jake sought his horse in the dark. He slipped the bridle over Sam's head and reached back for the blanket. Seth stood quietly beside him with the colorful blanket and saddle held in either hand.

"You walk like an Indian, old man," Jake said, half irritated.

"Who's to say I ain't?" Seth replied with pretended testiness. "White folks is come lately. Mostly only Indians out here until the 50's. Live among 'em long enough, pretty soon you can't tell the difference. I can't!"

Jake could feel the old man's sharp eyes pierce him in the dark. Seth said, "You look a decent sort, son. This here town's a snake pit and if you're a friend of that youngster in Jail, you're running against a stacked deck."

"I appreciate the warning," Jake told him as he tightened the cinch and stepped easily into the high saddle. "But I want to know who sent you."

"Nobody sent me," the old man snapped, suddenly angry. "I just got me a pocketful of my own good intentions. Don't be lookin' a gift horse in the mouth, young'n." He squinted at Jake accusingly as Jake reined Sam around, pointing him out of the yard.

The two scruffy Yahoos he'd seen earlier lounging against the corral were no longer there. He had bad feelings about them but seriously doubted they were more than bit players. It took money to get the five of them bushwhacked the first time and quite a lot more to finance fourteen men across more than a thousand miles of wasteland to catch him coming out of Colorado. Between those fourteen men, they still had more than two thousand dollars in their pockets. That's more than five years of cowboy wages and they hadn't looked to be the kind of men who saved for a rainy day.

Sam picked his way between clumps of sage, moving away from the buildings toward higher ground.

It was no two-bit rancher paid them to chase him, Jake knew. So money was no problem and it was money connected each assault on his life. A common factor. For that matter, once Jake was out of the way, this unknown person could pull that much gold out of the diggings in one day. That claim was rich diggin'.

How much had been stolen since the takeover, he wondered? Certainly a lot if the claim produced the way it had the last days he was there, when Harry was still alive.

So far, no one talked openly, just the veiled warnings by well-intentioned people like Seth. Wherever he went, the town's people got all tight-faced. Could be just because he was a stranger, but Jake doubted it. Somehow the whole community was tied into the bushwhacking and claim jumping. Those not directly connected were cowed by those that were. It didn't add up!

Jake remembered what Altimera said about asking for directions to the claim before digging him up from under the sand hill. Whether or not people recognized Jake, eventually they would remember José and they'd all get lumped together as troublemakers who had to go. How long would they have before it reached that point? Days maybe, but certainly not a week.

It made no sense to Jake that the whole town sat down to plan these things out. No one building with a room big enough, he knew. Somebody at the top pulled the strings. Jake's first guess was Big Bill Zachary, the Mayor. That man had been a maverick from as far back as anyone could remember, writing his own rules. His reputation and his influence reached all the way down to Sacramento. He figured to push folks around and get away with it.

Nobody ever proved anything against him. Well, I know folks in Sacramento also, thought Jake, wryly. That 'n a nickel three-cent piece otta get me a cuppa coffee.

His second guess for ringmaster was the Sheriff, 'cause nothing happened in a town like this to which the local lawman wasn't a party. He'd seen that seedy, son of a cur watching up and down the street and fairly felt the wheels of his mind a turnin' even at more than fifty yards. Same man as shot Tia's beau, Johnny Lobo.

Could be, Johnny knew who hired him, but that was not for sure. Funny, Jake thought, he no longer felt so strongly about his erstwhile bushwhacker. Sam's steady gait and the sweet night air cleared Jake's head as he'd hoped. Felt just like clouds lifting from his brow. Jake raised his eyes to the starry sky. Creation winked back at him from a thousand brilliant points. The lights of town disappeared behind a hill over his shoulder, as Jake rode forward into velvet darkness. Johnny was only a tool and maybe there was some way he could be turned to help the man he'd tried to kill.

This whole thing was tangled as a cat's cradle in the hands of a master string twister, maybe more. Suddenly Jake felt out of his depth again. He thought of Bobby Tattum, or Robert L. Tattum, Esq., as he was listed before the Bar of California. Bobby saw the law the same way Jake saw fists and firearms, a way to get things done. Jake didn't want a legal battle over the claim, but since the ground was occupied by the claim-jumper, it had already come to that.

Bobby might also stall proceedings against Lobo if the Sheriff tried to railroad the young man. It did look as though Laszlo might get him hung before Lobo caused other problems for the conspirators. That would make sense were the tables turned.

Jake's mind drifted back to the gold strike. Ownership of the claim would revert to Harry's partners if Jake showed original documents, which he believed he could, and motive for the murder, which was obvious. Heck, Jake realized, he had to show there was a murder. That would be enough, he thought.

The first priority was to throw the whole mess open to sunlight. Rats, snakes and scorpions all run from the direct light. That meant he must return to Bodie. Just one stop to make in the morning. Two, Jake corrected himself.

The land dropped away in front of him as Jake found himself atop a hill above the trail to Bodie. Below him, he saw two men in a horse-drawn buggy obviously headed from Bodie toward Nazareth far below. By his remarkable size, one must certainly be the Mayor, the one Harry had described to Jake when he first arrived. The other was a mystery. With the darkness flowing around him like cool water, Jake looked downward at the unsuspecting men.

"You're in big trouble, Mr. Mayor," Jake muttered softly, "You just don't know it yet," he promised.

In the rented buckboard, Big Bill's frame shuddered with a chill of premonition.

"What's wrong, Mayor?" asked Judge Hoagland. "You got a spider in your britches?" Poking through the big man's self absorption had lately become a hobby for the Jurist, a hobby with suicidal aspects.

"I don't understand you, Ezra," said the Mayor, finally irritated. "You're easily the most educated man I know, yet you speak at times like a common stable hand."

"That's just for your benefit, Mr. Mayor," the Judge smiled to himself. Nothing the Mayor could do to him mattered. He just didn't care anymore.

Their conversation terminated as they topped the last hill to see the remaining lights of Nazareth. The horses picked up their pace with the promise of their goal in sight.

Next morning, Jake found himself outside the Judge's Chambers, waiting his appearance. When he did arrive, Judge Ezra Hoagland lost his dignity to sudden surprise when he saw the visitor. That almost never happened in Nazareth, where people generally had reason to fear the authority of a bought Judge and a crooked lawman. Secondly, there weren't that many people who needed help, and thirdly, anyone with sense went elsewhere.

"I'm Jacob Tallon," Jake introduced himself, "Can I have a moment of your time, Your Honor?" Jake held his hat respectfully before him, trying unsuccessfully to cover the bullet hole in the crown.

He saw the Judge's eyes go swiftly pale at the mention of his name. "Doubtless, there are many things to discuss," Jake prodded, feeling the energy of the moment move in his direction. "For the time being, I wish to ask you about the Jail's only prisoner, Johnny Lobo."

"Come on in," the Judge juggled his keys, dropping them to the dusty boards of the floor with a clatter. Bending to retrieve them, he fumbled momentarily in his panic. Finally sliding the correct key into the lock, he turned it with an oily click and pushed the door open. It swung wide with a loud squeal, contradicting the earlier smoothness of the tumblers. Early light from the high windows lanced diagonally through the mote-filled air, reminding Jake of swarming insects in the way the small glowing points seemed to dance around each other.

What in hell's name is this man doing here, Ezra asked himself? Does he know he's inquiring about the man who shot him? Has he figured out that the Mayor's behind it all? Does he know how involved I am? What does he know?

The many questions made the Judge dizzy as he shuffled 'round the desk and placed his leather case against the wall. Jake watched in silence as the Judge settled into his chair.

Clutching at the shreds of his composure, the Judge focused on ritual as he removed his coat and rearranged papers on an already tidy work surface. He fought for calm before opening his mouth again. "What can I do for you, young man?" he asked, finally looking into Jake's face with a strength of will, attempting a bored frown.

None of the Judge's unease was lost on Jake, but Hoagland's guilt or lack of it was not the first mission on Jake's mind this morning. "You're aware of Althea O'Connell?"

"Perky young woman," the Judge smiled in spite of his terror. This was an easier question than he expected.

"She's my sister-in-law," Jake let that fact sink in. "She's concerned that Mr. Lobo is too ill with his wounds to stand trial and would like to see him receive better care."

Each revelation registered like a slap in the face. The Judge felt ill. "Nothing we can do about that, Son," he managed. "The trial is scheduled in two days."

"I thought I'd give you first crack at doing the right thing, Judge," Jake said, stepping forward until only the bulk of the desk separated him from the frightened Jurist. "Why don't we ask the Circuit Judge for a better schedule and while we're at it, move the trial to Bodie where Lobo can get a fair shake? For that matter why don't we bring the Sheriff up on charges of public mischief with women?" Both palms flat now on the front of the desk, Jake leaned threateningly forward, his face tightening with unrestrained anger.

"You're loaded for bear, aren't you son?" The Judge couldn't help but admire this young man. Not many had the gumption to stand up to the authority he represented. In spite of his own involvement, Ezra Hoagland smiled. "You think he'll go your way, do you?"

"Yes Sir. It's the right thing to do!"

"Okay, I agree," Hoagland surprised himself. "You got the delay 'til I hear from Pearson in Sacramento," the Judge sidestepped the threat of charges against Laszlo. He figured this was Laszlo's problem anyway. No skin off his nose. "I'll give you ten days."

"Thank you, Your Honor," Jake rose to a more respectful posture, with his hat held once more in front of him. "Now, what about access to the prisoner for medical attention?"

This boy can sure push his point, mused the Judge, lips pursed, his annoyance momentarily overcoming his fear. "Maybe you're in the wrong profession, young man?" He squinted his eyes up at Jake, his own guilt completely forgotten.

"I'm asking Bobby Tattum to represent Mr. Lobo," said Jake. "Thanks anyway for the compliment but I know what I'm best at and I know what Bobby's best at."

"I'm sure you do, Mr. Tallon. Tattum's a good lawyer. I've seen his work." Removing the inkwell stopper, the Judge dipped a pen, clicking it one too many times against the glass lip as he removed it, and scratched noisily on a small sheet of official looking paper. "Take this note to the Sheriff and you can doctor Mr. Lobo all you want."

"One more thing, Your Honor."

Hoagland's blood went cold. Tallon's visit had been too easy thus far.

Jake saw the Judge wince. "Four people were killed outside of Nazareth, little more than a month ago. Far as I know, few people except me and the perpetrators know that a crime has been committed. That's gonna change shortly!" Jake leaned forward again for emphasis, "I'm putting out a reward for information that'll lead me to the Killers."

"There's been no killing, I know of," protested the Judge.

"Like I said, that'll change soon enough," Jake asserted. "Money makes people talk and I'm offering a serious reward. I think two thousand dollars otta loosen a few tongues. Up to now, the murderers have avoided serious scrutiny, but the wheels are about to come off that buggy!"

Shock waves rolled through the Judge as he fought desperately for control of his face. This had to be his worst fear come true.

Watching the reactions of Judge Hoagland, Jake could only feel sorry for the man. He felt the Jurist did not possess sufficient evil to engineer the killing of five men. At worst, he was controlled by someone else and merely allowed it to happen. At some point the Judge might be a help to him and Jake didn't want to burn that bridge. "Thank you, Judge. You've been a big help," said Jake. "I really mean that."

Hoagland only nodded numbly in dismissal, terrified at the turn of events. I can only take so much at one time, he thought. William Zachary has his work cut out for him if he wants this fellow out of the way. "Good luck, son." Hoagland took his first breath once Jake had left the room.

He had to tell the Mayor. Stepping spryly from his chair, Hoagland sidled around the false partition at the rear of the room and made for the back door of the courthouse. Entering the alley from behind, he found the stairs to Zachary's lofty office and glanced once nervously over his shoulder before ascending them. He saw nothing but knew that meant little.

≡◻≡

Vernon Laszlo cast him a weary eye as the Judge stormed through the door, slamming it breathlessly behind him.

"Glad you're both here," he panted. "That boy, Jacob Tallon, is full of surprises," Hoagland began over the angry protests of the Mayor.

"Don't you knock?" Big Bill Zachary screwed up his face in anger and tilted his head to underline his question. He detested emotion run out of control worse than he hated interruptions.

"When things are normal, I knock. When things get crazy, sometimes I don't." The Judge pulled up a Captain's chair with a rounded back and gracefully curving armrest, so he could face the Mayor. "That boy's got all of his brains intact, if you ask me. He doesn't act like he's been head-shot at all. He's about to put out a big reward for information leading to the conviction of the person or persons who hired the murder of Harry Harmon and his friends."

The Sheriff smiled a lopsided smile and the Mayor sat bolt upright. "He what?" sputtered Zachary.

"Will post a reward is what I said."

On impulse, the Mayor stood abruptly and walked to the end of the room where he looked down into the alley just in time to see Jake stand away from the building against which he leaned and walk slowly out of sight.

Cursing under his breath, he turned back toward the desk and accused, "You just made it that much easier for him by coming directly here."

"He saw me?"

"Apparently so." The Mayor once again lowered himself into the fancy swivel seat and leaned forward, putting his elbows on the desk with a thump.

"We could just kill him," said Laszlo, "but with all of his friends, I count six more killings."

"I'm not so sure anymore, that can be easily done," reflected the Judge, "given our recent experience with the young man."

The quick appearance of the nervous Jurist at the Mayor's office wasn't ironclad proof, Jake understood, but it reinforced his strongest suspicions. Jake's mind raced. The Judge and the Mayor and maybe even the Sheriff were in this together. In what? Was there any ironclad connection between their obvious fear and the mine? Whoever owned the mine had motive. How could he make a connection?

Johnny Lobo might be more of a blessing than he knew. Without his difficulty, Jake might not have thought of Bobby Tattum so rapidly. The lawyer could help him research current mine ownership as well. Speed was very important because he didn't know how many more attempts on his life he could survive before he untangled this complicated mystery.

Jake put Nazareth City Hall behind him and turned left, looking for the Trapadera Restaurant. The shades of the Gunsmith, he noticed, remained drawn. The town wasn't that big. The restaurant was only across the street, halfway down to the boarding house. Nazareth had no real hotel. Beyond Molly's Boarding House, the only other rented rooms were on the second floor of the Oro Fino.

When Jake walked into the restaurant, he saw his friends and family in the far corner, light from the windows dividing the table into long misshapen squares before them. Crossing the open floor between diners, he lifted an empty chair from a table nearby and straddled it, facing the group.

The conversation stopped abruptly as he sat down. He looked at each friend in turn, amused he had so much attention all at one time. "Don't go all quiet on me," he protested. "You look at me like I was a ghost!"

"I just have such a hard time understanding," said Sarah, "why you take so much trouble with the man who tried to murder you, Jacob. I love you for it, but why do you go out on a limb for Johnny Lobo like you do?"

"Me too," agreed Tia. "I wonder also. I'm so grateful. It's just hard for me to believe that the man I know would do such a thing, but I believe you, brother Jake." She cradled her open hands tenderly in her lap like a living thing. Kind of like a little bird, Jake thought.

Jake took it all in before speaking. "Riding out last night gave me a chance to think things through." Jake removed his hat and smoothed back his hair. "The fact is, Johnny Lobo didn't kill me, only laid me up for a while … in a strange sort of way, he may have done me a favor." Jake allowed the quiet for a moment, then spoke again. "Had he succeeded, I may have felt differently. When he recovers, we will find he had his own reasons for doing what he did that had nothing at all to do with me. Chances are it was only paid work." Jake broke eye contact and rotated the hat in his hands. "Only paid work," he mumbled into his chest.

The women continued to regard Jake respectfully as he reached into a vest pocket and extracted the neatly folded paper, penned by the Judge. Opening the piece, he flattened it deliberately with the palm of his hand, then reversed it, and shoved it across the table to Night Walker, seated between the women.

"What's this?" the big Cherokee asked Jake as he picked it up.

"This is the Writ the Judge gave me, allowing us access to Johnny Lobo. Gather your supplies, herbs and magic, my friend. See what you can do for the youngster. That paper will get you through the door whenever you want."

"What about the trial, amigo?" interrupted Altimera. "That Writ does him no good if Walker heals him only to hang in two days."

"That's solved also," Jake looked down at his hands and up and around again at his friends circled around the table. "The Judge set the trial back ten days so I can get a hold of my lawyer friend in Sacramento, Bobby Tattum, and the Circuit Judge, Pearson."

"That means you have to get to a Telegraph Station or learn to fly," commented Night Walker dryly. "That won't happen. You aren't even Cherokee."

Jake smiled. "That's very true. Not yet."

"It means we must get to Bodie, again," observed Sarah.

"Not all of us. Night Walker must stay for Johnny, and I expect Tia would like to stay also," said Jake. "Things will get exciting very fast now. Finding the killers may not take ten days. This whole thing will be flushed out into the open if everything works the way I expect."

"Maybe we will not like it so much that way," mumbled the Mexican. "I work so hard to make you well, keep you from harm's way. Then the first thing you do is stir up trouble. Trouble means pain. You are too much loco, I think."

My Woman at My Back

The chill started in Jake's fingertips and raced, like ball lightning, up his arms to clamp his heart convulsively in a sudden icy grip. He rocked in his saddle from that impact, so like an internal thunderclap. He looked around him, desperately. Small hairs raced in ridge-like ripples across flat areas of skin beneath his clothing.

"Ohhhhhh!," he moaned, biting his lips to contain the sound. What the devil, he wondered? The landscape remained peaceful around him, yet the feelings of apprehension remained.

Removing his hat, Jake craned his neck in every direction, looking for the cause of the intense cold that drew his attention. A shadow maybe? No single cloud obscured the hazy blue above him. No bird wheeled before the sun; still the dreadful feeling persisted.

Sarah rode just off his left knee, chatting gaily with Altimera, oblivious to his distress.

No need to bother the others, Jake thought. It's just a feeling I have, so far. Probably nothing to worry about, although little has gone right this past couple of months.

That thought suddenly struck Jake as ungrateful, when he remembered what had been so generously returned to him. Just having Sarah here, next to him on her horse, settled him in ways he found difficult to explain. Still, it felt as though someone else rode with them and could not be ignored. He had to reason it out, find out who was behind the murders.

He figured that the Cruz Brothers had been party to the ambush in the beginning but were certainly not behind it. So while they were no longer a threat, someone else was. That person worried Jake mostly because he or they were still unknown to him. A secret stalker or a puppet master, someone was still out there making plans that affected his health and the health of those he loved.

"Isn't that right, Honey?" The words barely registered but the touch of Sarah's hand on his brought Jake around with a start. He realized just how preoccupied with his dilemma he had been.

172

"What's that Sweetcakes?" he muttered lamely.

Sarah leaned from her saddle, extending her arm to touch his cheek with a gentle hand. Concern showed across her bright smooth features. "Where've you been Jake Honey?" she asked, "Somewhere, way far away?"

"Not sure," Jake mumbled. Her tenderness made him smile. "I don't know that I'm feeling all that good. I get these spells every once in a while, since I was wounded last. That's what it is, just a spell. It's getting better. This is the first time since we've been together that I've had one this bad."

"Could be you just need a hot meal and some rest," she squeezed Jake's hand gently and turned her attention back to Altimera.

The path they followed wound its way down the toe of a ridge to join the main trail that twisted across the sagebrush flats in front of them toward Bodie Town in the distance. Jake watched the skyline with the intense interest of a person bent on survival. He seemed alone in his concern and glared at his companions with a small measure of resentment. Sarah enjoyed company and José's culture made him more social than Jake. Jake was surely feeling sorry for himself.

Once the first of the town's outbuildings passed on either side, he felt easier. Ambush wasn't so simple among people and in broad daylight. Things had been too easy for his enemies for too long. The fact that he could be bushwhacked so easily in the first place still stung.

How are things going to change, he wondered? I'm in worse shape now than I was when I was shot. Bingo snuck up on me and Buster caught me off guard. It seems like my weakened condition has opened the door for one life-threatening fiasco after another. What's next?

Jake brooded, head down, watching the trail pass under Sam's hooves without really noticing. How long can that go on, before somebody I care for catches trouble meant for me?

José turned them left down a side street then right again after a hundred feet. They found themselves in front of the Seneca Fire Pit, an eating-place of which Jake had heard but never visited.

"They do not know civilized food here," said the Mexican, "yet it is ver' good!"

"By civilized food you mean tortillas and beans?" asked Jake, dismounting and tying Sam's reins to the rail with a slipknot.

"Si," Altimera smiled broadly. "Tacos and frijoles. Man's food."

Sarah grinned through this exchange, allowing Jake to open the door for her. She slapped her hat against her clothing before stepping inside and then slapped it urgently against Jake's shirtfront, reminding him to remove his own headgear.

"You'll make a better man out of me, Sarah." He knew he was distracted. "What were the two of you talking about back there on the trail?" Jake tossed the question over his shoulder at his Mexican friend.

"Your wife is interested in broadening her horizons," Altimera paused. "Unlike yourself! She is learning Spanish from me. I am learning French from her."

Jake grunted, refusing the bait.

They walked to the back of the room, away from the windows and the direct sunlight. Against the wall it felt cool and dark. Jake breathed more freely in the absence of oppressive shadows and unknown threats.

"You speak French?" he asked Sarah, moving a chair back for her.

"Si," she said, cocking her head coquettishly, "and now, I am learning Spanish, Señor Tallon."

"Sometimes," said a frustrated Jake Tallon, "the two of you together make life for me more difficult, instead of easier."

Sarah giggled, her beautiful eyes sparkling. José, seated opposite, started to lean forward with his elbows on the table but was interrupted by the arrival of their food, sloshing in a large, black, two-handled pot.

"We haven't ordered," Jake protested to their whiskered server.

"You don't have to," came the belligerent drawl, mouthed around an unlit cigar stub. "People come here, want what we got. This here," he looked downward into the fragrantly steaming contents of the pot, "is what we got!"

"He's right," said Altimera with innocent eyes. "The food here is always good. Delicioso!"

Jake looked into the pot where the contents still bumped and swirled. He saw chunks of meat in a dark broth, thick with spices and small vegetables. José was right, delicioso. The smell reminded him of Creole cooking he'd experienced in New Orleans.

"Where are the bowls?" asked Sarah.

For an answer, their waiter dropped a handful of pewter forks and spoons on the table. "This here is the way you eat it," the server said. "We got ambulance." He emphasized the last word, drawing it out and hooking his thumbs in a soiled apron.

"I think you mean ambiance," said Sarah.

"That's French," Sarah and Altimera said at once, laughing.

Removing the stub from his mouth, the cook glared his dislike of their correction, humphed loudly and turned from the table.

Chattering happily, the three friends fell to spearing chunks of meat floating in the broth which dripped across the oilcloth covering on the table. Jake forgot his previous unease and enjoyed one of the finest meals he could remember with his two best friends. Like Sarah, he suspected the suggested atmosphere was no more than a shortage of dishes but kept his suspicions private.

Sarah was right, thought Jake, as he felt himself warming to the meal. The food helped a lot. Conversation flowed freely across the table between bites. His fears slipped into the background. Sarah had a way of enlivening any gathering. For the moment, she seemed to have put the incident that occurred on the mountain, Buster's shooting, behind her.

They shared the broth, tipping the kettle into their coffee cups until not a drop remained. Pushing away from the table, Jake asked, "I wonder what kind of meat that was?"

"It is a cultural recipe, my friend. It might be impolite to ask," said José soberly, lifting his sombrero from a nearby chair and turning toward the door, hoping it seemed, that the topic might disappear.

"That reprobate was no Seneca," Jake protested innocently, reaching for his friend's arm.

Altimera halted and tried again patiently to explain to Jake. "Don't tell him that. It would be well not to ask." He cast his eyes suggestively in Sarah's direction.

Seeing the implication, Sarah blanched and raised a hand to her mouth. She took a deep breath, forced herself to stand straight and shrugged off her surprise and distress with obvious effort.

"Oh," Jake said, too late.

"Marvelous," muttered Altimera under his breath as they made their way among a scattering of early diners. "Too much curiosity spoils a perfectly good meal."

"That was certainly an uncomfortable moment," Jake said to no one in particular, once outside. "I really put my foot in it, didn't I?"

Sarah was smiling now, "You big, insensitive oaf."

Altimera guided them to a space between the Seneca Fire Pit and the building next door where they could talk privately out of the sun and out of the bustle of the crowded walk.

Altimera spoke so quietly that Sarah was forced to lean forward to hear. "It's your money Compadre," the Mexican said. "Why don't you make the deposit and set up the reward fund. I'll talk to your friend, Colt, about printing the posters and maybe we can flush this bad hombre out from under whichever rock he hides."

This was the whole purpose for their journey to Bodic. Jake knew that a crime must be reported for it to be known, and the size of the reward he posted meant that it was a serious crime. A $2,000 reward created a lot of credibility. At last, the murder of his friends would be in the open and no longer a community secret of the town of Nazareth. Even without bodics, the murder would be accepted as truth.

As one they stepped from the shadows of the alley up onto the creaking boards of the walk. Jake felt a familiar chill despite the bruising heat of the sun. He touched Altimera's gun arm lightly. "We are watched, my friend. Before we got here, I felt it. Now I feel it again. Walk with care."

"Si, amigo." Altimera glanced carefully both ways before stepping into the street.

While Jake continued to scan the busy street, Altimera crossed in front of a long wagon and strode slightly uphill on a graveled path between two buildings. Jake searched for anyone who appeared too curious. Even off the main street the walks were crowded. Lifting his gaze he saw the low white building at the next intersection with the I.O.O.F. emblazoned on the sign, a landmark in Bodie. Though he knew little of the organization, he believed these were some of the good people. Odd title to join up under, he thought. Odd Fellows. Maybe I just don't understand.

Many men who followed the easy prosperity of new gold were shiftless, and worse. Today he saw much cause for suspicion but nothing that shouted outright danger.

Looking left again he saw a boot heel and pant leg disappear into an alley up the street. "Step into the Seneca," he whispered urgently to Sarah, "Hurry!"

Jake spun and dashed up the crowded boardwalk, creating a commotion and drawing more than one curse. Entering the alley, he crouched low against the opposite wall, while his eyes adjusted to the gloom trapped between the buildings.

Gun drawn, he waited, listening. Whoever owned that pant leg entered the alley and left the other end very quickly. Jake imagined a dozen logical reasons for the disappearance but believed none of them. The combination of his internal warnings and the disappearing pant leg were too real for him. Hair on his neck and arms rippled electrically.

Reluctantly holstering the Remington, Jake stood with a mixture of disgust and disappointment. Whoever watched, whoever ran, was too far ahead now for him to catch. Jake knew he and Sarah would be at the mercy of this stalker until the man exposed himself again by running or a direct challenge. The thought produced little comfort. Looking one more time toward the end of the alley, he kicked at the trash littering the ground in frustration.

There in the dirt lay a large, domed, silver button, big as a half dollar, the same kind that Mexicans often used to decorate their chaps. It hadn't been there long, because it still retained the luster of care and wear. Jake bent to pick it up. Had this belonged to the watcher? Slim chance but who knows, he thought, putting the button in his pocket.

Easing his way among the afternoon strollers, Jake stepped into the street and dodged horses and wagons, making his way again to the front of the Seneca where Sarah waited.

"I thought you would be inside," he challenged her over-loudly, his frustration bubbling over.

She reached down and calmly slipped the rawhide loop over his gun hammer. The woman knew him too well, he fumed inwardly. "You just have to be in the middle of everything, don't you?"

"I worry about you, Jake Honey," she cupped her hand around the back of his neck, looking intently into his eyes. "More than you need to worry about me. After all, you're the one with all the bullet holes. Let me take care of you for a change."

"That's not the way it's supposed to work. You're pregnant! I should be protecting you," he tried to growl at her. Jake knew he would lose any argument with Sarah. Too much time in the company of horses left him ill-equipped for a contest of wills with this woman. Smiling his resignation, he gently removed her hand from his neck and pointed her down the street away from the alley and toward the bank.

"If you persist in exposing yourself to danger," said Jake, "you should carry that little pistol at the very least."

By way of answer she nearly bumped him off the walk shoving her hip against his leg. Jake felt the hard shape of her small Remington and glancing down, noticed that she had shoved the entire holster into the large side pocket of her blue canvas trousers.

"Oh," he mumbled lamely.

"I watched your back for you, husband," she said accusingly. "This obsolete little pistol of mine helped us one time already. You might speak more appreciatively to me in the future."

"You're right, of course," Jake mumbled, feeling very small. "I was just thinking how you were sure to win any argument so I thought to prevail by ignoring you, and you come out on top anyway."

"You're lucky I love you," said Sarah. "That alone assures you of a place in my life, no matter if you're right, wrong, win or lose." She moved closer, hooking his elbow with her arm as they walked the uneven boards, letting her shoulder catch the hollow of Jake's right armpit. Moving his arm to her opposite shoulder, he pulled her to himself in a brief walking hug.

Jake felt warm all over, their immediate predicament eclipsed by her show of affection. He knew Sarah loved him but still he had a difficult time believing it. She had a way of making him feel small and big again without breaking stride. How did he live before meeting this woman, he wondered? Those were sure lonely times.

∃⚏∃

The Antelope Bank was the only brick building on the street. Two carved speckled granite steps rose off the boards to an elaborately framed double door set deeply into the corner of the building. No hitch rails stood before the structure and wide glass windows permitted any passerby to observe what transpired inside.

"Smart," thought Jake out loud. This bank cannot be robbed behind closed doors. He guided Sarah up the steps, holding her arm, and glancing once over his shoulder. Just inside the door, he dropped his hat back on its chinstrap to hang between his shoulder blades, thinking the hole in the crown might not be so easily noticed behind his back.

Banks always had a way of making Jake feel like he needed a bath and a change of clothes, at least a new hat. A person doesn't recover so quickly from being killed and buried that he begins to feel clean enough to enter a bank anytime soon. He patted his vest pocket and felt the reassuring bulge of paperwork. Altimera had earlier obtained a letter of credit from his bank in Colorado to insure the funds.

Two windows with wooden bars broke the paneled wall in front of them. Men stood before each, so Jake moved to the shortest one, standing patiently with Sarah on his arm. The transaction at the teller's window in front of them had ended and the clerk continued to converse with the miner, casting an occasional glance over the man's shoulder in Jake's direction. Jake suspected disapproval in the man.

When he saw the little man's eyes flick to Sarah and light up, he knew for sure. This hombre is too quick to judge others, he thought, his mouth forming a thoughtful frown.

"Perhaps another bank would better appreciate my deposit," Jake observed half aloud to his wife.

"Not at all, sir," said the teller, quickly recovering his poise. "Until next time then, Mr. Blackstone," he touched his eyeshade in salute and turned his full attention to Jake and Sarah.

Stepping up to the window, Jake reluctantly unwrapped the papers from their oilskins and shoved them under the bars of the window.

As he read the letter of credit, the clerk glanced over his wire-rimmed glasses at Jake with new respect. When he returned his attention to the second sheet, he whistled low in appreciation of the size of the reward.

"Marshal McKenzie will take charge of the …" Jake never got a chance to finish. His instructions were interrupted by a shrill warning from his woman.

"Jake!"

Palming a gun, Jake spun and crouched against the wooden teller's cage. He felt and heard the blast of Sarah's gun behind him as the wood next to his cheek exploded into a fistful of flying splinters. He saw the gunman in the doorway cranking furiously at his rifle's loading lever, obviously nonplused at having a sure thing spoiled by a woman's handgun. Sarah fired a second time, only a heartbeat behind Jake's shot, both shots dusting the center of the gunman's shirt.

The young man froze briefly, then collapsed backward against the door jamb, the rifle sagging heavily in his grip as his sky blue eyes glazed over. He slid to the floor and fell onto his face with a distinctive thump. Abstractly Jake noticed two exit wounds within a couple of inches of each other in his leather vest, between his shoulder blades.

The worn shotgun chaps and beat up gray hat of the man were too familiar. Jake remembered the two cowboys standing outside the Livery in Nazareth. It wasn't over yet, he realized. The young Mackinaws had played a card and one brother yet remained.

Shoving Sarah forcefully to one side, Jake moved toward the door even as one big window beside him exploded inward!

Merely curious at first, people on the street now dove for cover wherever they could find it in doorways or behind wagons and horse troughs. The second gunman stood alone on the walk directly across the street, powder smoke trailing away in a light breeze.

The rifleman fired again from the hip, the slug striking the sill just below the ruined window directly in front of Jake.

The range was long for a handgun but Jake had little choice. "Make him duck," he yelled. "Maybe we'll get lucky." He fired once, and drawing his left hand pistol, fired again. Dust and splinters flew from the wall behind the man, causing his third shot to go completely wild.

Jake stepped behind the brick column separating the two windows and used his gun barrel to strike the remaining glass from the frame for a better shot.

Now the rifleman found himself in the open, dueling with a man behind cover. Whatever advantage the rifle provided initially was gone. The Mackinaw levered and fired as fast as he could, throwing one slug after another at Jake's position. As he moved to his left, a single shot from the end of the room struck the rifleman in the left thigh, halfway between the knee and the hip. His leg folded under him, sending his next shot into the dust of the street as he fell forward.

Jake stepped from behind his bricks and fired one shot after another at the wounded man, striking him finally in one ear as he struggled to rise, painting the boards behind him bright red. Even at fifty yards, Jake new the wound was fatal. The gunman fell forward again on top of his smoking rifle with an arm cocked awkwardly under his armpit, one elbow pointing into the air over his back.

Gunsmoke moved sluggishly in layers about the room and snaked in broken tendrils through the shattered front window as the breeze in the street sucked it slowly outwards. Glass fragments crunched noisily under Jake's moccasins as he turned toward Sarah at the end of the room.

She crouched frozen over the sill of the bank window, her nickel-plated revolver hanging limply in her hand, her eyes fixed on the spreading pool of gore leaking from the first rifleman near the door.

Heads rose slowly here and there behind furniture as people realized the shooting had ended. Jake counted six bullet scars in the front of the teller cage where he had stood.

"You all right back there, Partner?" Jake asked, worry in his voice. Glasses askew and hair mussed, the teller's head rose nose high above the counter.

"Thick wood," he said. "God bless the owner for thinking ahead. Fact is, we have extra windows downstairs also." The man picked up Jake's paperwork and tipped it forward, letting the glass and wood fragments slide onto the counter.

"Are those the fellas you was after?" he asked shakily, peering between the bars at the carnage in the bank lobby.

"Unfortunately," Jake replied, "those men were grudge fighters. I'm sure of that. They're not the men I'm looking for."

"You got yourself a genuine situation, Mr. Tallon. It's a good thing you got help." He looked over at Sarah, who stood slightly behind Jake and leaned her forehead against the back of his shoulder, holding onto his arm and breathing unsteadily.

He knew how she felt. Jake also was upset by the violence, something that those who did not know him would not have guessed. He put his right hand over her two smaller ones on his biceps and felt great pride. This encounter had not been only one shot. It was a gun battle with shots flying both ways, a situation difficult for the bravest of men.

It must have been all she could do to keep her head up and keep shooting. He knew he owed his life to her watchfulness and bravery, yet again. Jake moved her hands and encircled her shoulders with his arm. She leaned in against him, staring vacantly.

"I need to get Sarah away from this, sir. Can you handle the money transfer?" Jake asked. "And take this." Jake handed over a bandanna with fifteen hundred dollars given up by the Bushwhackers in Colorado. "Just wire my account in Cumberland Crossings for the difference."

"Yes, Sir." The clerk straightened his glasses and used his fingers to brush at his mussed hair. "If I have any questions, I'll talk to Marshal McKenzie."

"Fine by me," Jake turned away from the window, guiding Sarah to the door and out onto the street where she took her first deep breath. Color seemed to flood back into her skin as he watched.

From the alley across the way ran a concerned José Altimera with Colt McKenzie close behind.

"Who was doing all the shootin'?" asked the tall, broad shouldered Marshal, his face gone cold and humorless.

"They did most of it," said Jake. "They also did all the missing." Jake saw a twinkle bloom again in McKenzie's eye.

"Shore do leave a mess behind you, don't you, young Mr. Tallon?" the Marshal put hands to hips, in mock disapproval.

"Sometimes."

Two of Colt's Deputies appeared through the same alley just used by Colt.

"See what you can find out about those two," McKenzie indicated the motionless forms.

Leaning Sarah against the wall, Jake glanced to Altimera pleadingly, then seeing his response, followed a Deputy to the body of the man with the chaps near the bank's door. "I don't think I'll be surprised by what we find. Please let me have a look," he stepped around Colt's Deputy, gently using his hands on the stocky man's arms to guide him to one side.

Kneeling, he put his hands under the armpits of the corpse and straightened it out. This action had the unforeseen consequence of dropping the body full into the puddle of its own gore. Jake grimaced. "Sorry," he apologized more to the Deputy than the body. The Deputy would likely have to clean up when they were done. A fancy-dressing McKenzie was unlikely to dirty his own hands, Jake thought wryly.

Rolling the body onto its back, Jake looked into a younger version of the man he killed with the staff in the clearing on the mountain so long ago. One of Bingo's brothers, sure enough. Looking down the right leg, he found the third button missing from the chaps.

Jake reached into his pocket and removed the button he found in the alley. Placing it over the missing spot, Jake saw that it was a perfect match with the others.

"There's one small mystery don't need solving any longer. We don't need the identity of these men," Jake said to a towering Colt McKenzie.

"Why's that Jake?" asked the Lawman.

"These are grudge fighters, the last of the Mackinaws."

"Heard that story," McKenzie smiled. "Seems they were less handy than the older brother."

"It just wasn't a fair fight," Jake looked at a recovering Sarah. "I had my woman watching my back."

She smiled brightly for the first time since the screamed warning and quickly wiped a single vagrant tear rolling down her cheek.

Lazlo's Undoing

Big as he was, the Mayor ate sparingly. Long ago he learned a person could eat as much as they wanted if he worked for a living and that's no longer what he did.

Eyes locked on the empty space above his plate, he remembered his time on the big city docks with fondness, smiling.

His experience hadn't started out happily. Thousands of immigrants, fleeing hardship and poverty, flooded into New York from Europe only to find more of the same. His parents died of a fever the winter he turned seventeen and he spent February hiding in an alley, covering himself with garbage to stay warm. Never again, he promised himself.

Waiting outside a bar, he smashed the head of a drunken laborer and stole his clean clothes. The following morning he got in line for jobs unloading ships.

Young and strong, Zachary came early to the understanding that not everyone played with a full deck, and decided he could use that knowledge to his own advantage. People were too trusting, by far. Starting small, he gained favor with the foreman. In a few short months he was the foreman himself. Labor was something done by others, by the ignorant.

Within a handful of years he ran the docks and graduated from character assassination to actual murder. Eventually the trail of bodies led right to his door. Big Bill Zachary learned an important lesson, two actually.

He learned there is a limit to how far a person can take advantage of others without trading something back, and he learned that when it all finally falls apart, you cut and run. Slowly his head rose and fell, savoring the familiar wisdom. There are some things I must never forget.

Zachary chewed slowly, thoughtfully. Planning ahead was a skill he learned early, so when the time came to run he lost only a fraction of his accumulated wealth when he pulled stakes and came west.

They looked for him, they did, but in all the wrong places. He joined a railroad work gang headed west to finish the iron road, linking the coasts. Since the laborers were mostly immigrants, Bill learned to fit right in, picking up the old accents, joining in the common banter. His body responded to the rough life, slimming down and toughening up. He felt fierce and proud as a young bull, like he had been in his youth.

As the road inched toward California, Bill saw opportunity in the rush for gold in the northern Sierras. Many of the early fields had already played out, but enterprising men continued to dig wealth from the earth. New strikes came in all the time.

Big Bill never thought to dig for himself but rather to use the cleverness of others, much as he had done on the New York Waterfront. California was a new land with teeming masses of people just like himself, looking for a fresh start and a new name.

Big Bill dropped his fork with a clatter. Stanislaus Borinsky had become a forgotten man. That thought troubled him. Even Borinsky was a created name, made grander over time as Zachary invented a more noteworthy history. His beginnings may have been fraudulent, not so the present. Nazareth was real, he told himself. It was real and it was now. His accomplishments in Nazareth made him proud.

He clenched his huge beefy hands into fists, staring into space, a tiny doubt nibbling away at the dream. Jake Tallon would not go away and Johnny Lobo continued to live. That damned big Indian, Night Walker, reminded him constantly of his failings whenever Zachary saw him standing in the shade, staring silently, accusingly, as the Mayor walked about his business. Anger and frustration bubbled over, causing him to forget his food.

They would be dealt with in their time, he thought resolutely.

Bill Zachary picked up his fork and focused on his plate once again. Calming his breathing, he forced himself to cut and lift a piece of meat mechanically to his mouth. This was as hard as he worked these days. Without hard work, food went to fat.

Food allowed him some pleasure in the face of the storm clouds that gathered on his own horizon. He pictured the delicacies he'd once experienced in cities back East, exotic vegetables, sauces, glazes, spices, fish eggs and bakery items.

The Mayor had a good memory, but these tasty images left him dissatisfied. If a person desired something special in this remote country, he thought with distaste, he'd have to go kill it himself. Most foods he really desired were simply not available. This disgusting cafe passed for luxury on the eastern slopes of the California Sierras. Probably as good as anything to be found in Bodie. The help dressed up fancy but the food was not that good. Maybe I'll buy a chef and set him up, thought Big Bill, his spirits momentarily lifting.

Glancing up, the Mayor watched a shadow cross the large windows at the front of the building, heading toward the front doors. Zachary heard a whispered conversation with the proprietor and then the heavy, hurried footsteps across the worn floorboards approaching his private booth. He knew the footsteps as those belonging to the seedy Sheriff, Vernon Laszlo. Unbidden to his mind came the moving picture of the man's slouching gait.

"You're interrupting my lunch, Laszlo," he said to the presence now shadowing his table. "I hope it's important." So confident was he, that Zachary never even looked up to confirm his guess.

The Sheriff hated the Mayor. Zachary saw it in his eyes as the lawman stepped around the partition. He'd known the Sheriff's feeling but cared not a whit as long as the man did his job the way Zachary wanted.

When that changed the Sheriff would be replaced by someone better. No feelings involved. That's just the way it worked.

"Well?" prompted the Mayor.

"I wouldn't stir m'sef during the heat of the day less I figured it'd get your blood in an uproar, Zachary."

"Sit," the Mayor commanded. "What's so important it deserved my immediate attention?"

The Sheriff took off his hat as he sat and motioned with irritation to the waitress for an extra cup. "Looks like the last of the Mackinaw Brothers is comin' home in boxes."

"Ha!" exclaimed the Mayor before sipping at his coffee. "Are they as messed up as Bingo?"

"Just holes so far as I know, Mayor."

"This is lukewarm," Big Bill complained to the waitress as she brought the cup for Laszlo.

"I'll get you a fresh pot straight away, Mr. Mayor." She hurried toward the kitchen with the offending vessel.

"How'd they get themselves killed?" Big Bill asked, bending toward his plate with a utensil in either hand.

"Seems like they started out right enough. They set up a crossfire when Tallon went into the Antelope Bank, but some woman saw Jesse's rifle and banged off a couple of shots to spoil his aim."

The Mayor looked up with sudden interest. "Some woman sprung the trap early? What kind of woman carries a handgun anyway?"

"Lots! This ain't like back East, Mayor. Women get respect in the West but much of it's because they also pack iron." The Sheriff shook his head knowingly. "If they don't pack it themselves, they all know someone who does."

"Like Lobo," the Mayor pretended disinterest but his comment was prime bait. It worked.

"Look here, Mayor. I don't take that …"

"Simmer down," interrupted Zachary, inwardly satisfied. "You can't do your job if you can't keep control of your temper. I didn't mean anything anyway," he soothed. As a boy he'd seen a man with a yo-yo spin it down, pull it back. A yo-yo, just like this Sheriff. Zachary found private pleasure in the torment of others.

The Sheriff settled back into his seat with a vague suspicion of the Mayor's insincerity.

"That man's too lucky," the Mayor pushed his plate away with sudden exasperation. "Did they get lead into him at all?"

"Not by all reports. Lobo came the closest of anyone I ever heard of puttin' Tallon down permanent."

"And you shot Lobo up too bad to be of any use to us. Over a woman," accused the Mayor.

"The man had it comin'," hissed the Sheriff through his limply hanging mustache.

The poison in the Sheriff's reply made the Mayor smile. "You're evil, Laszlo, and I love ya for it."

Both sat silently, each lost in his own thoughts for long moments.

"You don't suppose that was his wife with the gun, do you?" asked the Mayor.

"Makes sense to me but the third man didn't know her by sight."

"Only thing will work for that man is stick a gun in his mouth and pull the trigger," said the Sheriff.

"Or use a shotgun," suggested the Mayor.

"Or stick the shotgun in his mouth."

"You may have something there," said Big Bill Zachary, putting both heavy forearms on the table in front of him. "Who do you know could do something like that? Nothin' fancy, just close-up killin'."

"You're right there, Mayor. That's how things got screwed up every time. Too many people and complicated plans." Laszlo thought again, studiously tilting his head of unruly gray hair to one side.

"The Breed could do the job, if you paid him enough."

"Whiskey isn't enough for him anymore?" the Mayor narrowed his eyes to emphasize the question.

"The Breed's not stupid. He sees the list of your bullyboys getting shorter just like you 'n me. He'll ask for whiskey as well as money." The Sheriff was busy calculating exactly how much he'd ask of the Mayor and how much he'd actually give the killer.

"Five hundred bucks otta do it," he said, thinking he'd only have to give the Breed a hundred and he could put the rest in his retirement fund. Laszlo was on the downhill side of life now. His knees and hips hurt too much to ride for a living. The Mayor had given him a steady source of easy money for the last half dozen years and he'd managed to set some aside. He figured, he only needed a little more.

Laszlo didn't start out as an evil man but years with the Mayor had taken their toll. It had been a long time since people stopped him on the street just to chat. The mirror showed him a man with a mouth gone hard and eyes grown cold. Laszlo didn't know that man anymore. How could he find the way back? Shooting Lobo was something he would never have done ten years ago, for any reason, much less a woman.

Nodding to the Mayor, he pushed back his chair to leave. The Mayor picked at his teeth industriously with a matchstick. He won't even notice I'm gone, Laszlo thought, picking up his hat and leaving through the door by which he entered. Gotta get free of that bone-picking buzzard, he cursed to himself.

Talking with the Mayor left Laszlo in no mood for the company of other people, but then the Breed wasn't really people. He was a disease waiting for someone upon whom he might inflict himself. Laszlo didn't want to be the Breed's next target, so he mostly kept his distance from the man. No one seemed to know where he came from and the Breed never spoke of it to anyone now alive.

Why folks called him the Breed, Laszlo never understood. He wasn't half white; he just didn't really belong anywhere. No tribe of his own, Laszlo guessed, certainly no friends. Maybe he was half evil.

If he had any money he'd be behind the saloon drinking it up or in the loft above the Livery sleeping it off. Unlike most drunks, he didn't beg. The Breed had pride and industry. Give him a sharp stick and he hunted food. Problem with the Breed was that he'd eat most anything.

Laszlo shuddered. He'd heard stories he didn't want to believe or recall. The Sheriff's queasiness only made the Indian smile when confronted with questions of his diet.

Laszlo didn't remember leaving the cafe. He'd been too preoccupied with disgust for the object of his search. Next thing he realized he was stepping into the alley next to the saloon. At different places old bottles, refuse and rotting garbage collected against the building, hip-deep like snowdrifts. The oppressive heat did nothing to diminish the smell. His mind on the Breed as it was, he forgot to hold his breath and nearly gagged as he inhaled.

Stinking garbage drifts, he chuckled. What this place needs is a good fire. Of course, that's a danger also, he thought more seriously. The town was a tinderbox of explosively dry wood.

If someone keeled over back here right now, we'd never find the body amid all the trash. Never find it by the smell. Might be one under one of these piles right now, he mused.

The Sheriff stood hands on hips, surveying the back lot. Tufts of grass and occasional brush grew between the piles of garbage. I'll have a chat with Barnaby Rufus, Laszlo promised himself.

Don't nobody in this town have a regular name, he wondered, shaking his head. Of course, there's Zachary but he knew for sure that name was made-up. The Mayor was too slimy to have kept the same name all his life.

Like the devil, he thought, who had so many names. Satan, Lucifer, Beelzebub or the Beast. A man like Zachary kept a name until it was so weighted down with sin, he was forced to give it up for a fresh one.

The sun hit Laszlo like a hot slap in the face as he walked out the end of the alley. "Jésus," he cursed, wiping at his clothes, "I hope this stink comes off." He looked all around in the brightness of the noon sun and saw no living thing among the weeds or the trash that littered the yard behind the saloon. Laszlo walked to the arroyo that ran across the back of the yard and all up and down the length of the town parallel to the main street. He kicked at a clump of dead grass uprooting it with the toe of his boot.

No bodies here, that much he could see.

That was good news. This is where they'd be if there were any. The bad news was no Breed either. Hadn't run out of options yet but it only got harder if he wasn't found here. The Sheriff mounted the two stairs at the back of the saloon and shouldered his way through the heavy door with the sound of protesting hinges. In contrast to the yard and alley, the back room of the saloon was the picture of neatness and organization. Crates and boxes climbed to the ceiling in orderly rows.

A sudden motion in the shadows made him claw for his gun in panic. Gus the bar cat sauntered without concern into a downward slashing beam of light from the high windows.

"Whew," the Sheriff exhaled. "I ain't a young man no more." He gingerly lowered the hammer on the Colt and dropped it back into leather. Suddenly, like a splash of cold water across the face, the Sheriff realized, "I ain't gonna get any older neither, if I don't get shut of this town." He shook himself physically free of the feeling and reached for the iron knob on the door that opened into the area just behind the bar. Stepping through the portal, he turned smoothly to close it behind him.

"Barnaby!" he yelled without looking up, knowing the proprietor would never be far from his cash box. He didn't expect a response so much. Saying the name out loud was more of an announcement of his arrival than anything else. He was also thinking of the ten-gauge scattergun Barnaby kept under the counter. The man loads that thing with carpet tacks, Laszlo thought, scares the hell outta me.

When Laszlo looked around he saw Barnaby cozy the "sawed off" back into its niche next to the cash box. The Sheriff smiled to himself. Couldn't have been more right!

"Want a beer, Sheriff?" the white-aproned, sleeve-gartered proprietor offered.

"Shore do, if'n it's cold," Laszlo responded automatically, then remembered how, with uncommon inspiration, Barnaby had dug his cellar for a fifteen foot deep ice cave before the saloon was built and run a thaw drain out to the arroyo behind the place. That hole was likely a spring at some point in its history. The far-seeing Saloon Keeper only widened it at the bottom to fit the perfect image he had in his mind.

It snowed thirty feet deep here in the winters, so ice was no problem. It was storing it for the long hot summers what made Barnaby a lot of money.

"God built that sink hole for me," Barnaby said when he saw the gapping hole in the middle of the lot. No one else had the foresight to use it in exactly that way. At the time, Big Bill Zachary thought the man a fool for buying a lot so badly flawed. He let it go cheap, something he lamented frequently afterwards.

The Sheriff sipped at the cool, bitter liquid, appreciating Barnaby's surprising foresight. "People come for miles to get one of these," he pointed out.

"I know," Barnaby nodded smugly, "That's the idea."

"I want you to clean out your alley and backyard," Laszlo interrupted his gloating. "They're a fire hazard."

The change of topic shocked Barnaby profoundly. "Why do you care anyway, Laszlo?" Defiance flavored Barnaby's response.

"The first name's Sheriff! And it's a hazard, is why. One of your customers could fall unconscious and die back there. That brush is so high, we'd never know. I may start a fire there myself if I don't see it improve shortly," he threatened.

"You were never interested in that kind of thing before."

"I know! Something's changing. Maybe I'm just getting older." Laszlo shifted his weight from one elbow to the other on the bar top. Absorbed in his own problems, the Saloon Keeper's upset was lost upon the Sheriff. "Why don't you push it all down into the arroyo and burn it? You might have to clear some brush from the edges to keep it from getting away from you."

Barnaby regarded the Sheriff with wide-eyed wonder. "You're gettin' pretty civic-minded for a cranky old lawman."

"Maybe I just want Nazareth to be a real town, instead of a pretend town." Laszlo rotated the glass in a pool of its own condensation. "Have you seen the Breed?" Laszlo wanted a different topic as well as the information.

"Not really." Barnaby blinked several times, adjusting to the new request. "If the man doesn't have a bottle in his hand, he drifts like a shadow. If you're looking for him, chances are he'll find you first. He's spooky that way."

"I know," Laszlo squirmed. "Gives me the creeps."

Half an hour passed, along with the hottest part of the day. Barnaby never offered another free beer so Laszlo pushed himself resentfully away from the bar and walked loose-jointed toward the bat wings.

Several men had entered the bar while he drank. They regarded him with shaded eyes as he passed on his way to the door. Makes a man feel like a stranger, Laszlo mused, always on the outside. That's not a good way to live. Gotta get shy of this place, he thought yet again.

Pushing against the tall, dry frame of the door, he stepped sideways through the opening onto the deserted boardwalk. Laszlo settled the hat onto his head with one hand fore and one aft. Startled, he found himself staring into the smoldering coal-black eyes of Malvado, the Breed, as the man slouched contemptuously against the awning support.

"How ya doing, Mal?" Laszlo did his best to hide the upset he felt.

"You're not my friend, Laszlo." Standing away from the post, the Indian folded his arms belligerently across his glistening chest. "Don't be using any cute 'nick-names' on me either. It's Malvado," he drew out each syllable of his name. "You can even call me Breed. That's okay too."

Malvado did not say, "or I'll kill you," but the implied threat made Laszlo's flesh go goose bumps all over. "What's the name mean?" he tried to sound conversational as he stepped into the sun beside the Breed.

"It means Death." Malvado seemed to enjoy the answer, lingering overlong on the "th" sound at the end of the word, savoring his obvious contempt for the White Man before him.

"Figured as much." With effort, Laszlo tore his eyes from the hypnotizing gaze of the creature before him and looked down the street with what he hoped was a casual posture.

"You got work for me? That's why I'm here."

"How'd you find out?"

"I know is all. You don't need a better answer. You wouldn't understand if I told you."

If he could find a way to safely kill this man, Laszlo knew he'd do the whole town a favor. Maybe the entire territory. The Breed wore no visible weapon other than a big-bladed knife. He dressed mostly Injun in leather pants and breach clout, yet he wore the threat of instant violence like a velvet shroud hanging in generous folds from 'round his shoulders. He drank behind the saloon because he preferred solitude, not because Barnaby asked him to do so. No one Laszlo knew had the nerve to deny Malvado a seat at the table if he really wanted one.

"You know Jake Tallon?"

"Yeah, I know him. Seen him before too. Bad man to cross. Big Medicine. Ver' Big Medicine."

"Folks say you're not good enough to take him," Laszlo let that statement sit alone out in the open. He picked at his teeth.

Malvado smiled thinly. Laszlo fooled no one with his childish taunt, but he felt boxed by the big Sheriff nonetheless.

"Sure, I can take him, only not so easy as most White Man. I become his shadow. Steal his Medicine. It takes time is all."

"It's worth a hundred bucks."

"Two!" Malvado didn't miss a heartbeat, "And two cases of good whiskey. Not that cheap stuff they sell to other Indians."

Laszlo blanched. "You'll drink yourself to death before you kill Tallon."

"I'm not that stupid, Laszlo. He will eat steel before I drink the whiskey. That's the way you want it, don't you?" Malvado rasped a callused thumb across the bright edge of a naked blade.

Where'd that come from, Laszlo shuddered, staring helplessly at the shimmering metal. The Breed sure knew how to create an impression.

"Give me fifty now."

Laszlo fished in his pants pocket for a couple of double eagles. Pulling them out, he counted three into the Breed's outstretched palm.

"He killed the Mackinaw Brothers," said the Indian.

"Yeah, I hear he did."

"I told them, the Mackinaws," clarified the Breed. "They did not understand Medicine. They not listen to Malvado." The Killer wiped unconsciously at his nose with the back of his hand.

"What you gonna do so different?" Laszlo really wanted to know.

The Breed's contemptuous gaze struck the Sheriff with near physical impact. Laszlo shrunk back a half step. Leaning forward into the lawman's face, Malvado said, "You do not need to know, Sher-rifff, but when I'm done I will give you his eyes. If Tallon comes back one more time from the Spirit Lodge, he will be blind."

"G-Good plan," stuttered the lawman. Laszlo understood this time. His stomach turned over. He tried his best not to show it, but his mouth twitched anyway. He couldn't say what he wished, for he feared the blade too much himself. "Fine," he muttered, "I'll see you later." Laszlo turned on a heel.

Behind him he heard, "Maybe. Maybe not."

"Crap," he muttered real low. In spite of the blistering heat, Laszlo wrapped both arms around his thin torso. Gratefully, he walked into the full sun, letting the intense heat soak down through his shirt to his skin.

Something was changing in Nazareth. It was only conversation with Barnaby but something real had happened. He couldn't put his finger on it precisely. Losing half the town's bad men over the course of the summer was part of it, Laszlo knew. Was it just the change of faces? They got replaced as fast as they were lost, but it created ripples of doubt he could feel as he walked slowly down the street.

Laszlo thought it might be Tallon himself, undermining Zachary's authority as Tallon killed or crippled each assassin sent after him. Yeah! The final authority is the last man standing; he scowled with one side of his mouth. Code of the West. That's changin' too.

Jake Tallon was widely known as a reasonable person until riled. He didn't come on like a tough man. But once angered, he just kept on coming and wouldn't be stopped. He did something in Bodie that was sure to have a big effect. He made a reward for information. In his mind the Sheriff saw an hourglass turned over. The sand in the top was finite. Eventually there would be no more sand, no more time. That's what had changed. Tallon unstopped, represented the end of all of Zachary's scheming.

Somewhere deep down, the Sheriff wondered if indeed the Breed could cut the mustard this time and he was not sure he would enjoy informing the Mayor of another failure when that happened. No, that wasn't it. The Mayor didn't scare him so much as more like make him feel dirty, real dirty. He'd been thinking about a bath since seeing Big Bill over his lunch. He couldn't put it off no more.

Firelight

"It was all so fast," she said, "and so sudden." Sodden-faced, Sarah Tallon stared into the fire, red-rimmed eyes blank. "So much shooting!"

"I'm sorry you had to go through that gunfight, Sarah," said Jake, truly concerned but confused. How does a person deal with the onslaught of conscience after violence? The conscience is right after all. It's wrong to shoot at people. Now she's had to go through this twice with hardly a break in between!

Jake understood life and death struggle. Years of surviving such conflict had taught him how to cope with the aftermath. Jake also remembered that the first killing weighed upon him for years. Only recently had he put it into perspective. Only recently had he understood and forgiven himself. That was Man Above's doin', he realized.

Comprehending her dilemma and the process still left him no closer to helping her. If anything he ached with sympathy but felt unable to reach out to her. Sarah had been the sweet link that brought him back to a world broader than anger and revenge. Now she needed time, and she needed his patient understanding … once again. Hooking his thumbs in his belt, Jake allowed his feet to lead him in a relaxed circle of the small camp.

His restlessness brought him eventually to a point directly across the fire from Sarah. He watched her agony, as flames danced in between the two of them, periodically obscuring her features. How strangely the fire is symbolic of her torment, he thought, as the silence weighed like a rock between them.

Jake cast his glance into the darkness of the peaceful desert on the road between Bodie and Nazareth. The violence of the Main Street shoot-out seemed at odds with the softness of the velvet night. Insects clicked and sung in the sage all around them. Somewhere beyond the firelight, Altimera prowled the dry landscape, giving Jake privacy to heal Sarah's shock.

Yet, Jake felt awkward. "I thought for sure, Sarah, that time on the mountain would be all the violence you'd ever need go through. No one wants what happened to us today at the bank. Most folks never have to shoot at each other," Jake said half to himself as he finished circling the fire. "I've been through it before, more times than I care to remember. The shock value is gone now but it seems to get no easier. I hate the blood. I hate it worse when you have to see it.

"What right-thinking man would put his wife through anything of the sort, Sarah, much less his wife who is pregnant with their first child! I should put you into a convent!"

The lines in Sarah's face softened as he spoke. She glanced up at Jake, as he stood again beside her, and sniffed. Maybe he was helping after all. Gently, Jake stroked her hair, her shoulder. "Yeah! There's the ticket, Sarah. I'll put you in a convent, where you'll be safe!"

"I don't think a convent will work, Jacob. I'm not that kind of girl." Sarah spoke for the first time in a flat, tired voice. "I would be very uncomfortable there."

"The first part is certainly true. And I'm glad you're the way you are. Sometimes, I just have a hard time figuring out just what that is."

Spontaneously, Jake knelt and looked directly into her face. "You did well, Honey, in spite of being so very terrified."

Jake's words had soothed her. Sarah stared dry-eyed into the middle distance but was now relaxed enough to lean back against him. Looking down, he saw her chest expand with a deep relaxing breath.

"Today you became a hero, Sarah. You saved the life of another person." As he spoke, Jake felt more than saw the spectral figure of Shantee, watching, approving.

"Why do you haunt me, Old Man?" he focused his frustration on the standing figure.

Shantee smiled gently back at Jake. "I've always been around, Jacob. You have only recently learned to notice."

"Where were you this afternoon?" Jake couldn't hide a note of bitterness.

"Sarah needed me, Jacob. She did well, as you just told her. You picked a strong-hearted woman."

"Help her now, Old Man," he pled in frustration. "She feels so bad."

Shantee merely smiled his wonderful, knowing smile.

Sarah shook Jake's arm. "What's happening Jake?"

"Can't you see him? Feel him?"

"Him, who?" she asked perplexed.

"Shantee, the Old Man from the Spirit Lodge." Spell broken, Jake looked quickly around the brushless area lit by their fire. The whole thing had happened in his head.

"Where?" she asked, trying to look everywhere at once.

"Over there," he gestured vaguely. "Didn't you hear any of that conversation?"

"Mostly mumbling on your part," Sarah held his arm and looked intently into Jake's face. Her distress had passed just that quickly and easily.

"This is what miracles look like. I guess he did it after all." Jake smiled warmly at his wife.

"What do you mean by that?"

"Man Above said he was with you today, and I was mad at him because you needed him now. I guess he helped you in a way I couldn't predict."

"I was going to be okay eventually," said Sarah. "It's only that the moment in the bank kept coming back on me with the crash of guns and that big pool of blood. It was so loud indoors and I've never seen so much blood. It wasn't like the shooting on the mountain. Then I didn't even feel like I was part of the fight, part of the solution, until I looked down and saw the smoking gun in my hand at the very end."

She went quiet for a moment, thinking. "During the gun fight, I felt oddly at peace. The guns of those men threatened us. I just wanted to stop them any way that I could. It was afterwards that things got so messed up in my head."

"Shantee said he was with you during the fight."

"Ahh," smiled Sarah, "Could be. Do I have to do gun battles to be close to God?"

Jake found himself chuckling at her semi-serious question. He brought a hand up to his nose to help with his composure. "No Sweetie. Though I know he holds special anyone who helps others." In his mind Jake thought about warriors' work because that's what he did. "Mothers are always special to him."

"I know that much," she said irritably, "but now I can do both."

"Both what?" Jake eyes narrowed with concern. He was suddenly worried.

Sarah jumped up and bounded over to her saddlebags, discomforting Jake with her sudden change of mood. "What are you doing, Sarah?"

"I'm gonna load my gun!"

"Good grief," Jake moaned, "What happened to knitting and women's doin's?"

"You like me to reload my gun, remember? Besides, I don't have to knit if I can get store bought goods," she said, "You are my rich husband. You have mucho dinero, Señor Tallon!"

"Throwing Spanish at me now, are you?" Jake covered his eyes with one hand, now frustrated.

Sarah sat again, working industriously over her nickel-plated Remington, with Jake watching over her shoulder. This is how Altimera found them when he walked quietly back into the firelight.

"How are you two lovebirds doing?" he asked softly, hands on his hips.

"She's writing letters to Sam Colt."

"She can't do that! He's dead," objected the Mexican.

"It's more complicated than that," moaned Jake.

⊒⊟⊑

For all her brave show, Sarah remained deeply troubled. She scrubbed and polished at her nickel-plated Remington until it shined brightly by the light of the fire. Finally repacking each chamber with powder, patch and ball, she weighed the deadly instrument deliberatively in both hands.

Sarah understood that Jake owed his life to her help and the little five-shot pistol. But, try as she might, she could not love the gun. Every time she looked at it, Sarah saw the spreading pool of red under the dying gunman in the bank. She saw Buster falling face first into the fire and the rifleman on the street, collapsing under the repeated discharge of her pistol.

She loathed the pistol and everything it stood for. Why not throw it into the brush and be done with it, she asked herself? Unbidden, the answer sprung from the deepest part of her, as she stared blankly into the distance. "Because the mark upon your soul cannot be erased by abandoning the instrument, and your beloved husband will certainly need your help again. You must live with your acts and somehow keep them in perspective."

Still the impulse persisted. With strength of will, she remained seated. Sarah heard Jake and José Altimera, now her friend also, talking lazily just beyond the flames of the campfire. Her heart ached for Jake. Recovering from the head wound had been a miracle adorned with his ongoing pain. He bore it all so courageously.

Placing her hand upon her abdomen, she felt the tiny life it contained moving feebly but consistently. That life needed her protection but she could not see herself raising a baby without Jake. She loved the man with her whole heart and had from their very first meeting.

⊒⊟⊑

Unbidden, that image sprang to mind. A crisp winter day in Sante Fe, Sarah stood upon the boardwalk, billowy dress and heavy, royal blue cape, waiting for her father who had business in the bank. Down the street rode a trail-tattered young man on the biggest saddle horse she'd ever seen, a Grulla, they called them out here. Though gaunt with travel, the mouse-brown horse danced with the energy of a show animal.

Stepping quickly, she arrived at the hitch rail in front of the Livery as the man dismounted. Either he had not noticed her or had the breeding not to stare. Sarah was accustomed to the stares of hot-blooded men. Who was he, she wondered, plainly miffed, that he would not stare?

"Quite a horse, you've got there, Cowboy," Sarah observed, hoping for a conversation.

"I'm no Cowboy," unintended anger spilling into his reply, the young man spun to confront the young woman at whom he could barely avoid gawking.

"Oops," Sarah giggled, holding her dress, moving back a step in mock fear. "Touched a sore point, did I?"

"No! I mean yes," Jake felt the heat rise in his cheeks. "I mean, I'm sorry." He fiddled with the reins held before him in both hands and suddenly remembered to wrap the reins around the hitch rail. Even more consternated, he now had nothing to do with his nervous hands. The horse regarded them both with a wary eye, uttering a low wicker.

"What are you, if you're not a Cowboy?"

The question galvanized the young man. Nervousness sloughed off him like butter from a hot knife. Suddenly clear-eyed and calm, he answered, "I don't know yet."

The change startled Sarah even more than his flashing anger. This was a thinking man. Looking more closely she saw a ridge of white tissue along his right jaw and a raised circular scar like a permanent pimple above his left eyebrow. He wore cross draw guns. Two of them!

"Are you a gunfighter?" she brought a hand to her mouth in pretended horror.

"No Miss, I'm no gunfighter, but I am wondering if you're an actress?" The smile remained but the quality of expression shifted, reflecting some underlying consciousness.

Fascinated, Sarah's artifice dropped away. "I'm no actress," she admitted humbly, knowing that she had severely underestimated the man before her and regretted it.

"I can see that now," the young man observed, no longer defensive. Deliberately correcting his posture, he drew himself to his full height, removed the hat from his head, smoothed his unruly hair with splayed fingers and finally held the hat in both hands before him. "I am Jake Tallon, Miss. I am many things and right now don't have the first idea who you might be as I only now got into town."

"I'm Sarah Anne O'Connell." No longer in haughty control, Sarah hoped only that the opportunity to meet this very interesting man would not slip through her hands because of a thoughtless beginning.

Of course, it didn't. Jake quickly moved from interesting to central in her life and now she had killed to protect him.

Dropping her pistol back into its holster, she lay down where she was and pulled the blanket up snugly around her chin. The sound of voices swelled and faded in the background. Sarah must have slept, for when she opened her eyes only bright coals glowed where the cheery fire had burned before. As she sat upright the heavy blanket fell to her waist. Chill night air nipped at exposed skin where her shirt had pulled free of her trousers as well as her hands and neck. Sarah shivered.

Standing, she tucked her shirt into her pants and buckled a belt left unhooked for comfort in the night. Jake and Altimera snored softly where they lay nearby. From under the corner of Jake's blanket peeked the stock of his Henry Repeater. The omnipresent hardware only served to remind her of the man she had killed. Men, she corrected herself. Her heart constricted into a painful little knot and a tiny sob escaped her lips.

Bleary-eyed, nearly tripping on her saddle, Sarah fled into the brush just beyond the light of the dying embers. Like most people attuned to wilderness living, she knew how easy it was to become lost. Even in her upset, she glanced over her shoulder to fix the position of the cottonwoods against the stars in the background. The Big Dipper loomed above and behind them so she knew she was headed south. The Milky Way spread like a bucket of spilled diamonds above her, but she could not feel its beauty tonight.

Through the brush on either side the wind seethed and rustled. Each step produced an abrasive rasp of sand against her leather boot soles. As she paced forward, Sarah detected a kind of rhythm to the passage of air, almost a singsong chant, hay-na-na, hay-na-na. What, she questioned the silent darkness, could that be that sounds so familiar?

She smiled for the first time since the meal at the Seneca Fire Pit. The wind sounded exactly like Night Walker. A perfect image of the secretly smiling Cherokee came to mind. Sarah ducked beneath a blocking branch and aimed her steps toward a clear path of sand extending in the direction she walked.

Now beyond the light of the fire, she became aware of the sound of horses and peacefully breathing men, the perfect quiet of the night touching her heart like the feathery caress of goose down against the skin. So soft. So very soft. Sarah looked around herself, suddenly free of the torment of guilt that first drove her past the confines of the camp.

She sighed, letting loose the air she felt she had held forever. With it went the last, she hoped, of her bad feeling. Some part of her wished it well as it left. Breathing deeply once again, her gaze shifted left where she found an unobtrusive man standing quietly with hands clasped before him, head slightly bowed, just out of arm's reach.

"Do not be frightened," said the quiet man, gently smiling.

Sarah felt the pistol tucked into her waistband, but the man appeared neither armed nor ill disposed.

"You have many friends, Sarah, wife of Jacob," he fell into step beside her. "May I walk with you?"

"How is it that you know me?" She inquired, intrigued, wondering why she felt no fear. "And how did you find me in the middle of nowhere?"

"My name is Shantee. I have always known you. Wherever you are, I am also."

"Are you the same Shantee of whom Jake sometimes speaks?" Sarah interrupted, feeling uncommonly stupid.

"Different people call me by different names, Sarah. Each sees me in a way that is comfortable to them, yet I am one." Shantee's perfect smile reflected some secret irony he felt at that statement.

Sarah was so confused that she failed to notice. She could not lend words to the questions overwhelming her thinking. "Why?" was the best she could manage.

"Your heart is heavy, my sweet, sweet child." Shantee ignored her question and went straight to her concerns.

Sarah heard the word "child" but felt no anger, only the over-whelming warmth and love contained in that word.

"The events of the last days trouble you greatly."

Tears sprang to Sarah's eyes. She trembled and then stumbled. Shantee steadied her with his hand under her arm. His peace flooded though her like a tide of cool refreshing water. Turning into his shoulder, she cried with real abandon, finally releasing the deep hurt and remorse she believed she had already conquered.

Shantee seemed to grow as she leaned into him, as she accepted his comfort. He was big enough to absorb the enormous grief she felt. In a rush she gave it all to him.

The arms of Shantee circled round her trembling shoulders, pulling her close. His soothing words, like a calming tea, eased then replaced her agony of spirit.

"All life is precious," spoke Shantee. "I understand and share your feeling over the taking of life. Even with that regret, you know that the lives of your loved ones are the most precious of all." Gently he patted her shoulders as her sobs softened and decreased. "Defending your family against those who mean you harm is no sin at all."

"Thank you, Shantee," Sarah looked up and discovered herself with a fading image of Man Above, yet Shantee's benevolent smile remained brightly in her mind and in her heart.

"I will remember," she promised the newly empty night. Deliberately, she worked to steady her breathing. Eyes moving once more to the heavens, Sarah found the North Star and turned to retrace her steps. She could sleep now. As she dropped her eyes to chart a path through the head high brush, she was startled to find the figure of Night Walker, the Cherokee Shaman, before her, limed in a strange light.

The very size of the man was enough to give most people pause and inspire absolute terror in those with reason to fear his wrath, yet Sarah felt only joy in this surprise reunion with her husband's great friend.

"Night Walker!" Sarah greeted him simply with a sunny smile.

"Sarah Anne O'Connell Tallon," the big Indian strung all of her names together in a kind of ceremony she failed to grasp. So busy was she attempting to follow his greeting, Sarah nearly overlooked his unusual appearance. Though the Cherokee was illuminated only by starlight, he glowed brightly as though standing in the light of day, almost whitely.

"You're not really here, are you?" questioned Sarah, now deeply confused.

"No, I'm not."

"Where are you?"

"Far, far away."

"How …" Sarah fumbled for understanding.

"The explanation would make little sense to you now. It's a Shaman thing that has to do with dreaming."

"Ah," Sarah's response reflected the vagueness she felt.

"The miracle," explained Night Walker patiently, "is that you can see me at all. This surprises me." He smiled at the continued mystery, calmly folding his bare, heavily muscled arms across his massive chest.

"Those that love you, worry for you, Sarah. All of us understand that taking a life is no small thing. There are great responsibilities. Even making meat, the Indian learns to thank the animal and the giver of life, Can-Lun-Lun-Ti-Ah-Ni. In this way we do not become callous to killing." Standing quietly, the Cherokee allowed Sarah to absorb the meaning of his words.

"I pray for you in the Cherokee fashion, wishing to ease your pain, Sarah. I see the peace of Man Above already upon you. He must have come and gone. In that case, my prayers have been answered." During his entire monologue he had made no attempt to reach out to her, to touch her in even the smallest way.

Stepping forward tentatively, Sarah passed a hand through the image of the Indian. Startled, her eyes flashed upwards from the phenomena before her to the face of the image. "Wha …" she stammered, stumbling a step backwards. The action produced only a smile from Night Walker.

"Your bravery is the other half of the event which the killing itself cannot diminish. You are a worthy woman, Sarah Anne O'Connell Tallon." Unfolding his arms, Night Walker opened a leather pouch at his belt, removing a beaded necklace with a one-inch long, notched, eagle feather made of hammered copper. "I have something for you," he said. "I am thinking now I will be able to give it to you without waiting." As he reached to fasten it about her neck, Sarah felt the very real weight of the piece settle onto her throat.

"Of all birds, Sarah, the Eagle circles closest to heaven yet fiercely defends its young with talon and beak. To many peoples the Eagle is holy and an absolute symbol of courage. I know," he said, "that you are shocked at my appearance this night. It shouldn't be possible for me to appear before you in this fashion, but it is. Nor should it be possible for me to manipulate solid objects, while I am not solid myself. But it is."

Turning her with a seemingly solid hand upon her shoulder, Night Walker guided Sarah unerringly back to the camp and her blankets. As she pulled the heavy wool to her chin, he knelt beside her, placing a soothing hand upon her brow. "In the morning you will wake, healed. Sleep well this night, Sarah." With that benediction, she closed her eyes on the darkness.

⊐◼⊏

Sarah woke with the sun a full hand above the horizon, an unfamiliar weight about her neck.

Sitting up straight, she fingered the simple copper ornament.

"What's that?" queried a puzzled husband as the morning's first greeting.

"It's magic," said Sarah, her voice full, once again, of its natural soft strength.

Lobo Behind Bars

hortly after Jake had obtained the Writ from Judge Hoagland, Night Walker visited Nazareth's Jail, carrying only his buckskin parfleche. Nobody waited in the front office. He closed the door behind him and called out, "Anyone home?" Only silence answered the soft, strong query.

Looking cautiously left and right, the big Indian used his left hand to gently ease open the inside door that obviously led to the cells in the back of the building. Dust tickled at his nose. He smelled the rotting blood first. Deep in the shadow of the far cell, Lobo's long dark shape clung unmoving to the slat-bottomed bunk that hung sloppily downward on chains anchored loosely into the stonewall.

The iron door resisted the big Cherokee at first, causing him to pause in his forward motion. Frowning, he placed a hand flat across the locking mechanism as though to feel the heartbeat of tumblers cased in the heavy iron, then slapped the metal surface and lifted the barred door seemingly in one fluid motion.

The door creaked loudly as Night Walker let himself into the small dirty enclosure. He sat down his burden next to the rickety, slanting bed. "This would be simple if you just gave up and died."

"I'm not dying." The words came so low they might have been the sound of a draft through the bars in the window above. The Cherokee could see nothing of the wound with the young man facing the wall as he was.

"Smells like you're dying."

"I'm not dying," Lobo reiterated. Night Walker heard the knife-edge of defiance. At that point, he knew he could help this young man. Permission to heal sparkled within the denial of death.

"Turn over, boy. Don't make excuses. If you want to live, you're going to try harder than you have so far."

"I don't know how to try harder than this," Lobo replied.

As the young man rolled over, the pins pegging the chains to the wall threatened to pull free, dribbling dust onto his blankets. Moving quickly, Night Walker braced the sagging platform with his lower leg and snatched a short stool from the corner of the cell. The platform stabilized instantly with support under its frame.

The cell was far too dark. Without light, Night Walker realized he could do nothing for Johnny Lobo. Sliding his arms under Lobo's knees and shoulders, he picked him up and carried the young man like a limp, weakly protesting doll out the narrow cell door to the front office, where he laid Lobo gently across the top of an extra desk.

Lobo moaned as he settled onto the unforgiving surface. The feverish look in the eyes told the Shaman that even now the young man fought for his life. Turning to the stove, Walker kindled a fire for water, and threw open the front door, emptying the coffee pot into the street with an energetic toss. He found a bucket of fresh water next to the stove, filled the pot, placed it atop the hot flat surface and returned to his patient.

Noisily the big Indian shoved the desk and man at once across the uneven floor boards closer to the windows, leaving long deep scratches across the hardwood. Gently he straightened each limb and unbuttoned the shirt. He couldn't imagine a worse situation. The wound had gone untreated from the beginning. Blood pooled, soaked the clothing, dried and rotted right up against the skin. Flies buzzed thickly above the mess. The clothes were a loss. In frustration, Night Walker tore them effortlessly away and tossed the shredded cloth into the remains of an abandoned crate in the corner of the office. Now the flies have a home, he thought.

Johnny Lobo moaned where he lay, sickly and gaunt, unable to resist.

Holding him carefully on the shoulder and hip, Night Walker rolled Lobo onto his side so he could see the man's back. "Good," he commented mostly to himself, looking at a hole an inch and more across. "The bullet came on through."

"Could'a toll you that mysef," came a barely audible slur. "Don't be tossin' me around on this torture rack. Ask first."

"You know so much, Mr. Mouth. You know why I'm here?"

"Heal me or kill me." Lobo laughed, coughed and groaned again. "Feels more like the latter," he wheezed.

"I'm here because the man you tried to kill, Jake Tallon, cares for his sister-in-law, Tia O'Connell, and she cares for you."

The enormity of this fact stunned Johnny Lobo to silence. The eyes remained closed.

After three heart beats, the breath eased out of the body under Night Walker's hands. The Cherokee put an ear against the still chest. Because the heart beat on, he surmised that Johnny Lobo had only passed into unconsciousness.

"Best pain killer I know," mumbled the Indian. Rolling Lobo roughly onto his back and rising, he walked to the stove where the water in the soot-stained pot bubbled energetically.

Pouring a measure into a handy basin, he swirled the steaming liquid over the lip of the basin, and finally satisfied with the cleanliness, threw the rinse water onto the floor by the desk. "It'll dry soon enough," he told the empty room, refilling the basin from the bubbling pot and returning to his patient.

Nothing about Johnny Lobo's wound looked good. Night Walker had seen the inside of a warrior too many times during his efforts to heal. The entrance wound fell halfway between the belly button and the ribs, slightly left of center. Depending on the load the Sheriff used, it could be a blessing or Lobo could die of blood poisoning or Gangrene.

Certainly, if he died, he would die very slowly.

A conical bullet pierced the intestines and produced infection no medicine the Shaman knew could deal with effectively. A ball with a moderate load might shoulder its way past the strong, slippery tubes of the intestines without too much damage. He'd seen many gut shot men survive for that reason. It was impossible to tell the difference between normal infection and a pierced intestine only by smell. They were both long on bad bouquet. Maybe the pierced intestine was worse, the Cherokee speculated thoughtfully with a single nod of his head.

Night Walker broke the dried stalks of a soap plant into the steaming water. He smiled with satisfaction as little bubbles began forming on the surface and gathered at the edges of the basin. Clean was always an excellent place to start.

Dropping a handful of cotton cloth into the steaming concoction, the big Cherokee drew his knife and used the point to push the clean material beneath the soapy surface, then hook it once again and pull it out. Most of the water drained downward into the basin. The cloth itself remained too hot to touch. Holding it by either corner, he spread the steaming fabric flat over the stomach of the unconscious man. Using another cloth, he continued to dribble moisture onto Lobo's stomach.

Obviously, the man needed a bath after being left to rot in his confinement. This was likely as good as he would get for a while. What the heck, thought Night Walker. While the wound soaked, be began gently washing down the man's arms and face. Under the layer of grime and pain he began to see a surprisingly gentle visage.

Don't be fooled, the Indian counseled himself to caution. The devil frequently waits behind kind eyes.

The water in the basin had cooled considerably. Night Walker rose to reheat it from the pot on the stove. Sitting down once more by his patient, he removed the soaking cloth and gently washed at the areas around the insignificant looking hole, allowing some of the fresh mixture to drain into the hole. Can't hurt, he thought.

The Cherokee Shaman cocked his head to one side thoughtfully. The skin was red and inflamed just around the hole but normal looking other places.

Turning Lobo over, he repeated the cleaning process on the exit wound. The young man might live after all. Lobo was badly injured but seemed stable. That was only a guess, of course, but a guess based upon personal experience and a strong Shaman intuition. All that remained was to bind the wounds and provide the young man with something to eat and drink as he was able. An injured or unconscious patient, the Shaman knew, could die of dehydration or even malnutrition.

Briefly leaving his patient, Night Walker rose to refresh the basin. This time the Cherokee emptied the bloody mixture that filled the shallow container by casting it decisively into the street with a long splash that raised dust two feet into the air with its plopping impact. The action drew a number of curious stares from different points around the street. Night Walker stared boldly back until each citizen returned to his previous task.

He opened another packet of herbs and emptied it into the clean basin, covering it with the last of the steaming water from the pot on the stove. While the mixture steeped, the Indian used the razor edge of his big knife to scrape away the sparse body hair near either wound. He wiped the area clean with the herbal broth and wrapped Lobo's torso twice around with a wide swath of clean white bandage.

Gingerly grabbing a handful of the soaking herbs, Walker placed them over the exit wound in back between two layers of bandage and did the same in front. The patient's breathing evened out. Lobo already looked improved. Wonderful, Walker thought, what changes a little attention can produce. But this young man is not yet out of the woods.

By the time Tia and the Sheriff showed up, Night Walker had Lobo in a new shirt and was patiently shaving away at the unconscious man's whiskers with his evil-looking knife.

"I'm only shaving him," the Cherokee announced without looking up. "And I've almost got him decent again."

Just stepping though the door, Tia appeared not to hear a word. Hands to her mouth, eyes round as saucers, her concern for Johnny Lobo was evident. Shaking off the Sheriff's restraining hand, she rushed forward.

"Johnny," Tia said simply and his eyelids fluttered open as if on cue.

"He barely lived for me," said the Indian with disgust, "and he wakes up for you at a single word." Night Walker made a show of noisily repacking his supplies while the Sheriff looked on. At the end, he extracted the Judge's written permission and presented it to the lawman with a flourish.

"Already heard 'bout that," Laszlo said, pushing away the unwanted paper. "Don't bother showin' it to me. Can't read it no-way. Anyway," he corrected himself.

Skeptically, Walker refolded the document and carefully replaced it in his pocket as the Sheriff shouldered past him. "Borrowed the desk for an operating table," the Cherokee said.

"So I see," Laszlo frowned. "Is that scum gonna live?"

"No thanks to any effort you made in his behalf!"

"Don't push your luck, Redskin," Laszlo stormed. He hadn't yet learned to deal with his own guilt in the matter, and he wasn't about to have any stranger, much less an Indian, shove it in his face.

Night Walker smiled lazily and drew himself up to his full stature, dwarfing even the big Sheriff, who suddenly realized he'd just threatened someone who might crush him without effort. With a shudder of dread, the Sheriff also suddenly realized he'd run into this Indian's powerful presence before!

Laszlo mumbled a few inarticulate words and retreated hastily, without grace.

⊰▣⊱

Night Walker had left Jake, Sarah and Altimera in Bodie four days earlier. During that time, Night Walker had dream-walked to speak with Sarah, and had also ridden the terrain between the towns for other reasons. Now he watched the end of the street with increasing concern about their impending arrival and well-being. He didn't like all this worrying, he thought, as he approached the Jail for his third visit.

Entering the barred enclosure, he found Lobo sitting up in his rickety bunk, without support, as Tia sat off to one side, spooning a meatless beef stew carefully into his mouth. Night Walker watched genuine affection given and returned. It made him think.

Nothing like being gut shot to humble a man, he thought, casting an appraising eye toward Johnny Lobo. If he is true? If he remains true, Walker corrected himself, the couple may just work out. Pushing the door wider with a squeal of protesting hinges, he shattered the tableau. Both Johnny and Tia looked up guiltily to watch him approach.

"How's the patient doing?"

"Great," said Lobo.

"Very good," Tia's nervous answer overlapped her suitor's like children caught at mischief.

Were they aware how much they cared for each other, Night Walker wondered. Both transfixed him with wide, innocent eyes as he entered the six by eight cubicle.

"Stand up," Night Walker ordered a surprised Lobo.

Doubt flashed in Lobo's eyes, but his pride would not allow any hesitation. Tia backed out of his way as he swung his legs off the bunk.

"What you got in mind, Cherokee?"

"We're all going for a small walk."

"I'm in jail, remember?"

"And I'm your doctor. Also, I've got a note from the Judge, says I can do what I need to make you healthy. I'm bigger than the Sheriff anyway," Night Walker smiled crookedly. He engulfed Lobo's right biceps with one big hand and helped him almost roughly through the narrow door. On the way through the office, the Shaman snatched a length of peeled aspen trunk from atop the Sheriff's desk, left there for this purpose.

The Sheriff looked up doubtfully as they passed. Night Walker's backward glance nailed him abruptly to his chair.

"Nothin'," Laszlo shouted. "I ain't sayin' nothin'."

Night Walker grinned as they filed out onto the street. "A shave and a change of clothes, there might be a decent man hiding under all the lawman's bluster."

"Don't know about that, Cherokee," Lobo wheezed in obvious pain as he clung to the aspen held at either end by Tia and Night Walker. "How can a decent man do what he did and try to cover it up with a hanging?"

"You're certainly right, Lobo. The Sheriff should know better, but sometimes basically good people make mistakes, even smart people." They walked and stumbled a few steps before Night Walker observed, "The evil in this town runs deep. It poisons all who touch it. In a different place, Laszlo might be a better man."

"I think you're wrong, Night Walker," said Tia bitterly. "The Sheriff had a hair trigger. I saw him shoot Johnny just for defending me from his unwarranted advances!"

"I hear what you say, Miss O'Connell, yet I know what I know. This man holding the pole between us once shot someone dear to you for doing nothing at all."

The statement hung like smoke between them. Tia's face flooded crimson. "Oh," she said. "Perhaps you're right after all." They walked in silence for a few moments, using small halting steps to accommodate a gradually weakening patient. Johnny Lobo struggled valiantly for each deep breath.

"Still hurts," he grunted.

"As it must," said Night Walker. "You've never been shot before?"

"No, never had that pleasure," Lobo grimaced.

"Now you know."

"I've always known, Cherokee. Never took any pleasure in dropping a man."

"I believe you." Night Walker looked straight ahead as they walked, brooding. "It will take some time for me to forgive you. I don't know how Jake does that so easily."

Lobo walked straighter, drawing on some previously untapped, inner reserve of strength. His breath came more easily. When finally he spoke, the words stunned both Tia and the Indian. "I'm truly sorry, Walker. I'm sorry for shooting your friend."

Night Walker realized that this was the first time Lobo had actually used his name. But then his ears caught a new noise.

The sound of horses laboring up the steep side of the arroyo reached them before the horses themselves. Three big animals spun around the corner of the building and came to a disorganized stop before them, dancing and spinning in a moving cloud of dust kicked up by their hooves.

"Knew I'd find you here."

Night Walker narrowed his eyes against the glare of the sun behind the riders. He knew the voice like his own.

"Is that the prisoner?" asked Jake Tallon.

"We're taking him for a walk, to find his strength."

"He'll live, will he?"

"Do you doubt my healing ability?"

"You certainly have a gift in the way you answer questions, Walker." Dismounting, a grim, dusty Jake Tallon handed his reins to Altimera as Sarah did the same.

"I want to speak to Mr. Lobo privately," Jake said more sharply than he intended, grabbing Lobo by his only unbruised bicep, decisively guiding the stumbling Lobo away from the group of reunited friends. Behind them Sarah and Tia put their heads together in an intense, whispered conversation.

After a few steps Jake slowed up and Johnny grabbed at an awning post for support. "I owe you twice," he gasped to Jake before he could be interrupted. "I want you to know that shooting you was not personal and if I had to do it over again, I wouldn't."

"What do you mean, twice?" Jake was confused about several things.

"Once for not shooting me straight off and the other for saving me from the Sheriff."

"You're not quite saved yet, Lobo. You only got a ten day reprieve from your trial."

"Well, thanks anyway, Tallon," Johnny was getting all choked up, avoiding Jake's eyes in an effort to hide his sentiment. Suddenly he felt himself slammed up against the post with a horse kick in the chest. He looked down to find a trail-hardened hand bunched in his shirtfront. His eyes traveled up the arm into the angry face of Jacob Tallon. Yellow fire flickered in the eyes of that Legend.

"Get it straight, Lobo. You can survive this but your life is good only as long as Tia is happy. She's my family. I don't have that much family left and she's special to me."

Johnny understood Jake, but pride would not allow this handling. "Remember yourself, Tallon," his voice showed sudden steel. "Roughing me up wouldn't be so easy were I healthy."

"Oh! You're right." Jake's face registered a series of subtle changes as new understanding altered the way he thought about the man in front of him. His smile mirrored the sun emerging from behind dark clouds as he released him. "How 'bout I kick your rear once you're recovered?"

They both smiled now. "How are you doing?" Jake asked sincerely, almost solicitously.

"Nearly as good as new," Johnny's emotions stumbled all over each other in an effort to sort out the apparent changes in Jake Tallon. "I would be dead now without your Indian friend's help." Johnny realized he had never been required to thank anyone for his life before this time and now it seemed he thanked everybody in sight.

Jake tried to let him off the hook. "I've been there a couple of times myself. That Cherokee works miracles. He's a good one to have on your side."

"I believe you are also, Tallon."

Delay of Hearing

J ake felt unsettled after his encounter with Johnny Lobo. He might forgive the man, yet any kind of trust must come slowly, Tia or no Tia. That would be strange, he thought, having his one time assassin as a brother-in-law! But Jake felt that Tia deserved better from her older sister's husband than bitterness. Besides that, he just had a feeling about Johnny. That feeling was hope.

He would make every effort to be fair, he promised himself. Wasn't he, after all, on his way to see Hoagland, the crooked Judge on behalf of the man? The edge of the boardwalk passed under his feet as he aimed himself for the front door of the Nazareth City Hall. As usual, no one waited in the front office. Jake tapped lightly on the door to the Judge's chambers. It was a moment before he heard a reply.

"Come on in! Don't stand outside that door like a potted plant. Oh, it's you, Mr. Tallon!" In spite of his wasted physique, Judge Hoagland cultivated a speaking voice that controlled a courtroom and created an impression of power. It served him well, now facing the man he feared so much.

How strange, thought the Judge. The object of all our scheming stands before my desk, here in my own office, talking like nothing at all was amiss. "I thought you might like to know I put my agreement with you in writing."

"And that was?" Jake asked.

"Delay of Hearing! It's the only way to insure the proper outcome for young Mr. Lobo. The trial would have gone forward legally if it were not delayed legally. The Sheriff has no choice but to obey the word of the court. That's what this paper represents."

Finally moving his piercing gaze from the nervous Judge, Jake carefully examined the paper Hoagland presented. "Ten days it says."

"Yes," said the Judge, "Ten days from yesterday."

"I had a surprise waiting for me in Bodie," Jake managed with forced nonchalance. "Did you happen to know anything about it, your Honor?"

209

"Heard about it after the fact." The Judge shifted the papers before him unnecessarily. "Seems like you took care of two more of the Mackinaw Brothers."

"The last two!"

The Judge froze, "I understand there's two more in Colorado, somewhere." He met Jake's eyes briefly, looking for a reaction that never came.

"I already met them," said Jake in a flat unemotional tone. "One ain't getting up again and the other will take some time to heal."

"News to me," the Judge, noticeably paler, looked down again and back up. "Sounds like you and that Mackinaw family are having some kind of war." Under his uneven smile the Judge choked back his reaction. There seemed to be no stopping this young man, he thought.

"Not of my making," said Jake evenly. "Bingo started off playing the bully and his brothers tried and failed to make good his brag. All I've done is defend myself and no one will say different."

"Seems like you're rather an efficient young man," a smile fought fear for possession of the Judge's expression and pulled both corners of his mouth toward the ears.

"I try not to start anything I know I can't finish."

Judge Hoagland didn't know how much he wanted to tell young Jake Tallon, but something in the clear-eyed young man reached out to him. This was how he had wanted to turn out, all strong and brave. Looking backward at his life he saw only indecision and weakness. After fifty years he was no better now. A good education gave him a mind but not much of a soul. Maybe some of this young man could rub off on him?

"You're up against a stacked deck, Mr. Tallon."

"So I've heard. I've seen some of it and it hasn't amounted to much yet." Jake knew the Judge was part of the problem. If he kept the man talking, maybe he could find out just how much.

"Judge, you surely knew I went to Bodie to telegraph Sacramento. While I was in town, I put wheels in motion to find and punish the people who killed my friends and tried to kill me. "

"Put wheels in motion?" echoed the Jurist hollowly.

"Yes, I established the reward fund, we spoke of, for $2,000 for information leading to the people who hired the killing. I also made the complaint to the Marshal in Bodie, Colt McKenzie."

"Hired the killing?" questioned the Judge, suddenly sick.

"Half a dozen people I never met took part in the original ambush. Fourteen more showed up in Colorado huntin' my scalp. Not to mention assorted Mackinaws coming after me. I'd have to believe two dozen people woke up hating me one morning, to think they did it on their own."

"You got a point there, son," the Judge heard himself say from a vast distance, his heart pounding in his ears. His mind scurried like a furry rodent from one dark corner of a closed box to another. The walls drew in on him.

"They seemed to have quite a lot of traveling money to boot," continued Jake. "Nothing I did to those people accounts for their attitude, other than the gold Harry Harmon found that someone else now controls."

"Gold is the motive?" ventured the Judge half-heartedly.

"Appears so, to me."

"Who do you suspect?"

Standing suddenly straighter, Jake realized the Judge was getting more information from him than he was getting in return. He needed to build a fire under the man and smoke out additional clues if he could. Fear was the tool of choice.

"Don't rightly know who's involved, Judge." Jake's eyes narrowed. "There's a good possibility that some decent people will get caught in the middle if they're not careful. I think that the reward money will begin to loosen some tongues and I'll get information that will lead me to the real killers." Jake let the proposition and the unspoken threat settle on the table between them, then drew the noose taught. "You can count on that!"

"Of course you're right, son."

Zachary doesn't know whom he's dealing with, thought Judge Hoagland. This young man is more than fists and guns. He's got brains and he won't crumble under pressure, the way the Mayor believes. This fellow's not dead yet and he don't look like he'll go easy.

The Judge leaned forward in his chair and put one hand over the other on his desktop. "You'll have to excuse me, Mr. Tallon. Many tasks beg my attention before the office closes today and as much as I enjoy talking with you, I have to get at it."

"Certainly, Your Honor." I'll just bet, Jake thought to himself as he picked up his hat to go. "Thank you for the written agreement and for your time." Showing his teeth in an animal-like manner he intended as a smile, Jake nodded the respect he didn't feel.

Sky Fire

For the most part, Night Walker had stayed in Nazareth. But earlier in the week, before the healing of Johnny Lobo, Night Walker had ridden the return trail between Bodie and Nazareth, sometimes on the heels of Altimera and sometimes a mile or more distant. He had wandered aimlessly on the flanks, constantly seeking the high ground from which the surrounding country might be viewed.

For this Indian the sun had dimmed. Color had faded. The occasional game animal held no interest as his spirit reached ever beyond the obvious.

Night Walker perceived a threat not shown him by his dreams. Did this mean the threat was not serious? Was the threat immediate or distant? He failed to grasp the source, no matter how hard he tried.

"Great Spirit!" the Cherokee invoked Man Above, "Show me the enemy. Give me eyes to find his sign."

Before his mind's eye, future events gathered on the horizon like ominous clouds, piling, tumbling darkly, just out of reach. No one need tell him that they were stalked. That much was obvious. To Night Walker's Shaman mind this was fact as clear as sunrise or full moon.

He walked one foot always in the Spirit World.

As a boy he had run with others of his age, hunting and at play. He had dreamed a boy's dreams of manhood, casting wishful eyes at the maidens of another lodge. But in the moon of the Vision Quest everything had changed.

His friend Two Whistles, and Deer Foot (as Night Walker was then called), left camp together with little more than moccasins and breach clouts, a knife their only weapon.

The Vision Quest was more the custom of other tribes, but it appealed to the two young Cherokee friends. Maybe their feet needed to wander new trails, elders of the tribe speculated.

"Many trails find the same destination," said Walker's mother, Sees Far Woman, with a wise twinkle in her eye. "You will reach your goal, my son, if only you persist."

For a pair of days Two Whistles and Deer Foot shared the same path. Walking together, they worried as boys will. Which animal will be the spirit guide? Will our visions find each of us with a warrior's bear or a humble rodent? They laughed long at a warrior of another village named Man-Afraid-of-Beaver. Such things had happened. And the ultimate worry – would they see anything at all?

Pointing toward the forested mountains south and west, Two Whistles insisted they continue together. But inexplicably, Deer Foot felt drawn toward the prairie.

"Such a thing is not done," complained Two Whistles, irritated at his friend's ignorance. Yet the young Night Walker could not be swayed.

"Great Spirits live only in the mountains!" tried Two Whistles once again, stamping an adolescent foot with frustration.

"I am not so sure," countered the young Deer Foot, as he felt pulled gently but consistently toward the grassy wastes. "Something waits for me. It turns my eyes constantly in that direction. I cannot go to the high places!"

So speaking, he bid his friend and his boyhood good-bye at those crossroads. With certainty, he faced away from the mountains and began walking. The stride lengthened and became a run lasting for hours. The first night in the open, without fire, he nested into the high grass like an animal, curled tightly against the chill, covering himself with uprooted stalks for warmth. In the morning he drank his fill from a small spring puddling the prairie nearby, then walked and ran again.

All his life he had run, yet this run hardened his muscles and lengthened his bones like none before. "Ayiii," he intoned, observing this sudden growth with astonishment, "I become a man overnight!" He felt the touch and the pull of Spirit with each stride and paused only with a small hill in the near distance.

The feeling of the here and now swarmed in the very air around him as he stopped and stood, arms outstretched to thank Man Above for the boon of physical maturity and to embrace an unknown future.

Weak and a little dizzy with lack of food and water, the young man climbed the modest hill, which allowed him an equal view in all directions. As he sat gently upon the rolling summit, Deer Foot promised the waving grasses carpeting the land on every side, "No food passes my lips, nor will it until the purity of my heart allows me an introduction to the Guiding Spirit of my life."

Sitting, legs crossed, he waited eagerly. Breathe in. Breathe out. Tension drained from his body like rainwater from the surface of a glossy leaf. All his life he had prepared for this moment without a clue to the outcome. How would he change?

Day faded into evening and the darkness of night, yet he waited. A strengthening breeze teased at the seed-topped grasses around him as the stars above winked out one after another, eclipsed by clouds scudding through the night sky like great silent ships running before the rising wind. During the late hours of the night, the full fury of the storm smashed against the young man seated serenely upon the rise of ground.

Wind-driven rain ran in glistening sheets down his bare chest and arms. Lightning flashed and thunder rolled as a continuous drum. The young man's heart rose to the test.

"I will die," he thought, "or I will be touched by Spirit."

On the heels of that thought, he was slammed to the ground, then sent flying by an explosion of sound and light. The world tilted and collapsed. Night Walker knew the thrill of fear.

Opening his eyes, the young man found himself ringed by fire. The wind had died and he was no longer alone. Arranged before him, limed in eerie light sat three Spirit messengers: the Eagle, the Owl and the Coyote.

Cautiously, Night Walker sat erect. Though his body steamed and smoked, he seemed unhurt.

"Sky Fire," the animals addressed him as one. "Many seek the gift and few are they who receive. You have been chosen among your people to be the Spirit Talker."

"How can this be?" asked the shaken young man. "I do not seek this gift."

"You are not asked," the animals replied with a note of irritation, "You are chosen."

"Surely I need only one Spirit Guide. How am I to choose among you?" he asked.

"You are not to choose," spoke the animals imperiously, "you are chosen. Through you, all Spirit Guides from the Great Spirit will speak to your people according to their need and the situation. You cannot be as the other young men. Know that one day you will pass this singular duty to another. For now it is yours. You are the custodian of the Power."

Rolling the new name cautiously across his tongue, the young Sky Fire realized he would get nowhere fighting the assertion of this trio. Surprising or not, like it or not, this was the outcome of his man's journey. It was what he came to find.

Finally giving the task his full mind, the newly named Sky Fire composed himself.

Questions were asked and answered, both ways. The meeting moved from one hour to the next when the Eagle, responding to an unheard signal, snapped his regal head to one side. For the first time he spoke with a single voice. "It is now!"

Spreading his great wings as if to fly, he brought them together in a tremendous burst of sound. The young Spirit Talker was bowled unceremoniously onto his back. When at last the young man dared open his eyes, he found only daylight and the freshness that follows the storm.

No tracks might be discerned within the burnt circle of grass. He did find the three areas where blades and stems lay matted in patches like the nesting spots of small animals. As he watched, the grass struggled to stand straight.

His vision was true! Sky Fire sucked air between his teeth. It was true!

Also within the ring were the warm bodies of two freshly killed hares. Gifts. It could be no other way. Laying his hands on the small bodies, he turned his eyes to the sky and gave thanks. He dressed them with his stone knife where they lay.

Wrapping their meat in the fur, Sky Fire jogged down the hill to the smoldering remains of a lightning struck cottonwood. He fed the smoking stump with twigs and leaves till at last he had a blaze over which to cook the gift meat.

⊒⊒⊑

Moonrise many days following found Sky Fire seated outside the lodge of Dream Thunder, the current Shaman. At sunrise a tall, spare old man with a solemn, weather-lined face pushed aside the hide covering his door to find Sky Fire waiting attentively.

"It has been long," the white-haired Elder said, "waiting for you to arrive."

"And now I am here, old man," Sky Fire replied, smiling respectfully. "You will teach me the skills of the High Shaman."

"So it will be," answered the Elder without hesitation.

The two lived as father and son for many winters. With a smile in his eye one morning, Dream Thunder touched Sky Fire fondly on the arm. "It is time, my son, that I journeyed to the Council of the Wolves. My summers as Healer to the tribe have passed and another must continue where I leave off. It is now your time, Sky Fire."

"I am not ready for this burden, my father."

"More ready than I, when the robe of Healer was passed to me. Though you may not want it, your time is now." In his mind, Sky Fire saw the Eagle of his Spirit Quest saying the same thing, "The time is Now."

Contented silence passed between them. Sky Fire had waited this day of Dream Thunder's departure. It came as surely as the sun in the east. As the old felt their failing, they were allowed the solitude of the forest to take their passing in dignity.

Dream Thunder asked that privilege of his young friend.

Sky Fire clasped him strongly on the shoulder, eyes moist. He couldn't help but notice how thin was his friend under his hand. With certainty, he understood the truth and the finality of the request.

"Good-bye, my good friend," said Sky Fire, knowing that his acceptance was the greatest gift in his power to give. "Man Above will watch over you until we meet again in the warmth and plenty of the Spirit Lodge."

Rising, turning from the lodge fire to go, Dream Thunder hesitated. "We will meet again, Sky Fire, before your final death." The old man's eyes twinkled with his private mystery.

"Don't torment me with riddles, old man. I may prevent your passing to find the answers you hold now in secret."

"That is not possible my young friend," the old man smiled. "The riddle is yours to puzzle over in my absence. I have been shown our meeting in the place beyond death. That is all I know."

Seemingly rooted where he sat, Sky Fire watched the door flap fall into place behind the old man as he left. How like his friend to leave him with reason to think. How like his friend to make him grow.

Invisible

Fearing that his feelings of alarm might give him away, Night Walker refocused on the present, retreating, hiding behind the calm heart of the careful hunter, while he sought the source of the disturbance. Who knew if the power of this malevolent presence might perceive him by the very nature of his reaction?

This was no simple evil, Night Walker thought, such as might be found in a dark alley or at the bend of a trail. This was the practiced evil of a man who has chosen to live his life without a touch of beauty, a dark life choosing always the base pursuits of pain, suffering and cruelty.

Walker felt the dark tendrils reaching and exploring along the trails between boulders and among the stunted trees of the dry landscape, sometimes touching the party of friends as they wove single file into the outskirts of Nazareth. Whenever possible the Shaman avoided the sickly-silken touch of the filaments only half seen. Surprised more than once, he steeled his heart to smallness and silence as they brushed closely by.

Can other men not sense these fingers of darkness, he wondered? But Night Walker remembered when he'd had to leave his own people, for all purposes captive in the Indian Territories, so far from their real homes. He remembered how he'd decided to become somewhat invisible himself, so he could move in the darkness of the night, and be free to help his Cherokee Nation. It was then he took his new name, Night Walker, and assumed a new responsibility, even following the messages in his dreams to find Jake Tallon. Besides the best gift of newfound friendship, they'd both eventually decided to use some of Jake's gold to benefit the Cherokee, the people of Night Walker's heart.

Night Walker knew that all this time spent alone had heightened his senses even more than when he was known as Sky Fire. I will accept my responsibility, he thought, as he looked back and saw the connections that brought him to this time and place. Now the Cherokee Shaman paid attention to subtleties others might not notice. Had he felt them or heard them? In some illusive way, a crackle and hiss alerted his senses as the evil fingers of darkness passed near him. For a Shaman, they were much too obvious to be ignored.

So intense in his study, he was surprised when the first outbuildings of Nazareth appeared, drifting starkly through the edges of his awareness, like architecture from a different life, a different experience.

What kind of evil is this, he wondered again? Pain and cruelty are not so rare in themselves. Among the Kiowa, the Comanche and Apache, these were often considered survival virtues born of hatred for any person outside the tribe, but softened by the integrity that honors courage and bravery.

Night Walker felt none of those higher elements in the evil that now hunted them. This was evil for its own sake - evil somehow intertwined with the criminal forces of the town currently arrayed against them. He knew that this evil, this danger, was a unique threat that must be singled out and extinguished. To ignore it would ensure the defeat of his friend, Jake Tallon.

This evil probed cautiously, yet relentlessly, seeking out the pattern of the group, looking for weak points. On some level Walker understood he was not the object of the search. Likely Jacob was the target, since he represented the most tangible threat to the killers themselves, blunting their best efforts with his resourcefulness. The Shaman must remain unknown, tracking the source of evil intent secretly.

Becoming aware of his immediate circumstance once again, Night Walker found himself near the Livery in Nazareth, at the hitch rail in front of the Mercantile. Dark tendrils climbed around the area, winding to the sky. He need fear nothing in daylight, Walker knew. He now barely afforded the snaking tendrils any notice. Gathering the leather reins from his horse, he turned toward the Livery, taking that excuse to separate himself from the loathsome touch of the evil filaments.

With his horse in tow, the Cherokee walked boldly down the street toward the Livery. He breathed deeply again, finally free of the slithering, hateful bands.

The Hosteler saw him coming with his beautiful horse, but with a disturbingly serious grimace on his face. At the man's greeting, Night Walker mumbled little in return, his mind moving ahead to embrace the next steps of his self-assigned task. The menace must be surprised, trapped and smashed. It had lived long to become so powerful. Night Walker did not intend to fail by underestimation.

Evil this substantial was bound to leave some mark of its passing, a trail that might be followed or understood. The Cherokee determined to find whatever he might that he could better know the adversary and gain some small advantage before the final confrontation.

Having surrendered his horse, Night Walker strode quickly, head down in his intensity, to the corner of the Livery. He ducked around the corner and ran along the side of the building for a hundred paces and straight out into the sandy hills and scattered sage. Avoiding trails, he ran furtively, bent at the waist and always south toward the big lake, seen shining brightly between distant trees.

With distance he relaxed, running more upright.

People lived around the lake, both white and red keeping mostly to themselves. Walker found a likely ravine leading down to the water. The dim trail snaked between boulders, widening gradually to open upon a broad beach at the water's edge. Tall pines walked up the steep sides of the ravine, screening it from view on both sides. The tracks of birds, deer and porcupine dotted the trail under his feet. Satisfied it met the need for the privacy he desired, the Shaman quickly built a brush Hogan and covered it over with tall grasses.

Out front he built a sizable fire and inside a pit. He carried a dozen hefty rocks to the fire and covered them over with more fuel. As they heated he contemplated the purification he sought. He needed all his strength and skill to find and conquer the unknown foe that stalked his friend.

The sun passed two hands across the sky before the rocks were hot enough for their purpose. Standing, he stripped from his White Man's clothes and moved the smoking rocks to the pit inside the Hogan with a pair of inch-thick sticks. The language of his ancestors rumbled forth in musical rhythm as he tossed fresh boughs of sage and cedar upon the rocks, their fragrance rising thickly on the heat.

Using his shirt like a buckskin bucket, he carried water from the nearby lake to ladle by the handful upon the smoking rocks until a fragrant steam filled the Hogan. Walker's voice climbed in pitch and volume as he repeated the ancient song taught him by Dream Thunder, years before. Experience and emotion fell away, leaving him as clear and new as glass.

Time lost substance. The Cherokee danced with spirits and breathed the air of another world. The modest fire before him was replaced by that of the Spirit Lodge. He conferred with the warriors of Shantee, helpmates to guide his earthly quest. He prayed for help and insight.

Finally confident, he allowed the netherworld to dissolve to the tones and solidity of his more familiar, Earthly sweat lodge. His chin rested against his massive chest, now expanding with the first pure breath after cleansing. Strength flowed back into arms and legs, moving him from the ground and driving his body through the loose brush opening.

With a massive thrust of legs, Night Walker's body stretched out straight from the shore like a thrown lance and hit the cold water of the lake headfirst. The late rays of the sun lit the water aqua from above. Underwater, he rolled slowly to his back, exhaled bubbles rising languidly from his nose and the corners of his mouth. Savoring the light and color until the need for air became imperative, he headed strongly toward the surface, breaking the smoothness of the water like a feeding trout aiming at the sky.

Never had sweatlodge worked so well. He felt remade in his finest form as Spirit Talker, stronger than a bear, keener of vision than an eagle, a true warrior of the Spirit Path.

Once more on shore, Walker stood, allowing the water to run from his powerful body before dressing in moccasins and buckskin pants. Now clothed, he turned his back on the brushwood lodge and ran with easy grace once more into Nazareth.

Using senses unavailable to normal men, the Cherokee Shaman reached outward for information as he ran, searching for anything out of the ordinary. Quickly Night Walker found what he sought. Occasionally at first, traces only, here and there he saw the touch of evil, like the glittery fragments of finely powdered glass under a full moon. Mostly it poisoned the soil of the streets and paths between buildings where feet had passed, and rarely on a post or wall where a hand or shoulder had brushed.

Nazareth was not that big after all, maybe twenty major buildings along two perpendicular streets. In a matter of minutes the Shaman circumnavigated the entire village. What he saw convinced him this evil was only a human with a twisted soul. The traces seemed to cluster around the stable and behind the saloon.

Intuition shouted Indian. Walker's normally expressionless lips curled upwards away from his teeth in an expression of distaste. He slowed to a walk behind the saloon where he found the largest accumulation of experience with this individual.

It seemed obvious, all at once, that this person was unwanted or uncomfortable on the inside of the drinking establishment, but spent much time nearby. The story was too common to Night Walker, who, though he himself enjoyed a beer, saw the saloon as filled with a White Man's poison and death for his weaker Red brothers. But the sickness of this individual went well beyond the White Man's firewater.

Hate and anger filled this trail, along with the blood of uncounted killings, fountains and lakes of blood. The picture tightened as he searched. Almost like dream reading, Night Walker peered inside this twisted man. No individual knew how this evil entity worked or who had felt the bite of his knife and lived. The long history of this man's sickness made the name "killer" sound like a schoolyard taunt.

While impressions assaulted the mind of the Shaman, he stood as he had left the sweat lodge, stripped to the waist. Arms at his sides, he held his big hands palm outward next to his legs. His head bent slightly forward and to the right in an attentive attitude as he listened to his whirling inner voices. He must find out everything he could before Jake, Sarah, and Altimera came back to town.

It was in this posture, behind the saloon, Vernon Laszlo found the Cherokee Shaman standing. Ignorant of Walker's true nature, the Sheriff saw only another Indian. Drunk, he figured.

"Hey Redskin," the Sheriff bellowed, "Best not be hangin' around where you're not wanted!"

Walker's eyes flashed open. Not only was he not surprised by the approach of the Sheriff, he had taken time to evaluate the entire aspect of the lawman with the eye of the Spirit Talker.

At that instant, Laszlo had no idea of the trouble he stirred. He watched the dark eyes snap open, and stood waiting a verbal response with one hand casually on the handle of his big six gun. The Indian seemed to grow as he watched, standing now well above six feet. A tremble of apprehension swept through the Sheriff's lanky frame.

"Must be the dark playin' tricks on me," Laszlo mumbled nervously.

In a blink, the Indian once comfortably at a distance, now stood suddenly flush up against him. Not a small man himself, the Sheriff was forced to look upward into the benign, but somehow threatening countenance.

His confidence melted away like butter dissolving across the bottom of a hot pan. The gun at his side seemed useless and puny.

"You can stay as long as you want," his voice trembled uncontrollably despite his best efforts to sound forceful.

"A little late to change your thinking, lawman." Night Walker was less concerned with the man's rudeness than the miasma of evil that swirled about him, dripping from his clothes. Not for a moment did he attribute all of it to Laszlo.

For his part the Sheriff was unaware of evil as Night Walker's eyes perceived it. He knew only that the big Indian made him mighty uncomfortable but felt powerless to do a thing about it.

Seconds ticked by.

"Where is this man called 'Death'?" The question, like a piercing knife in the heart, caught Laszlo flatfooted.

"What the hell you talkin' about?" the Sheriff gagged through a throat constricted with the sudden fear.

"Death! A man called Death. You have been with him. His mark is upon you." Night Walker became impatient, grabbing Laszlo's shoulder, pulling him uncomfortably close.

Laszlo babbled, bereft of composure. He had been unable to get Malvado out of his mind but was now so upset he was slow making the connection.

"You mean Malvado?" the Sheriff would do or say anything to obtain release from this strange, overpowering being. "A man don't find Malvado 'cept by accident or he wants you to find him."

"What is he to you?" demanded Night Walker, shaking the lawman's shoulder urgently.

Summoning bravado from some deep resource, Laszlo spit, "He's a killer and my business is lawbreakers." His eyes leaked a solitary tear of humiliation, one on each side. His nostrils seemed to snap shut on a huge intake of air, causing his breath to shudder like a sobbing boy. "Ahhh," escaped his lips. Can't do nothin' proper, he raged inwardly at his lack of control, staring resentfully upwards at the big Indian.

"You're right as far as that goes," the Shaman ignored Laszlo's distress. "There is much more to it." With brisk, short movements, Walker began suddenly to brush at the surprised Sheriff's shirtfront and shoulders. Stamping his foot near the Sheriff's boots, causing Laszlo to dance away, Night Walker grabbed and pulled the lawman close once again, pursing his lips and focusing a breath along each stubbled cheek. Laszlo's head cleared momentarily like the bright sun peeking from behind piled storm clouds, his eyes opening wide in astonishment.

"The evil with which he marked you says he bought part of your spirit. You must avoid this man or lose your soul for all time." This was no idle rhetoric on Walker's part. As a Spiritual Healer, a High Shaman of the Cherokee, he knew well the despairing wail of souls lost to lack of principle.

The Indian's words struck deep into feelings Laszlo had carried since talking last with the killer. He wanted a bath and he wanted to shuck this whole town and everything in it. The Sheriff also knew that departing this berg sounded easier to accomplish than it was. Zachary wouldn't let him go if he didn't want to and if he did, the retirement was certain to be final.

Staring down at the crooked Sheriff, Night Walker watched the wheels turn. He was not concerned with making the man guilty. The whole story lay plain on Laszlo's face. Should the Shaman confront Laszlo with his guilt, he might well be forced to kill him as the Sheriff defended his pride.

"Go!" commanded the Shaman abruptly.

The Sheriff spun on his heel and jogged down the alley toward the street, eager at any cost to be away. Walker suppressed a smile over the Sheriff's lack of dignity. "This way is easier," nodded the Shaman.

Masking his power in a subservient posture once again, Night Walker used the weed-choked back paths to the stable where he found a cotton shirt and a sidearm among his gear. Leaving the horses in their corral, he walked into the night without a sound. Small light from distant windows flashed across his form as he melted like quicksilver into the brush outside of town.

Tirelessly, Night Walker circled the town in widening arcs seeking fresh additional signs of Malvado that might point the way toward a lair. This evil could not hide from the searching eyes of the Shaman, who for the moment found nothing fresh.

This confirmed the Shaman's feeling that Malvado marshaled his strength and waited an opportunity to strike. The Cherokee was likely to find the man, Death, when he least expected it, maybe when he least wanted it.

He must be ever on his guard.

Malvado

moke curled and snaked before Malvado's sightless eyes in a place as naked of life as the face of the moon. No insects or rodents troubled the solitary human, for honest animals avoid evil by instinct. A fire popped and hissed near the center of the Hogan as the Indian swayed to the rhythm of some inner drum for endless moments.

Without the smallest apparent transition he sagged limply onto the skins beside the fire.

From his supine position Malvado cursed vehemently in the language of a dead people. Something I cannot know waits for me along the way, he fumed.

"Spirit warned me," he remembered out loud. "Choose the dark way and someday meet someone stronger. Ayiiii!"

Still he would do it all again. There was a time before he took the name Malvado. A kinder time. He had started his journey as a good boy that some part of him still admired. His manhood quest took him to a mountain barren of Spirits. Certainly empty of the Spirit Guides he believed were destined to come to him, to help him on his trail.

Instead, after a dozen days waiting for revelations, he had nearly died of starvation. No vision brightened his eyes but he refused to quit.

A band of desert Indians found him, nursed him to health and he stayed with them rather than return home to admit that no Spirit sought his company. Over time, the blistering sun and arid hills of their home range became his.

Joaquin, Shaman of the tribe, took him as apprentice. The old man had much to teach, and before Malvado, had no heir to whom he might pass his magic.

Seven times, once in the spring of each year, the tribe journeyed to the mountains where they first found Malvado, the boy. Each time Malvado thought of his boyhood home to the northeast and his childhood friends. He thought of the Spirit Guides who denied him a proper manhood and directed his steps with those of Joaquin's people.

He was a man now, tall and strong. He knew no other home. The people of the lost desert gave him respect he had never known and promise of a future he might never have with his own people, now far to the north and east. The old man praised him for his mastery of magic. This must be my path, after all, Malvado decided. Joaquin and his people are the destiny I sought all along.

The spring of the eighth year with the People everything changed. A band of beaten Comanche drifted down from the north after the snow disappeared from the mountains. They cursed the Rangers of Texas who gave them no peace.

Privately, Malvado smiled at the irony. Even as a boy he knew of the suffering this hostile tribe brought to others. Now they meet someone even more warlike than themselves.

Their stories caused a stir among the People.

Before the moon was full, hunters returned with stories of other burned villages. Terrified, the people packed lightly and headed early for the mountains. It was none too soon, they learned, when their empty lodges lit the sky behind them. The next two years they likewise failed to find peace. They ran always from the rumor of Rangers. Joaquin worked a strange magic tracking the Rangers from a distance.

Exclusion from these mysteries produced only greater curiosity in Malvado.

This magic Joaquin would not teach when asked, but Malvado watched when the old man thought himself alone, memorizing each observed step. Joaquin valued the younger man who learned at his side and sought to protect him from spells he said would eat the young man's soul. The Apprentice scoffed. Malvado saw enough that he pieced together an understanding based on what he knew and small clues provided by casual conversation slyly contrived. So concerned was he, that Joaquin never noticed.

Even a High Shaman, like Joaquin, could not protect the People forever. One day dawned with the Rangers suddenly in their midst, dealing death on all sides of their charging, sweating horses.

Joaquin and Malvado dashed from their lodge to the rattle of hooves. Joaquin was kicked violently backwards into Malvado's arms by a horse pistol in the hands of a White Man in black clothes. Like a springing cat, Malvado was upon him before he could ear back the big pistol's hammer for another thundering shot.

They fought silently atop the same saddle as the horse moved beneath them, through the camp and out onto the plain. Malvado found the man's belt knife and rammed it home beneath his ribs again and again until the man slumped lifeless against his chest. Throwing the body from the saddle, Malvado landed astride the corpse and thrust his fist into the heavens with each victory shout. This was Malvado's first test as a warrior and his first killing.

But victory was stale. All he could see was the death of his teacher and his father of the last ten years. Without his mentor, the future was empty of promise.

Malvado knew the horse had taken them beyond the village and beneath the level of the desert, where the other Rangers could not see him. The animal had stopped only because it found itself boxed by impenetrable thickets of head-high cactus.

Malvado stripped the man's lifeless husk of its gun and ammunition, the first tools of a lifelong quest of revenge. Finding the stirrups and the reins, he returned to the village, prepared to do battle until death claimed him as it had his teacher. Overwhelming grief clouded both his judgment and his vision.

Towering smoke gave him a destination. The journey seemed far longer than the ride coming out, but who could tell time while struggling for his life? No movement could be seen among the smoldering remains. Quickly Malvado found the body of his mentor as he had left it.

The tragedy was too great. Men, women and children lay where they fell, fourteen bodies in all. At least twice as many ran, pursued by the Rangers. Dimly Malvado heard shots in the distance.

Holstering the pistol, he searched the ruins for weapons of a quieter nature and the herbs of his father. Vengeance burned within his heart. No reason he knew justified the murder of these peaceful people. All they desired was solitude and a humble existence granted them by the Great Spirit. Someone would pay. Someone must pay.

That night Malvado would find them where they slept. Every Ranger, he promised silently, would fall by his hand. These wandering desert people had accepted him. They had been closer than blood.

Rangers had hunted the people like animals from the backs of their tall horses, mindless of the trail they left. By nightfall they gathered once again. As the fires of the White Men died, he transformed himself into the stalking spirit. He built his own shelter a distance from their camp using broken limbs and dry grasses. He burnt the herbs of his teacher and rubbed his face with the ashes.

Smoke swathed his body. He relaxed. His breathing slowed and his body approached sleep while his mind surged forth. He found himself above the lodge, headed for the stars. In a moment of crippling fear, he crashed to the Earth with the sound of a great tree striking the ground. Closed eyes flashed open. Icy sweat erupted from each pore. "Ah-hee," he breathed.

Of course, there was no great tree. This is wrong, he thought. Many times have I watched Joaquin slip away. I am undone by my own fear! Maybe another night I'll try again.

Much too alert to sleep, Malvado slid into the shadows, circling the camp of the Rangers. He watched from each side a few minutes to discern their numbers and location. One lay wounded near their fire. The Indian watched another Ranger feed him. Something no healthy man would allow. With inspiration he realized the guard remained unrelieved during his entire transit of the camp. The night becomes sleepy for a man without companionship, he thought.

Absent conscious decision, Malvado drifted downwind, toward the spot he knew the guard waited. Even yet the horses stirred. Malvado cleared his mind, becoming the rocks, the sand and standing cactus. He was rewarded as the animals quieted once more. His mind held no judgment, no victory, no plan. He drifted as the air, ever closer to the dozing guard.

Warned by some inner sense, he glanced down in time to see the spiny leaves of the Prickly Pear cast about behind the guard, waiting the unwary step. These were seasoned warriors, he realized, accustomed to desert fighting and long lonely vigils.

With the point of his knife, he lifted the spiked leaves from his path, until he stood only inches from the dead tree against which the man reclined. Slowly, Malvado circled the whiskery neck with a long left arm and thrust the knife home below the third rib, straight into the heart.

Beneath his hand the body stiffened. Malvado's arm clamped it vice-like against the tree. Without a groan it sagged backwards in permanent repose. Even as his knife pulled free, the Indian heard the approach of the changing guard. A smile lit his face.

The sound of steps drew nearer. "Mordecai, you old war dog, I'm here to relieve you … Damn it, Mordecai! You're already asleep. How you gonna protec' us in your dreams?"

Shadows of the night shifted until the hatted form of a man reached down and forward to shake his friend. "Mordecai! Wake up! What's wrong with you, boy? You don't want me to tell your Daddy you slept, do you?"

Birth had gifted Malvado with the arms of a tall man. Reaching around the narrow bole of the tree, he drove the knife deeply into the throat above the collarbone of the man bending forward and down. Surprise ripped the knife from Malvado's hand as the man reared backward.

Confident, the Indian let go the blade. The man was dead though he still stood. The ten-inch blade pierced his enemy's heart from above as it had pierced his friend's from behind. No sound yet, the man wobbled where he stood and uttered a despairing groan, hardly loud enough to draw notice. Yet, as he collapsed, the horses stirred in surprise. This worried Malvado. Slipping quickly around the tree, he retrieved the knife and the man's gun. He heard a voice from the camp.

Acting with haste, Malvado strode to the picket line and selected a worthy mount.

Fully disturbed now by the presence of a stranger among them, the horses snorted and tossed their heads wildly, some pawing the air against the restraint of the picket line. Malvado wrapped the halter of his chosen mount around his arm and secured the end of the braided rawhide rope to the halter of the last horse in line. Mounting his own horse, he cut the remaining end of the picket rope and led the entire string into the night.

A chorus of yells and a single gunshot followed him into the desert. Malvado rode straight away at first then circled back to his rude shelter that he might collect his few belongings. Dismounting before the Hogan, he tied the horses that fretted constantly at the care and capture by unfamiliar hands.

The Indian did not want the horses. He wanted the Rangers who rode the horses and brought death to the People. Counting idly, the horses numbered thirteen. Only ten Rangers left, he realized, and one of them wounded. Only as many as the fingers of two hands, and far from the protection of their own people.

Bending to his quiver he counted only eight arrows. Enough. They might not let him so close again, but they were on his ground. Malvado smirked. The night was his friend.

Mounting, horses in tow, Malvado chose a path of rocky ground in the direction they traveled, that he might meet them once again on their way. He pushed hard, riding away the cool hours of the night, seeking the shelter and water of low hills to the east. He stopped only when he felt comfortably beyond the reach of his query. They were killers, these Rangers. Vengeful men. Men to be feared! Malvado would not underestimate the danger they posed.

He boxed the horses in a grassy enclosure used in happier times by the People and slept. When he woke, he found he lived in a world with a single purpose. The previous life receded, like the memory of someone else's dream. Malvado knew he must find a way to use the magic of Joaquin. But that was for the time of shadows. Now he must live.

Leaving the horses, he ran, bow in hand, to the broad desert floor. Wild pigs lived close to this water. Each year the People killed a few but never too many. He needed one now. Within an hour he found fresh spore and before dusk the point of his arrow found the heart of a boar.

Over the next days he would be a hunter of men. There would be lean days with little time for hunting. He cut the best meat from the body of the wild pig and wrapped it in the bristly hide. Waste goes against the grain of anyone who lives from nature. Life is hard and frequently hungry. He looked with regret at the carcass. Much meat remained but there was no help for it.

Standing, he turned his back on the remains of the pig and returned to camp, building a fire to cook and cure the precious meat. As he ate, Malvado planned every move of the magic in his mind, for he did not wish to repeat the mistake of the night before. He saw himself flying not like a bird, but like an arrow. Unlike the arrow, he knew he might change directions. Might, he smiled bitterly. I've got to do so. Old Joaquin alluded many times to "flying" but neglected to teach me the skill.

Malvado's mistake was in flying too high because the act of spirit flight depended much upon his personal confidence. "Fear," the old man said, "ties us to our bodies. The Novice must stay close to the ground in the beginning." Malvado saw himself cruising among the cacti like a rider without a horse, stretched along an invisible neck. It will be so, he pledged. A rider without a horse and an arrow shaped as a man, these images he conjured brought a smile to the harsh lines of his face. It was the first smile since the death of the People and maybe the last smile for the rest of his life.

He built a crude oven of flat rocks to bake long thin sections of pork so it might be useful over a longer period. As the meat cured, he tended the horses in their enclosure. They had grass and water. In the light, he saw they were good horses. Worth much. Glancing upward, his eyes automatically sought what the White Man called the Big Dipper, invisible in a sky waiting the death of the sun.

As a boy, Malvado knew the White Man and spoke the language. These horses might be too dangerous to trade on the American side of the river. The Rangers had other useful items. They had money and rifles.

Joaquin had known every weakness of his adopted son's heart. The old man protected Malvado from himself as long as he lived, and while the choice for good was now Malvado's to make, the bitter young man felt too compromised with grief to choose well. That very thought began his long slow slide into evil.

Malvado sensed the Spirits of the night crying out over his choice. This was not the proper use of Joaquin's magic. The Spirits had never shown themselves to Malvado and now they sought to bend his will against darkness. The Indian knew this moment was the cusp of his choice. The very reason the teacher never shared the deeper mysteries was that Malvado had yet to choose the light, to make a commitment.

Growing up, he had watched his brother-cousin-father stand for the true path. Somehow, deep inside himself, Malvado believed it was not his own destiny, that the die was cast early while still in the cradleboard. Things might have been different, had Joaquin lived. Now, the only people to show him kindness had been killed. My duty, he thought with conviction, is vengeance. It clearly makes my choice for me. In this way, he justified himself.

As darkness gathered behind the hills, in the arroyos and in the deadly thickets of spiny cactus, Malvado prepared the Stalking Spirit.

Joaquin had his private cave in this seasonal place of the People and now Malvado sought it out to repeat the ceremony of the night before. He brewed a tea he knew Joaquin sometimes drank. As he sipped, he felt it move his blood. He burnt the herbs, rubbed the ashes and soon slept sitting before the fire. At least he supposed he slept as he had seen the old man do when he claimed to fly. Malvado's mind seemed wondrously alive. Far too alive to sleep. Every inch of his skin tingled. Soon he felt the brush, dust and rocks in the countryside all around the cave as though they were part of him. He heard the insects in the night. He heard the birds in the brush beyond the corral. The horses stomped restlessly as though they stood right next to him. Impossible though it seemed, he was everywhere at once. Release!

Ah, this is it. With wonder, Malvado stepped cautiously from the body of the young man before the fire and coasted to the cave entrance. New light bathed every feature of the desert landscape. Not sunlight but spirit light. No shadows! The differences made him dizzy. He felt himself falling back toward his body.

"No!" he exclaimed with conviction. "I will not fail this time." New confidence allowed him to exit the cave.

Expectation moved him forward, slowly at first, then more rapidly. Ahh, he thought, this is something I can do. His spirit form soared over hills and sand bathed in a light of another world, light meant for spirit eyes. Faster now, with the speed of thought, he found the Rangers where they camped and overshot their bivouac in his haste. Cautiously he circled back.

They are too close, he thought with surprise. The Rangers had traveled far for men without horses. Tentatively, Malvado waded amongst them. This was wrong, of course. They cannot see me. Magic should never be used unfairly. This was one of the old man's chief concerns.

Nonetheless, he was here. Now was now. These men had killed the People and they must pay. One at a time, but ultimately they all must pay. The injustice they had worked was too great. Malvado stood among the huddled forms near the fire. Reaching down, he touched a blanket gingerly with a pale, glowing hand, not knowing what to expect. Empty, he realized. Every blanket held only brush and extra clothes. Ah! A ruse! Were I hiding close-by to watch for intruders, where would that be?

Looking right, looking left, he found a rock formation not fifty yards distant. There would be large pools of shadow near its base, even from starlight. A perfect place to hide.

Obviously, he could not be seen by their human eyes. They would have shot him by now, were that the case. This much he knew from Joaquin.

All was plain in spirit light. With the mere thought, he found himself transported to the crest of a rocky prominence nearby, where he found half a dozen of them cleverly hidden by brush and boulders. The balance of the force, somehow he knew, circled the base of the rocks. He sensed their tension. Though he crouched close by an alert Ranger, Malvado remained undetected.

For Malvado this was a great experiment. He ran his transparent hand before the face of the intent, staring man. No reaction! The Ranger's tension and fear etched deep lines in his white skin, made harsher in the spirit light. The face looked carved from pale wood.

Malvado stood slowly. He paced the crest, noting the positioning of guns. Descending, he circled the formation. Those below were protected by the guns above, who were protected in turn from approach below. Brilliant, thought the Indian, but effort wasted nonetheless.

Down the hill, away from the camp, a ravine ran away into the distant desert. The last two Rangers crouched at the head of this ravine, protecting the group against surprise from that quarter. Maybe they knew their enemy was few. Certainly they could not guess how few. They took such great care for only one enemy. The irony made Malvado smile.

He thought of his body, sitting before the fire. Just that quickly, he was there. The fire had died to coals.

Slowly, Malvado stretched, testing his body by slowly straightening each arm and swiveling his head around on his neck. Everything worked fine, just as he had left it. All that remained was to confirm the truth of the adventure. He felt compelled to prove his flight was not the empty dream of the old man's tea.

Two hours before dawn, Malvado walked his horse near the rim of the ravine, half a mile from where he believed the Rangers camped. Only as he dismounted did he realize with great distress, that so intent was he on the proof he sought that he carried no weapons. He carried only his knife.

It is enough, he thought, consoling himself. The Ranger upon the tall horse died by my blade and the Rangers of the horse guard died likewise. It is all I will ever need.

Before yesterday he had never killed in anger. He had never killed another man at all. Now he found he enjoyed it. He even relished it. The curving fingers of his hand ached for the rush and flow of fresh blood around his blade.

In panic, the young man that he used to be, the young man raised by Joaquin, grasped after some disappearing fragment of gentleness. It slipped away with a kind of finality and a despairing wail that left Malvado gasping.

Feeling somehow hollow now, Malvado knew that it was gone forever. He was changed.

The evil of his future laughed arrogantly at the boy's discomfort and slipped with certainty into his moccasins. At that very moment, the young man became Malvado. He forgot the name he once owned and fondly caressed the hide-wrapped handle of the long iron knife. He tied the horse and walked with a new and harder certainty toward the encampment.

The Rangers had planned well. They addressed every possibility except that of the Stalker Spirit. How could they have known? The two men so cleverly placed at the head of the ravine became the greatest vulnerability because Malvado knew they waited. No surprise existed for him.

The night was so quiet that even moccasins were a liability. Malvado tucked them into his belt and let the tough skin of his footpads caress the sand as one part of nature to another. Breath rushed between his teeth like desert wind around worn rock. Restless eyes picked apart the night, finding the landmarks shown to the Stalker Spirit.

In the intensity of his hatred he became less than an animal, for he could not hear Joaquin's spirit, crying next to him.

The Last Straw

Jake knew Night Walker had been coming and going in his own mysterious kind of way, even as the Shaman healed Johnny Lobo. But now that they were all together in Nazareth, Jake felt the bonus of their friendship. The extra confidence it brought him allowed him to more clearly think things through. After replaying some of the images in his mind, like seeing the Judge and the Mayor together, Jake pointed his feet decisively toward Nazareth's Jail, absorbed by the implications of their involvement. The Sheriff was also certainly a part of the conspiracy, but Jake wanted to check in on Johnny Lobo again.

He had no proof. Those three weren't likely to confess anything voluntarily.

Should he brace them one at a time or all together, the whole town would probably come down on him. The Judge, Mayor and Sheriff - those three held the triangle of power in this village and they weren't about to let go. Besides, without proof, all he had were ugly suspicions.

Though few of the reward handbills remained posted, most of the town already had a chance to ponder the printed information. Small groups of people huddled together in quiet conversation, hiding from view, speculating, Jake supposed. No bold townsman hailed him from across a sunny street. No potential ally gestured furtively from the shadows. Jake was not entirely sure what to expect, but something stirred within the town. He felt it.

The announcement of the reward let everyone know a crime had been committed and people killed. Now, it was no longer a secret to the world outside of Nazareth. Though he was prepared to pay, the substantial size of the reward was purely for credibility.

As he came abreast of the Jail, Jake paused, slowly pushing open the door, expecting the worst. This time no Sheriff sat behind the desk. The door to the cellblock stood ajar. Without touching the door, Jake peered through the narrow opening. He found Tia talking quietly to Johnny, seated together on his bunk. If they noticed him at all, they made no outward sign.

233

The sweethearts reminded Jake of the private world that he and Sarah shared during the first few months of their courtship. Truth be known, he was still goofy over the woman, now his wife. Turning, he left as quietly as he came, hoping he had not disturbed the two of them.

Jake had a lot on his mind. If he were to prove anything, somebody other than himself must stand up and accuse the Mayor or the Sheriff and claim the reward. Until that happened he was at loose ends and vulnerable to any attack.

Consumed with this confusion, Jake closed the outer door to the Sheriff's office quietly behind himself. As the latch snicked into place, he raised his eyes to spot Altimera across a wide expanse of dusty street. The ordinarily alert Mexican didn't seem to notice Jake's approach. Altimera's entire attention was focused on a white-haired man of indiscriminate age, a worn straw hat hanging over his back by a chin cord, now circling his throat like a brown rawhide necklace.

They spoke in Spanish. Jake found he could pick out more than a few words here and there, even at a distance. As he stepped onto the boardwalk, his shadow fell between the two men. They both looked up at the same time.

"Hola, amigo," Altimera greeted him.

"Jacob," stated the other gently.

About to say something, Jake found himself transfixed by the greeting of the second man. "Who?" he started to ask as the kind eyes locked his own. "Ah … Shantee!"

"Bueno, Jacob. You are surprised. No?"

"Yes and no." Jake turned to face him fully, ignoring Altimera for the moment.

"I talk to others, also. Not just to you." Shantee seemed to read Jake's mind.

Before Jake could articulate a response, Altimera pulled vigorously at his sleeve. "Many pardons, amigo, but I must borrow Mr. Tallon for urgent business."

Jake found himself speechless, looking over his shoulder at a smiling Shantee as Altimera guided him away.

"Do you know who you were speaking with, José?"

"Sure, a nice old man. A man of refined sentiments. A compatriot."

Altimera gave Jake only half his attention as he shifted a sheaf of flyers from one hand to another. "We had a nice talk about the way things were before you Gringos messed 'em up so bad."

"That was Shantee!"

"No!" The Mexican stopped cold, face flooded with amazement. "You're kidding me! That was just a nice old guy I passed the time of day with."

"No. That was Man Above!"

They both looked back open-mouthed at the bench where the old man had sat. He was no longer there, of course.

"Man Above? The same Hombre who helped you with your head wound? That was God?"

"The same one, amigo."

"The hell you say! I had a chance to talk with God and all I do is bullshit? I could have ask him why you are so loco or who shot all your friends or why there is no good eating place in this town? Caramba!" Altimera stomped the dust with pretended frustration.

"Look at this," Altimera dismissed Jake's concern with an open-handed gesture down the street, then shook a fistful of crumpled flyers with the other. "The Sheriff already take down all our posters."

"That seems to be part of the answer then, doesn't it?"

"No. It jus' means that he don' like us putting up posters in his town."

"Maybe we should go talk to him," Night Walker seemed to materialize out of the dirt. This was a phenomenon with which Jake was accustomed, but his sudden appearance and disappearance continued to upset Altimera.

"Aiyii! I wish you wouldn't do that."

"Good idea. Let's pull his teeth!" Jake ignored Altimera's upset, spun on his heel and the three of them headed back toward the office Jake had left bare moments before.

Crowding through the door, the three of them found the Sheriff with his hat back, his boots on the desk and one of Jake's posters in his hands. Color drained from Laszlo's cheeks, leaving him sickly in appearance.

"What do you know about that?" Jake demanded, pointing at the paper the lawman held.

The Sheriff had spent all his courage in the foiled face-off with Night Walker in the alley behind the saloon the evening before. Now the whole crowd of them stood over his desk, staring down at him.

"If what you claim happened, I know it happened outside my jurisdiction," he equivocated. Below hollowed eyes, the Sheriff's lips moved of their own accord.

"Not sayin' it did or didn't," Jake said. "I'm asking you if you knew who did it. Do you know, Sheriff?"

"Sounds like a whole bunch of fellers is involved, if they gunned down five men at once," Laszlo tried his best to avoid a direct answer.

"Frankly Sheriff, I don't care who did the shootin'. I want to know who paid to have it done."

"If I knew that, Tallon, I might have to arrest 'em and I can't figure how that would be healthy." There, the truth was out. Part of it anyway. Laszlo's cowardice overwhelmed him. He could no longer meet Jake's eyes.

With an uncharacteristic explosion of fury, Night Walker thrust-kicked the desk violently, sliding the furniture solidly into the lawman and the wall at the same time. The building reverberated on its foundation. Laszlo looked up through stricken eyes, speechless, wind knocked from his lungs.

"If you say you don't know and you won't help, maybe you jus' stay out of the way." Altimera caressed his tooled leather holster as he stared the man down.

Laszlo sincerely wished he were someplace else. No matter how bad Bill Zachary was, he knew he couldn't face these men across a gun on the Mayor's behalf.

And now they knew it also. Laszlo felt like he'd been to the dentist.

The Dutchman

Jake Tallon's thoughts tumbled over one another without direction. First confused by the ambush outside Nazareth that caught him so by surprise, then the fracas on the return trip from Cumberland Crossings, and finally the cross fire in the bank that had caught him off guard once again. He realized he was only reacting to situations instead of controlling them. From which direction would the next assault come? When would it come? What would he do about it when it happened?

The attacks were almost constant. Now Jake didn't know where to turn that would not lead immediately to another deadly confrontation. That worried him because others depended so much upon his clear judgment. Sarah and the baby must be protected though she fought so hard to walk at his side.

The answers he desired lived here in Nazareth. Jake felt them lurking somewhere in shadow. Nothing jumped right out at him. The Gunsmith was closed again today. Why? Every time he checked, the office was locked. This was the man who had warned José.

Traffic moved before him on the street as his eyes lazily wandered but no one returned his gaze, even when he stared. It was like he wasn't there, he thought. From the corner of his eye he caught a merchant glancing covertly in his direction. When he turned his head the merchant abruptly, even guiltily looked away, sweeping nervously.

Even strangers got more notice. Especially strangers got notice. The word was out on Jake and his friends. Why should he be surprised? Altimera had said as much from his first visit to this poisonous little berg. It had only gotten worse as the table stakes increased.

Posting the reward for information stirred the nest as he'd planned. Still, nothing definitive had happened. The tension bunched between his shoulders like a bruised muscle. He felt the skin of his face tightening over his cheeks with each passing hour. For a moment he wished he smoked tobacco, then instantly dismissed the thought as nonsense. He wagged his head side to side at such foolishness.

Sarah stepped quietly to his side, hooking her small arm through his left elbow. She seemed self-conscious of the pistol she now wore openly, thrust behind the belt over her hip.

Jake watched the roofline across the street covertly from under the brim of his hat. He expected no trouble but took no chances. This town was closed up tighter than a Wells Fargo cash box. The same man that held the lid shut would empty the street, before he struck. Jake was certain. The constant traffic reassured him in that regard. Still he wanted no repeat of the bank shoot-out. His luck might not last through another such incident.

Sarah turned her face into his shoulder and held her modestly growing belly against his arm. "The baby moves," wonder colored her voice. She placed his right hand over her midriff. Jake felt nothing but understood how distracted he was at the moment. Certainly Sarah could feel more than he. Men were ever outside of this miracle of life, destined to be merely observers.

Jake looked away, pursing his lips as his feelings of frustration persisted. What should he do next? Where should he turn? He squinted his eyes against the glare from the street. Who all was in on this? Who pulled the strings? How could he find out? Standing here accomplished nothing, yet he could imagine no additional action.

Thoroughly involved in her own delight, Sarah failed to notice his obsession. He worried about Sarah. Many times he had felt the sting of bullets. He could not stand to see her hurt in such a way, much less the baby. Sarah had been lucky so far, real lucky.

Fortunately, Jake's enemy concerned himself only with Jake. Sarah would not be hurt unless she happened to get in the way. Jake knew he could best protect her by leaving her behind, but if anything, Sarah wanted just the opposite. Jake furrowed his brow in frustration. This was the crux of his problem.

A shadow thrown by the tall figure of the Cherokee crossed the boards at Jake's feet. Jake looked up to find Night Walker standing before him. Face unsmiling, the big Indian pressed a handful of sand and gravel into his fingers, much of it spilling through.

"Remember what is real, Jacob!"

"What's that supposed to mean?" Jake snapped, puzzled and irritated.

The Cherokee was gone as easily as he appeared, but Jake's mind held his image. Concern had shadowed the Indian's face. Relaxing his fist, Jake allowed the rest of the sand to trickle slowly to the boards below his palm, retaining a single irregular pebble that he rolled thoughtfully between a finger and his thumb. A shroud lifted from his eyes. In his own enigmatic fashion, Night Walker had unlocked Jake's prison of inaction.

Jake sucked in a single slow deep breath, trembling slightly. He tried again. "Ahh," he exhaled, expelling imaginary poisons from his lungs. Tension seemed to leak outward from his neck, cascading downward, following the previously held grains of sand to the boards of the walk beneath his feet.

With both hands he gently moved his wife away from her warm nest against his ribs. "Why don't you and Tia find that doctor?" the words sprung from Jake's lips of their own accord.

"There's no doctor in this town, Jake Honey," Sarah sounded puzzled.

"Well, find a midwife and see about that baby. I have a little errand out of town."

"Where?"

"The mine. I want to see who's running it and how they're doing."

"Is that smart?"

"Maybe, maybe not. It's the only thing I can do right now, to flush these Polecats out. We put up the reward poster and nothing's happened. I'm tired of waiting for them to move against us. Most of these townsmen are buffaloed by someone they see as stronger than themselves. Until I show the strength of my own resolve, nothing here will change for the good at all."

"You're right, Jake. I see the fear in their eyes. Who do you think can make them that frightened?"

"Wondering that myself, Sarah. That's why I need to take some kind of action. Here in town they won't try much. Maybe they will if I make it easy for them."

"Didn't stop them in Bodie."

"Those were the last of the Mackinaws. Good sense was never part of their strong suit. The Mayor here is smarter than that."

"The Mayor?"

"Yeah, Big Bill Zachary. That's what I'm thinking. He and the Judge got together after I went to the Courthouse," Jake confided. "I watched the Judge when he thought himself unnoticed. Everyone either works for Zachary or owes him. Who will stand against the Mayor when he owns the town?"

"You're right, Jacob." Sarah leaned affectionately, once again, against his arm. "As long as the Mayor looks stronger, no one's gonna take your side against him."

Jake looked up and down the street. Sarah followed his gaze. The moments began to stack up. "Okay," she reached for his hand. "But be careful." She squeezed it briefly.

"Ow," he complained comically, "you're bruising my gunhand." Jake looked downward. Like a flash, in that instant, his eyes made a picture not unlike one of the new tin daguerreotypes. He noted the contrast of her alabaster skin against the weathered brown of his own. With a tiny smile, she let his hand drop. The moment was gone but he knew he would not forget the picture it made. Life, it seemed with Sarah, was a vast collection of such beautiful images.

Jake stood away from the wall and stepped into the full sun. People watched Jake covertly as he watched them. Zachary would know he was on the move by the time he threw a saddle over Sam's back. No matter!

Let 'em come, he thought. I may need some help, Shantee, if you're around.

Walker and Altimera came around the corner of the stable as though on cue, walking together toward Jake. He pushed the hat up off his forehead and stretched his shoulders to get the kinks out of his spine, watching as his two friends approached.

Jake took a moment to appreciate the vast gulf each of these two men had crossed to be his friend. Night Walker forgave the many sins of the White Man and Altimera forgave everyone, both Red and White. The magic of forgiveness, Jake realized, is that once learned, it may be repeated. So beneath the hard visage that each friend presented lay the forgiving heart. Who would know just by looking at them?

Such charity is forever tempered by common sense, Jake knew. No man had the right to expect it of others without sincerity. Jake understood that he could always expect it of these friends. They were worthy men for whom he would do the same, at any time, without their asking.

"I'm going out to the claim," he announced as they arrived before him and stopped. "We will find answers there that we can't find standing around here."

"Good!" Night Walker's lips pulled away from his teeth in an expression that resembled no smile Jake had ever seen. It was his battle face with which he confronted death. Its very presence told Jake the Cherokee believed they neared some dramatic confrontation.

Altimera was far more pragmatic, echoing Sarah's caution. "Is it wise, Jacob? Surely they wait for us."

"Maybe not. Although, each time before, they have come for me. Perhaps they will not expect me to come for them."

Within moments the three friends rode out of town toward the looming, blue-hazed mountains of the Basin Range. As they neared the hill at the curve of the trail, the site of the ambush, Jake raised his eyes to see the slight figure of an old man atop the rise, who raised an arm, pointing away from the trail at right angles.

Without a question Jake guided Sam through a break in the horse-high brush beside the trail, in the direction Shantee had indicated. Walker and Altimera followed, much puzzled by Jake's change of direction.

Shortly the brush thinned out against the sand hills and José pulled up alongside. "This is where I found you, amigo." He nodded toward four piles of stones.

Walker held the nervous mounts while Altimera helped Jake tidy the stones above each grave, talking as they worked. "I am surprised they do not move these graves. They are proof of the murder!"

"I know, José, but I am glad for other reasons." Jake's sadness was tempered by his recollection of the Starry Path and his friends beside him as he climbed toward the meeting with Shantee. He recalled his initial confusion. There was much of that, this side of the Spirit Lodge, not so much once he got there. The Spirit Lodge felt like home to Jake, a place of peace and safety. The thought warmed him as he explained, "My friends are no longer under this ground, maybe never were. These stones are only for their memory."

Rising from the simple task, Jake was startled to hear the unmistakable voice of Harry Harmon. At first it was as though heard from far away, so much like the wind it sounded. Standing stock-still, Jake strained with each of his senses.

"Howdy Partner. Can you hear me, Jake? It's Harry. I want a word with you."

Jake's surroundings dimmed out. A tremor of nervousness betraying his voice, Jake replied, "Sure. Howdy yourself."

Harry chuckled. "I'm not exactly sure how this works either but I want a favor from you." Harry never beat around the bush as Jake remembered the man.

"Sure, Harry. I feel so guilty. I'm not there with you. That part's not fair. I really want to be there."

"I'm not sorry, Jake, but I know how you feel. My situation isn't like yours, anyway. You still have a job to do."

"What's that?" Jake only had half a notion of what he spoke.

"In time, Jake, you'll find out."

Riddles! This was just like having a conversation with Shantee, thought Jake. "You're not going to give me a good answer, are you, Harry?"

"No answer I give you will make any sense to you now, Jacob, without the right time or without you knowing the answer yourself. If you think about it, you already know most of what you want to ask."

More Riddles! "Guess I'll have to find out for myself."

"That's the joy of it, Jacob." Jake could hear the humor in his "voice." Harry would make him work for an answer. Was making him work for an answer. Deep inside he had the sense that the very purpose of his life was unraveling these fundamental mysteries, mysteries like, "Why am I here?" Or "Why do I suffer so much?"

Harry's voice abruptly ended his musing.

"I want you to find my wife, Jacob. My death put a hardship on both her and my daughter and they need your help."

"Minnie was her name, if I remember right."

"Minnie Heycock Harmon and she's still in St. Louis where she washes and sews for a living, though she don't need it. That was as far east as I could bear to go when I returned from California years ago."

Jake scuffed uncomfortably at the sand around his moccasins. "Seems like a dream since I left the Spirit Lodge. I've had so much trouble keeping my feet on the ground. I'm sorry I didn't remember Minnie before now, Harry."

A moment passed before Jake could continue, "Finding the killers seemed the thing to do right at first. After I found a few, killing them just seemed like more of the same. I kinda lost my taste for that. But me changing my mind about vengeance don't make any real difference because someone still wants me dead again, real bad. It's like I'm trapped in a circle of killing that won't stop."

"You're in the middle of their plans, Jake. That's all it is. No one wants to kill you but they don't figure they can have what they want without doing you in first. You've made a career out of being an obstacle for bullies and dishonest folks. That's why I'm counting on you to survive this particular difficulty. A portion of that mine belongs to Minnie. Make sure that she gets it, Jacob." Harry paused. "She has the papers. All of them."

Resolution flowed into Jake like water after a long thirst. He stood up straighter, expanding his chest. Now he had the answer to the missing deeds and paperwork. His sense of purpose solidified for the first time since Altimera talked him out of a coma. "Thanks, Harry."

"I know you'll make it right, Jacob."

"I will make it right, Harry. For sure, I'll make it right!" Jake turned from the piles of sand and stone to find his two friends watching him with intense interest.

Altimera crossed himself vigorously, invoking the Mother Church. "Madre Dios. What am I to think, amigo, when I stand here watching you converse with the dead?"

"It's nothing to get in a sweat over, José. The dead are never very far away and in many ways they live better than we do anyway. To live in the world of flesh and blood is to endure pain and suffering. The spirit has no pain, but also they have less opportunity. Real learning takes place only when there are consequences."

"Pain is a good thing, Jacob? You are telling me this? Is that why I collect bullet wounds when we are together?"

"I understand, Jacob," the Cherokee added a sober note.

Jake angled his head thoughtfully to one side. "There is much to be said for either condition. Talking with Harry cleared up my thinking. I now know better what must be done for the living but still not all of the how."

As he spoke Jake was in motion, stepping into a stirrup and hauling himself upwards into the saddle atop his big Grulla, Sam. With a twist of the reins he pointed the horse toward Harry's claim and kicked the horse into forward movement, trusting that his friends would be close behind.

In short order they found the stream and a now well-worn trail leading to the claim first developed by Harry Harmon. It seemed only yesterday that Jake and his four friends had ridden unknowingly to their end. With the crystal purity of perfect memory, Jake replayed those moments. He saw nothing he would have done differently.

There had been no hint of danger, no one nosing around to cause suspicion. There had been no threats and no failed attempts. Yet someone had watched, calculated and planned. When the Bushwhackers had figured the time right, they had taken Jake and Harry's lives and their gold.

The coldness of the execution chilled Jake. It colored his thinking. The man responsible must pay for the deed. Lobo was a tool who may be forgiven his part but the planner must answer to Shantee. Jake winced. It would be tough for any man to face that gentle smile with dirt on his hands.

Jake had been reluctant to press Lobo for that information so far but his heart had changed. The new attitude fell into place with a palpable thump. Jake now felt that if Lobo wanted to be part of the family, he had to hold up his end, even if it meant giving up a previous associate. The fact the Sheriff shot Johnny was proof of his expendability, if Johnny needed any.

The three riders climbed a long shallow grade leading to the claim. Jake abandoned his reverie and focused intently upon the moment. Knowing others now worked the claim made his approach seem inappropriate, as if it was he who was the trespasser. Though he knew this was not the reality, the feeling persisted.

Tension built in Jake as they rounded a last corner and found the corral full of horses. There were fifteen if there were a dozen. Several stood in the shade of cottonwood trees with their heads over the rails, watching the three men approach. A rifleman with an unshaved face and dirty, misshapen hat stepped from a stand of close-growing pine to confront the three riders.

Jake recognized him immediately as one of the ambushers he had yet to confront. Curiously he felt no real animosity toward the man. Regardless of what happened here today, it was plain to him this man's future was neither long nor full of portent. A dismal end waited for him that Jake felt no compulsion to hurry.

The man's initial bluster melted away as he realized who it was that he confronted. Clearly, he didn't want to be anywhere near Jake Tallon.

Altimera and the Cherokee swung out to either side, creating a difficult choice of targets. Nervously the gunman's hand had dropped away from the firing mechanism of the Spencer rifle he held. He retained hold of the weapon by the barrel, dropping the scarred wooden stock to drag in the sandy dirt.

"You got it right, Gammell," Jake answered the unspoken question. "You didn't bury me deep enough the first time and you won't be the one to do it anytime soon."

The man's eyes danced back and forth like two bees trapped in a bottle. "I don't know you mister and I don't know how you heard my name."

"You know me all right and I know not only that Gammell is not your real last name, but your given name is Elmer. You were the least of those who bushwhacked me and my friends that night on the road to Nazareth. If you want to know, Elmer, your bullet missed. You killed Harry Harmon's horse. You can't even shoot straight. You sure 'nough weren't meant for this kind of life, Elmer."

Gammel obviously wanted no part of this conversation but the last comment made him pause even as he turned to run. "What ya mean by that?"

"Your friends had little respect for you and made you shovel sand while they watched and laughed. It was my fortune you didn't dig deeply."

Jake saw bits and pieces of that long ago night as though he watched through the eyes of another. He heard the derisive laughter of the Cruz Brothers and their cruel banter as Elmer labored over holes in the sand along the base of the low hill.

"The Cruz Brothers are dead, Elmer." The words dropped with the finality of stones into water. "They won't trouble you or anyone else ever again."

Mixed emotions crossed the man's tortured face in waves, distorting his features as they passed. "That's impossible," he stuttered. "Those fellers is too mean to die. No they didn't. You're funnin' me."

Jake sat quietly in his saddle as the man absorbed the truth of his words. Elmer's features cleared momentarily as he understood. His eyes brightened.

"My bullet missed, you said? That means I didn't hurt nobody. Iffen I didn't hurt nobody, what are you going to do with me?" he wheedled, looking sideways at Jake through suddenly crafty eyes.

"Nothin'. I'm not going to do anything with you, Elmer." In spite of his pitiful attempt at manipulation, Jake continued to bear him no ill will. He saw one narrow hope for the man, like a spark of light in a distant corner of a dark room. "Stay away from whiskey, Elmer. Drink makes you weak. Not drinking is the only way you'll see a new moon."

Jake heard the Cherokee grunt agreement behind him. Maybe he had seen the same thing.

Elmer didn't need convincing. He dropped the Spencer and ran bandy-legged for the corner of the corral, glancing fearfully over his shoulder like a beaten, frightened animal.

Sam stepped on the rifle as he moved forward, on purpose, as if he understood the threat inherent in the firearm, splintering the stock under his huge hoof. It would never be the same again.

The three friends passed in and out of shade as they moved up the slope toward the mineshaft. A small ore crushing operation, a stamp mill, worked with a heavy, continuous thump down by the water where Jarred had broken rock with a hammer so recently in Jake's mind. Smoke from the boiler fire hung in the air around the building and trailed down the watercourse, seemingly drawn by the race of white water along its tumbling path.

A man disappeared over the hump in front of the shaft, running toward the chimney of rock Jake remembered so well. They were announced, he knew.

The stamp mill ceased its hammering. Three or four curious men stepped from the front door and stood, hats back, hands on hips, to watch Jake approach the mine.

The horses stepped down into the broad, worn path used by mule-drawn ore carts and turned uphill and slightly to the right. Jake remembered a time when the path had been more modest, worn only by his single wheelbarrow. In spite of the coming confrontation he smiled at the memories. They were all that remained of his friends and for the moment all that he had with which to celebrate their lives, their good lives.

Slowly, noise from the mineshaft diminished, then ceased altogether. The only sounds came from the steady shuffle of shod hooves as the three horses moved forward. Though tense with expectation, Jake rode loose in the saddle, reins in his left hand, his right hand resting limply against his leg.

A bearded, bobbing head appeared above the rise in front of the shaft. Jake knew the path descended slightly on the other side before it reached the hole. Soon other heads appeared as a group of miners moved to meet the horsemen. In the lead was the biggest man Jake had ever seen. The man's chest and arms were massive; his forward stride was choppy. The short thick legs might have belonged to someone else. Were the situation different, Jake might have thought the combination comical, but no humor graced the man's harsh Germanic features.

This person was his sworn enemy. No other way to cut it. They might not know Jake but even the slowest intellect must be suspicious of the sudden acquisition of such a rich strike. This man was in charge of a stolen claim and he didn't look like he cared.

As he strode forward, the bullet-headed behemoth scrubbed at his dirty face and neck with pieces of roughly woven, equally dirty cloth. He came to a stop before Jake and stuffed the rags into a back pocket. Jake couldn't help but notice that he stood a full head taller and twice as wide as any other man in the group. A chill of apprehension shot down Jake's spine.

"Who be you?" the stocky giant asked without preamble, squinting his eyes against the sun and cocking his shaggy head slightly to one side.

"Might ask you the same thing," Jake tossed back as his big horse shifted nervously under him. "I own this hole and you don't work for me."

"You own nuthin' less you prove different, little man." The monster put his ham-like fists on his hips and thrust his jaw forward. A torrent of German accented words poured from his mouth. "You're right, I don't verk fur you. I don't effen know you. You better turn dat horse 'round and leaf dis ground before me angerr happens."

Apparently the man had saved those words just for this occasion. They came at Jake so fast, he had no time to respond. Nor would he get any opportunity. As the big man finished speaking, he lunged forward with the miners at his side. He made a slashing grab for Sam's reins that barely missed as the big horse danced backward.

As Sam reared in surprise, he violently bumped the horses behind him. Jake saw that if he didn't start shooting, the three of them would be quickly overwhelmed. The miners were unarmed but he knew better than to disregard the danger of their numbers. These men worked hard, with naked rock, all day long. They could easily kill with their hands.

As one, the three spun and galloped quickly out of reach. Jake pulled up and turned once again to confront the man-giant. A confusion of angry retorts whirled in his mind. "Who do you think you are? You can't steal a man's claim and his life and get away with it." Sam danced under him with excitement. "Not forever you can't."

"I tink I am Dutch Honnicker," the monster rumbled, words like giant rocks tumbling down a hillside, "and I verk for da man dat owns dis ground. And as long ass I am here, he vill own it! Possession is all! You are only anoder little man."

"While I am alive, possession is nothing," Jake spat back. "You and the man you work for are thieves and worse." He felt the futility of his words. This man understood only violence.

"Dan vei don't you get down off dat pretty horse, little man. Ve see who iss alive and who possess da mine." Honnicker's wicked smile betrayed no possible doubt in the outcome of the suggested confrontation. The men at his side snarled and mumbled their evil appreciation like the scurvy pack dogs they were.

Jake was stymied. They were three against many and strangers in a town where they were unwanted. Only the thin influence of distant authority had protected them thus far. One misstep was all that was needed. No one in this town would stand up for him. Should he shoot an unarmed man, he would run for the rest of his life.

He fumed with tortured indecision.

"Some day, Dutch, you may get what you want."

"You can't mean that," Altimera was horrified.

"He's big but he's only a man. I can fight him alone but I can't do it on his ground with all of his friends."

"He'll break you like kindling," predicted Altimera with certainty.

"Sure, little man," the giant taunted. "Ven you get brave enuf ve verk it out." Honnicker's derisive laugh was echoed by his cronies.

Though Jake burned with humiliation, he knew the best course was to back off. Retreat simply went against everything that raged inside him. "Another time," he mumbled, through tight, bloodless lips.

"Another time," echoed the Cherokee.

Face burning, Jake pointed them back toward town.

"Sure, little man," the giant taunted. "Ven you get brave enuf ve verk it out."

Eliza Crombe

The sun bounced along the mountains behind them as they followed the trace into Nazareth. Glancing to the side, Jake shuddered as they passed the site of the ambush in fading light. There were too many unpleasant memories here, always would be.

They found Nazareth nearly deserted. Most people would be eating their suppers. As they tied their horses outside the Livery, Jake saw a candle in the Gunsmith's window.

Oh, he thought! This was a first. Had the Gunsmith been away and now returned? There was a question here and Jake wanted the answer. He mumbled an excuse to his friends and strode toward the shadowed storefront. His feet found the boardwalk, and the door swung easily and quietly open at his touch.

Deeper into the shop, behind an ornately carved customer rail, sat the old Gunsmith at his heavy worktable. In a pool of light from an overhead lamp was a single object. Not a customer's gun as Jake might have suspected, but a heavy crystal glass, half full of amber liquid.

Bald on top, the Gunsmith's wiry white hair spun a cloud that circled behind his head. Brass-rimmed spectacles sat on a small nose above his bushy white mustache. The nervous motion of his hands as he toyed with the tumbler betrayed his inner turmoil.

The old man suddenly looked up, though Jake had made no sound. "Keeping that door oiled sometimes works against me, said the Gunsmith. "Can't hardly help it though. It's not in my nature to let good metal go to rust."

"You did some work for my friend, José Altimera, a while back, fitting a couple of Remingtons with bored-through cylinders. It was good work." This was the first time Jake had talked to a townsman that they had not immediately disengaged the conversation. Jake likened the experience to playing a big fish on light tackle. If he made the wrong move, it might spit the hook or break the line.

"I remember that fancy Mexican and I know who you are anyway, young fella." The old man smiled with one side of his mouth. "You're the one can't duck fast enough. My name's Eliza Crombe."

"Jake Tallon." They shook hands. Jake felt Eliza's pent-up need to talk, so he waited quietly without speaking. Maybe this fish wasn't running.

"I'm a trouble-maker," Crombe began. "Can't keep my mouth shut. When you showed up, the Sheriff asked me, no he told me, to take a vacation. Coming back early worries me some, I'll admit. I'm just glad you showed up first."

"So, why'd you come back?"

"Partly 'cause I couldn't stay away. Also 'cause there's other people don't like the way things are run in Nazareth, but are too afraid to do anything about it. Someone has to say something!"

Jake's heart hammered in his ears. He was afraid to ask too much too fast, and spook the old man into silence.

"What's there to fear?"

"Don't play games with me youngster!" The Gunsmith reached into the shadows beyond the light and with a rustle of paper pulled out a copy of Jake's reward flyer.

"They tore all these down 'cept what folks got to first. Everybody knows about the claim changin' hands. Anyone with half a brain can draw a conclusion. The Mayor is up to no good. Again!" The Gunsmith slapped the scarred tabletop for emphasis.

"Why do you say the Mayor's behind this?" Jake probed, raising a single eyebrow.

"Because Big Bill Zachary is behind everything that goes on in this town. He built Nazareth as his personal cash machine ten years ago and he's been cranking the handle ever since. Weren't too bad while the boom was on. He could milk every prospector and new claim was filed. When that died out he pressured local business for cash to finance his own ambitions.

"Last few years, everybody's felt more of the squeeze. He'd send the Sheriff around with suggestions for this or that contribution. If'n a man didn't ante up, things started happening. Property would be stolen or broken. Maybe a fire. Not so much is happenin' lately. He's gettin' his money somewhere else." The Gunsmith looked up meaningfully from under his bushy white brows. "Like that new claim of his. And he's been leaving the rest of us alone."

"So what's that supposed to do with me?" Jake asked.

"You're a cautious one, aren't you?" the old man peered up at Jake, adjusting his spectacles as though to see more clearly, squinting in the process. "You don't need to be so careful with me. I'll tell you everything you want to know. It's like I said before, I can't keep my mouth shut.

"You and your friends are the first folks had gumption 'nough to stand up to that bully and his hooligans. You're the first to survive the

Mackinaw Brothers. Ha!" The old man smiled into his whiskey. "Nobody's gonna miss that brood of nasty brats. They been ornery as long as I can remember. I wouldn't sell them guns 'cause I knew they would use them for no good. Let 'em go somewhere else to buy their killing tools."

"So you think the Mayor arranged that ambush? Did he do it alone?"

"The Mayor pays for everything and does nothing himself." Crombe gestured Jake into a chair. "He owns all the riffraff in this town. Dutch Honniker is his muscle boy down at the mine. I gather you already met him. He still alive?" Crombe asked.

"Yeah, he's still alive but I'm not sure he's gonna let things be. The only reason one of us didn't die was we still had our horses and could ride away."

"Honnicker won't wear guns. He'll kill you with his hands if he can get a hold on you. No man in his right mind wants to come within reach of those big hands of his." The Gunsmith shook his head, frowning. "Dutch'll be after you now that you've been down to the mine. Up to now, they've just been hoping you'd go away."

"They killed my friends," Jake spat, "I'm not going away until I've found the responsible person and nailed his hide to the wall." Jake found himself clenching and unclenching his hands uncontrollably.

"Yup." The old man regarded the younger cautiously while his anger subsided. Behind Jake he saw two shadows enter the room and spread out to either side of his visitor. As they entered the pool of light, he identified them as Jake's friends, the Mexican and the Indian.

Eliza lowered the hammer on the Remington Army and lifted it from under the table where he had held it until the advancing shadows became known. His caution did not go unnoticed.

Jake brought a hand to the wound on his head, pushing the hat back in the process. He felt it pulse under his touch. "I don't think I'm completely well yet," he apologized. "I can't stop without justice, but I still feel like I'm working in the dark. I have plenty of suspicion but no certainty."

"Here, take this. It's a mate to the one you have in the right holster." The Gunsmith handed over the converted Remington Army he had held under the table.

Jake grinned his appreciation as he hefted the piece. "Yeah, the other one got shot up a bit by the Cruz Brothers. Been meanin' to drop it by for repair. That's why I wanted to see you in the first place, but it seems like you might have something else on your mind right now."

"You're a perceptive young man," observed Crombe with narrowed eyes. "I was telling you about our crooked Mayor. He's responsible for everything around here. I'm sure he arranged the ambush and controls your claim but he will certainly have covered his tracks. He's real good on the details. I'm sure the Judge helped him there. You won't be able to prove anything." The old man seemed to slump against the table.

Staring dumbly at the bare, polished work surface, Crombe continued, "Living in this town makes me sick. Every morning I wake up hoping things will change but they don't. If anything, they get worse. Then you came into town. This is the first time Zachary hasn't got his way from the outset. His bully boys keep showing up in the back of someone's buckboard with canvas on their faces."

The Gunsmith's features creased into a brilliant smile, the first real emotion he'd shown since Jake walked in. "You really did a job on that Bingo Mackinaw. What did you hit him with?"

"Well, just a stick really."

Altimera looked at him with astonishment, "It was a really big stick. Maybe ten feet long."

"It was only seven feet long, José." Jake found himself smiling over the incident. "I don't know how I can laugh about killing somebody. He was so full of himself, I can't say he didn't deserve what he got."

"Hey, Señor Gunslinger, you want a toothpick?" José pantomimed the throw with realistic intensity. Even the taciturn Cherokee smiled.

The old man lifted his frail body from the stool and disappeared into the shadows. He returned with a bottle and extra glasses. Looking first into each face, he poured drinks all around with studied care.

Jake and Walker sipped politely from their glasses. Altimera tossed his back with gusto. "I never drink," José explained, "but I'm not sure I like the direction this story takes."

"I don't know about that," said the Gunsmith. "For the first time, people around here have a little hope. Just by surviving, you've shown them that Big Bill Zachary can be beaten."

"I don' see them throwing flowers at us yet," said the Mexican cynically, pushing his glass forward for a refill.

"Don't look to me like he's beaten," Jake agreed.

"But except for Honnicker and a few at the top, all the faces are new," the Gunsmith cocked an eyebrow in Jake's direction. "His lieu-tenants are all pushin' up daisies or disappeared after that Utah trip. Those that you see working for him now are all brand new hired guns. They have no real loyalty. The Sheriff and the Judge stay indoors a lot. Everyone can see they're scared. First sign of serious trouble and the gunmen are gone."

"Yet they are many," said Altimera. "What can we do?"

"I'm not sure there is much of a choice," Jake offered. "I had to run from that mob out at the claim and I'm not running again. I say we smoke 'em out right here." His eyes were bleak with his resolve.

"What about contacting authorities in Sacramento? What about the trial?" Walker questioned, entering the conversation for the first time.

"If we fail tomorrow, Lobo won't stand a chance anyway." Jake paused, casting his eyes around this circle of friends. "Eliza's right about Honnicker. He'll be after me first thing and I know that Zachary is aware of my reward for information. They cannot afford to wait any longer, so we don't have to worry about proving anything. It'll be a showdown."

"You will need much help," the Mexican spoke up again.

"Gunsmithing's an art and I'm an artist, not a warrior. I'm no good at a stand-up fight but I'm a fair shot with a long gun. Maybe I can cover your back." The Gunsmith turned from the table again. This time he returned with his hands full of rifles. He laid a brand new Winchester on the table along with a full length Sharp's breechloader.

"I fitted that Sharp's for cartridges. Make 'em myself. It'll throw a four hundred grain slug out to about thirteen hundred yards."

"I have never seen this before," Altimera hefted the Winchester.

"Same company as makes the Henry," said Crombe. "Uses a bigger cartridge. They started makin' 'em last year. It's the Model 66. Only just now starting to see 'em out here."

"That's just two guns," the Mexican pointed out.

"I don't know how much help you can expect on the street, but this town is fed up with Big Bill Zachary and that rotten Sheriff. You'd be doing everyone a big favor."

"Chihuahua! If we live, that would be great also."

Jake stared downward at the table top, appearing deep in thought.

The Cherokee stepped forward, touching the desk with extended fingers. "Free Lobo, put a gun in his hands, Jacob, and lock the Sheriff behind his own bars."

"Lobo's the marksman that started this whole shindig. Why not cut loose that wolf and turn the tables on the Mayor and his bullies!" Jake's features brightened. "The Sheriff was what had me worried. Even a bad Sheriff carries a lot of weight. This will work if we do it the way you say, Walker!"

"I will do this now, myself," muttered the Cherokee almost to himself, "He is afraid of me and because of this, I own his soul."

The Indian paused as he stepped toward the door, "There is yet one other loose end to which I must attend before I deal with the Sheriff!"

Spirit of the Night

The Rangers had been the first victims of the Spirit Stalker. Over the course of that first week, Malvado hunted and killed them by ones and twos. Though the revenge was complete, his hatred and contempt of the White Man only expanded.

His murders since that time had been increasingly less memorable and even less honorable, causing Malvado to grow more distant from other human kind and even more disturbed. Turning to the White Man's whiskey, he sought to dull the hurt and fill the void left by the absence of honor.

It became more difficult for him to hold the memory, the image, of the kind old man who taught him in the beginning, the Shaman Joaquin. Whenever he did succeed in summoning that vision, Malvado was forced to shake off his mentor's stern disapproval. At this time in his life he hardly possessed even an image of himself to fall back upon.

He no longer knew the young man from which he grew. His life was reduced to drinking, murder and the chronic misuse of magic that helped him perform those murders.

This was an exceedingly dangerous, downward-spiraling cycle. In particular, something troubled him about the current assignment, something to which he could not pin a name. Even the Sheriff could not have known. Perhaps Laszlo should have grown a suspicion based upon the difficulty involved in tracking and removing Jake Tallon. But Tallon, himself, was not what troubled Malvado.

The trouble was that the Spirit Stalker had never been "seen" before. Ahh, Malvado thought. There it is! I have never been seen and now I am seen by another. But by whom? Not a White Man! Certainly, not a White Man.

The question of "who" continued to disturb him as Malvado prepared for the approaching evening and the successful completion of his brash pledge to the Sheriff.

The young Tallon never stayed long in one place, but now he was back in Nazareth. The Black Shaman planned to catch him and extinguish his life this very evening before he moved on once again.

253

Crouching in a rude Hogan near the outskirts of the small mining settlement, Malvado fed the fragrant herbs to a small fire. As always, he had a twinge of conscience using Spirit magic for such ends. It was wrong but he did so anyway. Somewhere inside, Malvado knew this violation was responsible for his slow decline. No matter now, he thought. The pattern has long since been set and was now unchangeable.

The fascination with Spirit Travel remained. Settling fully upon crossed legs, he breathed deeply of the wild smoky perfume, relaxed easily and slipped into the nether world of Spirit Flying. As his body broke free, he soared again into a night curiously lit as though by day with the unique silvery Spirit Light. Swooping across the brushy flats and into the town of Nazareth, he cruised the main street from one end to the other like the hunting owl, sliding through the night air.

At that very moment Malvado saw Jake Tallon enter the shop of the Gunsmith. None of the previous danger surrounded the White Man. Malvado drew no conclusions from the observation but was instead filled with exhilaration and the desire to strike. A perfect time, he thought.

But in the spirit form, he might do nothing except observe. With the speed of thought, he slammed home to his body, slumped forward over crossed legs near his lonely fire. Reentering that body, Malvado uncurled with the silky sinuousness of the desert Sidewinder.

Standing above the dying embers, he stretched and bent to each side, unlimbering every muscle. A demented smile lit his face ear to ear, the black eyes glistening with unnatural anticipation. This was the most difficult task he'd ever undertaken. Tallon was a known man, an adversary thought by many to be nearly invulnerable. There were other wrinkles, like the feeling of exposure he experienced almost constantly when stalking Tallon, yet he felt as confident in this mission as of any previous. No man before Jake Tallon had stayed his knife, nor would Jake Tallon.

Spirit flight gave Malvado the ability to scout without discovery. Now he must execute on his own and it was that for which he labored, for which he most yearned. The excitement of the moment gave him momentary pause, as he realized he was most alive when he killed. Other men have women and children to lend meaning to their lives. Malvado experienced that understanding only as a flickering regret, gone as soon as it bloomed.

Stooping purposefully, he grabbed handfuls of cooling ash and smeared them liberally across his sweat-streaked body. The uneven coloring let him blend more effectively into the night. With sudden energy, Malvado burst from the Hogan, sticks flying, and ran eagerly on naked feet toward the sleepy town in the near distance.

He circled the village that he might approach the shop of the Gunsmith from behind. Dim starlight piercing the night from a cloudless sky above showed him an open space between the Mercantile and the building where Tallon sat in quiet conversation. Stepping cautiously forward, slowing his breathing and even his heart, Malvado embraced the darkness betwixt the buildings that concealed his progress. Though trash filled the alley through which he moved, he stepped on none that caused the slightest sound. A small skill among many, he sneered silently.

At the window, back from the light, which might expose him, Malvado saw Jake Tallon talking with a Mexican and the Gunsmith, the man Crombe. He recognized the Mexican as Tallon's sometime companion. Malvado had killed many Mexicans over the years and he held no fear of this one, though he wore his guns like a natural extension of his will.

Watching the Mexican toss off another drink, Malvado hissed his derision softly into the night around him. No problem here, he thought, as Tallon would be the first to fall. The small seconds allowed by the shock of the attack and the Mexican's dulled senses would give him time for the second. This was almost too easy.

Slowly Malvado crouched and spun from the side of the building, seeking the even deeper shadow within the alley. High walls blocked the starlight from above, providing Malvado nearly total darkness in which he swam like water. No human ear could hear him approach the head of the alley near the front door of the shop.

From inside the building the sounds of chairs scraping and men standing reached him through thin walls. He heard booted steps approaching the door and the sleepy goodbyes of tired men.

Drawing the long, wicked blade, Malvado grew intent with the singleness of his purpose. As the Gunsmith's door closed, its oiled lock clicked smoothly into place. He now distinguished the whisper of moccasins along with the heavy thud of the Mexican's boots on the boards of the walk. The sound of moccasins would be the footfalls of his principal target, Jacob Tallon.

Like a shadow, Malvado moved forward, bent at the waist and knees, left hand feeling for the wall behind him. Doubt, like the distant sound of lonely wind, tickled at the back of his mind. His eyes twitched. A cloud blocked the light of stars. A cloud? Acting on the premonition of imminent danger, prey forgotten, Malvado spun away from the head of the alley, hearing behind him the whistle of split air as if someone had swung at him and missed.

Absurd! Who that knew of him would challenge Malvado in the moment of his attack? Who had the strength and courage to risk certain death at the hands of Malvado? Had Malvado even time for such thoughts, he wondered, as the initial sound of splitting air was followed immediately by the light but insistent footfall of pursuit, first one then another as quiet as his own.

Malvado danced silently amidst the garbage of the alley with steps that soundlessly avoided a can, a bottle, a pile of rotting food, seeing each without the aid of his eyes, seeing with a sense he depended upon but had never defined. Suddenly spinning, skidding noisily to a stop, Malvado lashed out with the broad-bladed knife at the end of his overly long arm. Dim light caught and reflected from the flashing steel showed him a huge figure arching away from instant death. Perhaps he had nicked the abdomen of his agile pursuer. Perhaps not.

Reversing his grip and the silvered edge of doom, Malvado stepped energetically forward and slashed downward at legs that would perhaps not move so quickly. Crash! Lights danced in time to the musical tinkle of glass as his unseen assailant smashed the side of his head with the bottle over which he had just leapt.

Back and forth. Up and down. The knife of Malvado sought the flesh and hot blood of his unseen enemy while the stars above regained their stability. "No!" shouted Malvado as he realized the struggle took him only further from his most important target, Jake Tallon. Saliva collected, spilled from the corners of his mouth and spattered outward with the rush of his labored breath as he fought his way once more toward the entrance to the alley. Perspiration born of his exertions flowed liberally down each limb, oiling the air through which he slipped.

Skidding past his right cheekbone, a rock hammered the boards at his back. Then, even as he bobbed and wove, a sharp point scored the shoulder of his opposite arm. Malvado folded his legs beneath him, leapt and slashed simultaneously, fighting the best and the most futile fight in which he had ever been involved.

No! This can't happen! Who is this dangerous, illusive shadow? Is he even human, he wondered desperately. This enemy is more invisible, more insubstantial than the spirit body in which I sometimes walk, though he torments me with constant attack. Try though I might, I cannot even touch him.

"Ahhhrgggh!" with the suddenness of a thunderclap, the breath exploded from Malvado's lungs. In his mind he cursed vividly. This would ruin everything! And at the same time, he realized there was more involved than an involuntary rush of hot breath.

Malvado felt himself pinned helplessly to the rough vertical boards of the building behind him, and glancing downwards, found a very large hand crushing the bleeding flesh and broken bones of his chest into a tight fist. For the first time in his experience, the knife at the end of his nerveless right arm failed to respond to his command. Distantly, he heard the now useless blade strike the ground at his feet with a dull thump.

Desperately looking again to the fist in his ruined chest, he followed the long muscular arm all the way to the shoulder and the face - the face of a long-forgotten friend! Sunlight buried deeply in the Stalker's soul broke through the obscuring clouds of evil. His heart turned over in sudden despair as he saw the length and breadth of his wasted life reflected through the eyes of his boyhood companion. "I ... am ... sorry," Malvado whispered with his last wisps of breath.

"I am sorry as well, Two Whistles," spoke the Cherokee Shaman Night Walker in the forgotten language of Malvado's youth. "You choose unworthy tasks for your great talent."

The eyes of Night Walker's childhood friend had already dimmed in death but the Cherokee knew that he had been heard. Relaxing his death-hold, he sagged backward onto his heels, allowing his eyes to unfocus, seeking the drifting cloudlike form of his friend's soul that he knew hovered nearby.

Loose Ends

Tensing for action, Jake turned at the sudden commotion in the alley. After only an instant, he heard a muttered exchange in what he knew was the Cherokee language, having picked up a few words from Night Walker here and there over the years.

Still cautious, he edged around the corner of the building to find the Cherokee easing a long limp form to the ground, stretching the legs straight in repose. Jake's eyes adjusted slowly to the darkness after so much lamplight. "What's happening?" he asked of his Indian friend.

"Someone who was once a brother," said the Cherokee briefly, sorrow cloaking his voice. "He was a threat of which I have not spoken but he has now abandoned his mission after a brief disagreement."

Jake felt a curious absence of the oppression that had dogged him these last days. Intuitively he felt Walker's actions were connected with that change. "There's more to it than that, isn't there?" he asked.

"Yes. I must care for Two Whistles, Jacob. I had to stop him from hurting us. He was a friend of my childhood. He is dead now."

A silence ensued while Night Walker fumbled for words. He seemed consumed by a grief that had caught him unawares. "Perhaps I'll see you in the morning, Jacob." With effort, the Cherokee shrugged off his emotions and disappeared quietly into the darkness of the alley, carrying his sad burden.

A lot of ground to cover with so few details, thought Jake. He wanted to cure the obvious hurt of his friend but also felt the intense pressure of events driving them all forward. Jake shrugged off his emotions and followed the Mexican. It was time to act.

So leaving the Cherokee to deal with his friend, Jake strode, Altimera at his side, toward the office of the Sheriff. Only a few lights brightened the street at distant intervals. Dust, illuminated by the moon, puffed silently around the impact of each rapid footfall.

A single lamp shone in the Jail's office.

One stride across the boardwalk, and Jake hit the door with an outstretched palm, breaking the simple mechanism holding it shut. Loose

258

on its hinges, the door hit some object in mid-swing and careened drunkenly back toward Jake on one remaining hinge. Gun in hand, Jake strode past the door, leaving a surprised Altimera to block it with a raised forearm.

Half asleep, stunned by the sudden violence of the intrusion, Laszlo sat, hands flat on the desk, staring wide-eyed at the stormy approach of an angry Jake Tallon. Laszlo saw trouble he felt powerless to stop.

Bang! The desk slid straight into him, struck him in the stomach and pinned him against the wall again. Deja vu from the onslaught of Night Walker two days before washed over him in waves. "Haven't we done this before?" he wondered out loud. "Look's like I'll have to nail this damned desk to the floor, always moving like it does. Doggone thing hurts when it catches me under the ribs."

"I've had just about enough out of you and this crooked town," Jake came across the desk and grabbed the larger man by the shirtfront. Hauling the unresisting Sheriff face down over the littered surface, Jake snatched the lawman's single gun from his holster and jerked the shirt from his belt, looking for a hideout piece.

"You got 'em all, Tallon. What you gonna do with me?"

"I'm gonna trade you for Johnny Lobo and make sure you don't get involved in whatever happens tomorrow."

"You won't get no fight outta me," protested Laszlo, "I'm done."

"You bet I won't." Coming around the desk, Jake pulled the man out of his chair and threw him with surprising strength against the door to the cell room. "Keys," he demanded.

Unwilling to look away from the legendary Berserker, Laszlo patted the wall above him in the shadows until his hand found the key ring on its ten penny nail. The collection of iron keys rattled as he hauled them down. "Here! I'll open the door for you myse'f."

"No! I don't trust you! José, get a lantern and check the cell before we put him into it."

"Si, amigo." José lifted one of the two lit lanterns from its peg and thrust it before him as he entered the cellblock, gun drawn. Jake handed him the keys on the way through.

Altimera found Lobo waiting, face pressed against the bars, awakened by the commotion in the outer office.

"What's up?" Johnny asked.

"Not only are you a free man," Altimera answered, "you're gonna help us." He scanned the cell as Lobo buttoned his shirt and picked up his hat.

"It's clean," said Johnny Lobo. "I've been looking for something since I got here. There's no way out for even an enterprising man like myself."

"Please don't tell me it's clean," said the Mexican. "This place stinks to high Heaven. You say the Sheriff can't escape once we lock heem up? Is that what you say?"

"Yes," Johnny's face brightened. "I'll take care of him."

"No," Jake cut through Johnny's expectant joy with a single word and pushed Laszlo in front of him. With a foot in the small of his back, Jake propelled the Sheriff viciously into the small barred enclosure.

Laszlo hit the far wall below the window and sprawled gracelessly onto the floor.

"You dint have to do that!" mumbled the beaten Sheriff.

"Like I said before. I've had enough of this fandango. You're gonna stay in here and you'll be quiet. This treatment is good, compared to what I feel you deserve." Jake jabbed a trembling finger in Laszlo's direction. "If Lobo hears a whisper, he has my orders to shoot you. Heck! I'll have him shoot you a couple of times."

Laszlo blanched at the suggestion. The last thing he wanted was Lobo with a gun. His life wasn't worth five cents with the scales so drastically turned.

The same idea occurred to a broadly smiling Johnny.

"You betcha, Boss," Lobo said.

"Take it easy, Johnny," said Jake. "Don't kill him unless it's absolutely necessary. I mean it, Johnny!"

Laszlo pulled himself off the floor and came to the door as Altimera locked it into place, grabbing two vertical bars, one in each hand. "What about the Judge?"

"What do you mean, the Judge?" Jake asked him curiously, stepping forward again, squinting his eyes in suspicion.

"I mean you want him out of the way just like me, don't you?" Laszlo knew the Judge was as unhappy with the direction of events in Nazareth as he and would also benefit by being locked up while things came apart. Sort of like professional courtesy, he thought, and smiled.

"Makes sense to me," said Jake cautiously. "This window opens on the alley," he pointed out, "and Johnny will hear you before anyone else."

"Like I toll you before, Tallon, you won't get no fight outta me. I'm done. I wanna know, what do you plan to do with me after?"

"After?" That question made Jake think beyond the moment. After only a brief pause, Jake answered with a measured delivery and slightly narrowed eyes, hoping Laszlo would understand the seriousness of his dilemma. "If you find some way to square yourself with Lobo, we'll let you leave the country."

"You mean apologize?" Laszlo made a face thinking about the apology, but quickly resigned himself to it as the lesser of all unpleasant possibilities.

"Let me do it now!" an involuntary gagging sound issued from his throat, but he looked at Lobo through the bars with a face wiped consciously free of expression.

Johnny stepped close to the bars, expectantly. "How do you apologize for gut-shooting a man? I want to know."

"I've been mullin' it over for some time, Lobo, is how," said Laszlo. "I've been in this town too long, an' I been hooked up with all the wrong people."

"Zachary?"

"Yes. You know how he is, if anyone does. I wasn't always like this … this kind of man. And I wouldn't have shot you had I been thinking right, especially over a woman and right in front of her like it happened." The Sheriff blinked several times looking away, and then composed himself once again. "That flat makes no sense to me."

"Or to anyone else!" Johnny understood the corrupting effect a man like the Mayor could have on others. Hadn't he sat in his office feeling like a fly poised above the web of a very deadly spider? Zachary numbered among the most evil men with whom he'd ever dealt. "What was it, that he offered you, Laszlo?"

"Just the lawin' business at first. Then he'd ask me to fudge a little here and there. It kinda wore me down. I needed the money or thought I did. Before you know it, I was his creature and it was too late. I saw my life had slipped away from me. He pulled all the strings." The words tumbled from the lawman's mouth. "I did whatever he'd ask. I've seen it happen to others. It makes me sick to think I let it happen to me."

Laszlo drew an uneven breath as he finished and sagged against the bars, the truth of the situation coming to him as he spoke. "I can be a different man, Lobo." He paused meaningfully. "If you let me. I'm honestly sorry for what I did to you. I'm sorry."

"Sounds like you mean it," Johnny smiled nervously, warring with his conflicted emotions, unconsciously running a hand over the healing wound in his midriff. It was plain, even to Lobo, that the Sheriff spoke the truth.

"I'm sorry," the repenting lawman repeated himself.

Lobo started to say something but stopped before words could leave his mouth. Spinning abruptly, he abandoned the cellblock and its new occupant.

Laszlo starred at the floor, hope flickering as a small vulnerable flame behind his eyes. "Better get the Judge," he reminded Jake. "His days is numbered, otherwise."

Altimera patted the lawman's fingers limply and set the lantern down inside the door to the office. Pushing Jake out the door before him, he left Laszlo to his misery and reflection, closing the door behind them.

As he turned into the office, Jake went directly to the desk, straightening and stacking paperwork to put into a drawer.

"I'll get the Judge," Altimera said. "I saw his light burning in the Courthouse."

Jake nodded agreement to Altimera. "Why don't you come with me, Johnny?" Tallon said to his one-time Bushwhacker. "Let's go talk to the girls. The Sheriff'll be okay while we're gone."

After Lobo stepped through the front door into the street, Jake wedged the front door into a semi-shut position behind them. Light bursting into the darkness from the upper left corner spoke of the busted hinge. He smiled crookedly. "Don't know my own strength sometimes."

At a loss for words, Jake realized there was no longer anything he needed to hear from Johnny that he hadn't concluded for himself. Almost companionably, they walked together down the dark and dusty street, finally mounting the steps to Molly's Boarding House. They found Sarah and Tia over tea in the colorfully wallpapered parlor. Stripes and bright bouquets of small flowers ran floor to ceiling. Seeing them enter, the hostess rose and left, leaving the men with their women. Johnny hadn't heard a word since leaving the Jail and waited anxiously for Jake to begin as they took their seats on upholstered chairs across from Sarah and Tia.

Jake felt uncomfortable with any outward show of affection in this formal room, in front of two unmarried friends. And only the fact that Jake blocked Johnny's path kept the young man from rushing to Tia's embrace.

For her part Tia rose part way out of her chair before she clamped an iron control upon her runaway emotion. What was Johnny doing free from his cell, she wondered desperately?

"What happened at the claim?" asked Sarah, eyes wide. She wanted to hug Jake so much, her arms ached. He lived! He lived, her heart screamed!

"Nuthin' much. They got quite an operation going out there with a new portable stamp mill and all. I didn't get many answers from them." Jake couldn't bring himself to mention the way they were chased off, or the overwhelming size of Dutch Honnicker. He was still red in the ears. Sarah would know these things soon enough.

"The Mayor's behind it all," Johnny volunteered, eyes still hungering for his love.

"Could'a told me before now," Jake glared at him, suddenly hard. "I had to figure that one out for myself."

"You never asked and you sure never confided much in me, Tallon," Johnny bristled in outrage. "Never even knew what you wanted."

"How can that be true, Johnny? How could I not want to know who was behind the murder of my friends?"

"You have more friends in this town than you know, Jake," Sarah interrupted, suddenly drawing the eyes of both men. "Molly was talking with us when you came in. Everybody's fed up with the Mayor and the Sheriff but they're so scared of that pair, they feel powerless to change anything."

"We figured the same thing. Walker, José and I been talking with Eliza Crombe, the Gunsmith. Johnny's with me because the Sheriff is in his cell right now. Shortly, the Sheriff will be joined by the Judge."

"That's legal?" Sarah asked.

Jake chuckled as he turned his hat in his hands. "No. Sure ain't legal but I want 'em out of the picture when we confront the Mayor. That way I figure more citizens will feel free to side with us when they see the Mayor standing alone. "I don't need legal so much as I need the sympathy of this town. I can be a hundred percent right and get lynched if nobody stands up for us during the showdown."

Tia leaned forward in her chair and reached for Johnny's hand. "What's going to happen to us Johnny?" she asked, more than a little worried.

"Can't say for sure, Tia, but I know I'll admire standing alongside your brother-in-law." Johnny nodded toward Jake. "We have our differences, but he's a stand-up fella!"

Tia colored at his use of such a familiar use of her first name, then smiled guiltily at the others. "We talk a lot," she explained.

"That'll sure 'nough get you into trouble," said Jake. "That's how we started and look at Sarah now." He gestured to her visible pregnancy.

Sarah kicked at his ankles but was blocked by the leg of the parlor table. "Yeah, but we're married, Jacob, and that's where these two kids are headed also. Plain as anything."

"Like I said, Partner," Jake turned to Johnny, "You're in trouble, for sure!" He nodded his head knowingly.

Sarah kicked at him again and connected this time. "Ow! You haven't done that since the stable yard in Sante Fe." He paused as though reflecting, remembering the confrontation when Sarah had made him promise to return to her, once he'd found the gold he'd sought. That was the turning point in their relationship. "Kinda makes me warm all over, when you get mad at me like that."

It was Sarah's turn to color for no good reason. "You make that sound like fun, Cowboy. We can go 'round again if you thought that was such fun."

Jake tucked his legs under the chair. "No thanks!"

As if on command, each party averted their eyes as the artificial good humor evaporated and reality reasserted itself like an ominous presence among them.

"Stop clowning around, Jake," Sarah showed her real worry, "And tell us what will happen tomorrow."

"I don't know," Jake looked at the floor thoughtfully. "With the Sheriff and the Judge out of the way, it might be as simple as a town meeting in the street outside Zachary's office. Things never seem to work out that simple, so we'll prepare for the worst. I don't want the two of you women involved. Do you understand that, Sarah? The last thing I need is the distraction of worry if things get dicey."

Sarah squirmed under her husband's hard gaze, trying not to meet his eyes.

"Johnny'll be looking on from the Jail's front window with his Blue Mountain Long Gun, just in case. Also, Old Man Crombe will be someplace up high with a new Winchester. José and Night Walker will walk beside me. Anyway, I'm hoping the Cherokee will be there. Something happened as we left the Gunsmith. He had some sort of ruckus with a past friend of his."

"What sort of ruckus was that?" queried Sarah.

"Don't rightly know. He was only half with us when we went into the Gunsmith's shop, hanging back in the shadows, like. Then he disappeared. Next thing I know there's a terrible crash back in the alley and the Cherokee is carrying a body out of the dark."

"Oh no, Jake. That sounds awful!"

"Whoever it was, it seemed like the Cherokee knew him. Maybe someday I'll hear the full story but he was kinda short on explanations."

"Didn't you say that he'd promised to be back in the morning?" Johnny interjected helpfully.

"Which morning, is what I'm wondering." Jake was obviously concerned.

"I trust him to be there when you need him, Jacob," Lobo spoke up.

"You know him so well, do you Johnny?"

"I trust the Cherokee, Jacob. He healed me when I shoulda died. As a friend of yours, he had every right to let me die. I trust him with my life."

Suddenly guilty over his lack of confidence in Night Walker, Jake broke eye contact with Lobo and looked away.

"You're hoping the town will side with you?" she reached for his hand.

"Mostly," Jake warmed to her touch, "I'm just hoping they keep out of the way and come to court on my side. I want to see the Mayor hang for what he did to my friends, Sarah. If puttin' him behind bars is all I can get, that's enough." Jake had few illusions about how much help he might expect in a showdown, but held his tongue.

Sarah wore a gray traveling dress, a gift for her from Tia's luggage. Sitting there as she was, she looked very much the lady, not the gun-toting vixen Jake knew from the last two weeks, yet he was not fooled. "You're clear on all this, Sarah?" he asked again, eyes narrowing with his intensity.

She looked demurely downward at the tops of her beautifully shaped hands. "I understand, Jacob. This is something you want to do on your own. You're telling me that you won't be needing my help, at all."

He patted her layered hands reassuringly. This was too easy. Deep inside he had a terrifying feeling he had failed and there was nothing he could do to keep her out of the fight. "It's for the baby," he reasoned, a lone note of desperation betraying his fear, causing his voice to waver.

"I know," she said without meeting his eyes. "We'll be okay, Jacob."

Though there was nothing in her reply with which he might argue, his awful, desperate feeling persisted. Sarah had her own mind and would do whatever she darn well figured necessary. Jake shook his head ponderously with the immense weight of resignation suddenly shrouding his shoulders.

Sarah nodded once, finally meeting his eyes, confident she was understood. Jake got up to leave, and with an insistent thrust, put Lobo's hat in his hands that he should leave also.

"You won't be bothered here," said Jake, not at all reassured by his own words. "José will be disappointed, but it's best if we sleep near the horses. It's more open there and we can see who comes and goes from town.

"Damn," Jake cursed under his breath, his words sounded so darn hollow.

Altimera found the Judge at his desk, sitting in the pool of light from a single desktop lamp. He faced off with a small empty glass and a full bottle of good whiskey centered before him on the clean blotter.

"Buenos noches, Señor Judge," Altimera left the door open behind himself.

The Judge didn't seem particularly surprised by the interruption. After looking up, he went back to staring at the amber liquid in the bottle.

"Find any answers in there?" José stood respectfully, hat in both hands.

The Judge's eyes flicked to the Mexican and back. "This is the way it starts?"

"Si, Señor. The Sheriff respectfully requests your company." Altimera purposely omitted any mention of the Jail or the cell, but it must've shown in his eyes.

"I'm not fooled by your courtesy, young man. I've been waiting." The Judge stood and picked up his hat. Looking for a brief moment at the bottle, he grabbed it by the neck and picked up the cork from the blotter beside it, ramming it home decisively with the palm of his hand. He and the Sheriff could entertain the bottle in his more humble chambers. The Judge smiled at the thought. Maybe the whiskey will take the edge off the stink.

Secretly he was relieved. The Judge knew his usefulness to Zachary had ended and he only waited for a gunshot through the window. When Altimera found him, he had been saying good-bye to life, doing a mental balance sheet just to see how his life stacked up at the end. He didn't like the summary.

This way was better. He'd have some time … a chance to recalculate the totals before the end. Maybe he could add to the column of good to compensate for what he'd not done these past years.

Smiling to himself, lifting the sooty glass chimney and blowing out the lamp, he allowed the dapper Mexican to show him, unresisting, out the door. Maybe he could even change, become a stronger, better person. There might be time enough for that. Now he would have time.

⊐⊂⊐

Sarah watched her husband close the door behind him.

The sister before her represented a life in which she was raised and her man represented the life she had chosen. Having both in the same room, at the same time, left her emotions in shambles. She felt as though she straddled two worlds with a tea tray in one hand and her nickel-plated pistol in the other. The contrast caused a nervous giggle to bubble from the back of her throat, embarrassing her immediately.

"You didn't mean all that, did you?" asked Tia, wide-eyed. "You lied to your husband. Darn it, I know you too well. Sarah, you're scaring me." The words tumbled over each other in an effort to get out.

Althea witnessed foreign emotions suddenly at war on her sister's face. A kind of giddiness fought with inner pain for possession of her sister's normally composed features.

Sarah moved her lips but seemed unable to speak.

"Tell me, Sarah," Tia prompted gently, whispering, folding her sister's hands softly within her own.

Looking at her captive hands, Sarah gathered her control once again. The breath staggered in her throat. "I think I've killed." She paused, fearfully searching her younger sister's face for signs of condemnation.

Hesitantly, she began again, "That's wrong. I know I've killed." Sarah paused, examining the truth of the revised statement. "I've killed not once, Tia, but twice." She looked away and down, her hands flexing within her sister's grip, reflecting her inner turmoil. "Although Jake helped on one." Her eyes, full of moisture, drifted back to Tia's face.

Now it was Tia's turn for unease. Now it was she who tried withdrawing her hands but Sarah resisted. "You always were stronger than me," Tia complained.

The demons tormenting Sarah seemed to run through that connection, causing Tia to writhe uncomfortably.

"It's too horrible. Isn't it Tia?" Sarah begged.

"Ah! Ahhh!" Inarticulate sounds surged through Tia's tightening throat. "I don't want this," she managed finally, eyes squeezed tight. "First, I find Johnny. Then he's shot. Now my own sister is part of the violence I hate." She pressed her arm against her face in a futile effort to block out the painful images. "Too much hurting!"

From her baby sister's agony, Sarah found the connection that tied them together. She remembered what Shantee and Night Walker had told her. Releasing the hand, holding Tia with her gaze, she reached within the high, lacy neck of her traveling dress and extracted the beaded necklace with its single copper ornament.

Tia ceased her sobbing at the release of her hands and stared, transfixed, at the gleaming red-gold colored feather.

"Of all birds," Sarah repeated to her sister, "the Eagle circles closest to Heaven yet fiercely defends its young with talon and beak." The words seemed to galvanize Tia, who now sat straighter. Torment drained away, leaving her countenance clear and open.

Choosing her words carefully, Sarah knew she had one good chance to gain the complete understanding and help of her closest sister. "How did you feel, Tia, when Sheriff Laszlo shot the man you love? You don't want him shot again, do you? Maybe killed this time? Well, I don't want anyone hurt, but I don't want a tragedy to continue either. All of the killing must come to an end and I've a feeling that my Dear Heart will need all the help he can get."

In the shadows of the stairwell door a diminutive figure hugged the oaken casing. Boarding House Molly watched the two sisters in silence, feeling the ache of her own love, lost so many years ago to murderous violence. As she listened, resolve bloomed and grew deep within her heart. She would prepare, she decided, as she quietly climbed the beautiful boarding house stairs.

Purification by Fire

Big Bill Zachary stood, face nearly touching the multiple-paned windows looking out over his sleepy domain, early sun painting his face an eerie shade of red. He'd heard nothing about the Sheriff's most recently hired killer, the Breed, concerning the success of that mission. For that matter, he'd neither heard from nor seen Vernon Laszlo since last evening. The Mayor strained his eyes, searching for some sign among the lingering shadows or a movement from the Jail that might give his mind ease.

Why didn't it all just go away, thought the Mayor. No single adversary had stood so long against him in his memory. Zachary's resources dwindled as Jake Tallon ate away at his army of ruffians by one's and two's. He was now down to his last resources and his best defense, the Dutchman.

Dutch Honniker was easily the cruelest man Bill Zachary had ever met. The hard rock claim of Harry Harmon was the perfect place for the behemoth to work. There the granite of the Basin Range absorbed all the anger and energy that might otherwise fall on some unlucky and unsuspecting man. Those who worked with Honnicker were relatively safe as he drove relentlessly, ferociously through the endless yards of solid rock in pursuit of the spidery, winding veins of gold.

The men who worked the ore face with the huge Honnicker regarded him with unreserved awe. He was a monster, an unstoppable mining machine when pointed at the rock, a man-machine who produced all the ore and debris they could carry. He kept a dozen men busy for as long as they worked each day, then drove them out of bed and started early again the next morning.

The Mayor and the Dutchman were two of a kind. Because of that, Honnicker never stopped being valuable. Zachary's schemes always required someone sufficiently without principle to carry them out.

As the sun splashed fire across the horizon, he watched the big German rumble toward the Courthouse in his high-sided ore wagon, drawn by the six big Missouri mules. In his wake followed every man who shared work at the claim. Must be a gold shipment, thought the Mayor. That's the only reason to leave the mine deserted. Zachary took his first full breath of the day and a great deal of the dread he felt over Tallon simply fell away. There was safety for the Mayor when Honnicker was around.

Dutch promised him a month ago, when he had too much dust to keep at the mine, that he'd bring it to the Courthouse, where Zachary kept a safe big enough and strong enough to protect it. Constructed specifically to hide and support the iron monster, the City Hall, which also contained Zachary's office, was built upon a solid rock foundation and sported dozens of 12" x 24" beams in the load-bearing walls on the ground floor.

Today was the day!

Zachary remained at the window while the big man climbed the stairs, each footstep booming on the frail wooden steps like the steam-driven stroke of the stamp mill, his stamp mill. That man needs a stone staircase, thought the Mayor. Ordinary wood stairs were not intended to take that kind of punishment!

The Mayor remembered many visits from Honniker. Looming over the desk of the Mayor, Honniker would stand with his short, thick thighs flush against the edge. Zachary could see where the edge of the wood creased the fabric of his pants horizontally. Not much however.

In the beginning they had fought as rivals on the docks of New York. The Mayor knew exactly how hard those short legs were. Just like a peeled log, he remembered. Although they had not fought in years, there was an ongoing test of wills. Big Bill Zachary could no longer stand a physical test against Honnicker. Both of them knew it! Zachary's power rested instead, in the men he controlled.

Honnicker would stand, not out of politeness but to emphasize his height and bulk. He loved looking down on the Mayor.

So while the Mayor controlled him one way, Honnicker enjoyed reminding his boss he could break him like any other runt. Dutch stopped short of calling Zachary by the term he used so freely with other opponents, "little man."

Behind him, the door opened and closed as Honnicker entered. Zachary turned and assumed his seat without looking up at the German giant. "So you chased him off, did you?" The Mayor was pleased and worried at the same time. The Dutchman had to know it wasn't because Tallon feared him. "He only let you win because he didn't feel like shooting an unarmed man. You realize that, don't you, Dutch?"

"Dat ist his veakness, not mine! Next time, I make him fight. I break him!" Little drops of spittle flew from the big man's mouth, arching through stabbing beams of early morning sunlight to fall on the desk in front of Zachary. "In town it vill be different. His voman vill vatch. Den he mus' fight! Maybe today he vill fight."

This is what Zachary liked so much about his protégé, he thought, smiling at the Dutchman's passion. "What about his friends? After you break him, what's to stop them from cutting you to pieces with their six guns? ... I would."

"I send to the ranch. Peale vill bring more guns."

"Peale Stokes. There's a real snake," Zachary admired, rubbing at his chin. He leaned back into his big chair, satisfied, reflecting on this good news. "Fresh outta Texas with his whole crew is he? I know of him. He's made big tracks since the war. He couldn't have come at a better time."

"The Rangers chase Herr Stokes. He calls vat you do in Nazareth, a company-owned town." The Dutchman smiled. "He feels he vill be effen more comfortable here than Texas."

"He knows what happened to the Cruz Brothers, the Mackinaws and the others?" the Mayor arched his generous black eyebrows with the question.

"Dey ver incompetent, he says. No discipline! No organization."

"How many are they?" asked the Mayor.

"Elf," Honnicker spat in his native language. "Eleven," he corrected himself.

"Good," gloated the Mayor. "Tallon is the last obstacle to my clear ownership of the diggings and I'll not stop until the mine is completely under my control. I've worked too hard."

Honnicker watched as the Mayor sank inside himself, weighing all the factors and possibilities. The seconds stretched into a minute. The Dutchman's mind wandered onto more pleasant topics. Years had passed since the giant had last dismantled a man with his bare hands. That particular talent created trouble for him in New York, when his enthusiasm resulted in the deaths of three of the Mayor's enemies in one evening. They were not the first to die by his hands, but they were the "one too many" responsible for Zachary's flight west. Dutch had always worked for the Mayor as his enforcer.

So lost in memory was he, that Honnicker was startled when the Mayor suddenly spoke. "And Dutch," Zachary said, bringing the Dutchman's vicious imagination up short, "we will make absolutely sure that Tallon does not live at the end of this day."

"How vill ve do dat?" The Mayor's very tone told Honnicker he would not get first shot at Tallon's dismemberment and he was angry.

"The Colonel gets first play. You're too valuable for me to risk you without first trimming the odds. I need you, Dutch," Zachary sought to soften the stern instruction. "If Tallon lives after Stokes is done, you can tear him up in little pieces at your pleasure."

"No!" Dutch erupted, "Me first!" He thumped his chest with terrifying force. "I do not vant da Colonel's left-oafers." The beady, close-set eyes sparked fire, showing the big man's frustration and disappointment.

"Don't argue with me on this," Zachary shouted back, both hands slapping flat on the desk before him.

The big German slumped defeated into the high-backed chair facing the Mayor, bitterness creasing his face. "You are wrong ..." Honnicker almost said out loud what he always thought, "little man," but bit his tongue barely in time. "Guns are not so sure," he reasoned. "Dese hants," he held the massive engines of destruction up before his face, are the only sure solution. No man ever survived dese hants. No mountain survives dese hants. Bullets miss too much der target!" He glared acidly at his employer.

"You're right but my decision stands. It's the Colonel first, then you."

⊒◼⊑

Flat on his back in a pile of straw, Jake woke with a hollow feeling in his stomach. Hunger wasn't the issue, he realized. A day stretched before him filled with unknown peril.

"The Mayor is behind it all," Johnny had said.

That sure made sense to Jake. Something he might have expected all along, though he could have had no certainty. It fit all the facts.

According to Crombe, the Mayor built this town and ran it for ten years with absolute control. Jake was certain it was the Mayor who had made several attempts on his life and finally had sent more than a dozen guns after him in Colorado. Though he had failed repeatedly, the Mayor remained a force to be reckoned with. Zachary would resist any kind of change, especially one that so threatened his quality of life.

Legal strategy fell to the background. Jake sensed that if he waited, Zachary would end his life before the authorities in Sacramento could become involved. Jake intended to "bell the cat" to smoke the Mayor out, make it impossible for Big Bill Zachary to pull the strings quietly, anonymously, behind the scenes, and he did not expect this day to go easily.

Rising, he brushed the straw from his clothes and kicked gently at the huddled form beneath a colorful Aztec blanket. "Buenos dias, amigo. Time to greet the rising sun."

Altimera groaned and mumbled a response liberally sprinkled with Spanish curses, which Jake chose not to understand.

Swinging the belt around his waist, Jake buckled on his guns and descended the ladder to the ground floor of the stable. Rungs polished with age and the passage of many feet slid beneath his hands. Few horses remained inside the building, but nowhere could he find the old man who loved them so much. The memory of the Hosteler pleased Jake, because it made him think of Shantee. Sam was in good hands here. Seth must be at breakfast, he concluded.

Running a hand across his stubbled jaw, Jake thought how good a close shave might feel. His eyes settled on the enameled basin next to the stove. Cold water he could have any day of the week, out of any fresh running stream. Hot water would sure feel good for a change. He remembered Sarah heating water for him in the early mornings at their home near Cumberland Crossings. The thought made him smile. In his mind he saw her standing near the iron cook stove, wearing the long skirts she loved so much, steam swirling around her upper figure. Shaking his head, Jake cleared his mind of past images. Today was today. Today could be his last day.

The Hosteler likely wouldn't mind him heating water. Jake removed his shirt and guns and rummaged in his bags for a razor. If he died today, it would be clean-shaven. It occurred to him that most all the known men, real honest-to-goodness gunfighters like Wes Hardin, lived clean-shaven. A few had mustaches, but that was about it.

They all wanted to look good, if and when they died, he figured. The thought amused Jake. Though dying was not uppermost in his mind, Jake did want to feel as good as he could on a day when he faced so many challenges.

Jake listened to the greedy flames trapped within the stove. They sounded crisp and busy.

Many times since the Spirit Lodge, he had balanced the merits of mortal life against the freedom of living as a free soul on the Starry Path. With the pain of his wound now a memory, he decided that such small things made life worth living. Yet the crackle of a simple fire and the smell of pines were the first things forgotten in a busy life.

He liked the way the hot towel made his face feel so clean and alive. The scrape of the razor was something he heard as well as felt. His clean face smiled back at him from the fragment of mirror nailed to the wall. Life is good!

The coming confrontation cast common tasks into sharp contrast with each other, giving each moment an added value. Jake wasn't afraid of dying. He'd been there. Maybe he should be more worried than he was, but everything he knew to do had already been done. The Judge and the Sheriff were under lock and key. Lobo knew his job as did Crombe.

Sticking his head briefly out the door, Jake realized that morning had dawned without any trace of Night Walker. The big Cherokee had been absent since the scuffle in the alley the night before. Where could he be, Jake wondered, staring with knitted brows and pursed lips through a fly-speckled, greasy office window along the main street fronting the Livery.

"Don't worry about your Indian friend," Altimera's reassurance drifted through the door to the loft. "He's always there when it counts."

"How do you know what I'm thinking?"

"Your silence shouts at me, even through this floor. Plus, I am not stupid. You worry and you need each one of your friends." Seconds of silence measured Altimera's own inner thoughts. "I am concerned also, my friend. We need more help than we now have."

Jake turned away from the window, chaffing at the goose-bumped flesh of his bare arms. A fresh, heavy, cream-colored shirt hung on a peg against the wall. It slid easily over his shoulders and torso. Maybe I should wear scarlet, he thought, like the Romans, so no enemy will see my blood.

"You want breakfast, José?" yelled Jake. "The cook promised to smother your eggs in jalapeños."

"Wha . .?"

"Jalapeños!" answered Jake to the incomplete question. "I don't know when you'll have such a chance, ever again."

"Sainted Mother!" José exclaimed, "There is a woman who knows how to feed a true Vaquero!" Boots and sombrero dropped downwards through the hole in the ceiling, like colorful comets followed closely by a rumpled Mexican with uncombed hair. "She will teach you how to eat like a real man."

"Yeah, I may have some too," said Jake, pushing the sombrero into his friend's hands before he finished slipping on the boots.

Together they walked across the grass-strewn stable yard into the early light of morning. Not so early, thought Jake, I can see the sun. Too much indoor living will make me a late sleeper.

Drawn by thoughts of breakfast, Altimera turned left upon reaching the street, toward the cafe. Over the background noise of birds and other early risers, Jake thought he heard the sound of horses. After only a few moments, he became more certain. Glancing over his shoulder, Jake saw the horses and riders appear around a distant corner.

Pulling José toward the boardwalk, they turned to watch three riders following a well set-up gentleman with West Point written all over the way he forked his horse. His posture expected respect and obedience. Reins in his left hand, his right rested across tailored riding pants tucked into polished knee-high boots.

"Cavalry," said Jake.

"Si, amigo. That is Peale Stokes, a bad man with good manners. The wimmen, they like him, but he is ver bad."

"What's he doing here?" Jake wondered out loud.

"He never go anyplace without he is paid."

"Did you hire him, José?"

"Maybe you lend me dinero, I hire him, but no. Not me."

As he passed, the gentleman with the officer's posture glanced sideways at the dapper Mexican standing beside an average looking man with the long Apache moccasins over canvas pants. The man's thigh-length buckskin jacket concealed his guns. Was this Jake Tallon, he wondered? He'd know soon enough.

Stokes touched his hat and rode on toward the Courthouse and the Mayor's office.

Jake hooked his thumbs in his gun belt. "Seems like trouble to me," he speculated. "After all we been through already, I expected the Mayor to run out of Bully-boys before now."

"As long as he got money, he got more trouble for us," observed the Mexican.

"Trouble is, José, that's my money!" Jake scowled after the horsemen.

Johnny Lobo waited their arrival over breakfast. The man looked right perky, thought Jake, walking up to the table. "Freedom seems to suit you well, Mr. Lobo."

"Sure 'nough!" Lobo said between bites, "A man can get his food hot if he's able to cross the street on his own power. I figure Laszlo made a point of waiting 'til it cooled 'fore he carried it back to me."

"That being the case, why don't you trade him back the same as he gave you?"

"I won't treat a dog like that, Tallon." Johnny shook his fork at Jake for emphasis. "Both he and the Judge will get hot food like he should'a got me."

Jake smiled at Johnny's passion. Whenever he was able to forget about the ambush, Jake liked Johnny, but he wondered what Tia saw in Johnny. For that matter Jake wondered what Sarah saw in him. "We saw Peale Stokes on our way over," said Jake casually.

"Colonel Stokes? Know him I do."

"How?" Jake's interest showed in his eyes and his posture as he leaned involuntarily forward.

"Rode with him at Chancellorsville and some after."

"What do you know of him lately?" asked Jake.

"Still fightin' the war, seems like," Johnny talked around his food and went on chewing.

Jake noticed Altimera in animated conversation with the cook near the kitchen doors. He'd forgotten about food but his friend hadn't. "How many men does the Colonel run with?"

"If it's one it's a dozen. Lot of men still believe in the Colonel. They'll follow him anywheres." Johnny froze, as though snake bit. "Oh!" he blanched, setting down his fork and trying desperately to swallow his last mouthful.

Jake pushed Johnny's coffee cup closer to his hand.

"Thanks," said Johnny, gulping at its hot contents. "We got trouble, don't we?"

"That's the first time I ever saw understanding sneak up on a man, like that," said Jake, smiling. "Kinda like a puma-stalked deer. One minute facedown in the grass. Next minute head pops up to get a tooth necklace."

"I know. I know," protested Johnny Lobo, "Puma still attached. You're right, I was eatin' and not payin' attention to what you was sayin'."

"You weren't payin' attention to what you were sayin'."

"We got us a peck o' trouble, compadre," said Johnny, face now serious.

"We got food now, trouble later." Altimera pushed a big plate of steak and eggs in front of Jake.

Jake noticed the food was smothered in sliced Jalapeños.

"You two are so full of jokes," said Johnny, white around the lips. "Aren't you worried about Peale Stokes and his boys?"

"We got you backin' us up from the Jailhouse," said Altimera. "Why should we worry?"

"You should worry because everything Stokes does is a military campaign. He might know about me and he'll spot a sniper up high somewhere just to take care of me. Even if he doesn't know about me, he'll use a sniper. I've done that for him more than once."

"Probably thinks you're still in Jail. Nonetheless, it's worth thinking about." Jake's eyes lost focus as he forked food slowly into his mouth and chewed automatically. "There's five of us and at least a dozen of them," he mused.

"I'm not worried," said a feeding Altimera, gesturing sideways at Jake with a fork-filled fist. "I witnessed firsthand as this Gringo busted an ambush of a dozen men with only three."

"Yeah," said Jake, "and one good man is buried back on that mountain who didn't make it out the other side of that ambush. Who's volunteering to be left behind this time?"

"Don't go and spoil my breakfast," said an angry Mexican. "I had it all figured out how we win and now you spoil it all by asking for details."

"Your ideas are always welcome, amigo. I'm just curious." Jake had stopped smiling.

Suddenly downcast, Altimera could do little save look at his half-empty plate, rotating the china self-consciously. After another moment of silence he threw his hands expressively into the air, "You get crazy and kill all of the bad guys. That is what I see before. There, I said it. The Cherokee, he don't kill so many."

It was Jake's turn to be downcast. "That was all luck and desperation, my friend. I can't plan that and we can't depend on that." Again the moments ticked away against the constant background sounds of cooking and eating. The waitress came again with fresh coffee, looking nervously from one downcast face to another, then leaving.

"Nobody knows about Crombe," Jake said quietly after she had left. "Maybe he's our ace-in-the-hole."

Altimera brightened perceptibly, "I like that."

"And Maybe we could fort-up the Jail just a bit," said Johnny. "We'll kick apart those old benches on the boardwalk and put the extra planks around the front windows on the inside. That'll stop most all of the pistol balls and some rifle balls. If I'm back from the window some, I don't make so good a target from above," he added helpfully.

"I like that also," said a pensive Jake Tallon, standing, pushing his plate away. He laid his linen thoughtfully beside his plate and dropped some silver coins onto the table, the seated Liberties flashing back at him as they bounced, spun and settled.

Returning to the Jail with Johnny, Jake used long iron spikes from the Smithy to mount an extra four-inch buffer of wood all around the windows, blocking out the upper half entirely. Reduced light from the windows cast an unnatural gloom around the office. Before leaving, Jake grabbed a couple of ten-gauge muzzleloaders from the rack behind Laszlo's desk. Dropping a rod down the first barrel, he was rewarded with a hollow metallic thunk as the hickory struck the back of the empty chamber.

Lifting a can of powder from the bottom corner of the rack, Jake asked his future brother-in-law, "How much can these pieces take without coming apart?"

"A lot," answered Johnny. "It's the lead you hafta watch. I wouldn't put more than a handful of pellets and maybe half that again in each barrel."

"That's a lot of pellets," mumbled a dubious Jake.

"You wanna make a big impression, or what? I'm thinkin' we do whatever extra we can to balance the scales." Johnny slid a loading tube into the butt of his Spencer and cranked a cartridge into the chamber, standing it up against the edge of the desk.

Once loaded, Jake didn't bother with additional powder and shot for the big scatterguns. After those barrels were expended there would be no opportunity to load again. It would all be pistol work after that, if he remained standing. He checked the cartridges in his reworked Remington Armies and filled the empty chamber in each.

As he turned to the door, Johnny Lobo called out to him, "Jake. Take an extra." With barely one hand free, Jake caught the cap'n ball Colt Johnny tossed his way. With a grateful nod, he tucked it behind his belt.

Arms full of hardware, Jake left the Jail and stepped into the street. Clouds shouldered against the Basin Range to the west, looking dark and angry. A small wind kicked up dust here and there, giving the open area between the two rows of facing buildings a restless, unsettled look. Sensing the seriousness of the coming confrontation, pedestrians scattered like starlings, each finding a hole in which to hide. Furtive eyes watched from behind drawn curtains, slightly cracked doors and attic windows.

As Jake stepped off toward the Courthouse, Altimera appeared by his side on the return from his visit with Crombe. "Where's the Cherokee?" Jake wondered out loud, looking right and left. "He said he'd be back and I don't see him."

"Hey! Do I get one of those or you gonna use them both?" the Mexican asked.

Smiling, Jake handed over the extra scattergun. Carefully, the Mexican lifted the hammers to check the copper percussion caps and settled the gun across the crook of his arm, pointing away from Jake. Altimera was at his best during times like these, thought Jake. He knew loyalty and he knew fighting.

Jake glanced sideways at his friend, who smiled back, tight-lipped with tension. He knew that the hard times are when you found your friends. "Muchas gracias, amigo," Jake said.

"De nada," Altimera answered. "You scared, amigo?" Their matched footfalls thudded against the dusty street like seconds ticking irrevocably off the face of Destiny's clock.

"I'm always scared," said Jake, trying to keep his teeth from chattering. "So often, fights are sudden." He swallowed. "There is no chance to think about them beforehand." They walked with scatterguns pointed outwards.

As they passed the saloon on the right, half-a-dozen hard cases crowded through the door to watch them pass. The first through the door hawked and spit loudly into the street toward them. His friends laughed appreciatively.

"Did we count those?" asked a concerned Altimera, shifting his eyes meaningfully between his friend and the crowded saloon doors.

"They'll be the ones behind us," answered Jake disconsolately. "Somehow there's always more where they come from."

Sweeping along the street before them like a dodging, darting phantom, the wind picked up, tugging at the hair sticking out from under Jake's hat. The corners of his coat flapped upward against his arms as he held the scattergun. He felt the long buckskin fringes dance along the length of his sleeve.

Down the alley Jake caught a glimpse of Barnaby Rufus, the saloon owner, burning trash in small piles. The man glanced nervously at the sky, blissfully unaware of the drama in the street at the front end of his building. That'll change soon enough, thought Jake.

The open windows of the cafe appeared and slid by on their left. It took everything Jake had to keep his eyes straight ahead. The point was soon moot. Peale Stokes stood before the courthouse, hatless, gleaming white shirt and tie, with a tied-down gun against his right leg. Other men stepped from doorways and alleys, as if by some signal, assembling on either side of the former officer as though called to morning formation.

The man knew what he was doing. He didn't even bother to see he was being supported. He'd assembled his troops by increments to demoralize the opposition and it was working!

"What do you want, Tallon?" he challenged in a voice adorned with studied boredom.

This was not as Jake had planned. He intended to make the challenges. "You've got no part of this Stokes," Jake yelled. "We're here for Zachary, the Mayor. Not for you!"

"You've got no business with the Mayor, Tallon. You're not even a resident of this town. You own no property here."

Jake counted fourteen men including Stokes. Quickly, eyes flicking left and right, he did a mental inventory of his strategy and assets, including surprise.

"There are too many, Amigo," whispered an agitated Mexican, reflecting Jake's own concern. Altimera drifted back half a step.

"If we turn, they'll kill us anyway. I think it's too late." At those words, Altimera stopped in his tracks, then moved forward, even with Jake.

"Besides, the manner of this south-country martinet makes me unreasonably angry." Jake's fear and uncertainty drained away.

"Martin ... what?" the Mexican mumbled, confused.

"You're more wrong than you know Stokes," Jake yelled, interrupting the musings of his friend. "I sure 'nough own the ground four of my friends lay under and the claim the Mayor stole from them after he had them killed."

"That's something you'll have to prove, Tallon, and I don't think you'll get the chance." Stokes needed a quick gunfight. The men behind him exchanged nervous glances as the promised confrontation turned into conversation.

"We didn't come here to talk, Colonel," the man at Stoke's side complained bitterly from beneath an excessively wide-brimmed hat that sagged forward, partially concealing his eyes. "Maybe we should all sit down over coffee."

"Maybe you should shut your mouth," snapped Stokes, "unless you wish to be flogged on the spot ... before the eyes of our adversary!" A handful of seconds expired as the subordinate stepped slightly back, assuming a more subservient demeanor.

"The way I hear it you used to be respectable, Colonel," Jake used the military title with emphasis.

"Respectable," Stokes repeated, his mouth twitching into an ugly sneer. "The war was a long time ago, Tallon, and you will recall that my side lost."

"Oh, I don't know Colonel. A lotta folks still swear by you. Johnny Lobo, I know, still believes in you."

Nothing could have shocked them more than had lightning struck at their feet. All up and down the line, men looked to the trees and rooftops. "How do you know Johnny?"

"He's related by marriage," smiling slightly, Jake stretched the truth, "and my on-going health is a concern of his wife. I think he probably has that tie of yours framed in the sights of the squirrel rifle that served you so well during the heroic conflict."

Stokes squirmed where he stood but pride would not let him run. With a gleam of sudden arrogance, he puffed out his chest and threatened, "If he cares for your health, he'll come out and lay down that long rifle."

"Maybe it's the health of your men you should worry most over," Jake felt a shift of energy in his direction.

"They've fought before," boasted Stokes defensively.

"Have they died before?" drawled Jake, following a bare heartbeat. "They don't stand half a chance against snipers, out in the open like they are."

The impatient, big-hatted man standing just beside the Colonel swept back his long coat, palmed his gun, staggered and fell to one knee as the report of Johnny's rifle echoed back from the storefronts! The hat fell forward concealing his face as he examined the fatal wound in his chest, before he toppled forward into the dirt.

"Carmichael!" shouted the Colonel, recovering his poise and falling back a step. At his command, shots boomed from the parapet atop the Courthouse. Two men fired downward into the Jail, where wisps of smoke from Johnny's shot trailed from the glassless window to be shredded by the breeze. Splinters flew from the boards above the opening as they bucked and split under the impact of repeated hits.

Rifle shots cracked from opposite ends of the street. One of the shooters dropped his rifle into the gutter and sagged backwards onto the roof. The other reeled, grabbing at his throat. All along the line before Jake, men pulled at their six guns, but now their attention was divided.

"Where are you Shantee?" Jake cried, leveling his scattergun and letting one hammer fall. The blast of shot cleared a hole in the line of men facing him.

Even above the roar of gunfire, Jake heard the quietly spoken words, "Always here."

Off to his left a terrific explosion blended with the twin detonations of Altimera's shotgun on his other side. Up and down the opposing line, as though in slow motion, men wilted or reeled with the impact of large pellets. They're not all ours, Jake realized. He fired the other barrel in the direction of men still standing.

Altimera grunted with a bullet impact and collapsed. Dropping his shotgun, Jake pulled a pistol and somersaulted in José's direction, bullets kicking up dust all around him. José was down but firing from the ground. Jake grabbed his collar with one hand and returned fire with the other.

As the two collapsed behind the shelter of a bullet-thrashed water trough, Jake glanced back toward the saloon to see a collection of mounted riders and riderless horses milling in confusion. On the veranda of the boarding house, two hundred feet distant, Tia and Sarah stood calmly, firing slowly and deliberately at the riders with Henry repeaters that looked far too large for their small stature.

Many among the mounted saloon scum could not bring themselves to return fire at the women and those that did were ineffective with their six guns. Their pistols would not reach that far.

Jake's anger fought with his great relief. Now everybody was undercover or out of range, save the desperados before him lead by Peale Stokes.

Beside Jake on the ground, Altimera fired his pistol, stretching his forearm and gunhand over the top of the trough, without looking. Jake lifted his head in time to see Colonel Stokes drop his gun and raise his one working arm in surrender. He stood head bowed in abject defeat, clothing torn and blood splashed across his brilliant white shirt. It had been a hard day for the men of Colonel Stokes.

"Hold your fire!" yelled Jake Tallon. "Hold your fire!" he yelled again. The gunfire slackened and stopped as he stood. Two remaining riders still atop their mounts dodged down the alley next to the saloon and beat a path for the open plains.

Barnaby, the saloonkeeper, dodged to one side, barely avoiding the desperate horsemen as they ran pell-mell through the middle of his fires. Horror cloaked his face as burning debris scattered upwards carried afield on the freshening wind.

Jake surveyed the carnage before him. Only one enemy besides the Colonel remained standing. Smoking rifle in hand, the Cherokee approached from Jake's left. Crombe stood from behind the parapet on his own building. Leaving the cover of the riddled Jail front, Johnny Lobo moved the Colonel's men, whenever he found those that could walk, back into the confinement of cells behind the office. Many of the erstwhile Cavalry could not move, would never move again.

Striding cautiously up the street, Tia and Sarah moved in Jake's direction. Sarah's gait had assumed some refinements, he noticed, reflecting her pregnant condition. "That woman takes too many risks," Jake raged. "She's got to start thinking about more than herself! Or me," he added with some chagrin. She too, had helped save his bacon.

Looking back to the Shaman, Jake saw him bending next to a pile of dark clothing, crumpled incongruously in the dust of the street. As he watched, the Cherokee raised Boarding House Molly to a sitting position with his arm behind her small shoulders. In her hands she cradled the huge sawed-off shotgun that Barnaby had previously kept under his bar, near the cash box. Maybe it just looked big because she was so tiny. The weapon's recoil must surely have knocked her unconscious.

Jake did not remember seeing her before the confrontation with Colonel Stokes. It was the blast of shot from both barrels of her gun that turned the tide. With admiration, Jake noted the carnage at her end of the line.

The wave of shot shredded the three or four men closest to her and whipped on down the line across the very front of their rank. They had been spread out in such a way that only raking fire from where she stood could effectively balance the odds. In his heart, Jake knew he lived because of her brave deed. "Thanks be to Man Above," he mumbled, "and a good woman."

Even as Jake mused, a booming yell interrupted Jake's train of thought. "Little man!" His vision swiveled immediately right to find the street peopled once again by the opposition. A dozen or fourteen miners, armed this time, led by the cartoon of a man he hoped never to see again, Dutch Honnicker.

Smoke billowed from the back of the saloon, Jake noted. Somehow that observation was very important, but not so important as the task now before him.

"You're pretty good vit da guns, little man. Maybe you afraid to face a man like a man," the big German taunted, thumbs in his belt. "Dutch vill show you how a man fights."

"Just shoot the bastard," groaned Altimera, at Jake's feet, holding a bleeding thigh in both hands. Counting the Cruz Brothers' wound, the Mexican had now been shot in roughly the same place on each thigh.

"I can't," said Jake distractedly. In his heart Jake heard the words of Shantee and had come to recognize the difference between his own ruminations and that curious outside voice always quietly pointing the direction of higher good.

"This is the evil for which you have been spared, Jacob," Shantee was saying. "He wants to learn that violence is not the best way to manage his affairs. Merely dying will not teach him this necessary lesson. He must experience defeat on his own level for him to learn how each of his past victims felt at his own hands."

"That's the stupidest thing I ever heard," Jake scoffed, yet inside he knew differently. The very size of the man made fighting him an insane proposition. "How can I do that?" he asked out loud.

Time ground to a halt during this internal conversation.

"Remember, you killed a deer and a very dangerous gunman, Bingo Mackinaw, with only a stick," Shantee needled Jake. "I will never give you a task beyond your ability."

"Pain is temporary and justice is forever," mumbled Jake, unbuckling his gun belts and stepping out from behind the water trough with clear-eyed commitment.

Honnicker ran eagerly to meet him with his short-legged ambling gait, so much more like a buffalo than a man.

No matter how funny this man may look, Jake reminded himself, he is more dangerous than any four men I have ever faced! Even at a distance, he saw the shine of greedy anticipation in the black, beady eyes. It 'minded Jake of being caught in the headlamp of an on-coming locomotive.

Uncurling an immensely powerful palm thrust that met the face of Dutch Honnicker, Jake stepped into the charge even as the massive arms reached to encircle Jake's spine. Though blood splashed from under both sides of Jake's hand, it was Jake who recoiled from the blow as though he had struck a stone wall. Finding himself flat on his back in the dust of the street, Jake held a jammed right wrist in his left hand. "Ow," he complained, astonished!

Honnicker stamped his short legs alternately in enraged pain, both hands to his bleeding face, before charging Jake where he lay. The distance too short, Jake had no time in which to recover.

Bending at the waist, Honnicker lifted Jake like an inconsequential length of cordwood and threw him horizontally through a four-inch post supporting the awning to the Saddle Shop. The whole building reverberated with the impact as Jake's legs, from the knees down, crashed through the front window. Jagged glass bit sharply through the thick leggings of his elk hide moccasins.

"Ow, again," he said as he fell in an absurd tangle of arms and legs to the boardwalk, one ankle caught on the sill of the now glassless window.

"The town's burning! The town is burning!" Above his own pain and fear, Jake heard the cry repeated by many voices. Distracted by the same cries, Honnicker hesitated in his follow-up rush. It was all the time that Jake required.

Springing to his feet, Jake ducked the sagging awning, vaulted the hitch rail and rolled into the street, pain lancing once again through his lower leg. Bouncing to his feet, Jake turned barely in time to catch Honnicker's backhand across his left shoulder, numbing Jake's arm and sending him ass over teakettle in a good imitation of an acrobatic cartwheel. Jake's world turned upside down once and then again as the wind whipped away the dust kicked up by his passage. He looked back after skidding to a shaky stop, incredibly, still standing.

Jake's initial blow had a substantial effect on the big man. As the artificial energy of the Dutchman's rage wore off, he moved much more slowly. Blood flowed generously from his mouth and nose, staining the entire front of his shirt, starting narrow at his collar and widening to each side of his massive stomach at the belt, hiding his suspenders against its dark color.

Jake had also paid. His two arms were now both nearly useless, leaving him only his legs with which to fight. Noting the severity of these injuries, Jake realized this man was far more dangerous than he could ever have imagined.

Stepping into the charge once again, Jake bent away at the last possible moment, twisting at the hips and driving his right leg straight up into Honnicker's throat like a vertical pile driver, stopping the big man cold. Honnicker stumbled back two steps, gagging and holding the crushed throat.

Standing straight, then wobbling, Jake saw people running for buckets and equipment. Smoke and wind-driven fire now dominated the scene behind his antagonist. Before Jake could sort out all of the distraction, Honnicker had covered the ground between them. Even injured, the Behemoth was simply too quick on his short legs.

He wrapped Jake in a killing hug that had been his obvious strategy all along and Jake felt his spine bend over impossibly backwards. Lungs squeezed flat, he could get no air. Huge quantities of blood, saliva and fetid breath assaulted his face.

With the last of his remaining strength, Jake first pushed fiercely against the crushing embrace, then pummeled the bullet-like head of his attacker with both hands, even trying a head butt that failed to reach the mark with enough force to be effective.

Impervious to Jake's assault, Honnicker responded with even more force as he stumbled forward and back, intent upon the crushing destruction of the man in his grasp.

Weakening, Jake's right arm swung free behind him, brushing a sharp, hard shard of glass protruding from the large muscle of his lower leg. In desperation, he yanked it free. The pain was nothing compared to the smothering death now encircling his chest, preventing his breath, crushing his life.

In a last great effort, Jake brought the four-inch shard of jagged glass in a wide-armed arc aimed at the side of the huge man's neck. In a dream of fading consciousness, Jake saw firelight flash from the ragged edge as it bit deeply into the tough, whiskered, hide-like skin beneath the jaw of the big man.

"Argh," the Dutchman roared, releasing Jake to fall limply from his grasp. With fierce determination, Jake retained his hold on the biting glass, slashing it downward into Honnicker's collarbone as he fell. Blood gushed from a mortal wound, yet the Man-Mountain failed to collapse. Clawing at the offending shard, Dutch spun and ran shambling, bleeding and crying like a wounded beast into the alley of fire next to the Courthouse.

A collection of incredible pain, Jake raised feebly up on one elbow in time to see the Courthouse collapse with a fountain of flaming embers into the fiery tunnel through which the Dutchman ran!

"So it ends," said Jake.

"Not ended, Jake," sounded the sympathetic words of Shantee. "It is but one battle by which you confirm your choice of good."

"Oh," Jake groaned. "How should I feel about that?"

"Tired maybe. It's okay to feel tired, Jacob." Jake heard the smile and the mercy in the words and sagged backward into the dust, giving up consciousness to the comforting blackness.

Ashes

ake had a dream and in the dream Altimera cursed and badgered him at their campsite in the mountains as he healed from his head wound. "I don't much like this dream," he heard his own voice saying at a great distance. But waking was simply not that easy. Sluggishly, he swam to the surface, struggling through heavy unending waters, in pursuit of the elusive beckoning light of consciousness.

"Ahh," painfully Jake sucked air into his damaged chest. "Oh my."

"Stop complaining, Compadre," groused Altimera from a nearby bed. "I have all the bullet holes this time! Not you. Stop your crying. Bear your wounds like a man if that is possible!"

This was no dream, he realized. Gingerly lifting the covers with his left hand, Jake saw his chest swathed in tight dressings, his right hand bandaged like a mitten with only the tips of the fingers showing.

"Jake!" the door burst open and Sarah fell through in her eagerness to find her man once again awake.

"Oh, Sarah!" Jake's face lit like a freshly fired lamp.

The bed rocked under Jake as Sarah swung around the brass end post with swishing skirts and collapsed into a chair at the bedside, throwing herself half across his chest with a kind of hungry abandon.

"Yow, that hurts!" Even as the words left his mouth, Jake realized he'd endure any pain just to have his love close. The last thing he desired was the absence of her touch.

"Oh, I'm so sorry," Sarah raised her head from Jake's damaged torso, stroked it gently and pursed her lips into the pretty pout of a confident woman, a woman who had fought for her family and won. The smile on her face bloomed and just wouldn't go away.

"My whole chest must be crushed," Jake exaggerated, raising his head slightly from the pillow, looking down at the bandages. "I could use some more sympathy, Honey."

"Oh, Jake! That ugly beast treated you soo bad! You never told me he was so dangerous and so mean." She tenderly sought his undamaged hand with both of hers.

"I didn't want to scare you, Sarah." Jake's eyes softened as he thought about what they'd survived, together.

"I was plenty scared when I saw him run at you like an enraged bull. And he threw you against that building as if you were a toy doll. I was so surprised when you got up and hit him again! And so very glad!" Sarah tried to lay her head against his chest again, this time more gently.

"Being in the middle of the fight, I didn't have the luxury of surprise, Sarah. It was the only thing I could do." He stroked her hands with his bandaged one, feeling greatly at peace again.

"I'm soo happy you're okay, Jake." Sarah kissed Jake's forehead. "You're too old for this kind of thing. At least you didn't get any new holes in you. I hate when that happens."

"Me too!" Jake relaxed again into his pillows.

"It's nice to have you awake again but I have pots boiling on the stove. I'll be back to feed you in a while." She patted his bandaged chest, rose to her feet, turned and swept from the room with a rustle of skirts.

"That 'splains the whole thing!"

"What do you mean José?"

"That fight at the pass, when I first see you, was a one-time thing. You are too old now. At last I understand!"

"You have a bad mouth for such a broken down Vaquero," Jake groaned. "Do you borrow that disrespect from a much younger man? Where do you get it, anyway?"

"The disrespect comes from my pain and frustration! Look at this," Altimera threw aside his covers to show the bandages covering his right thigh. "I may never walk again!"

"You exaggerate. You have both legs, don't you?"

"Si," replied Altimera, reluctantly. "I have both my legs."

"And you still have your mouth, don't you?"

"Si," replied a more cautious Mexican.

"Well as long as you have your mouth you will walk because you will drive all your friends away and you will walk or you will starve." Jake smiled.

"Anyway, now you know this is no dream, amigo."

"Oh, I certainly know that."

⊰⊡⊱

After only a day, Jake could no longer endure confinement with the irascible Mexican. Slowly pulling on his clothes, he discovered that if he was patient with himself, he might hobble down to the cafe, whose window now overlooked a field of ashes.

"Lost some and saved some," Jake commented, leaning on his cane as he stood upon the boardwalk before entering the eating establishment.

"Looks like it," said the voice at his elbow.

"Johnny!" Jake was surprisingly pleased to find the reformed Bushwhacker at his side again. He'd seen him in the morning for a private conversation. Johnny had wanted to, and indeed had tried in vain to give Jake what they all now knew was money that had come from the Mayor, as the new Johnny wanted nothing of it. Only a clean start. Maybe the conversation wasn't so private. Even José seemed pleased, Jake saw out of the corner of his eye, as José joined them. Now, after all that had happened, thought Jake, here we stand, shoulder to shoulder.

"When the saloon went up," Johnny pointed incredulously at the scene in front of them, "it all collapsed into the ice house in the basement! A great hiss of steam and spray from exploding barrels dampened the flames on either side of the building. The loss of last winter's ice and all that cold brew didn't make Barnaby very happy but it may have saved the rest of the town."

"Anybody ever find the Mayor?" Jake queried.

"No and funny thing is, nobody found the big guy either, Dutch Honnicker. I figured that neck wound was mortal, the way it bled so bad."

"Seems like a guy that big would be found no matter how bad he roasted."

"I know," said Johnny, "kinda like trying to hide a horse carcass."

"Sure hope we don't see him again," wished Jake. "Almost did me in." Hesitating only a moment, he focused his gaze on the man now before him, the good man. "How do you feel about running the mine for me, Johnny?"

"Where did that come from?" Johnny asked, his sudden surprise draped like a blanket across his features.

"I don't know, I've had a lot of time to think, that is whenever José shuts up for awhile."

"He only talks because he likes you, Jacob. Notice, he never talks so much to anyone else." There was warmth in Johnny's eyes, even in the midst of banter.

"He may grow to like you also, Johnny, 'cause he's stayin' too."

"Good, I don't know anyone I'd trust more." Johnny shifted his feet uneasily, trying vainly to regain his mental balance under the unexpected weight of responsibility conferred by the new faith of his one-time target. "And I'd be honored to run the mine and do you proud."

"I like you Johnny." Jake had not meant to say those words but found upon inner examination, they were exactly how he felt. Taking Jake's part in the fight against his previous employer counted for a lot. "You and Tia will do well." Spontaneously, each man reached out to shake hands, but allowing for Jake's injuries, they did so gently. Still, the action contained the power of what both men felt, and how both men had grown.

With a conscious, calming intake of breath, Johnny nerved himself to look into the eyes of his benefactor, exposing his soul. He hoped Jake could see the truth felt so deeply in his heart. "I can't thank you enough, Jake - for everything."

Both men broke eye contact and turned to look out upon the town. Silence between them stretched comfortably as they watched men working over piles of rubble across the way.

"I have to build Sarah a new house before the baby comes. We'll be heading back soon."

Looking at Jake scanning the desolation, Johnny began to understand the transformation Jake had undergone since meeting Sarah. He'd heard all the stories. Now, he'd seen the man in action. The stories must all be true, he realized!

Involuntarily, Johnny's head wagged in amazement. Golly, that man could fight. What other ten men would take on Dutch Honnicker with only their bare hands?

Shocked, like a flash of heat lightning, Lobo realized that no one he'd ever met had spoken of Jake's kindness. What else might he call that which allowed Jake to forgive him after what Johnny had done to him? Maybe the kindness was new, he guessed.

It occurred to Johnny, in that same moment, that Jake had always been a fine man. Kinda like a grand plantation house with pillared porches and marbled entry. Only now he'd had the inner rooms redone with fine silk wall fabrics. Ahh! The vision pleased him immensely, causing a slow smile to spread across his lower face.

Kinda had his soul dressed up.

Makes a man wonder, Johnny mused, hand now to his chin, deep within his reverie. Maybe that might also happen to me.

∃□∃

Interrupting Johnny's musing, Sarah stepped out from the restaurant behind them, casually slipping her arms through each of theirs and leaning her increasingly rounded body against Jake.

"What happens now, Jacob?"

Comforted by her nearness, yet absorbed in his own inspection of the desolation, Jake was slow to answer. The vertical creases on his forehead gradually relaxed their hold on his features. Poised upon his arm, Sarah drew his attention like the irresistible force of the strongest magnet. Remaining lines in his face rearranged themselves from concern to smiling joy.

"While you're still able to travel, I think we'll go to St. Louis to take care of a promise I made to Harry. His wife, Minnie, owns his interest in the diggings and she deserves to know what happened to her husband from my own lips."

"No! I mean here in Nazareth!" Sarah smiled while she stomped a small foot to underline her frustration. "Sometimes, Jacob, I don't know whether you're too smart or too slow."

"Mystery's what makes life so grand, ain't it?"

As she raised her hand to swat at his rambunctiousness, Jake arrested the motion with his unbandaged hand. "Haven't I been hurt enough? Look at me! I'm a mass of bandages! And you want to hurt me some more?"

"Uuwwww," Sarah stifled her outrage with noticeable effort. "Okay, Jacob. Not now. We'll let the when of my just revenge be our own little mystery." She winked playfully.

"Glad to see you're up and around son," Eliza Crombe had come up to Jake opposite Sarah. Taking Jake's bandaged right hand in his own, he pressed it gently, pumping it up and down with genuine gratitude beaming from his eyes.

"I helped bandage this hand," said Crombe. "It's not hurt so bad as it looks. The Cherokee figured to tape it up just to keep it clean." Dropping the hand, he shifted his gaze to the desolation and then back to Jake and Sarah. "You did a brave thing, Jacob."

"Stupid maybe, is what I figure."

"No. I wasn't thinking about Honnicker," the Gunsmith's eyes twinkled with humor at Jake's expense. "I'm talking about going after the Mayor. Altimera was right about the Dutchman. That was stupid. I woulda shot him myself but the Sharps overheated and the Winchester wasn't big enough to bring him down."

"Anyone find either one of them yet?" Johnny Lobo's curiosity brought them all back to real concerns.

"No," Crombe allowed. "Honnicker's boys joined the townspeople to fight the fire, much to their credit, but no one seemed to see either the Dutchman or the Mayor afterwards." Looking downward, the Gunsmith massaged the back of his neck thoughtfully. "And no one found any extra bodies either. The only bodies were right here in the street."

"Found the gold, I hear," volunteered Lobo.

"What gold was that?" Jake's interest was evident.

"From the claim," Johnny said. "Honnicker had brought it in that morning. When the fire started roaring through the alley, the horses on the ore wagon bolted. They ran the wagon against the Courthouse where it overturned next to the outer wall! The heat of the fire burned the bags and slagged the dust. There's a big puddle of precious mineral and charcoal out behind the Judge's back door. He's the one found it, in fact."

"It's still there?" Jake was aghast.

"No," said Johnny. "The Sheriff had some smelter experience in his checkered past. He's remelted the gold, skimmed off the impurities and molded it into little bars that are a lot easier to ship. I think he's trying to get back in our good graces."

"The Mayor's oversized safe is half buried in that rubble," Sarah added, pointing with her chin to the foundations of the Courthouse. "But it's open and empty. Looks like he got away with whatever he had inside."

"Good riddance," said Jake.

"May not be over yet, amigo," Altimera had wandered quietly up to the Gunsmith's side, speaking hushed but loud enough for everyone to hear. "Too many unanswered questions make me ver' uncomfortable."

Townsmen working on the rubble watched the conversing friends covertly, curiously.

Nothing much has changed here, thought Jake to himself. Trouble always waits in the wings. Zachary's just one more thug poised to spoil my day. He scuffed an undamaged toe against the boards of the walk.

"He won't return," said Crombe. "Town folks won't put up with it no more. They've seen he can be beaten."

"Good," Jake thumbed back his hat, showing eyes full of optimism and relief.

"That's really what I was thanking you for, Jacob. You gave us back our town." Crombe stood straighter and shot Jake a grateful look. "The others are still pretty embarrassed about their lack of courage so it may be awhile before they feel like they can talk to you."

"They're scared of me? Now, they're scared of me?"

"Jacob!" exclaimed Sarah. "You could be more generous."

"Naw. They're just embarrassed, not scared," said Crombe.

"But Eliza, there were some of you who got past your faint-heart-edness." Jake focused his entire attention on the Gunsmith, feeling the force of Shantee's words reverberating within him. "You decided it was one battle by which each of you could confirm your choice of good. The townspeople stood up for themselves! That made all the difference in how I succeeded in my own efforts."

Jake thoughtfully considered the frail-looking but now tall-standing man at his side, "You were one of those good people, Eliza, and could just as easily have shied away from this daunting task."

Pausing a heartbeat or two, Jake looked past Crombe to Lobo, "And you, Johnny, you were another."

Jake felt Sarah squeeze his arm and he knew, without looking, that she was smiling her heartfelt approval.

Always Here

Jake, Sarah and Night Walker guided their horses between piles of weather-rounded rock in the barren desolation east of the Basin Range. No birds circled in the sky. A single cloud floated like a brilliant white, flat-bottomed cotton ball against a cornflower blue background.

Jake had said his adieus, but felt good about leaving Johnny and José with the mine. Johnny was family now. Sarah was looking forward to St. Louis as the civilized honeymoon they never had.

Jake was in no hurry. The rocks and the wind and the sun were all that he needed right now to set things right in his mind. Nature's rhythms. In the distance, Jake noticed an old man walking among the stunted trees with apparent unconcern. So we are not completely alone, Jake thought. Improbably, their eyes met and locked across the great distance. Instantly Jake knew.

"You're never very far away, are you Old Man?" he mumbled under his breath, not really expecting an answer.

No I am not, the thought returned, clear as if the Old Man was standing right next to him. Jake swiveled his head to see if Sarah had heard, but she rode like a seasoned warrior, eyes scanning close and far, apparently unaware of this long distance exchange.

Who are you, Shantee, anyway? Jake really wanted to know. He felt his thought speed forward as clearly as a spoken word.

With the warmth of his gentle smile the Old Man returned his own reply without words, but like the sound of rolling thunder, filling the wilderness.

> *Who am I?*
>
> *I am the trees*
> *whispering to each other.*
>
> *I am the river*
> *knowing its way*

291

I am the fir needles
softening the path

I am the clouds
and the sky and the rain
all working together

I am the rock,
silent, still,
wise beyond my years

and I am part
of the forest,
a ribbon
a connection.
a center
a harmony
a peace.
          I am.

I am the One
          and the Many.

The Old Man turned and vanished as though stepping around a corner, down some alley.

"You didn't go anywhere," Jake silently challenged the figure, no longer there. "I know better now. You were the voice of the campfire!" he accused, remembering his convalescence after the fight at Big Mesa.

I was the voice you thought your own. I am here whenever you care to listen. I am in the campfire and in the winds. I am in the clouds that float across your sky. I am always here, my friend. Always here.

Gratitudes and Grins

A special thank you to cherished friends from everywhere, including the great circle of friends from Hillsboro, who contributed so abundantly, and cared so deeply. Just as Allen had, all of you became our Heroes!

I'm sure Allen is grinning as he sees all the people who have helped GONE TO GLORY come into being, despite enormous challenges. First, I want to thank Allen's late mother, Evelyn Stephens, and Don Alter, who both helped him grow into the man I was fortunate enough to marry. *Most importantly, I want to thank Julian and Jim for opening Allen's heart, and for loving their dad so much that Allen's friends cannot remember him without a smile on his face.* From days at soccer, to music, to cell phone calls and water-gun fights and more, Allen felt so blessed to share his life with his two fine sons.

Allen would also probably want to thank his good English teachers, the experiences he had as a Medic in the Army, as a tennis player for Portland State University and the Army's Asian Pacific Tennis competition, and his many years as President of his own advertising and communications business.

Next I want to thank all the wonderful friends at Schwan's, from Jack and Kathy Wood, to Jason and Scott, to ALL of his "brothers" there, and the nation-wide response from a company that cared. And thanks to Kathie and Dave Liden, Paul Kingsland, Bev and Jim Martin, Meridian Park's Grief Support Group and all our family and friends who helped light our path through difficult days.

Many people helped Allen with his research — such as museum directors, but especially friends in Hillsboro who gave him old books on history and life in The West, and who encouraged him as he made a transition into a writing career. As I edited my husband's book during a time of mourning, they helped me, too. Extra sustenance came from three people who deserve to be mentioned again - my dear friend, Kathie Liden, who walked each and every step of the way with me, as did my wonderful sons, Julian and Jim!

Thanks also to Rocky, E.T., Heidi, Shawn and Angela — just to name a few "Hillsboro angels" who loved Allen, and who now loved me and our boys. I simply cannot list everyone who we now know, or want to know better, because of the outpouring of Allen's friends at his Memorial Service — but know that each of you has a special place in our hearts, and are a part of the joy of this book.

Thanks for splendid editing assistance from Lisa Robertson, Sandi Jordan, and Dollie Mercedes, plus wonderful design implementation from Kim McLaughlin Designs, and Sheryl Mehary, and the kind coordination by Bob Smith. Other good-hearted people such as Will Goldstein, Kay Allenbaugh, Kelli and Bruce Sussman, Yvonne Brown, Heidi Truel, and friends in the NWABP — from Steve Jordan, Barb Whitaker, Nancy Kelley, Anita Jones, Jim Duncan, Marv Mitchell, Denise Arvidson, Louise Shaw, and Linda Beattie Inlow inspired me to complete Allen's worthy dream.

I'm sure Allen is grinning as I thank you one and all.
– *Sheila Stephens*

Allen L. Stephens 1947–2004

When Allen Stephens passed away suddenly in a pedestrian accident at the age of 57, he left us with an enormous legacy of love, and a series of extraordinary Western novels. GONE TO GLORY was, amazingly enough, about a Near Death Experience in which his main character, Jake Tallon, died in much the same way as Allen did, by an injury to the temple. But Allen's novel and life were about more than mere coincidence. As his family, it is our hope to tell you something about the man who made such a difference to so many people.

Because it is difficult for us to find words, we invite you to share in a portion of the Testimonial we wrote for *The Oregonian* newspaper after Allen crossed over:

Gifted Western Writer. Dreamer. Visionary.
Devoted Husband & Father. Healer. Friend.

Dear Allen, you filled each day with a joy that only comes from love.

You made us feel treasured, important, and vitally needed. You had words of wisdom that tumbled from you, like the most natural mountain stream. You will be missed, for you increased God's Love by sharing it in little and big ways everyday. You loved your wife and sons, and made them happy. You sincerely cared for us, and made not only adults, but also children, and dogs and cats your friends.

You made us laugh often and wholeheartedly. And just as quickly, you listened to us well, giving us compassion and hope. In so many ways, you healed us and made us better people. Now we are honored to hold you in our hearts forever, and share it with others, so we might carry on the tradition of a fine and loving man.

In conversations with other authors, Allen Stephens was often heard to say - "I like the way good *does* triumph over evil — *after a vigorous struggle!*"

May you enjoy his adventures, and the character he brought to them.

His wife, *Sheila Stephens,*
and sons, *Julian & Jim*

GONE TO GLORY
The New Western

"Celebrating the Spirit that Moves in All Things"

Allen Stephens believed that in the West, there were always men and women who loved and respected each other as equals, who worked together to create their dreams, and who listened to a sacred and natural intuition that directed their paths. Facing their fears, they refused to become cynical. For that reason, they became victorious. They became the positive and powerful legacy of The West.

Readers are saying… "Profound and Powerful!"

"Profound and powerful — this action-adventure set in California's gold rush era takes me back to an exciting, nearly forgotten time, the Old West, where men were often forced to settle their differences with a six-shooter. **Yet Jake Tallon becomes a legend not just because of his fighting skills, but because people became better through knowing Jake.** Their lives changed.

This Western is filled with **spirit lessons taught by the Cherokee Shaman,** Night Walker, with powers from beyond — and **a love story** between Jake and Sarah that makes you never want to put it down."
- E. T. Tawzer, Hillsboro, Oregon

"GONE TO GLORY is a **riveting story of courage, hope and the life-changing force of forgiveness.** True-to-life details of Western life sweep you back to another time — and **characters jump off the page** to become your instant friends."
- Lisa Robertson, freelance editor

"**Brilliant piece of work!** Had me from the first page! Allen was a man's man, but I never met *any* man with his compassion. In the way he had a lot of love for everybody and in the way he wrote, he praised God – only this time he did it in a Western! He's not gone, he just rode off into the sunset."
- Rocky Young, friend & former Bodyguard

To order additional copies visit the Web site:
FlowersOfTheSpirit.com

Or write to the publisher:
Flowers of the Spirit LLC, PO Box 1028, Sherwood, OR 97140